February, 1973

THE YOUNG ELIZABETH

She paused by the Beauchamp Tower and whispered: "Robert. Robert Dudley. Are you there?"

He was at the window looking through the bars.

"My . . . Princess!" he murmured.

He was pale through long confinement, but his pallor seemed but to enhance the beauty of that incomparable cast of features; the flesh had fallen away to disclose the fine contours of his face. How handsome he is! thought Elizabeth; and any man who admired her seemed to her charming.

ALSO BY JEAN PLAIDY

THE SPANISH BRIDEGROOM

Gay Lord Robert

Jean Plaidy

A BERKLEY MEDALLION BOOK
PUBLISHED BY G. P. PUTNAM'S SONS
DISTRIBUTED BY BERKLEY PUBLISHING CORPORATION

Published by arrangement with G.P. Putnam's Sons

SBN 425-02242-0

G.P. Putnam's Sons
200 Madison Avenue
New York, N.Y. 10016

Berkley Publishing Corporation
200 Madison Avenue
New York, N.Y. 10016

BERKLEY MEDALLION BOOKS ® TM 757,375

Printed in the United States of America

G.P. PUTNAM'S-BERKLEY MEDALLION EDITION,
OCTOBER, 1972

AUTHOR'S NOTE

In writing of what is undoubtedly one of history's most puzzling relationships, it is perhaps advisable to add a few remarks in order to justify the conclusions to which I have come. This is particularly the case with regard to the mysterious death of Amy Robsart.

All that happened on that Sunday morning at Cumnor Place will never be known. Was Amy's death due to accident, suicide or murder? After studying available records my verdict cannot be anything but murder.

Consider the facts: The Queen was being pressed by her ministers to marry. She could not bear to forgo the attentions of Robert Dudley, and Robert could not give up the hope of sharing the throne. Thus Robert's wife Amy stood in the way of two ruthless personalities. The Queen, in politics the soul of caution, had always been reckless in love. Scandal was circulating throughout the country concerning the relationship of Elizabeth and Robert Dudley. People remembered Thomas Seymour. Before Amy died there was a strong rumour that her death was being planned; and when it was said that Amy was suffering from a fatal malady, many believed that to be a false rumour set in motion in order to explain the death which was to follow. So persistent were the rumours, that a physician refused to attend Amy, fearing to be accused of administering poison should she die. This was the state of affairs when her minister, Cecil, returning from Edinburgh, found the Queen strained and nervous, and, to his astonishment, heard from her lips that Amy would soon be dead. Cecil, appalled, hurried from the Queen, and was so distraught that, coming face to face with the

Spanish ambassador, he could not keep his suspicions to himself. 'The Queen and Lord Robert Dudley are scheming to put Lord Robert's wife to death!' is what he said—according to the Spanish ambassador. And a few hours later Amy was found dead.

Why should the Spanish ambassador have written those revealing despatches if the contents were untrue? Spain was no enemy of Robert's at that time, and Robert had won Philip's approval at St. Quentin.

An accident to Amy resulting in her death at such a time so convenient to Elizabeth and Robert is surely too incredible a coincidence to be accepted.

As for the suggestion of suicide, if Amy had wished to kill herself would she have chosen a method which, she must have known, might not result in death, but merely add acute pain and misery to her remaining years? Would any woman destroy herself in such a painful way in order to avoid being murdered?

Everything points to murder, apart from Amy's strange conduct on that Sunday morning in sending all her servants to the Fair. Why did she—in perpetual fear of murderers—clear the house of all the servants on that day which was to prove so tragic to her?

I have looked to her maid Pinto for the explanation because from her first came the suggestion of suicide. It seemed that this suggestion came simply and unwittingly from Amy's maid; but was Pinto such a simpleton? What if the suggestion were not wrung from her, but deliberately given? Might she not have known the true reason why the house was deserted on that Sunday morning? Let us consider what a woman would do when the whole country was hinting that she was about to be murdered. How would a devoted maid behave? As for my interpretation of Pinto's feelings for Robert, it must be vemembered that, during his two and a half years' exile, he had lived in Norfolk and would have come into continual contact with Pinto; and if we can discover little of Pinto's character, we know much of Robert's.

It is the novelist's task to present a convincing story and, when the characters actually lived, to adhere to facts obtained by research, only diverging from them with good reason, e.g., when they are unknown, and then only making careful and responsible deductions as an aid to the completion of the story. Therefore I offer my views of what happened at Cumnor Place in the summer of 1560.

To reach these conclusions—and others—I have studied many books and documents. The chief among these are:

Calendar of Letters and State Papers (Spanish) relating to English affairs preserved principally in the Archives of Simancas. Published by the Authority of the Lords Commissioners of Her Majesty's Treasury under the direction of the Master of Rolls. Edited by Martin A. S. Hume, FR Hist S.

Elizabeth and Leicester. Milton Waldman.

Queen Elizabeth. J. E. Neale.

Lives of the Queens of England. Agnes Strickland.

Queen Elizabeth (Brief Lives). Milton Waldman.

Natural and Domestic History of England. William Hickman Smith Aubrey.

British History. John Wade.

Old and New London. Edward Walford.

England in Tudor Times. L. F. Salzman, MA, FAS.

King Queen Jack (Philip of Spain Courts Elizabeth). Milton Waldman.

Two English Queens and Philip. Martin Hume, MA.

History of England. J. A. Froude.

I

It was hot, even for August; the foul odours from the river, carrying the threat of pestilence, hung in the sullen air that sultry day; but the crowds who were assembling on Tower Hill were oblivious of discomfort. Traders had left their shops or stalls in Candlewick Street, East Chepe and the Poultry; horse-dealers were coming from Smithfield Square; the goldsmiths from Lombard Street, the mercers of Chepeside had deserted their houses, realizing that there could be little business at such a time. Apprentices, risking a whipping, crept out after their masters, determined to see what could be seen on Tower Hill that day.

Laughing and jesting they came. All men and women believed that the hardships of Henry VII's reign were behind them and the days of plenty were at hand. No more cruel taxes would be wrung from them; no more fines; no more impositions. The old miser King was dead and in his place was a bonny golden boy who laughed loudly, who jested and made sport, and loved to show himself to the citizens of London.

It was he who had provided this day's pleasure for them; and it clearly indicated what they might expect of him.

9

"God bless King Hal!" they cried. "See how he pleases his people! He is the one for us."

The cheers for the King mingled with the jeers for the traitors. Some apprentices had made two effigies which they held high above the crowd, to be mocked and pelted with refuse.

"Death to them! Death to the extortioners! Death to the misers, and long life to King Harry!"

Jostling, cursing, laughing, they surged about the hill. At the summit, close to the scaffold, members of the nobility were gathered. The bell of St. Peter ad Vincula had begun to toll.

At the edge of the crowd, not venturing into it, stood a boy. He was pale, soberly dressed, and was staring, mournful and bewildered, at the weather-washed walls of the great fortress which seemed to stand on guard like a stone giant. So grim, so cruel did it seem to the boy, that he turned his gaze from it to the green banks where the starry loosestrife flowers were blooming. He remembered a day—long ago it seemed to him now—when he had taken his little brother to the river's edge to pick flowers. He remembered how they had strolled along, arms full of blossom. The flower of the water betony was like the helmet a soldier would wear, and he was reminded that soldiers would soon be coming out of the great prison, and with them would be the men who were to die on Tower Hill that day.

"Death to the traitors!" shouted a man near him. "Death to the tax-gatherers! Death to Dudley and Empson!"

The little boy felt the blood rush to his face, for his name was John Dudley, and his father was one of those who would shortly lay their heads upon the block.

He would not look, this little John. He dared not. Why had he come? He knew not. Was it because he had hoped to see a miracle? His father had seemed to him the cleverest man in England; and not only did he seem so to John, but to others, for Edmund Dudley, a humble lawyer, had become chief adviser to the King. But kings die, and often favours die with them; and a friend to one king may be a traitor to another; and if that king is desirous of winning his people's love, and those people demand a man's head as a symbol of *his* love—then that head is given.

He was standing up there now, the father of the boy. Little John stared at the ground, but he knew what was happening, for he heard the shouts of the people. Then there was silence. He looked up at the sky; he looked at the river; but he dared not look at the scaffold.

His father was speaking. The well-remembered voice rose and fell, but the boy did not hear what he said.

Then all was silent again until there came a shuddering gasp from the crowd. John now knew that he was fatherless.

He stood, helpless and bewildered, not knowing whether to turn shuddering away or to run forward and look with the crowd at his father's blood.

Now the executioner would be holding up his father's head, for he heard the cry: "Here is the head of a traitor!"

He wondered why he did not cry. He felt that he never would cry again. The shouting people, the grey fortress, the sullen river—they seemed so indifferent to the plight of one more orphan.

11

Such a short while ago he had been John Dudley, eldest son of a king's favourite minister, with a brilliant future before him. Now he was John Dudley—orphan, penniless—the son of a man whom the King had called a traitor.

He felt a hand on his shoulder. "John," said a voice, "you should not be here."

Turning, he saw standing beside him a man whom he knew well, a man whom he had looked upon in the light of an uncle, one of his father's great friends in the days of his prosperity—Sir Richard Guildford.

"I . . . wished to come," said John haltingly.

"I guessed it," said Sir Richard. " 'Twas a brave thing to do, John." He looked at the boy quizzically. "And not to shed a tear!"

He slipped his arm through that of the boy and began to lead him away.

"It is better for you not to be here, John," he said.

"What would they do to me?" asked the boy. "What would they do if they knew I was his son?"

"They'd not harm you, a boy of . . . how old is it?"

"Nine years, sir."

"Nine years! 'Tis young to be left alone and helpless . . . and your mother with two others."

"They will take all we have . . . "

Sir Richard nodded. "But 'twas not done for the love of your father's possessions. It was done to please the people. Who knows . . ." He looked at the boy shrewdly, but stopped short.

"Did the people so hate my father then?" asked the boy incredulously.

"Kings must have scapegoats, my boy. When a king does what his subjects do not like, that is the fault of his statesmen; it is only when he pleases them that the credit is his. It is the late King against whom the people cry out. Your father and Sir Richard Empson are the scapegoats."

The boy clenched his fists. "To be a scapegoat! I like that not. I would be a man . . . and a ruler."

Then suddenly he began to cry, and the man, walking beside him, helplessly watched the tears roll down his cheeks.

Sir Richard understood. It was natural that the boy should cry. He did not speak for some seconds, then he said: "This day you shall come home with me. Nay, do not concern yourself. I have seen your mother. I have told her that I would find you and take you to my home."

They had now reached the river's edge where a barge was waiting; and as they went slowly up the river, the sobs which shook the young body became less frequent.

At length they alighted, and mounted the privy steps which led to the lawns before Sir Richard's home.

As they entered the mansion, and crossed the great hall, Sir Richard called: "Jane! Where are you, my child?"

A girl, slightly younger than John, appeared in the gallery and looked down on the hall.

"I have a playmate for you, Jane. Come here."

Jane came solemnly down the great staircase.

"It is John," she said; and the boy, looking into her face and seeing the tear stains on her cheeks, knew that she too had wept for his father, and was comforted.

"He has suffered much this day, Jane," said Sir Richard. "We must take care of him."

13

Jane stood beside the boy and slipped her hand into his.

Sir Richard watched them. Let the boy forget the shouts of the mob on Tower Hill in the company of little Jane. He was safe with Jane.

As Sir Richard Guildford watched John Dudley grow away from his tragedy in the months that followed, he recognized in him that strength of character which had been Edmund Dudley's. He was excited by the boy, sensing in him latent ambition, the will to succeed, the passionate desire to bring back honour to the Dudley name. Sir Richard could look with pleasure upon the growing friendship between his daughter and this boy; and nothing less than having John in his own house and bringing him up as his son would satisfy him.

It was not difficult to arrange this, for Sir Edmund's widow and her children were forced to look to relations and friends for help, and Lady Dudley was only too glad that Sir Richard had taken this interest in her son.

It was Sir Richard's custom to talk to the boy, to nourish that ambition which he knew was in him; and one day, as they walked in the City to Fleet Lane and over Fleet Bridge and on to Ficquets Fields, Sir Richard talked of John's father.

"Your father was a great man, John. When he was your age, his position was little better than your own."

"Nay sir," said John. "It is true that my father was the son of a small farmer, and himself but a lawyer, yet he was descended from the Lords Dudley; and I am the son of a man who is called a traitor."

Sir Richard snapped his fingers. "The connexion

with the Lords Dudley was never proved," he said, "and I doubt it existed outside your father's imagination."

The boy flushed hotly at that, but Sir Richard went on: "Oh, it was clever enough. Dudley needed aristocratic ancestors, but he found them for himself. No doubt he made good use of them. But between ourselves, John, there is more credit due to a man when he has had to climb from the valley to the top of the mountain than when he starts near the top."

John was silent and Sir Richard continued: "Just for ourselves we will see Sir Edmund Dudley as the son of a farmer, himself a lawyer, yet such a master of his profession that the King sought his aid and through him and his friend Empson, ruled England."

The boy's eyes had begun to shine. "The son of a farmer merely—and he one of those who ruled England!"

"What should that teach you? Just this: No matter how lowly you may be, there is no limit—*no* limit—to the heights to which you may climb. Think of the King. Dare he look too far back? Is it not true that his Tudor ancestor was the son of a groom, and a bastard? Think, boy, think! This is treason and I'll whisper it. Dudley or Tudor? Is one better than the other? Remember it. Always remember it. Your father had great ambition. It may be now that he looks down from Heaven on you . . . his eldest son. It may be that he asks himself: What will my son do in this world? Will he rise as I did? Will he learn from my mistakes? Has he the fire within him which will make him a great man? John, I doubt not that your father looks down from Heaven upon you and prays and hopes."

15

John did not forget those words. He was determined to be as great a man as his father.

In the games he played, he was always the leader. Already he was Jane's hero. Sir Richard was pleased as he watched the growing affection between John Dudley and Jane Guildford.

Sir Richard's position at Court had brought him into contact with the King, who was as yet a careless boy in love with pleasure, yet a boy with an awakening conscience. Sir Richard thought that the King's conscience might play its part in the future of his young protege.

Henry still frowned at the name of Dudley. He was well aware that the execution of his father's favourite and adviser had been carried out for the sake of his, Henry's, popularity. Henry had not yet come to terms with his conscience. It could not yet persuade him, as it would later, that Dudley and Empson had deserved their fate, so the very mention of the name Dudley brought discomfort to him. But when Sir Richard subtly begged royal permission to ask the Parliament for the repeal of the attainder against the Dudleys, Henry was almost eager to give that permission.

Let the boy inherit his father's wealth. The King did not want it; he had that vast accumulation of riches, which his own father had amassed through his thrifty reign, to squander. Yes, let the attainder be repealed. Let the son of Edmund Dudley have his father's riches. The King could then feel happier when the names of Dudley and Empson were mentioned; he could put aside the thought that those two men had been executed to placate the people from whom much of his

16

father's wealth had been extorted.

The first step was therefore taken. John was no longer penniless. He was a rich *parti* for young Jane; although he could not yet go to Court.

Sir Richard came home full of excitement. "See what I have done for you, John!" he cried. "Now it will be your turn."

"Yes, now it is my turn," said the solemn boy.

Jane watched them gravely, wondering what this was all about. But there was no need to explain such matters to Jane. She was happy because her father was happy; and she saw in John that deep brooding concentration which she respected although she could not share it.

As they went out to the stables together she said: "Something good has happened, has it not?"

He nodded but he said no more then for he did not wish the grooms to hear.

As they rode across the clover-starred meadows, he said: "I am no longer without means. My father's fortune is to be returned to my family."

"John . . . does it mean you will go away?"

He smiled at the fear in her eyes. "If I went away, I should come back. You know, do you not, Jane, that when we are old enough we are to marry?"

"Yes, John," she answered.

"You will be happy then, Jane. So shall I!"

He was sure of her contentment—as sure as he was that one day he would be a leader of men. It did not occur to her that this might be arrogance on his part; if he was arrogant, then, in her eyes, arrogance was a virtue.

As they cantered across the fields she was thinking

of their future, of their marriage and the children they would have.

He too was thinking of the future, but not of his life with Jane. Jane's love was something he took for granted. The thunder of horses' hoofs seemed to say to him "Dudley—Tudor!"

Those names implied ambition—the rise from obscurity to greatness.

They were married when John was nineteen and Jane had just reached her eighteenth birthday. They continued to live quietly at Sir Richard's house—so near Court and yet not of it.

The King had changed; he was no longer a careless boy; his conscience had begun alternately to torment and soothe him, and it now assured him that Sir Edmund Dudley had been a traitor who had imposed great hardship on the people. He had deserved his fate, and what, this King could ask himself, would his subjects think of a monarch who honoured the descendants of such a man!

No, the King would show no favour to a Dudley; nor could he receive at Court the son of a traitor.

Jane's first son was born; and John, who felt that the shame and humiliation of that day on Tower Hill were branded on him so deeply that only the dazzling accoutrements of dignity and great power could distract attention from the defect, determined that if he could not win favour at Court he would seek it on the field of battle.

Jane was tearful at the prospect of his departure for France.

"Why cannot you stay here?" she asked. "What do

18

you want of fame? We have all we need. We have our little son, your namesake, and we will have more children."

"Aye, we will have more," said John. Of course he would have more. Children—even girls—were useful to men of power, for through them links with the great and rich were forged. Jane had her task; he had his. She must provide him with many sons and a few daughters; but he must bring power and fame to the name of Dudley.

He distinguished himself in the service of Charles Brandon, Duke of Suffolk, who had married the King's sister Mary. John came back from the battlefield *Sir* John Dudley.

An important step forward had been taken.

Quickly the years passed whilst ambition smouldered. Jane was fulfilling her task more successfully than John fulfilled his.

She had given him four sons and three daughters; and she was about to bear another child.

Jane remembered the day long afterwards. She was happy enough in the garden of their Chelsea manor house with the river lapping at its edge. She was thinking of her beloved children—and wondering whether the one she now carried would be a girl or a boy.

How blessed she was in her four handsome sons!

There were many rumours about the King at this time. How he would have envied her her four if he had seen them! It was said that his eyes first lighted up, then smouldered when he looked at other men's sons.

Such excitements there had been of late! Such

rumours! Would the King really take Anne Boleyn to wife? Would he make her his Queen? Jane had seen the lovely Anne pass along the river in her barge. The King was growing impatient, it was said; the air was thick with rumour; and here was little Jane Dudley, peacefully awaiting the birth of yet another child, living remote from the Court, though so near it—peaceful and contented with her family about her.

Of course she would have liked John to have his heart's desire—a share in the affairs of the Court. Sometimes he frightened her. He seemed so fierce in his determination. She would watch him pacing their chamber, pacing the lawns, his eyes narrowing as he looked without seeing it at a barge on the river. Then she would be fiercely glad that he was outside Court matters. She often thought of that great man Cardinal Wolsey who had met his doom and died of a broken heart. She would not have her John become such a one as the great Cardinal. But what a ridiculous comparison! Her John and the great Cardinal! But Wolsey had been humble once, and so had John's father.

She wished that he were not a Dudley, that he had some happier background, someone who had a humble father who had not risen to greatness but who had died peacefully in his bed.

And that day John came home in great excitement.

The King had decided to forgive him for being his father's son. It was more than twenty years since Henry had beheaded Edmund Dudley; and after twenty years, the King evidently thought, he could forgive a man for reminding him of his own guilt.

Jane watched John alight from his barge, saw him

hasten across the turf crying her name; and never had she heard his voice so joyous.

"Jane! Dear wife, I am appointed Master of the King's Armoury."

She felt her heart fluttering uncomfortably. She must appear to be glad. She always took her cue from him; she must be what he expected her to be.

"What . . . does it mean, John?"

"What does it mean! It means that the King has decided that, if I am worthy of honours, they should not be denied me. It means that we are on the road, Jane, on the road."

"Oh, John . . . on what road?"

But he did not answer. He was smiling as he looked along the river towards Westminster and Greenwich.

And it so happened that in her new apartments at the Tower of London, Jane gave birth to her fifth son.

She called him Robert.

He was the most handsome of all her boys. In the first few weeks of his life she knew that he would be the best beloved. He was lustier than all the others; he had been born with a thick down of hair; his eyes flashed more brightly than she believed eyes had ever flashed before; he demanded his own way from the beginning.

His father scarcely noticed him. Why should he? He was "on the road" now. He was preparing to march on to greatness.

Robert was all Jane's in those first months of his life. No nurses should take him from her. He was her baby—her little Robin.

How sorry she was for poor Queen Katharine, living out her lonely life in the Castle of Kimbolton. A boy

21

like Robin would have made all the difference in the world to her happiness, poor lady. As if a baby like Robin would not make all the difference to any woman! But poor Queen Katharine desperately needed a son.

And now another Queen was praying for a son.

Queen Anne was lying-in at Greenwich, and the country was waiting for the birth of a prince to be proclaimed.

When the King passed along the river, Jane watched him from the shelter of an arbour—seeing but unseen—and she held up the little boy, murmuring: "Look, Robin. There goes a king. They say he would give half his kingdom for a boy like you. But then who would not give all the world for you!"

There was a mist on the river during those September days, and the trees of the orchards were heavy with ripening fruit.

"May the Queen be fruitful," prayed Jane; for, sorry as she was for the displaced Queen, yet she wished joy to the new one. "May the Queen give birth to a prince as bonny—nay, that were impossible—*almost* as bonny as my Robin."

The bells rang out in the City. A child was born to the King and Queen.

A prince! said the people. It is sure to be a prince. Nothing but a prince would please the King.

Ah, thought Jane, the King needs a son. It will be God's way of telling him that he was right to break from an incestuous union and set a new Queen on the throne.

John came home from the Court, sober and unsmiling.

"What news, John? What news of the prince?" asked Jane.

And he answered: " 'Twas not a prince that was born this day at Greenwich. 'Twas a girl." Then he gave that short hard laugh which, she had noticed, had developed lately. "It will not do, Queen Anne Boleyn," he muttered. "The King married you for sons . . . and you give him a girl!"

"Poor lady!" murmured Jane. "Poor lady!" And she thought: Oh dear, she is gay and wicked, they say; but I would not wish to see her suffer as poor Queen Katharine did.

Suffer? How could she suffer? She was young; she was the most attractive of women; she was not the sort to despair because her first-born was a daughter. The King was deeply enamoured of her; for her sake he had broken with Rome. Who was Jane Dudley to be sorry for such as Queen Anne Boleyn!

She whispered to Robert: "It is because we are both mothers, my love. But she has a daughter and she longed for a son. And I have you—the most handsome baby in the world."

She kissed him and he wriggled away. He was nearly a year old and only wished for kisses when he was in the mood for them.

"But what does Robert Dudley care for the new Princess Elizabeth?" crooned Jane.

In the next three years Jane often thought of the little Princess. So much honour was done to her at one

23

time. The King himself delighted to have her dressed in finery that he might carry her round and show her to the ladies of the Court, insisting that they admire his daughter, his little Elizabeth.

But the King still wished for sons; and Queen Anne, it seemed, could no more satisfy his wishes than his previous Queen had done.

Such rumours there were of quarrels between the King and Queen—and she was not humble as her predecessor had been, but fiery and haughty. "The Queen is riding for trouble," said John.

There was talk of the lady Jane Seymour and the King's interest in this pale, quiet girl. The King's conscience, like a monster drugged by the sweet intoxication of Anne Boleyn, was throwing off its stupor. Was Anne really his wife? he was asking now. Had she not betrothed herself to another before she had gone through the ceremony with the King? Was she the virtuous wife he had believed her to be?

If there were no longer a Queen Anne Boleyn there might be a Queen Jane Seymour.

But Jane Dudley's thoughts were for the little Princess—the once feted and the honoured. What would become of her? Those about the King were already wondering whether she would be designated Bastard, as her half-sister Mary had been.

"Poor little Princess!" said Jane.

But she had her own family to occupy her mind.

A new son was born to her. This son was called Guildford, after her father. Guildford Dudley. That pleased Sir Richard.

And one day on Tower Green Queen Anne lost her

head, and with unbecoming haste the King made Jane Seymour his Queen.

Jane wept when she heard the news. Robert and Guildford watched her for a few seconds before four-year-old Robert asked: "Mother, why do you cry?" He was precocious beyond the others. He listened to gossip and his eyes flashed as his father's did, "Is it because they have cut off Queen Anne's head?"

She was silent for a while, then she said: "No, my tears are not for the Queen, for she is past her pain. It is for the little one who is left, her daughter, the little Princess Elizabeth who is but three years old and without a mother to love her."

Robert was the centre of his world; he saw everything in relation to Robert.

He said: "I am older than the Princess. She is but three and I am four."

"Yes, my darling. And you have your mother left to you."

Robert laughed. He was important. He was the most important person in the world. He saw that, in the eyes of his mother and young Guildford who were watching him with such admiration.

The prosperous years had set in. Jane was rich in children; she bore John thirteen—eight sons and five daughters; some of them died when pestilence struck London but her darling grew bolder and more handsome every day.

There he was, a sturdy little fellow, strutting in the Tower gardens, calling to the guards and warders. They all laughed at his swagger. "Ha," they said, "he will get on in the world, will Master Robert Dudley."

Meanwhile John had continued with his spectacular rise. He had come a long way now from that boy—of Robert's age—who had stood on Tower Hill and heard the mob, shouting against his father.

Sir John Dudley was handsome, witty and clever; he distinguished himself in the tiltyard and at all those sports and pastimes at which Henry himself had once excelled.

"I like this John Dudley," said the King; "and it was ever my custom to reward those who pleased me."

Others received their rewards from the King. His fifth wife lost her head on Tower Green and was buried in the church of St. Peter ad Vincula beside the King's second Queen who had suffered a similar fate. At this time Henry made Sir John an Admiral of his Fleet and with that honour gave him the title of Lord Lisle. John Dudley had proved himself a good servant.

They were indeed rising in the world. Lord Lisle could look at his sons and daughters and be proud of what he had done for them. He talked to them often and his talk was always of ambition. "See how a man or a woman may rise! Your grandfather, the son of a farmer, was a humble lawyer, and he became the King's right-hand man. As a boy I saw my father beheaded on Tower Hill and knew myself a penniless orphan. And now, my sons and daughters, here you see me; Lord Lisle, Admiral of the Fleet, and for my services in the Boulogne battle I am to become a Knight of the Garter."

Robert was entranced by his father's conversation. He boasted to Guildford as they strolled in the Tower gardens or those about their father's Chelsea Manor house: "As our father rose, so shall we . . . higher and higher . . ."

There were places for the family at Court; and one day Robert was taken to the royal nurseries, where he met the pale Prince—quiet and delicate, full of wisdom he had learned from books; and with the little Prince were the two eldest Grey girls, Lady Jane and Lady Catharine. The girls were quiet and very pretty; and the Prince was fond of them. Guildford, who accompanied Robert, could not make up his mind who was the prettier, Jane or Catharine. Guildford was too young to appreciate the honour of playing with such noble persons.

One day when they were in the nursery, there was a visit from the Prince's half-sister. That was a day to remember—a day like no other, Robert thought it. When Edward was in command, the talk would be of Latin verses which he and Jane had composed together, or some such matters. Robert had never taken kindly to such arts and graces; he would show his prowess on a horse or at the games which he always won.

But on that day when the young girl came to the nursery everything was different. Her hair was red, her eyes blue, and she had a sparkling quality which would bubble into laughter or as suddenly into anger.

Robert was quick to sense that all the children were afraid of her, and that she was afraid of none, even though her brother was heir to the throne and she was called a bastard.

Her governess came with her; the Princess giggled with her and she might have been a serving maid until she remembered that she was the Prince's sister and became as haughty as a queen.

She was a year younger than Robert, and Robert was glad, for he felt that gave him some advantage.

"Who are you?" she demanded. "I have not seen you here before."

"I am Robert Dudley."

"Say 'Your Grace' when you address me. I do not know a Robert Dudley."

"You did not," he said, "but you do now."

"I do not think that I shall continue to do so," she answered turning away. She approached her brother and said: "Brother, what ill-mannered boys are these that you have allowed to be brought to your apartments?"

Young Jane and Catharine looked on in concern, and Edward was uncomfortable.

Robert was the most important person in the world. His mother and Guildford had always thought so. He was no ill-mannered boy; he reminded himself that the Princess was a bastard, but remembering also the gracious manners which his father had taught him, he knelt before the Prince and said: "Your Grace, I kneel before you. *I* am not so ill-mannered as to forget the honour due to your Royal Highness."

The Princess laughed and stamped the floor with her foot. "Get up, you fool!" she commanded. "We want no Court manners here."

Robert ignored her: "I was about to say, your Royal Highness, that I would not bandy words with another in your presence. Have I your gracious permission to rise?"

"Yes, yes," said Edward. "Get up."

"If I have the esteem of your Royal Highness, I wish

28

for no other," said Robert pointedly.

Then the Princess looked again at him and she continued to look. His dark hair curled about his neck. Beside him poor Edward looked more puny than ever. Robert's skin was pink and healthy; poor Edward suffered so from spots and rashes. And the other boy, Guildford, was frail compared with his brother.

The Princess then began to think that this Robert Dudley was the handsomest boy she had ever seen, and because of his personal beauty she was ready to forgive him his arrogance—and in truth she liked his arrogance, for it matched her own.

She went to him and tapped him on the arm; and when he looked haughtily down at her he saw that she was smiling at him in a very friendly fashion.

"Enough, Master Robert!" she said. "What games do you play?"

He showed her how to play "Pope Julius's Game" which he had learned from his elder brothers. She sat by him smiling at him. She set the pace; it was she who usually suggested what games they should play; the others, he could see, had always been ready to follow her.

"Now," she cried, "we shall compose verses. Each member of the party must add a line." She looked sternly at Robert; "And," she added, "it must rhyme."

She beat him at the game, but he said it was a foolish one and not a man's game. She retorted that if it were indeed a little foolish he must be very foolish since he could not play it even as well as little Catharine.

She herself was expert with her lines; but after a while she grew tired of the game and showed them the newest Court dances, although how she knew of such matters Robert could not understand.

She herself danced with Robert. "You are the only one of a size worthy of me," she told him, as she paired Jane and Edward, Catharine and Guildford.

"You would dance well, Master Dudley," she said, "with a little more practice."

"I would we could practise together," he said.

She fluttered her eyelashes and said demurely: "Your Grace."

And just to please her he said it. She was very satisfied, and so was he. It was indeed a very satisfactory occasion.

Often he met her in the royal nursery, but one day she was not there. She had been retired, Edward told him, to Hatfield where she would stay with her governess.

How dull it was without her!

King Henry died and the puny little Edward was King of England. John Dudley could view the new reign with confidence, for his standing was even higher under the new King than it had been under the old. Henry had appointed him a member of that Council which was to form a Regency and govern the kingdom until Edward was of age. John Dudley was climbing to the summit of his hopes, but there were two men who stood in his way. These were the uncles of the King, the Seymour brothers; Edward, now Duke of Somerset, the sober statesman, and Thomas, now Lord Sudeley, the handsome philanderer. The only characteristic these brothers appeared to have in common was their overwhelming ambition, and if Edward had the power, Thomas had the popularity. He was not only the favourite of the young King, but the Princess Elizabeth was said to blush when his name was mentioned.

During this time young Robert saw his father become one of the most powerful men in England. He was now the Earl of Warwick, which in itself was significant, for that title had been extinct since the death of the grandson of Warwick the King-maker. Had a new king-maker arisen?

The family was very rich, for the Warwick estate was now theirs. Jane Dudley was apprehensive; often she thought how happy she would have been if her husband could have been content with what he had won. In the last reign no man had been important, except the King; now there were several men all struggling for pre-eminence. She wished she could have talked freely to John; she wanted to warn him. How he would laugh if she did! He had never considered her opinion worth asking for.

Young Robert knew of her fears and tried to soothe her.

"Why, Mother," he said, "my father will win. He will beat the Seymours."

"Your father will beat all who oppose him," said Jane and her voice trembled. She could not dismiss from her mind memories of that day when her father had brought John home. Such sights as John had seen on that day were often to be witnessed on Tower Hill.

"I'll tell you why my father will beat them, Mother," said Robert. "He is now in command of the King's armies, and therefore his position is as strong as that of the Lord Protector Somerset."

And Jane had to be content with that.

The new Earl of Warwick lost little time in

arranging advantageous marriages for his children. His eldest son John should be affianced to the daughter of the Protector himself; his daughter Mary was to marry the King's friend, Henry Sidney.

"Your turn will come, Robin," said his mother.

Robert's answer was: "I, Mother? I shall choose for myself."

When he thought of marriage he thought of the red-headed Princess. Was he looking rather high? Robert did not think so. Who could be too high for Robert? Moreover she was a bastard. Yet he did not object to that. He had admired her spirit, the way in which she had commanded the children, the way in which she had cajoled him into calling her "Your Grace." What impudence, and yet what dignity! What arrogance mingling with a certain promise of . . . he was not quite sure what.

"Yes," he affirmed, "I shall choose for myself."

Strange rumours were afloat.

The younger Seymour was attainted of high treason. He had plotted, it was said, to seize the government and marry the Princess Elizabeth.

Robert was bewildered by the news. He had, of course, seen Thomas Seymour, Lord Sudeley, rich and magnificent, swaggering through the Court, the eyes of the women gleaming as they followed him. All had agreed that Thomas Seymour was the handsomest man in England; but at that time Robert was yet a boy and no one had noticed him.

The rumours were shocking, for they involved the Princess. Robert was angry when he heard of them. He did not believe them, he told himself; and yet when he thought of her, smiling at him, fluttering her sandy lashes, how could he be sure that what he heard was not true?

His mother talked of the rumours with the ladies of her household; she would sit in the gardens at Chelsea and talk with her friends.

"Was it true then . . . the Princess but a girl of thirteen and a Princess . . . so to conduct herself!"

It did not help matters that the man with whom the Princess was reputed to have behaved so disgracefully was the husband of her stepmother, Katharine Parr.

Robert heard it all, the story of the flirting and the rough horseplay; he heard of the occasion when the daring Seymour had cut her dress to pieces while sporting in the gardens of the Chelsea Dower House; there were stories of his visits to her bed-chamber, of tickling and smacking and kissing while the Princess was in bed. The Princess Elizabeth had been known to ride in a barge on the Thames like a light woman.

Robert thought of it all, pictured it, saw Seymour and the Princess in that embrace which it was said had exposed the guilty affair to Katharine Parr when she had come unexpectedly upon them and witnessed it.

There was no end to the tales, and snatches of conversation stayed in his mind.

"And have you heard the rumours? I had it from a very reliable source . . . someone who knows . . . from the midwife herself. Do not speak of this to any other. One dark night the midwife was awakened from her bed by men and women in masks and made to follow them, bringing with her the tools of her trade. She was blindfolded until she reached a certain house, and there she delivered a child. She was warned that if she spoke a word of what had happened her tongue would be cut out. The lady who needed her services was young and most imperious. She had red hair . . ."

Robert was more angry than ever then, but his anger turned to sadness when he heard that she was taken to the Tower.

There she was questioned, and it was said at that time that when Thomas Seymour lost his head on Tower Hill, the Princess Elizabeth would soon follow her lover.

Robert, at sixteen, was restless for adventure.

At that time the two most powerful men in England were jostling each other for first place; one of these was the Lord Protector Somerset, the other was Robert's father, who suddenly found that he had the advantage over his political enemy.

Thomas Seymour had been beheaded without being granted an opportunity to speak in his defence. This in itself was shameful, but carried out at the command of his own brother seemed ignoble in the extreme. The popularity of the Lord Protector was waning and that of his opponent consequently waxed.

Then came the rising of the peasants of Norfolk who were starving on account of the enclosure laws. They were marching on London when the Earl of Warwick, as General of the King's Armies, set out against them and defeated them on their own ground in Norfolk.

The insurrection had been suppressed with great cruelty, and trouble averted. The country was grateful to Warwick for his speedy and ruthless action. The Norfolk landowners considered themselves deeply indebted to him, and Robert, who was with his father in Norfolk, became a guest at the large country estate of

Sir John Robsart, lord of the manor of Siderstern.

Warwick returned to London, leaving his son to follow him; but Robert was in no hurry, and the reason was Robsart's young daughter, Amy.

She was plump and pretty—a girl of Robert's own age—and she had never seen anyone quite so dashing and handsome as this young man from Court circles.

Amy was the youngest of the family and rather pampered by her father and her two half-brothers and two half-sisters, particularly since the death of her mother which had occurred a short while before the Norfolk rising.

Her brothers John and Philip, and her sisters Anne and Frances Appleyard, were not her father's children; and Amy, being John Robsart's only legitimate child was also his heiress. She was used to having her own way, and she made no secret of her feelings for the handsome newcomer; and the more openly she admired him, the more good sense and charm she seemed to have in the eyes of Robert.

He liked the country; he enjoyed life in a great manor house; and he appreciated the honour showed to him by all these people. John and Philip Appleyard deemed it a compliment when he rode with them to the hunt. The girls—Anne and Frances—saw that all his favourite dishes were served at table. All the family smiled benignly to see his friendship with Amy ripen. As for Sir John Robsart, he was fervently hoping that Amy would make a good match, but at the same time wondering if he dared look so high as to the son of the most important man in England and the country's real ruler.

Meanwhile Robert and Amy rode out together,

hawking and hunting; her simple admiration was enchanting; she never failed to laugh when he indicated that he expected laughter; she always applauded, and she showed him in a hundred ways that he was more like a god than a man.

Robert felt gay and merry, basking in such adulation. He felt as worldly-wise as the young Princess whose name had been tossed hither and thither by sly rumour. He assured himself that this pretty and simple Amy was in truth far more desirable; she would never scorn him; she would always admire whatever he did.

One day when he and Amy were walking in the fields on her father's estate, Amy began to collect daisies to make a chain. She had many pretty gestures and everything she did was with a charming innocent grace, as she now made a daisy chain.

It was springtime and the country smells and sounds enchanted Robert. He felt suddenly that he did not wish for any other life than this. To wander in green fields, to hunt in the forests, to live a life of ease and comfort with these pleasant country folk from whom he was so different that he was something more than human, seemed to him the ideal life.

"You are very pretty, Mistress Amy," he said; and as she cast down her eyes and feigned great interest in her daisy chain, he continued: "Did you not hear me, Amy?"

She raised her eyes; they were large, limpid and somewhat sad. "But you will have seen so many who are prettier. What of the clever people whom you meet in your father's house?"

"You are prettier than any."

"How can that be?"

He shrugged his shoulders. "Do not ask me. I am not God. I did not make you all."

That sent Amy into titters of shocked laughter. It sounded like blasphemy, but it was so amusing. Robert was always amusing. She deemed him as clever and handsome as he considered himself to be. She reflected his own pride in himself. He was sure in that moment that he could be happy at Siderstern for the rest of his life. He dazzled her; he dazzled them all; and he was determined to dazzle them more than ever before.

"Amy," he said, "I love you."

She was a little frightened. What did he mean by that? Surely not marriage! He was the son of the man who was shortly to become—so she had heard her father say—Protector of England. No, Amy could never hope for marriage with a man such as Robert Dudley, even though she was the heiress of her father's considerable fortune. What then? Seduction? What else? And how could she say No? How could she resist his overpowering charm?

She stared at the crimson-tipped daisies because she dared not look at him, but all the same she was seeing his face—those bold eyes, the dark curling hair.

She had heard the servants talk of him; Anne and Frances whispered together concerning Robert. They had never seen any so handsome. As yet, they said, he did not know his power, but that would come.

Had it come? And was Amy to be its first victim?

"Why do you not answer me?" he said and the answer she gave pleased him more than any could: "I . . . I dare not."

He felt powerful. He was, after all, a Dudley. In him

was the love of power which had raised his grandfather from a humble lawyer to be the extortioner-in-chief of King Henry VII, the same love of power which had induced his father to step along the road which had led from Tower Hill to the Council Chamber and would take him before long to the Protectorate. He felt very tender towards her; he took her trembling hand and kissed it.

"You are afraid, Amy. Afraid of me!"

"I . . . I think I should return to the house."

"Nay," he said firmly, "you shall not."

He sensed the ready obedience in her and it delighted him. He wanted now to repay her for the pleasure she gave him. He said on impulse: "I will marry you, Amy."

"Oh . . . but how could you! Your father would never allow it."

She saw his lips tighten. "If I chose to marry I would do so," he said sharply.

"My father is rich and important, but that is here in Norfolk. We have our house and our estates, and one day they are to be mine. But . . . what of your father in London? He visits the King himself, and they say that even the King must do as he wishes."

"The King may do what my father wishes," said Robert boastfully, "but I shall do what *I* wish."

"But it could not be." She was too innocent to know that her attitude was stiffening his determination to have his own way.

"If I will it, it shall come to pass," he said.

Then suddenly he had taken both her hands, was drawing her towards him and kissing her.

"Robert . . ." she began.

"Your skin smells like buttermilk and your hair like hay," he said.

"We shall be seen."

"And do we care for that?"

"They will think you are a shepherd with your love."

He released her. He did not care that Robert Dudley should be mistaken for a shepherd.

They walked slowly back to the house.

She said sadly: "It is like a dream that will never come to pass in reality."

"We will make it come true."

"But I know your father will never consent. It is wrong therefore to hope."

"I tell you I will do as I please."

"But you have forgotten who you are and the grand schemes your father will have for you. You have forgotten that although I am my father's heiress and he is considered rich in these parts, you are Robert Dudley the son of the most important man in England."

"There is something *you* have forgotten. It is this: When I say I love, I love; and when I say I will marry, I will do so. No one shall stand between me and my desires."

It was bold and it was what was expected of him.

He kissed her as they stepped into the house, and he kissed her as though he cared not who might see.

Amy told her maid Pinto what had happened. Amy could not keep anything from Pinto.

"Pinto," she cried, "I am swooning. Bring a fan and fan me. I know not what is to become of me."

Amy lay on her bed, half laughing, half crying, while Pinto tried to soothe her frivolous young mistress.

"Now, now, sweeting, now, now! What is it? You must not be so excited. It's that young man, I'll wager."

"Clever Pinto!" said Amy with a smothered laugh.

"Oh, Mistress Amy, what has happened? What have you done? He is not for you."

"You must not let him hear you say that, Pinto. He would be angry with you. He *is* for me, Pinto. He says it, and he will be very angry with any who gainsay it."

Pinto felt sick with the horror of this. The family might think it great good fortune to have that young man as their guest. Pinto was a wise woman. She watched him often, and always with a fearful absorption. "What have you done?" she demanded. "Tell me . . . everything."

"I was in the meadow with him . . . making a daisy chain."

Pinto sighed and shook her head. "How many times has it begun thus?" she cried. "Making a daisy chain! There is some evil in daisy chains. So simple! So innocent! Thus was Eve when the serpent came along."

"He says he will marry me, Pinto."

"Never!"

"He is determined to do so."

"They are always determined at first. It is only afterwards that their determination wavers."

"You misjudge him . . . and me."

"Then you are still my little virgin?"

Amy nodded. "He swears he will marry me. Not even his father will stop him."

"A man who could deal so swiftly with the Norfolk rising not stop his son making the wrong marriage!"

"But this is the right marriage, Pinto."

"Nay, dearest."

"He says so and he is always right."

"I like this not, Mistress Amy."

"I shall never allow you to leave me, Pinto, wherever I go."

"I should think not!" said Pinto.

Pinto looked at the sixteen-year-old girl who had never been far from her country home. What did she know of the way of the world? And the young man had the air of knowing much.

Perhaps he would go away. He could not mean this talk of marriage. Pinto would know how to comfort Mistress Amy when he went. There was no fear that Robert Dudley would marry Amy Robsart. *Fear* of it? Yes, fear. For if innocent little Amy married Robert Dudley, how would it end?

Surprisingly the Earl of Warwick gave his consent to the marriage of his son with the daughter of John Robsart. Robert's powers of persuasion were great, and his father recognized that determination which he knew so well because he himself possessed it. Robert was his fifth son, so his marriage was not the important matter of that of a first-born; the Robsarts were rich. Moreover at this time the Earl had great matters to which he must attend. Every day seemed to bring the fall of Somerset nearer and he, Warwick, was preparing himself to become Lord Protector. The matter of a fifth son's marriage therefore seemed less important than it might have seemed at another time.

Jane Dudley, who could not accustom herself to her grand title, contemplated Robert's marriage with happiness.

"It is a true love match," she said, "and that is what I

would have chosen for Robin. Amy is a pretty girl, a little simple because she has been bred in the country, but I like that. Robert will spend much time in the country, and the country life—away from the plotting and planning of the Court—is a good life."

Jane pictured herself visiting them, resting in the lovely manor house, playing with their children, showing dear Amy how to make certain special preserves which could not be left to the serving maids, and how to grow herbs which could be used for flavouring and medicines. She saw that happy life for Amy and Robert which she had hoped might be hers and John's.

She scarcely saw John these days. But how unreasonable it was to expect him to give his time to her. She had served her purpose. She had borne thirteen children to enrich the Dudley fortunes and, although six of them had not survived, seven was a goodly number, particularly when they were such children as hers.

As for the Robsart family they could scarcely believe their good fortune. Their dear little Amy, their simple little pet was to be the means of allying theirs with the most powerful family in England.

The wedding was celebrated with much pomp and ceremony at the Royal Palace of Sheen, and King Edward himself attended. Never had the Robsarts believed such glory would come their way.

After the ceremony the married pair returned to Siderstern and prepared to live happily ever after.

And for a time Robert was happy.

Still greater power had come to his father. He had

brought a charge of treason against Somerset who on Tower Hill had met the same fate as that which a short while ago had befallen his brother, the fascinating Thomas. With Somerset headless, John Dudley was ruler of England, for the fourteen-year-old King—sick and steadily growing weaker—counted for little.

John's immediate action was to assume the title of Duke of Northumberland, although never before had any man, unconnected with royalty, had the title of Duke bestowed upon him.

Honours found their way to the Siderstern manor house. The Duke of Northumberland bestowed Hemsley Manor, which was not far from Yarmouth, on Robert and his wife. John Robsart was given jointly with Robert the Stewardship of Manor Rising. This was a sure sign of the King's favour; but the King's favour was in reality Northumberland's favour and it was small wonder that that fell upon his son and his son's father-in-law.

For Robert and Amy the long days were full of pleasure. Whether it was hunting, hawking, tilting or sport of any sort, there was none in Norfolk to compare with Robert. Wherever he went his smile was sought. He was called by the folk of Norfolk: "*Our* Lord Robert."

So he grew in strength and beauty, taking a great interest in local affairs. If his father was the greatest man in England, Robert was the greatest in Norfolk. There was scarcely a woman in the county of Norfolk who would not have been his for the asking. The young bridegroom of seventeen had become a handsome man of twenty—the handsomest in Norfolk, the most fascinating, it was believed, in the whole of England;

and if a search of the entire world were made, where would one so merry and gay, so full of charm and chivalry, be found to equal Lord Robert!

It was not his father's wish that he should stay for ever in the country. Now and then there would come a call to Court, and Robert would set out with his servants while the country folk—particularly the women—would sadly watch him go. They said that Norfolk was a dull place without Lord Robert.

A great welcome always awaited him in London. His mother wept with joy over him, and his brothers and sisters rejoiced to see him. Even his father who had little time for family affairs was not insensible to his charm and often would look at him with something like regret. The Robsart marriage was scarcely good enough for the most personable member of a powerful family.

One day during a visit to London Robert was at Hampton Court when his father took him into a small room and, with an air of secrecy, said he must have a few words with his son in the greatest privacy.

"I have had it from the King's doctors," said the Duke, after having ascertained that they could not be overheard, "that Edward is dying and cannot last the year."

"What then, Father?"

"What then indeed! Unless matters go our way, we are lost."

Robert was well informed enough of current affairs to know what his father meant. The Duke had, for political purposes, set himself at the head of the Reformers; and there were many in the kingdom who would say that Edward's lawful successor was Mary

Tudor—that fanatical Catholic.

It would be the end of his father's power if Mary came to the throne, and the Dudleys who had made their second rise to great heights would make their second abysmal fall.

Northumberland smiled grimly at his son.

"Robert," he said, "you have been a fool."

"I, Father?"

"You will see what I mean when I tell you what I plan to do. Mary Tudor is a bastard; so is Elizabeth. Their own father said so. England will not tolerate bastards on the throne when there is a legitimate heir. The Grey sisters come before Mary Tudor. Jane, the eldest, will be the rightful Queen when Edward dies. Is she not the granddaughter of Henry VIII's sister Mary? There is no taint of bastardy in Jane and, by God, she shall be Queen of England."

"Jane! Little Jane Grey Queen of England!"

"Certainly. It is the King's custom to name his successor here in England . . . and I have Edward's consent to this. With that and her superior claims over the bastard daughters of Katharine of Aragon and Anne Boleyn, she will indeed be Queen. But do not imagine my plans end there. Robert, had you not been such a fool as to rush into marriage with the daughter of a country squire, I would have made you King of England."

Robert for once was without speech. King of England! He saw himself in regal velvet. How that would have become him! Power! What did he know of power as yet? He realized his recent ignorance when he pictured what he might have been as husband to Lady Jane Grey—that fragile and most beautiful girl. It was true that she was a little too pious for Robert's taste, but she was an enchanting creature.

"Well, you have missed your chance," said the Duke, "and it will go to Guildford."

"I . . . see," said Robert.

His father laid his hand on his shoulder. He was regretful. What a king Robert would have made! Guildford would do his duty, but the Duke would rather it had been Robert. "Learn your lesson, my son. You are young, but it is never too soon to learn, as you now understand. See what your headstrong behaviour has done for you. You might have been the King, but you in your own youthful folly chose to be a country squire. Always look ahead. Always think of what the future may hold. No doubt your brother and his wife Queen Jane will bestow many honours upon you. But, you see, a little patience, a little foresight, would have brought you so much more. Now you know the position, but remember it is a secret as yet. We must succeed. The future of our house depends upon success. On the King's death there will be opposition to Jane's succession. We must be ready for that. You will return to Norfolk and wait there, but while you wait, you will gather together a goodly force in secret to be called upon if need be. You understand me?"

"Yes, Father."

That interview entirely changed Robert's outlook.

He returned to Norfolk in a very thoughtful mood. Nothing looked quite the same to him again. Amy was loving, but what a simpleton she was! He could not help comparing her rustic charm with the beauty of Jane Grey, her simplicity with Jane's learning; and he

46

could not help seeing beside Robert the Squire, Robert the King.

They saw the change in him when he returned. Amy was fretful and jealous. Pinto believed that he was in love with a woman whom he had met at the Court. Pinto had always sensed danger in Amy's marriage.

She tried to warn and advise. "Be patient. Do not flatter him so wholeheartedly. Hold aloof. Let him come to you for favours. Do not bestow them so generously."

Poor Amy tried to follow Pinto's advice, but how could she? When Robert was near her, she must beg for his smiles like a little dog performing her pretty tricks for him.

"Amy," he cried in exasperation, "when will you grow up?"

"But you used to say you loved my childishness."

"You cannot be childish for ever."

"But you used to rejoice because I was different from the girls you met at Court."

Ah, he thought, different indeed! Lacking the gracious enchanting dignity of the Lady Jane Grey, the fire and exciting qualities of the Princess Eizabeth.

Amy was shaking his arm. "Why do you not speak to me? Of what are you thinking? Why are you always staring out of the window, listening it seems. For what do you listen?"

"I . . . Listen! I listen for nothing."

"You do. I swear it. You are waiting . . . waiting for a message from someone . . . someone whom you met at the Court. Why do I never go there with you? Why must I always stay here in the country? Why, when you go to Court, do you go without me?"

How stupid she was!

He looked at her with mild distaste. Oh, what a fool he had been! He was the husband of a simple country girl, when he might have been married to a queen.

Her lips were trembling. He watched the tears roll down her cheeks as she fell on to a couch and began to sob.

Would he never learn? He was more foolish than ever. His father had entrusted him with a secret, and already he had almost betrayed it. She knew that something had happened on his visit to Court and, being the foolish child she was, she believed he was in love with another woman.

He sighed. He certainly had eyes for women—the women of the Court and the women of the country. Did silly little Amy think that since their marriage he had never looked at another?

Yet he must soothe her; she must not know that he had changed. She must not know of the thoughts which were now chasing each other through his mind. He who might have been the King of England would be the brother of a king; and Guildford had always admired him. He would be able to do what he wished with Guildford; power would come his way—but not if he allowed a simple country girl to know when he had a dangerous secret.

He bent over her, lifting the hair from her hot and tearful face.

"Amy," he whispered, "little Amy. What ails you? Why should you be jealous of the most faithful man in England?"

She raised her eyes to his face as he bent over her.

"But, Robert . . ."

"Why should you think these evil thoughts of me, eh? Tell me that."

"Because you have been away from me."

"On duty. Nothing but duty to my father would tear me from your side."

"But . . . there is something. Pinto says it is another woman."

"Pinto! What does she know of my affairs?"

"She knows much of the world, and she says that men are the same the whole world over."

"Come, kiss me, Amy. Let us prove that Madam Pinto, though she knows so much of most men, knows nothing of this one."

Now he was soothing her and she was ready to listen, so ready to believe what she wanted to believe more than anything on Earth; and he would not have been Robert if he had not been able to convince her.

It was night, and Amy awoke to find herself alone in the bed; the curtains about it were drawn, yet not so closely that they shut out the moonlight which filled the room. She put out a hand and touched the feather bed which still bore the impression of Robert's body.

She sat up. The fur rug which covered the blanket had been thrown aside. There was one thought in her head. He had crept out to go to a woman, she was sure; and that woman was not a lady of the Court, but one of her own household.

With tears in her eyes she got out of bed and put a wrap about her shoulders. She stood hesitating then, wondering whether to go and tell Pinto what she had discovered. Now that she was sure he was unfaithful she was miserably unhappy, and covering her face with her hands she sat down on a stool and began to rock to and fro. She sat thus, undecided for a long time until a noise from outside startled her. Hastily she rose and went to the window. In the moonlight she saw Robert, and with him was her father and another man. She was so delighted that she threw open the casement and called his name.

The men looked up. Her father waved his hand angrily at her indicating that she was to move away from the window. She obeyed in great perplexity.

It was only a few minutes before she heard the boards in the corridor outside her room creaking, and her door was opened by Robert who came quietly in. He was half dressed but she saw that his eyes were shining with excitement. She flung herself at him, sobbing with relief.

"I thought . . . I thought . . ."

He put his hand over her mouth. "Quiet . . . for the love of God, Amy, be quiet. What are you doing out of bed? You'll wake the whole household."

"But . . . I must know . . . I believed . . ."

He led her to the bed; he sat down on it and drew the curtains about them.

He was angry and his anger frightened her. "You will ruin everything," he said.

Even as he said those words they seemed to have a prophetic ring. She *would* ruin everything. Had she not already done much harm? His brother Guildford was married to the Lady Jane Grey; and at this moment, though few knew it, Jane Grey was Queen of England. He looked at Amy, pretty enough with her hair hanging about her shoulders and her wrap falling open to show those plump shoulders; but he had grown up; he had outgrown the simple country charms of Amy Robsart.

"You are going to leave me, Robert?" she said.

"Now listen to me. We had not meant that you should know. But since you have seen what you have seen, your father and I think there is no help for it but to tell you."

"What . . . what have I seen?"

He hid his exasperation. "Your father, myself, and the messenger."

"The messenger?"

"He comes this night from *my* father, and he comes with the utmost secrecy."

"Yes, Robert?"

How he wished at that moment that she was not there or that he had no wife, and that she was the young washerwoman who had caught his fancy in the kitchens not long ago, and who could, without curtailing his freedom, provide as much excitement and amusement as Amy ever gave him. His freedom! He felt hot with anger when he thought of his freedom. Guildford—King! And he, Robert, might have been in that exalted position. He could have put his hands about her throat and squeezed the life out of her.

"Robert, what is it? What ails you?"

When she spoke and he looked at her childish mouth, he was surprised at himself. As if such a creature could be allowed to stand in his way!

He said: "Poor Amy, I frightened you."

And he bent over her and brushed her mouth with his lips. Her hands came up to cling to him. Silly Amy!

51

She had no conception of what she had done to him. All she had said when she had learned about Guildford was: "What a great marriage your brother has made!" "Aye!" he wanted to shout at her. "And I might have made it!" She was too stupid to see that through her he had lost the great chance of a lifetime. All for the sake of a country girl who was no longer able to satisfy his carnal appetite!

"Don't be frightened, Amy," he said. "You do not think I would hurt you?"

"Nay . . . nay . . ." How she clung to him! He kissed her again; she was soft and warm from the feather bed. Poor Amy!

"Count yourself lucky," he said, "that you are my wife and not only your father's daughter. He would have made you smart for calling out as you did."

"But, Robert . . . I thought you had gone to visit a woman."

"Why did you think that? Do you doubt your powers to charm me?"

"No, Robert."

"Of course you do not! You have a high opinion of your charms. Do I not often see you simpering with Pinto as you look in the mirror?"

"But . . ."

"I am teasing, Amy. You must not be afraid. Can you keep a secret?"

"No, Robert, you know I cannot."

"You are an honest woman, Amy. But I know how to make you keep a secret, and because I know this I shall now trust you with a most important one."

"What do you mean, Robert?"

"If you betray this secret, Amy, you betray *me*."

"I still do not understand, Robert."

"You do not understand much, my Amy. But your father and I have decided to trust you with this secret. You have forced us to it. You have seen a stranger in your father's courtyard. You must say nothing of this man's presence here, for if you do it may cost me . . . your father too . . . it may cost us both our lives."

"How so?"

He put his hand on her bare flesh and felt her fluttering heart.

"Are you so frightened at the thought of losing me?" he asked. "Would it grieve you so much to see me mount the scaffold at Tower Hill?"

"I beg of you . . ." she began.

He interrupted: "I shall be leaving his house before dawn."

"Where will you go, Robert?"

"Great events are afoot. The King is dead but that is not generally known. My father has set a cordon of guards about Greenwich Palace; he has closed the ports. He wants this known only among his friends as yet."

"But what does it *mean*, Robert?"

"Amy, you have married into a great family. My brother will be King because his wife will be Queen. But we have to act before our enemies can. This night I leave with a few of my trusted followers. Can you guess on what mission, Amy?"

She shook her head.

"Of course you cannot." He stroked her hair almost tenderly. "What could you guess, dear Amy, but whether it would rain or the cream turn sour? Then like as not you would be wrong."

"Robert, what have I done to merit your displeasure?"

He looked at her sadly. Married me, was the answer. Closed the door which led to the highest power in the land. But he said; "Who told you I was displeased? Did I? Nay, Amy, I am not displeased, for I know that you will perform the most difficult task in your life . . . and all for my sake. You will keep a secret!" He laughed softly. He was so sure of her, so sure of himself. He could even succeed in making Amy keep a secret! "Now I will tell you, Amy. My mission is to capture the Princess Mary and take her to my father as his prisoner, thus making the throne safe for my sister Jane and my brother Guildford."

"But . . . Robert, these are great matters. They frighten me."

"You are too easily frightened, Amy. My father is unsafe, and so am I, until we have Mary under lock and key."

Amy's teeth began to chatter. "I am so frightened," she said.

He kissed her and laughed, thinking that it was just as well. "Be in good spirits, Amy. Now you will see what it means to have married a Dudley."

Lord Robert rested with his men at the town of King's Lynn. It was useless to keep up the pursuit. Mary had evaded him. She had too many friends in the country and someone had betrayed the Dudleys' intentions. When Mary had heard of her brother's death, and of the plot to capture her, she had gone at once to Kenninghall, the mansion which was owned by the Dukes of Norfolk—those sturdy Catholic enemies of the Dudleys—who had been out of favour lately, but were now preparing to return to it. The Howards of Norfolk, who thought themselves more royal than the Tudors, hated the Dudleys as they could only hate those whom they called upstarts. They were ready now to fight for Mary and the Catholic cause. So now, Mary proclaimed herself Queen, and hearing that Northumberland had sent his son Lord Robert Dudley to capture her, was gathering supporters about her as she went to Kenninghall.

At King's Lynn Robert heard that Mary had reached Framlingham, the heavily defended stronghold of the Norfolks; he knew that even if he pursued her, he could not take Framlingham with his present force. Therefore there was nothing to do but rest at King's Lynn and await his father's instructions.

Because the waiting seemed long, Robert began to lose a little of his confidence. He knew now that not only were many noblemen rallying to Mary's cause, but that the people were with her too.

What was happening in London? His father was to have joined him in Norfolk and he had not expected him to be so long in coming. At least one of his brothers should have come with the necessary reinforcements, that the soldiers might go on and capture Mary.

The anxious days passed slowly.

One night Robert was aroused from his sleep by the clatter of horses' hoofs in the cobbled streets. He sprang from his bed, shouting to his servants: "Hurry! The reinforcements are here!"

Soldiers were tramping up the stairs of the inn in

which he lay. Robert met them at the door of his room; but they were not the men he had expected; they did not come from his father nor his brothers. Two came forward and took their stand on either side of him. Robert was unarmed and helpless.

"Lord Robert Dudley," said another who stood before him—and beyond him he could see the stairs and corridors were full of soldiers—"you are my prisoner."

"What means this?" demanded Robert. "How dare you come there thus? On whose authority?"

"On the authority of Queen Mary."

"I know no such Queen," said Robert contemptuously. "I serve Queen Jane."

"There is no Queen Jane, my lord. Mary is Queen of England."

"My father. . . "

"The Duke has been arrested at Cambridge. He is now a prisoner in the Tower of London whither you are to go and join him with the other members of your family."

There was no escape.

During the journey to London he learned that the whole country had risen to support Queen Mary. Jane Grey's short reign was over. She had fallen and with her had fallen the Dudleys.

For many days Robert brooded on these events in his dismal cell in the Beauchamp Tower.

Crowds had gathered on Tower Hill that hot August day.

"Death to the Dudley!" they cried. "Long life to Queen Mary!"

Forty-three years had passed since John Dudley had stood on Tower Hill, a boy of nine, frightened and bewildered, not daring to look at the man who was mounting the scaffold. Then he had vowed: "I will be a ruler of men." And so he had been; he had risen from penniless orphan to be virtually ruler of England. He had started even lower than his father and he had climbed higher; but his steps had led him back to the same grim spot and it had taken him forty-three years—almost to the day—to complete his circuitous journey.

Even as he left the Gate House for the scaffold, he was wondering desperately if there was yet time to save himself. It had been such an arduous journey, and Ambition, his constant companion on that journey, would allow him no other. Love and Honour had to be cast aside to serve Ambition's demands. Now Ambition reminded him that little mattered except that John Dudley, Duke of Northumberland, saved himself and continued the onward march.

He was ready to abandon the Queen he had set upon the throne and swear allegiance to the new one. It mattered little if young Jane and Guildford went to the scaffold. There must be scapegoats. But if John Dudley lived he could start at once to rebuild the Dudley fortunes.

He was ready to lay before Mary's councillors all the information he had; he would show her who were her enemies; he would serve her to the end of his days; he would renounce the Protestant Faith. All he asked in return was his life.

But it was too late. He had too many enemies who remembered his arrogance and envied his genius; he had never cared that people should love him, only that they should serve him. It was no use asking for their friendship now.

The bell was tolling. John Dudley, Duke of Northumberland, such a short while ago the most powerful man in England, walked slowly to the scaffold and laid his head upon the block.

In the Beauchamp Tower, Robert listened to the bell's tolling, to the shouts of the people; and he knew that his father was dead.

II

At Hatfield House the Princess Elizabeth lay in her bed. She was sick, her household declared, of a malady which afflicted her from time to time. This malady never failed to come to her aid at those times when she was uncertain how to act; and there had been many occasions when, by discreetly retiring to the comparative safety of her curtained bed, she had avoided a trying situation.

Bed was obviously the place for her at this time; so, obediently the malady returned.

A courier had brought a letter to her that morning; it was from the Duke of Northumberland. Her brother, the King, was, according to the Duke's communication, urgently desiring to see his dear sister. "Your Grace should come with all speed," said the message, "for the King is very ill."

But the Princess, who had always instinctively bestowed her smiles in the right quarters, was naturally not without friends. Poor as she was and mighty as was Northumberland, she was the richer in friends.

Concealed on his person, the courier had another note for the Princess. It had been sewn in his shoe for safety, and when she read it Elizabeth saw that it had been written by a certain William Cecil, a man whom she believed to be her friend. "The King is already dead," ran the note. "It is the wish of Northumberland to place Jane Grey and his son Guildford on the throne, and to seize the persons of yourself and your sister. To obey the summons would be to place yourself in Northumberland's hands."

And so to bed went the Princess Elizabeth, after penning a note to the Duke regretting that she was too ill to leave Hatfield.

She was in danger. She knew it. But when had she ever been far from danger? She thought of gentle Jane Grey whom Northumberland would make Queen of England. Poor Jane! What did she think of these honours which were to be thrust upon her? Jane was learned, but what was the good of erudition if cunning did not go with it? Jane was a puppet. She would be no more Queen of England than Edward had been King. Her fate had been decided on when she had allowed Northumberland to marry her to his son Guildford. It had been obvious to Elizabeth what would follow as soon as that marriage had taken place.

Elizabeth remembered young Guildford well. He was a weakling. She, being strong, had an unerring instinct for smelling out weaklings. Now, had it been Robert . . . ! She wanted to laugh aloud when she thought of Robert who had married a simpering country girl. How could he have been such a fool! Yet was he such a fool? If he had not married his rustic bride he would have been married to the Lady Jane Grey. But was that such an enviable position? Only time would show. In any case Robert had no right to have married a country girl.

She laughed into her pillow, forgetting her danger,

for this short moment, in her memories. What a pity Kat Ashley was not with her. What fun they would have had with the cards . . . telling fortunes . . . seeing if anything came to light concerning Robert Dudley (a tall dark man) as they used to look for Tom Seymour.

How stupid to think of Tom now. She could never think of him and that dreadful time, without a tremor. Tom was beautiful with his great booming laugh, his mighty oaths and his strong arms. Tom Seymour . . . nothing but a headless corpse! And he had almost taken her with him to the grave, as in life he had wished to take her with him to the throne . . . to the marriage bed.

Never again must she be so weak as she had been with Tom. What an escape! She might have been tempted to marriage . . . to love. Tom was such a tempter. No one should tempt her in that way again. A Princess who is only a step or two from the throne must learn her lessons and learn them quickly, for there is often no second chance of doing so.

Now in this moment which she felt to be full of unknown dangers she must brood on that earlier danger still so clear to her.

She could picture him distinctly. She believed she would never forget him, the jaunty Admiral in his gorgeous garments who had come to her after the death of his wife, Katharine Parr, feigning great grief. But was it real grief, when all the time his eyes were pleading with her, telling her that he was now free?

Intuitively she had felt the inclination to hold back; it had ever seemed to her that the trimmings of courtship were more enticing than any climax could be. Elizabeth, almost seduced but never quite, was a much more attractive picture to her than Elizabeth conquered. It was an Admiral to woo her whom she had wanted—not a husband to command her. Men wished to be amused, titillated, enjoying in imagination that which she had the good sense to know could never in reality compare with such dreams.

Yet there had been times when she had been on the point of surrender to that fascinating man; there had been times when his cajoling ways had almost got the better of her good sense.

She was older now; she was wiser. When he had come to woo her she had been reluctant, aloof, in no way the same girl who had romped with him during his wife's lifetime. He had been clever in his way, but not quite clever enough. There had been so many ugly rumours connected with his name, and how could the Princess Elizabeth consent to marry a man who, it was said, had poisoned his wife that he might marry her?

No, the death of Katharine had been the first object lesson; the heartbreaking death of Thomas the second, and his had struck her so hard that it would never be forgotten.

How clear, in her memory, he was to her, as though he stood at the side of the bed now, laughing at her with passion in his eyes, trying to pull off the bedclothes as he had in Chelsea, to tickle, to slap, to kiss.

He had won Kat Ashley to his side. What had he said to Kat? Had he made light love to her with his eyes as he knew well how to do? Had he promised her rewards on the day the Princess Elizabeth became his wife? Kat was quickly his slave, as were so many of the women about their Princess. Kat began to find him a good influence in the cards . . . dear silly Kat! Elizabeth could hear her voice now with the trill of excitement in it. "Here is a good marriage for you, my darling; the best marriage that you could make. Now let me see, who is this husband I have here for you? He has a golden beard and he is handsome . . . how handsome! I believe he is connected with the sea . . ." Then Elizabeth would burst into laughter, and call Kat a fraud, and ask what the Admiral had given her to make her say that. They would laugh and giggle, abandoning the cards to talk of him.

She believed she had toyed with the idea. Yet had she seriously intended marriage with him? Already at that time her thoughts had soared high above him. Her brother Edward sickly, her sister Mary not very young and delicate too—and then . . . herself.

Was she glad that the Council would not agree to her marriage with the Admiral? When she had been asked if she would marry him her answer had been characteristic of her: "When the time comes and the Council shall give its consent, then shall I do as God puts into my mind."

And would she have eventually married Thomas? At that time he could flatter so charmingly; he could plead so passionately.

Dear Thomas! He always talked too much. Great power had been his through his charm and beauty, and the power was such a potent drug; it went to the head; it soothed the fears; it played tricks with a man's vision until he was twice the size he was in actuality. Thomas had boasted that he had ten thousand men ready to serve him, that he had persuaded the master of the Bristol mint to coin large sums of money which should be used in his service; he would marry Elizabeth and then . . . all would see what they should see.

And so Thomas was taken to the Tower on a charge of high treason.

What a time of terror when Kat Ashley and Parry the cofferer were also taken to the Tower, and she herself kept prisoner at Hatfield with guards outside her door, not allowed to venture out into the grounds without an escort! How apprehensive she had been for Thomas! How she had dreaded what Kat and Parry would say in the hands of the questioners!

And what had they said? How could she blame them? She did not. In fact she longed for the day when her dearest Kat would be restored to her. How could she have expected such as her dear tittle-tattling Kat or Parry to keep quiet? They were born gossips, both of them.

Soon the whole country was tattling. Out came the story—every little secret, every little scene, magnified, coloured, so that a little innocent flirting became an orgy of lust.

She flushed at the memory, but even so she began to laugh. Oh, why was not Kat here that they might chat together! She herself loved a gossip. She wished now to talk of Northumberland, and Jane Grey, and weak Guildford Dudley on whose head, Elizabeth doubted not, Northumberland would do his best to cram a crown. What fun it would have been during this "illness" to take the cards and to find a tall dark man—Lord Robert Dudley this time, as once they had found an Admiral—and for Kat to purse her lips, put her head on one side and mutter in that serious voice which could send Elizabeth into fits of laughter: "I think I see a handsome young man. He is about Your

Grace's age . . . and he comes out of the past . . ."

But how foolish to think of Kat, who had been taken from her, and of Robert Dudley, that foolish boy who had married a country girl!

Yet . . . how pleasant! And it was necessary to think pleasant and frivolous thoughts when at any moment life might become deadly serious and dangerous.

But now her thoughts had gone to the saddest moment of her life when they had come to her to tell her that Thomas was dead—her beautiful Thomas. She had been surrounded by spies; she had known they were watching her, trying to trip her, and she knew that every word, every look, would be noted and reported. Lady Tyrwhit (how she hated that woman whom they had given her in place of Kat!) had had her sly eyes on her, always watching, hoping that there would be some betrayal of feeling to report to her master the Protector, that false brother of dear Thomas.

She had faced them, calmly and courageously. Yes, she could look now with approval on that young Elizabeth who had not shown by a flicker of her eyes or a twitch of her lips that her heart was almost breaking.

"Your Grace," had said that spy Tyrwhit, "this day the Admiral laid his head upon the block." And she waited for the effect of her words.

Elizabeth looked back at the woman with no expression whatsoever on her face. Yet she knew she must speak. Lady Tyrwhit must not be allowed to report that her grief had made her speechless.

"This day," she had said, "died a man with much wit and very little judgement."

It was said of her that either she was without feeling or she was a magnificent actress. She was a great

65

actress. That was the answer; for without doubt she had loved Thomas.

And was she not acting all the time? Was it not necessary for her to act, to feign simplicity? How she had acted after the death of Thomas! She had lived quietly at Hatfield, giving up her days to study, reading Cicero and Livy, studying the Greek Testament, reading aloud the tragedies of Sophocles, studying Italian and French. She dressed simply, wore her hair unfrizzed—she who loved fine clothes and who loved to have her red hair frounced and curled, and to wear rich velvets and sparkling jewels. But she was clever enough to know that it was necessary to live down the reputation which the Seymour scandal had given her, and that to live in obscurity was the only way of preserving her life during those difficult days.

Her friends kept her closely informed of affairs at Court, and from the seclusion of Hatfield or Woodstock, she was aware of the heady progress of the Duke of Northumberland, thinking often of the gay Lord Robert who, had he not been so senseless as to marry a rustic girl, might have been a greater power in the land than a poor Princess who must keep as still as a lizard on a stone for fear any movement by her should attract the attention of her enemies.

She watched the tussle between Edward Seymour, Duke of Somerset, whom she would never forgive for what he had done to Thomas, and John Dudley, Duke of Northumberland, who was the father of that young man who interested her as no one had since the death of Thomas.

And now Somerset was dead. That which he had done to Thomas had been done to him. It was fearsome, thinking of the heads which fell so readily.

She needed to laugh in order to calm herself, to make light of her misfortunes so that when the test came she might face them with equanimity.

But what could she do now but lie abed . . . and wait?

The waiting was over sooner than she expected.

Faithful friends brought the news. The would-be Kingmaker had been defeated. Mary was proclaimed Queen of England. Now was the time for Elizabeth to recover from her malady.

She did so without any fuss; and her first move was to write a letter to the Queen conveying her congratulations and her delight in her sister's accession. There was an answer to that note: a command to meet Mary at Wanstead, that they might ride into the Capital together.

Elizabeth made ready for the journey. She was excited as always at the prospect of pageantry and a return to Court. Again and again she warned herself of her difficult position. Master Parry, who had come back to her service, also warned her. He flattered her in his sly way; she knew his words for flattery, but flattery was a luxury she would not go without.

"Your Grace must be careful to hide your beauty. The Queen will not be pleased at being outshone."

"Nonsense, Master Parry!" she retorted. "How can I in my simple garments outshine the Queen's royal velvet and glittering jewels?"

"Your Grace's eyes sparkle more brightly than jewels. Your skin is more soft than any satins."

She tossed her red hair, calling his attention to it;

and he smiled that sly smile which he did not attempt to hide from her. "Your Grace has a crown of gold more beautiful than any that ever sat on the brow of King or Queen."

"Enough, chatterer!" she cried. "I am right glad we bought new liveries for my servants this year, Master Parry. I do not grudge the forty shillings I paid for those new velvet coats."

"Your Grace is right, and we will make a brave show. But pray accept my warning: do not outshine the Queen."

She was demure thinking of it. She would wear white; she would cast down her eyes if the cheers for her were too loud. She would wear few jewels on her hands, for too many rings would hide their slender beauty; she would hold them so that the crowd might see them and marvel at their milky whiteness; and she would smile at the multitude—not haughtily but in that friendly way which had never yet failed to set them cheering.

No, she would not outshine the Queen in rich raiment or jewels, only in personal charm with youth and beauty and that subtle indication to the people that she was at one with them, that she loved them and one day hoped to be their Queen.

So, accompanied by a thousand followers—some of them lords and ladies of high rank—she came riding into London. Was it a good omen that she must pass through the City on her way to Wanstead, thus entering it before her sister?

The people of London came out to greet her as they always greeted the Princess Elizabeth. They caught their breath at the sight of her. She was so demure in her white gown; she looked so young; the people sensed in her the regality of her father and the vitality of her mother. She smiled and bowed and was clearly so grateful to the dear people for the homage they paid; she was so moved that there were tears in her eyes. About her rode her servants, all in green, some in velvet, some in satin, some in plain cloth, according to their standing in her household.

On through Aldgate she passed to Wanstead where she awaited the coming of the Queen.

Mary expressed her pleasure in this meeting with her sister.

How old she looks! thought Elizabeth.

Mary was not yet forty, but she looked older. Neither purple velvet nor jewels could alter that. She had suffered much and life had used her so cruelly that it had left its mark upon her.

"And is my dear sister recovered from her recent illness?" asked Mary.

"My humble thanks to your gracious Majesty. I am fully restored, and if I had not been before this moment, I could not fail to be now seeing your Majesty in such good health and knowing your enemies routed and yourself safely upon the throne."

"We cannot as yet say safely," said Mary grimly. "But we have good friends, we hope."

"And none more ready to serve your Majesty than your humble sister."

"I rejoice to hear it," said Mary; and she embraced Elizabeth.

They rode side by side towards London, these two daughters of Henry the Eighth, whose mothers had been such bitter enemies, and on that day the Queen was thinking how happy she was to have her sister beside her. She had been sorry for Elizabeth in those days when the girl had been in disgrace after the death of Anne Boleyn, neglected and unwanted, so that it had been difficult for her guardians to procure enough money to clothe and feed her. Cruel things had been said of this Elizabeth—far worse than anything that had ever been said of Mary. They had both been called bastards, but Elizabeth had suffered greater indignity, for some had declared that the Princess was the fruit of an incestuous union between Anne Boleyn and Anne's brother, Lord Rochford.

Mary hoped that Elizabeth would now conduct herself in such a manner that would enable them to live in amity.

Elizabeth demurely kept a little behind the Queen, now and then taking covert glances about her, throwing a smile at the crowds, letting her head droop when they cried too loudly for the Princess Elizabeth. She was thinking: What will happen now? She will marry, and if she bears a child, what hope have I of ever wearing the crown? Yet . . . how ill she looks! She is not strong enough to bear a child. And then . . . when she is dead?

The City was ready to greet the Queen to whom it had given its support. When Jane Grey had sailed down the river to the Tower that she might receive the crown, the people had been sullen; there had been few to cheer Queen Jane. The City did not want Queen Jane. She was young, beautiful, learned and noble; but right was right, justice was justice, and England accepted no other than Mary as its Queen.

From the windows of the houses strips of brilliantly

coloured cloth were fluttering. From over the old City Gate the charity boys and girls of the Spital sang the Queen's praises as she passed under. The streets had been cleaned and strewn with gravel; and the members of the City Guilds had come out in their full dress to welcome Mary to London. On the river was every sort of craft fluttering banners and streamers, some bearing musicians who played sweet music and sang victorious choruses which all had the same theme: the delight of the people of London to welcome their true Queen, the expression of their loyalty to Mary.

Down Leadenhall and the Minories to the Tower of London went the procession. The Lord Mayor greeted the Queen, and the Earl of Arundel was beside him with the sword of state. All about the Queen were her velvet-clad attendants; and next to her rode her sister Elizabeth.

Mary, to show her utmost confidence in the loyalty of her greatest City, had dismissed her guard at Aldgate and had accepted that of the City, and it now followed her and her ladies, each man carrying his bow and javelin.

Sir Thomas Cheney, warden of the Cinque Ports, greeted her as she came to the Tower. Elizabeth could not help but shudder as they passed through the gate and she gazed at the towers. She caught a quick glimpse of the Devlin, the Bell and the Beauchamp Towers, and she remembered that, in the Beauchamp, the handsome young man of whom she thought now and then, was lying a prisoner and that he would doubtless ere long follow his father to the block. It was a sobering thought for a girl who had so recently received the cheers of the crowd. She must think of all the noble men and women who had been shut away from the world in those grim towers, released only that they might take the short walk from their prisons to Tower Green or Tower Hill. She must think chiefly of her mother, who had come to this place by way of the Traitor's Gate and had left the world by way of Tower Green. She muttered a prayer as they went forward.

They had reached the church of St. Peter ad Vincula, and there on the very Green where Elizabeth's mother had received that blow from the executioner's sword which had ended her gay and adventurous life, knelt those prisoners of state who under the last two reigns had begged in vain for justice.

Among them were the old Duke of Norfolk, who had been saved by the timely death of Henry the Eighth and had been languishing in prison ever since, Cuthbert Tunstal, Bishop of Durham, and Stephen Gardiner, Bishop of Winchester; all were firm supporters of the Catholic Faith and they looked to the new Queen for honours.

The sight of the Bishops brought home afresh to Elizabeth the precarious nature of her position. Staunch Catholics, those men would inevitably view her with disfavour; and since the Queen had by no means the look of a healthy woman and, unless she had a child, Elizabeth was a likely successor, it seemed very probable that those two Catholic gentlemen would use all their formidable power to ensure that Elizabeth should never reach the throne. And what was their best way of doing that?

She imagined that these uneasy thoughts came from her mother's spirit—surely not far, on this summer's day, from the spot where it had departed from this Earth.

But there was one among those prisoners of state who turned Elizabeth's thoughts to pleasanter matters. This was young and handsome Edward Courtenay, a noble of great interest, not only on account of his handsome person, but because of his royal lineage.

His grandmother was Catherine, a daughter of Edward the Fourth, and he was therefore related to the Queen since Mary's grandmother, Elizabeth of York, had been that Catherine's sister. Courtenay had been a prisoner in the Tower since he was ten years old, which was fourteen years ago. His father had been executed by Henry the Eighth. Now the young man's hopes were bright, for Mary would never consent to the prolonged imprisonment of such a staunch Catholic.

He knelt gracefully before her now and lifted his handsome eyes to her face with such admiring devotion that the Queen was touched.

"Rise, cousin," she said, "you are no longer a prisoner. Your estates shall be restored to you. Your suffering is over."

There was a faint colour in the Queen's cheeks; and it seemed that even while she received the loyal addresses of men whom she could trust, such as Norfolk and Gardiner, her eyes strayed to the handsome young Courtenay.

Elizabeth, watching and alert, believed that there might be some truth in the rumours which had already begun to circulate as soon as it was known that Mary would take the crown. It was natural that her first duty would be to marry; and if she were wise she would please her people in this. The people of England wanted an English husband for their Queen; well, here was a young man of royal connexions, handsome, virile, surely capable of providing the Queen with the heir which all—except Elizabeth and those who followed her—must surely desire.

Mary was aware of this; Courtenay was also aware of it. But now it was the young man's duty to greet the Princess. Elizabeth extended her hand; he took it; her blue eyes were haughty, yet faintly coquettish; somehow they managed to convey a flirtatious message to the young man. You find my sister old? her eyes seemed to suggest. She is indeed many years older than you are, my lord. But look at me! I am younger than you are. What if I were the Queen whose hand in marriage you might have a chance to win? Ah, my friend, what a different prospect that would be, what a different and dazzling prospect, eh!

Courtenay rose and stood before her. Did he hesitate a little too long? Was the smile he gave the Princess a little too friendly, a little too overcharged with admiration?

The Queen had turned impatiently.

"Have a care," the spirit of Anne Boleyn might have warned her daughter.

But Elizabeth, cautious and clever as she habitually was, could never resist inviting admiration. To her it was life itself—as necessary as the sun and air.

Who could understand that better than Anne Boleyn? She would certainly wish to warn her daughter.

Jane Dudley, the Duchess of Northumberland, was a

broken-hearted woman. In a few short weeks she had lost most of what had made life good for her. John, her husband, was dead. He had shared his father's fate. The cruelty of that stunned her; and yet it was not wholly unexpected.

In the solitude of her house in Chelsea, which was all that was left to her of her grand possessions, she mourned bitterly. It was futile to weep for John, but what of her sons? With the exception of little Henry, who was too young to have been suspected of treason, they were lying in the Tower. John, the eldest, was already sentenced to death. Ambrose, Robert and Guildford were all awaiting trial.

As she walked from one deserted room to another she cried out: "Oh, John, why were you not content to live in peace and happiness? We had riches; we had comfort. You placed our beloved sons and daughters in danger. It was not only your own life that you risked."

She must act. She must do something to save her sons.

She had become like a miser, gathering together a little store of her precious possessions which had been overlooked when her goods had been confiscated. She intended to offer them as presents to any who would help her to save her sons. This was the only task which was left to her.

Dared she crave an audience with the Queen? Was it possible to ask Mary to pardon those who had plotted to destroy her? They had sent her to the Tower when they had taken John, but quickly released her, and she feared that if she tried to see the Queen she might be sent back to her prison. Not that she cared if she were. The discomfort of a cell would mean nothing to her.

But if she were imprisoned, how could she work for her sons?

In the days of her husband's greatness many had come to him with petitions for help; they had offered him money and costly goods. John had amassed a fortune in those years when he had ruled England. Now she herself would plead, as others had pleaded with him. She would offer everything she possessed. She would gladly live in poverty for the rest of her life if her sons might be free.

Each day she walked to the palace. Sometimes she saw people who in the old days had flattered her and thought themselves fortunate when she exchanged a few words with them. Now they turned away. It was not due to pride, or scorn, or unkindness. It was fear. Naturally they were afraid. How could they show friendship to a woman whose husband had plotted against the Queen, to a woman whose son was married to the girl they now called the impostor Queen?

"Oh, God, help me!" prayed Jane.

She was almost demented. She went by barge to the Tower; she would stand in great distress contemplating those impregnable walls.

"What will become of you all?" she murmured. "My John . . . Ambrose . . . my poor Guildford and my gay and handsome Robin!"

Elizabeth knew of the plight of the sad Duchess and wished that she could help her. But how could she of all people plead for the Dudleys' release? Her own position was too precarious for her to risk pleading for others.

Already the Queen was casting suspicious eyes upon

her. Already Gardiner and Simon Renard, the Spanish ambassador, were seeking to destroy her. And they were not alone in this endeavour. Noailles, the French ambassador, was as dangerous as the other two, although he pretended to be her friend.

He would seek her out when she walked in the grounds that he might speak to her alone.

He told her: "My master knows your position to be a dangerous one. You have my master's sympathy. He seeks to help you."

"The King of France is noted for his goodness," said Elizabeth.

"I will tell him how you speak of him. It will enchant him."

"Nay. He could not be interested in the opinion of such as I am."

"Your Grace is mistaken. The King of France is your friend. There is much he would do to save you from your enemies. He deplores that you are deemed a bastard. Why, he would do all in his power to reinstate you."

She looked at him coolly. "But alas it is not in your royal master's power to have me proclaimed legitimate. Such must surely be left to the decision of the mistress of this realm."

She left him and she knew that he was angry.

She was too clever to be deceived by an offer of French friendship. She knew full well that Henri Deux wished to destroy her, so that, should Mary die childless, the field would be clear for his own daughter-in-law, Mary Queen of Scots.

Elizabeth knew, as she made her way to her apartments, that danger was all about her. It would be so easy to become involved in plots with the French. She understood the schemes of the crafty Noailles. He wished to entangle her, to make her betray herself in a way which would lead her to the scaffold.

There was no friendship for Elizabeth in France or in Spain, and she would never be deceived into thinking there was.

Much as the Princess loved the gaiety of the Court, she began to yearn for the peace of her country houses, for only far from intrigue could she have any great hope of survival.

Gardiner was speaking against her to the Queen because she refused to go to Mass. Yet what could she do? She knew that a very large body of Protestants looked to her as their leader. If she accepted her sister's religion as wholeheartedly as Mary wished her to, it would mean that those Protestants would say: "What matters it which sister is on the throne?" She would lose their support and she would not gain that of the Catholics. So she must hold out against the Mass for as long as she could. But how long could she hold out? Gardiner was urging that she should either be brought to Catholicism or to the block.

The Queen sent for her.

Mary was cold and Elizabeth's heart quaked as she knelt before her.

Oh, to be at Hatfield or Woodstock where she could suddenly feel her old malady stealing over her, where she could beg for a few days' grace to recover before she made an arduous journey to see the Queen! It was not so easy here.

"We have heard that which does not please us concerning you," said Mary.

Elizabeth answered in a mournful voice: "I see plainly that your Majesty has but little affection for me, yet I have done nothing to offend you except in this matter of religion. Your Majesty must bear with me, must excuse my ignorance. Remember in what religion I have been brought up. Your Majesty will understand how I have been taught to accept my religion and no other."

"You are old enough to recognize the truth."

"Ah, your Majesty, if I had time to read and learn, if doctors might be sent to me . . ."

It was the old cry; "Give me Time." Time had always been her friend.

Elizabeth looked at the pale face of her sister. How ill she looked, how white and sickly! Only a few more years and then . . . Glory!

The thought gave her courage.

Mary was frowning. One of her dearest wishes was to bring England back to Rome. This girl, young as she was—frivolous and coquettish—could do much to prevent this. Mary must weaken the Protestants, and what weakened a force more than the knowledge that one whom they looked upon as a leader had capitulated? There were three religious sections in England now. There were the Anglo-Catholics, who followed the religion established by Henry the Eighth, which was the same as the old religion with the exception that the sovereign, not the Pope, was the head of the church; there was the Protestant Church, now established as the Church of England since the Protestant Protectorate under Edward VI; and there was the old religion which looked to the Pope as its head. The last, in the Queen's eyes, was the true

79

religion, and the one which she wished to see established throughout her realm.

Mary was not altogether displeased with Elizabeth's reply. She preferred it to a plain refusal which would have resulted in Elizabeth's being taken to the Tower.

"I will send doctors to you to teach you the truth," said the Queen.

"Your Majesty is so gracious that I would make another request."

"What is that?"

"It would be easier for me to study in the country away from the Court. I realize that I have gone far in my studies of the new Faith and that much concentration will be needed . . ."

"You shall not leave Court," said Mary grimly.

Was she beginning to understand this sister who had managed to extricate herself from many an awkward situation with the help of her old friend Time?

Well, thought Elizabeth, I must continue to be exposed to great dangers. But surely the Queen must understand that a great deal of time is needed if I am to assimilate such great truths to which I am now a stranger!

The thoughts of most people were now directed to the Coronation. Only such as Elizabeth and the Duchess of Northumberland had thoughts of more urgency.

Elizabeth's constant thoughts were of her own preservation. Jane Dudley was only capable of one desire, so overwhelming was it. She had seen a lady of the Court who had come to visit her out of kindness, leaving her barge at the privy stairs, hastening across the lawns wrapped in a cloak which disguised her. It was now as great a danger as it had been an honour to visit the Northumberland residence.

"Oh, Jane, Jane, you must not despair," cried this lady, embracing her old friend. "The Queen is of a kindly nature. It bodes good that so far your eldest remains in his cell. They say that she is reluctant to send the Lady Jane to the block, even though Gardiner and Renard are persuading her to do so. She wishes to show clemency and I feel sure that she will. Only . . . for a time they must remain prisoners. Wait until after the Coronation. Then Her Majesty will feel safe on the throne, and the safer she feels, the more merciful will she be."

Jane wept. "It is because I feel happier this day," she explained.

"As soon as the Coronation is over I will try to put in a word in the right quarter, dear Jane. Perhaps you may be allowed to visit your boys. Be of good cheer. The more time that elapses, the better, for the more likelihood there will be of their release. Remember, the three younger ones have not yet been tried."

After that life seemed more bearable. Jane longed for the Coronation to be over.

What rejoicing there was throughout the City when the Queen set out! In a litter covered with cloth of silver and borne by six handsome white horses, Mary was surrounded by seventy of her ladies all clad in crimson velvet. The Queen herself wore blue velvet trimmed with ermine. Her cap was of gold net ornamented with diamonds and pearls. It was so heavy that she could scarcely hold up her head—which was unfortunate, for she suffered much from painful headaches. Mistress Clarencius, her old nurse and the woman whom she trusted more than any other, glanced at her anxiously from time to time and longed to remove that heavy head ornament which she knew was causing pain and discomfort.

Mary suffered from more than a headache on that day. She was deeply conscious of her young sister. She knew that many in the crowds would be comparing them—the sick looks of one, the glowing health of the other, age with youth, Catholic with Protestant. Was Gardiner right? Was Renard right? Was it folly to let Elizabeth live?

Elizabeth was enjoying her state ride. She might be about to die, but such pageantry, with herself playing a prominent part, was the birthright of a daughter of Henry the Eighth. Beside her sat her father's fourth wife—Anne of Cleves—the only one of six still alive. They were dressed alike, which, for Elizabeth, was an advantage. Anne of Cleves had never been a beauty, and now she was an excellent foil for the radiant young girl of twenty as they sat side by side in their gowns of cloth of silver with the long hanging sleeves, not unlike those which Elizabeth's mother had introduced from France.

In Fenchurch Street addresses were declaimed by four men, all of whom were nearly seven feet tall. In Gracechurch Street the procession paused that a trumpeter dressed as an angel might play a solo to the Queen; Heywood the poet read some of his verses to Mary at the gates of St. Paul's School. The people shouted with glee and prepared to make merry as they cheered the Queen, the Princess Elizabeth and the young and handsome Edward Courtenay who had now been created Duke of Devonshire. Red wine flowed in the conduits, and this boon pleased the people as much as any.

A few days before the Coronation the Queen came to Whitehall from St. James's; and there she stayed until the first day of October, when she set out for Westminster Abbey for the ceremony of crowning.

Elizabeth with Anne of Cleves walked directly behind the Queen. Elizabeth's hopes were high. Surely, she reasoned, the Queen could not feel cold towards her since she allowed her to take such a prominent part in the ceremony.

Elizabeth could not help imagining, during that glittering occasion, that it was herself who held the centre of the stage.

She heard the voice of Gardiner: "Here present is Mary, rightful and undoubted inheritrix, by the laws of God and man, to the crown and royal dignity of this realm of England, France, and Ireland; and you shall understand that this day is appointed, by all the peers of this land, for the consecration, unction and coronation of the said most excellent Mary. Will you serve at this time and give your wills and assent to the same consecration, unction and coronation?"

And Elizabeth, with all those present, cried: "Yea, yea, yea! God save Queen Mary!"

But the name she seemed to hear was not Mary but Elizabeth.

Whilst the oraisons were said over Mary, whilst her mantle was removed, whilst she was anointed and her purple velvet ermine-edged mantle laid again about her shoulders, Elizabeth saw another in her place. One day it would be Elizabeth who was in robes of velvet, the crown on her head, the sceptre in her right hand, the orb in her left. It would be Elizabeth to whom the peers knelt in homage and allegiance, Elizabeth whose left cheek was kissed. "God save Queen Elizabeth!" would be the cry in her ears.

And when they left the Abbey, among the cheering crowds Elizabeth thought she saw a woman, with a white and tragic face and mournful eyes, who stood out among the gaily cheering people because she did not cheer, because she was sad in the midst of all that gaiety.

Was it the sorrowing Duchess of Northumberland?

Elizabeth shivered. Here was another reminder of how close disaster could be to triumph.

A few weeks later when winter had set in, many people waited in the cold streets to see another procession. This was in great contrast with the glittering spectacle of the Queen's Coronation.

Bishop Ridley led this procession, and among those who walked behind him was Lord Robert Dudley.

Robert held his head high. He, who longed for excitement, was glad even of this; he appeared jaunty as he walked through the narrow streets. Even at the Guildhall, he could only shrug his powerful shoulders. It was what he expected. Ambrose, Guildford, and Lady Jane had already been condemned and returned to their prisons. It was his turn now. And what could save one who had without doubt plotted against the Queen? It was useless to do anything but plead guilty.

It was no surprise to Lord Robert that when he left Guildhall for his journey back to the Tower, the blade of the axe should be turned towards him. He had been condemned to that terrible death which was reserved for traitors: to be hanged, cut down alive and disembowelled.

But Robert was by nature optimistic. It would be the axe for him. The son of a Duke would not die the ignoble death of common traitors.

So back to his cell in the Beauchamp Tower he went to await the summons to Tower Hill. But on the way he was aware of women in the crowd who had come to gaze at the prisoners. He noted their looks of sympathy and interest. Life in a dismal cell could not rob him of his powers to charm.

"What a handsome young man!" it was murmured. "So young to die."

And it was Robert whom their eyes followed.

There was one woman who watched him. She longed to call out his name as he passed; yet she hid herself, fearing that the sight of her there might distress him. How noble was his carriage, she thought; and how careless he seemed of his fate! That was what she would expect of her proud Robin.

As the procession passed on, Jane Dudley fell swooning to the ground.

There was perturbation at Court. The Queen had, after showing favour to Edward Courtenay, turned against him. Some said this was due to her discovery of the profligate habits in which he had indulged during his stay in the Tower. He was without doubt a libertine and could not be so enamoured of an ageing woman as he pretended to be. Others, more knowledgeable, believed the change in her manner towards this young nobleman could be explained by the secret conferences she had had with the Spanish ambassador, and the fact that Philip, the son of Emperor Charles and heir to vast possessions, was a widower.

Noailles, the French ambassador, secretly sought out the Princess Elizabeth.

"Your Grace has heard that the Queen considers marriage with the Prince of Spain?" he asked.

"There have been such rumours."

"Your Grace must know that a union with Spain would be most unpopular in England."

"The Queen is mistress of the country and herself. She will marry when and whom she pleases."

"There are many people in this country who would not tolerate a Spanish marriage."

"I know nothing of them."

"Does Your Grace know why the Queen has turned from Courtenay? It is because she suspects where his affections really lie."

In spite of Elizabeth's control her eyes brightened. "I do not understand Your Excellency."

"It is Your Grace of whom he is enamoured. He is so far gone in love for you that he is ready to throw away an immediate crown for the hope of a future one."

Elizabeth saw the danger. "I know nothing of this," she said.

"Yet others do. They are saying that if Courtenay married you, and you succeed to that for which you have a claim, the people would be happier than they would be to see a Spaniard the Queen's husband."

Her heart was beating fast. Again she heard the Abbey service and the cry of the peers: "God save Queen Elizabeth!"

She thought then of the woman she had seen in the crowd, of the Dudley brothers at this moment awaiting the penalty of ambition which had failed.

Noailles went on: "Courtenay has powerful friends in Devon and Cornwall. Your Grace, a great future lies before you."

I am crossing a chasm on a flimsy bridge, she thought. Walk with balanced care and I shall find a throne awaiting me; but one false step and down . . . down to disaster, down to a cell in the Tower, and the block.

Noailles wished to prevent the Spanish marriage at all costs because it was against the interest of France that it should take place. But would he wish to see Elizabeth on the throne? Indeed no! His plot would be to ferment trouble which would remove Mary and Elizabeth and leave the way clear for Mary Queen of Scots. Her lips were scornful. The French ambassador must think her a fool.

As soon as he left her, Elizabeth sought an audience with the Queen. Mary granted this, but as Elizabeth was kneeling before her she saw that Mary's attitude towards her was no more friendly than it had been on their previous meeting. The Spanish ambassador, knowing the unpopularity of the match he was trying to make for the son of his master and the Queen of England, was aware that there were some factions who would prefer to put Elizabeth on the throne and allow her to marry Courtenay. If such a thing should come to pass, England would once more be a Protestant country. Renard was therefore urging the Queen to send Elizabeth to the block. He was sure that the Princess was concerned in plots against the Queen, and he was determined to trap her and thus override the Queen's sentimental feelings for her sister. But the girl, for all her youth and seeming innocence, was more cunning than those ambassadors. Always she eluded them.

Renard had warned Mary, and the Queen, as she watched her kneeling sister, remembered those warnings.

"Your Majesty," said Elizabeth, "I crave leave to retire to one of my country houses."

"Why so?" asked Mary.

"My health is failing. I need the fresh country air."

"You appear to me very healthy."

"I suffer much, Your Majesty. In the quiet of the country I could study the books Your Majesty has set me to study. I feel that in the quiet of Woodstock or Hatfield I could come to an understanding with the truth."

"You will stay here," said the Queen, "that I may know what plans you make and whom you have about you."

Elizabeth was dismissed. She left the Queen's apartment with much apprehension, knowing that she was living through one of the most critical periods in a lifetime of danger.

Strangely enough the Spanish ambassador came to her aid though unwittingly.

The entire country now knew that the Queen was favourably considering a match with Spain. There was disquiet throughout the land, for the English hated the Spaniards; and there was much talk of the virtues of Elizabeth.

The Queen had stubbornly refused to acknowledge her sister's legitimacy. It seemed that she was afraid to do this because the people might decide that a younger, legitimate daughter who was a Protestant would be a better ruler for England than the elder, Catholic daughter of Henry the Eighth. But the real reason simply was that if she herself were legitimate, Elizabeth could not be, for the only way in which Elizabeth could be legitimate was by declaring her father's marriage with Katharine of Aragon void. Therefore it was not possible for both of them to be legitimate.

The Spanish ambassador, wishing to precipitate matters, unwisely sought to implicate his old enemy Noailles. It would be a master stroke to have Noailles sent back to France and Elizabeth to the block at the same time. He accused Noailles of visiting Elizabeth's chamber at night in order to plot against the Queen.

This was a ridiculous accusation and the plot was exposed, for not even Elizabeth's enemies could find a case against her.

On her knees before the Queen she cried: "I beg of Your Majesty never to give credit to the evil tales which are spread concerning me, without giving me an opportunity to prove myself guiltless."

Mary believed sincerely in justice, and Elizabeth's words were well chosen.

"My dear sister," said Mary, "I am sorry that you have been misjudged. Take these pearls as a sign of my affection."

Elizabeth accepted the pearls and was quick to take advantage of the situation. She lifted her eyes to her sister's face and said: "Your Majesty is so good to me. I know you will give me leave to retire from Court that I may live in quietness and hasten to do what Your Majesty would have me do. Give me your gracious permission to retire that I may study the books you have set me to study, the sooner that I may govern my thoughts and lead them whither Your Majesty would have them go."

The permission was granted and, with great relief, Elizabeth retired from imminent danger.

There was one way of escape from ever-threatening danger. Often she thought of it; always she rejected it.

The King of Denmark had offered his son, Philibert Emmanuel, the Duke of Savoy, as a husband for her. Spain favoured such a match, and therefore it received due consideration by the Queen.

While she lived her quiet life in her house at Ashridge, Elizabeth was filled with apprehension. If a stranger rode up she would be on the alert for a messenger from the Queen bringing a summons for her to appear at Court, which might be followed by imprisonment and death. Only by marrying a foreign Prince could she escape that constant fear. But to abandon fear was also to abandon her most cherished dream. As the Duchess of Savoy she would never hear those magic words which, perhaps next year, or the year after that, or in five or ten years' time, could ring in the ears of the Princess Elizabeth: "God save Queen Elizabeth!"

No, here she was, and here she would stay. All her hopes were in England, and if at times she felt she would never succeed in climbing the slippery path which led to the summit of ambition, well then, she would rather fall in the attempt than give up the climb.

Emphatically she refused the offer from the Duke of Savoy.

The Queen and her ministers were annoyed, but mildly; and temporarily the matter was allowed to drop.

She lived quietly in the country for a few weeks, eagerly learning all she could of what was happening at Court from her friends who were still there.

News came—wild news, news which might lead to triumph or disaster. Wyatt had risen in protest against the Spanish marriage. Letters asking for her support had been sent to her, but she would have nothing to do with such a rebellion. She knew that her hope of success lay in waiting. She knew that Courtenay was concerned in the Wyatt plot, and handsome as he was he was weak and untrustworthy; and if the plot were successful, the Duke of Suffolk, who was also one of the leaders, would surely hope to bring his own daughter Lady Jane Grey to the throne rather than help Elizabeth.

No! Rebellion was not for her.

And she was soon proved to be right, for Courtenay turned traitor in a moment of panic and confessed the plot to Gardiner, so that Wyatt was forced to act prematurely. The rebellion failed and Wyatt was under arrest; Courtenay and Suffolk were sent to the Tower, and the order went forth that Lady Jane and Lord Guildford Dudley were to be executed without delay. Unfortunately for Elizabeth, letters written by Noailles and Wyatt, intended for her, were intercepted and put before the Queen.

When the summons came, Elizabeth knew that in all the dangerous moments of a hazardous life, there had never been one to equal this.

There was one thing she could do. She could go to bed. Alas, she declared, she was too ill to travel; and indeed, so terrified was she, that her illness on this occasion was not altogether feigned. She could neither eat nor sleep; she lay in agony of torment—waiting, listening for the sound of the horses' hoofs in the courtyard which would announce the arrival of the Queen's men.

It was not long before they came.

They were not soldiers come to arrest her, but two of the Queen's physicians, Dr. Wendy and Dr. Owen.

Her trembling attendants announced their arrival.

"I cannot see them," said the Princess. "I am too ill for visitors."

It was ten o'clock at night, but the doctors came purposefully into her chamber. She looked at them haughtily.

"Is the haste such that you could not wait until morning?" she asked.

They begged her to pardon them. They were distressed, they said, to see her Grace in such a sorry condition.

"And I," she retorted, "am not glad to see *you* at such an hour."

"It is by the Queen's command that we come, Your Grace."

"You see me a poor invalid."

They came closer to the bed. "It is the Queen's wish that you should leave Ashridge at dawn tomorrow for London."

"I could not undertake the journey in my present state of fatigue."

The doctors looked at her sternly. "Your Grace might rest for one day, after that we must set out without fail for London on pain of Her Majesty's displeasure."

Elizabeth was resigned. She knew that her sick-bed could give her at most no more than a few days' grace.

She was carried in a litter which the Queen had sent for her; and the very day on which she set out was that on which Lady Jane Grey and her husband Lord Guildford Dudley walked the short distance from their prisons in the Tower to the scaffold.

Some of the country people came out to watch the Princess pass by, and she was deeply aware of their sympathetic glances. They thought of the lovely Jane Grey who was only seventeen; she had had no wish to be Queen, but the ambition of those about her had forced her to that eminence. And perhaps at this moment she was saying her last prayers before the executioner severed that lovely head from her slender body. The people could feel nothing but pity for that young girl; and here was another—this young Princess who might be on her way to a similar fate.

For once Elizabeth was desolate and afraid. She was delaying the journey as much as possible because she believed that Mary's anger might cool if given time. Therefore each day's delay was important. She spent the first night at Redbourn and her second halt was at St. Albans. Oh, that she might rest a little longer in the comfortable hospitality of Sir Ralph Rowlett's mansion! But they must go on to Mimms and to Highgate. She made a point of resting as long as she possibly could at these places, and the journey took ten days, far longer than was really necessary.

When Elizabeth reached London it was to find a subdued City in which many gibbets had been erected. Men were hanging outside the doors of their houses; there was a new harvest of heads on the Bridge. London had little heart to welcome the Princess who was sadly conscious of her own uneasy head.

But as she passed through the Capital, which had always been friendly to her, she roused herself from her melancholy. She had the litter uncovered that the people might see her all in white, a colour which not only set off the glory of her hair, but seemed to proclaim her spotless innocence; she sat erect and proud, as though to say; "Let them do what they will to an innocent girl." And if the people of London felt that at such a time it would be unwise to cheer the Princess, they did not refrain from weeping for her; and they prayed that she might not suffer the fate which had befallen the Lady Jane Grey.

She was taken to the Palace of Whitehall.

It was on the Friday before Palm Sunday that Elizabeth, in her closely guarded apartments at the Palace, heard from her attendants that Bishop Gardiner with some members of the Queen's Council was on his way to visit her.

At length he stood before her—the great Bishop of Winchester, one of the most powerful men in the kingdom and her declared enemy.

"Your Grace is charged," he said, "with conspiracy against the Queen. You are charged with being concerned in the Wyatt plot."

"This is a false accusation."

"Letters are in the Queen's possession which will prove that you speak not the truth, and it is Her Majesty's pleasure that you should leave this lodging for another."

Elizabeth could not trust herself to speak; that which she had most dreaded was upon her.

"Your Grace is to be removed this day to the Tower."

She was terrified, yet determined not to show her fear. She boldly answered: "I trust that Her Majesty will be far more gracious than to commit to that place a true and innocent woman who never offended her in thought, word nor deed."

"It is the will of Her Majesty that you should prepare to leave for the Tower this day."

An impulse came to her to throw herself upon her knees and plead with these men. Instead she stood still, looking haughtily at them.

"I beg of you, my lords," she said, "either to plead my case before the Queen or to ask her graciously to permit me to see her."

Gardiner answered: "The Queen's orders are that you shall prepare to leave at once."

The Earl of Sussex was moved by her youth, her courage and her desperate plight. He said: "If it be in my power to persuade the Queen to grant you an audience, I will do so."

They left her then, and when they had gone she collapsed upon a stool. She covered her face with her hands and whispered: "So did my mother go to the Tower . . . never to return."

All that night she waited for a summons from the
95

Queen. Her servants told her that the gardens surrounding the palace were being patrolled by guards; they were in the palace itself, for it was greatly feared that there might be some plot for her escape.

The next day the Earl of Sussex came to her to tell her that she must leave at once, for a barge was prepared and the tide would not wait. She wrote a note to the Queen and pleaded so earnestly with Sussex to take it to her that he was deeply moved.

"My lord Earl," she implored, "I beg of you to take it now."

He hesitated, but he could not resist her pleading and he took the letter to the Queen.

Mary was enraged. This, she cried, was a ruse of her sister's. Did not my lord Sussex realize that she had duped him into missing the tide for that day?

The next day was Palm Sunday and there was nothing to prevent her going to the Tower.

She had not been taken on the midnight tide because it was feared that in the darkness a rescue might be possible.

As she walked to the barge she murmured: "The Lord's Will be done. I must be content seeing this is the Queen's pleasure!" Then she turned to the men who walked beside her and cried out in sudden anger: "It is an astonishing thing that you who call yourselves noblemen and gentlemen should suffer me, a Princess and daughter of the great King Henry, to be led to captivity, the Lord knoweth where, for I do not."

They watched her furtively. How could they be sure what she would do? They—stalwart soldiers and statesmen—were afraid of this slender young girl.

The barge sped quickly along the river, while the

Londoners were at Church, that they might not see her pass by and show her that sympathy which they had never failed to give her. Quickly they came to the Tower—that great grey home of torment, of failure and despair.

She saw that they were taking her to the Traitor's Gate, and this seemed to her a terrible omen.

"I will not be landed there!" she cried.

It was raining and she lifted her face that she might feel the rain upon it, for when would she again be at liberty to feel its softness? How gentle it is! she thought. How kind in this cruel world!

"Your Grace . . ." urged Sussex.

"Must I then land here . . . at the Traitor's Gate? Look! You have misjudged the tide. How can I step into the water?"

Sussex put his cloak about her shoulders to protect her from the rain. In sudden pettishness she threw it off and stepped out. The water came above her shoe, but she did not heed it. She cried in a ringing voice: "Here lands as true a subject, being prisoner, as ever landed at these stairs. Before Thee, oh God, I speak it, having no other friend but Thee alone."

As she passed on, many of the warders came out to see her, and some of them brought their children with them. The sight of these small wondering faces calmed the Princess. She smiled wanly at them, and one little boy came forward on his own account and, kneeling before her, said in a high piping voice: "Last night I prayed God to preserve Your Grace, and I shall do so again."

She laid her hand on his head. "So I have one friend in this sorry place," she said. "I thank you, my child."

Then several of the warders cried out: "May God preserve Your Grace."

She smiled and sat down on one of the damp stones, looking at them almost tenderly.

The Lieutenant of the Tower came to her and begged her to rise. "For, Madam," he said, "you sit unwholesomely."

"Better sit here than in a worse place," she retorted, "for God, not I, knows whither you bring me."

But she rose and allowed herself, with those few women who had been permitted to accompany her, to be led into the Tower.

The Earl of Sussex still walked beside her. "Your Grace," he murmured, "you will understand that I like not this task which has been put upon me. Rest assured that I shall do everything in my power to ease your stay in this place."

"My lord," she answered softly, "I forget not your kindness to me."

She was conducted to the apartments prepared for her—the most heavily guarded in the Tower; and as her weeping ladies gathered about her, she felt her courage return.

So it had come—that which she had so often dreaded. Her thoughts were not of the trials which lay ahead but of her conduct during her journey to this place. Had any seen that when they had brought her through the Traitor's Gate she had almost swooned? She fervently hoped that none had witnessed that display of fear.

Now she felt so calm that she was able to soothe her women. "What happens now is in the hands of God," she consoled them. "And if they should send me to the block, I will have no English axe to sever my head from my body; I shall insist on a sword from France."

They knew then that she was remembering her mother, and they wept more wildly; but she sat erect, her tawny head high, while she calmly looked into a future which might bring her a crown or a sword from France.

III

Robert was pacing up and down his cell. He had been excited since that rainy Palm Sunday when he had heard, from the warder who brought his meals, that there was a most distinguished prisoner not very far from him.

How long had he to live? he wondered. Young Guildford had gone, alas! It was a sobering thought. Guildford and he had spent so much of their lives together. Father . . . Guildford . . . Who next?

When the threat of death hung over a man for so long, there were times when he forgot about it. It was some months since he had walked from the Guildhall back to the Tower, aware of the axe with its edge turned towards him. When his cell door had been locked upon him and he was alone with those two servants, whom, because of his rank, he was allowed to have with him, he had felt nothing but bleak and utter despair; he had almost longed to be summoned for that last walk. But such as Robert Dudley did not despair for long. He had been born lucky. Was he not Fortune's darling? Had she not shielded him when she had made him commit the seemingly foolhardy act of marrying Amy? If he had not done so, it would have been Robert, not Guildford, who had walked to the scaffold to be beheaded with the Lady Jane Grey, since his father would most certainly have married him to that most tragic young lady. The more he thought of it, the more convinced he became that he was preserved for some glorious destiny.

It was Easter time, always a season for hope.

The warder came in to bring his food, and with him he brought his small son. The little boy, not quite four years old, begged that he might accompany his father when he visited Lord Robert. The child would stand gravely surveying the prisoner, and although he said nothing, his eyes scarcely left Robert's face.

Robert was amused. He could see in the child's eyes the same admiration and sympathy which had shone in those of the women who had stood in the street to watch him on his journey from Guildhall to the Tower.

He bowed to the boy and said: "I am honoured by your visit."

The child smiled and hung his head.

"My lord," said his father, "he asks always if I am going to visit you, and if I am he implores to come too."

"I repeat," said Robert, "I am honoured."

And with a display of charm which was natural with him, he lifted the child in his arms so that their faces were on a level.

"And what think you of what you see, my little one?" he asked. "Take a good look at this head, for the opportunity to do so may not long be yours. One day, my child, you will come to this cell and find another poor prisoner."

The little boy's lips began to quiver.

"And this poor head which you survey with such

101

flattering attention will no longer have a pair of shoulders to support it."

The warder whispered: "My lord, my lord, he understands your meaning. He will break his little heart. He sets such store by your lordship."

Robert was immediately serious. He kissed the boy lightly on the cheek.

"Tears?" he said. "Nay, we do not shed tears. Do you think that I shall allow them to harm me? Never!"

The child smiled now. "Never!" he repeated.

Robert lowered him to the ground. "A bonny boy," he said. "I look forward to his visits. I hope he will come again."

"He shall, my lord. Always he pleads: 'I want to see Lord Robert!' Is that not so, my son?"

The boy nodded.

"And great pleasure it gives me to see you," said Robert smiling.

"He has another friend in the Tower, my lord."

"Ha! I grow jealous."

"It is a lady Princess," said the boy.

Robert was alert, eager to hear more.

"It is the Princess Elizabeth, my lord," put in the warder. "Poor lady! It is sad for her . . . though they have allowed her a little freedom. She is allowed to walk in the small garden to take the air."

"Would I could walk in a small garden now and then," said Robert.

"Ah, my lord, yes indeed. They were at first strict with the Princess, keeping her closely guarded. But my lord of Sussex and the Lieutenant have put their heads together and have decided to give her this freedom."

"It would seem that they are wise men."

"How so, my lord?"

"They remember that the Princess may well be Queen one day. She would not look too kindly on those who had, during her imprisonment, shown her something less than kindness."

The warder looked uneasy. He did not like this reckless talk. It was all very well for Lord Robert who had little to lose since he was under sentence of death, but a humble warder to be caught listening to such talk concerning the Queen's enemies!

He took the boy by the hand but Robert said: "And so my little friend visits the Princess in her garden, eh?"

"Oh yes. Her Grace is fond of children. She encourages them to talk to her: and young Will is almost as devoted to the lady as he is to your lordship."

Robert swung the boy up into his arms once more. "It would seem, Master William," he said, "that you are a gentleman of much discernment."

The boy laughed aloud to find himself swung aloft, but Robert was thoughtful as he lowered him to the floor.

The next day when the warder came, the boy was again with him; this time he brought a nosegay—flowers which he had picked from the patch of ground outside his father's apartments within the prison precincts. Primroses, violets and wallflowers made a sweet-smelling bunch.

The boy handed them shyly to Robert.

"Why," cried Robert, "this is the pleasantest thing that has happened to me for a long time. I need a bowl in which to put them, for they will quickly fade if I do not. A small bowl of water. Could you procure such a bowl for me?"

"I will bring one next time I come," said the warder.

"Nay, that will not do. I'd not have my friend's flowers fade. Go, like a good fellow, bring me a bowl and leave your son with me that I may thank him for his gift." He picked up the boy. "You will stay with me . . . locked in my cell for a little while, will you not? You are not afraid to stay with me?"

The boy said: "I wish to stay with my lord."

The warder looked fondly at his son and, seeing that to be locked in the cell with Lord Robert would delight him, agreed to go and bring the bowl. He went out, carefully locking the door behind him.

As soon as he had gone, Robert, who still held the boy in his arms, whispered into his ear: "You are my friend. You would do something for me?"

The boy was all eagerness.

"Bring me some flowers tomorrow?"

"Yes, my lord . . . bigger, better flowers tomorrow."

"And when you bring me more flowers, I shall take these which you have brought today, out of the bowl and give them to you."

"But they are for you."

"I would that you should take them to a lady." The boy's eyes were alert. "To the Princess," whispered Robert. "But you must tell no one . . . no one at all . . . not even your father. It must be thought that I give you a present of flowers, and so you in return give me one. No one must know that you are going to take a present from me to the Princess."

The boy was puzzled, but he was concentrating with all his might. His one desire was to do what his hero wished.

"Remember! It is a great secret. No one must know. In the bunch of flowers I give you, there will be a letter.

You must be careful that you do not drop it. And if no one is near when you give the flowers to the Princess you might say: 'I bring these from Lord Robert!' Could you say that?"

The boy nodded. "I bring these from Lord Robert," he said.

"Then you will do this for me? Tomorrow . . . bring more flowers for me. I shall give you these which you brought today. It is a game we are playing because we are such friends. It is a present from me to the Princess . . . but a secret present, and none knows of it but my little ambassador. Do you understand?"

"Yes, my lord."

Robert put his fingers to his lips and the boy nodded gleefully.

"And can you do this for me, my clever little friend?"

The boy nodded.

"Not a word," said Robert. "Here comes your father. Remember. It is our secret—yours, mine and the Princess's."

When the warder had returned, Robert marvelled at his own foolhardiness. What a reckless thing to do! For himself it was unimportant; he was under sentence of death. But what if he had involved the Princess in further trouble? He had trusted her life perhaps in the hands of a small boy.

But, he soothed himself, there was no political intrigue in this, he was not plotting rebellion or escape.

Moreover the plot was so simple. It could not fail. He sat down and wrote;

"Dearest lady, My cell in this dreary prison has

become brighter since you are close to me, grieved though I am by your misfortunes. If your walks should bring you past my cell and I might see you, that is the only boon I would ask before I die. This comes from one who has had the great joy of laughing with you, dancing with you, and would now find equal joy in a glimpse of your sweet face. From one who has never forgotten you, nor ever shall. R.D."

He hid the note in the posy, binding it fast; and eagerly he awaited the next day, wondering as he had through the night, whether the child had been unable to keep the secret or if he would remember to bring fresh flowers on the next day.

As soon as the boy entered the cell with his father, this time bearing a larger bunch of flowers, Robert saw from the brightness of the boy's eyes and the tightly pressed lips that he had not forgotten.

"You bring me a present," said Robert. "Now I shall give you one." He took the new bunch and pressed the old one into the child's hands. Their eyes met and the boy's were brimming over with excitement.

"God bless you," said Robert.

"God bless my lord," said the boy.

"I envy you this fine boy," said Robert to the warder. "I . . . who have no sons . . . nor daughters either, for that matter."

He thought with exasperation of Amy, waiting for him in the manor house which was their home—Amy who had saved him from marriage with the Lady Jane Grey and who now stood between him and he knew not what.

"Ah, he's a bonny fellow," said the father. "And he has brothers and sisters."

"You are a lucky man."

The warder shook his head, thinking of the splendours of the Dudleys which had ended so tragically and abruptly.

The little boy wandered out, tightly clutching the bunch of flowers.

A change had come over the Princess Elizabeth. There was fresh colour in her cheeks, renewed sparkle in her eyes. It was obvious that she looked forward to her walks in the Tower garden.

She would smile and kiss the warder's little boy who so often brought her flowers. She would pick him up in her arms and whisper to him, walking with him among the flower beds. Her attendants and the guards said: "She is very fond of children." And it was touching to see the eager way in which she took the flowers which the child brought to her.

She had thrown off her melancholy. It was difficult to believe that her life was in danger and that none was more aware of that dismal fact than herself.

"Ah, my little one," she would cry, on seeing the boy, "so you do not forget me then?"

"I would never forget you, Mistress," he would say.

She would take his little hand and walk away from those who attended her; she wished to be alone in the gardens with her little friend.

"How is my lord?" she would whisper.

"He says that he is in wondrous health since he has had word from your Grace."

"He looks for a letter from me, I doubt not?"

"Nay, Mistress. He says you must not write. *I* will tell him what you say."

"You are a dear good child and I am fond of you."

So she blossomed among the flowers and passed much time in her apartments—which otherwise would have been spent wearily—in remembering the charm of Robert Dudley, picturing what would happen if they met again.

Other children began to follow the warder's little boy into the gardens. There was so much talk of the Princess, that they too wished to see her and to tell her how sorry they were that she was a captive.

There was the son of the Keeper of the Queen's Robes, and little Susannah, the daughter of another warder, who came with the boy. They would run into the garden and stand before the Princess, who always had a word and smile for them; but little Will was her favourite.

There were many persons of importance who wished to show leniency towards the Princess. It was folly, said Bridges, the Lieutenant of the Tower, to offend more than need be, a lady of Elizabeth's rank. One turn of Fortune's wheel and she would be their Queen. He expressed his feelings thus in order to win support for them; for he himself was a kind man and the plight of the Princess had aroused his compassion. He swore to himself that while Elizabeth was in his charge she should have as much respect as he dared give her.

It was not long before the Princess was allowed to go where she wished within the precincts of the Tower; and thus it was that she saw Robert.

She knew that he was in a lower cell of the Beauchamp Tower, and that if she passed by he would be able, by looking through the bars of his window, to see her. On that first day of her new liberty, she curbed her impatience, but on the second she dressed herself with the utmost care and with her attendants about her and her guards nearby, she walked aimlessly in the direction of the Beauchamp Tower.

"Wait here," she said to her attendants. "I would be alone for a while."

The sympathetic guards allowed her to go on, but they begged her not to go from their sight or they would be forced to follow her.

She paused by the Beauchamp Tower and whispered: "Robert. Robert Dudley. Are you there?"

He was at the window looking through the bars.

"My . . . Princess!" he murmured.

He was pale through long confinement, but his pallor seemed but to enhance the beauty of that incomparable cast of features; the flesh had fallen away to disclose the fine contours of his face. How handsome he is! thought the Princess; and any man who admired her seemed to her charming.

"I cannot tarry long," she murmured. "My guards are watching. Have a care."

"You came . . . to see me! I shall remember it till I die."

"Robert . . . what will they do to us?"

"Time will tell."

"You do not care?"

"Life has to end sometime, sweet Princess. I have railed against my fate. But I am here and, because I am a prisoner, and you are a prisoner, I have shown you what is in my heart. How could Robert Dudley have said to a noble Princess what one prisoner could say to another?"

"You have been very bold," she said with feigned severity.

"It is well, mayhap, that the walls of a prison separate us, for if they did not, how could I, dazzled by your beauty, control what might be unforgivable boldness?"

She pretended to contemplate the April sky, and her eyes seemed to take colour from its blueness. She heard the call of the cuckoo from the distant meadows. Spring was in the air and in her heart; she could not think of death for herself at such a time. They were both so young. Prisoner as she was, this was one of the happiest moments of her life. She vowed there and then that she would never forget the man who had made it possible for her to be so happy in this grim prison.

"It is well indeed," she said. "I shall walk on a few paces and turn back. I see they are watching me."

His voice followed her. "If tomorrow I walk out to the scaffold, I shall not complain. I am a prisoner here under sentence of death, yet I rejoice . . . for the Princess has passed my way."

How handsome he was! How ardent his eyes! She had heard it said that he was irresistible. Yet because she was a Princess her royalty would resist him. But what need to think of resistance? They were separated by unbreakable barriers: her royalty, his prison walls, his marriage to a country girl. She did not resent these barriers; she wished for barriers. She saw herself as the most desirable woman in England, young, beautiful, yet unattainable. That was how she wished it to be.

She dawdled past his window once more.

"I was grieved," she said, "when I heard of your arrest. I was grieved because I remembered you and because of the reason you are here."

He was prepared. He had not mentioned politics in his letters; those spoke of nothing but love and devotion. He said: "I am my father's son. I had no alternative but to fight in my father's cause. I was young . . . without experience, his to command."

"And who may command you now?"

"The Princess Elizabeth. She may command me, body and soul."

She was delighted, but she said with asperity: "When was your allegiance severed from the Lady Jane Grey? When she went to the scaffold?"

"I can only say that I served my father."

"Robert, you are a fool. And so am I to linger here."

"But . . . you will walk this way again?"

She stooped as though to flick a piece of grass from her shoe. "Should I step out of my way to listen to you?"

"If you are merciful, yes."

"Merciful?" She looked round. Those who were watching her were growing suspicious. She dared dally no longer, but she was finding it difficult to tear herself away. Flirtation such as this was a game she enjoyed beyond all others. "Who am I, a poor prisoner, to be merciful?"

"There is none other whose mercy I would ask. I crave the mercy of a smile from your sweet lips. The memory of your beauty will stay with me . . . lighting my cell. If I die tomorrow I shall die happy . . . because you came to see me, my dearest Princess."

"I but passed this way."

"Then Your Grace is displeased because I wrote to you?"

111

"It was somewhat impertinent of you."

"Then if my letters have given you displeasure, I must deny myself the great joy of writing them."

"As to that you must please yourself."

"If I pleased myself I should write all day. You will come this way again?"

"My lord, do you think I shall go out of my way to avoid you?" There was a trill of excitement in her voice. She knew she ought to go, but she could not resist lingering there.

"To see you is the most wonderful thing that has happened to me," he said.

"I must go."

"I shall live for this hour tomorrow."

"My guards grow suspicious. I must tarry no longer."

"Would I could kiss your hand . . . Elizabeth."

"I dare stay no longer."

"I shall wait . . . and hope."

"It is a good thing to wait . . . and hope. It is all that is left to us poor prisoners."

She had turned her face to the sky so that the light fell upon it; she shook out her hair and touched her throat with one of those white slender hands of which she was so proud. She made a charming picture for him to see and retain in his memory.

"You are so beautiful," she heard him whisper. "Even more so than I remembered."

And smiling, she passed on.

Did they know, those guards and friends of hers, why her morning walks always took her in one direction? Did they know who the prisoner was on the other side of the grille? If they did they feigned ignorance.

She would sit on the grass outside the cell and, leaning back against the walls, look up at the sky while she talked to Robert Dudley.

She scolded him, but there was a warmth of tenderness always beneath the scolding. She was as excited as she had been during that most exciting experience with Thomas Seymour.

"So, Robert Dudley, you are a traitor to our most gracious Queen."

"Princess, I serve only one Queen."

"Then that must be Queen Mary."

"Nay, the Queen of my heart, the Queen I shall always worship to the end of my days. Her name is not Mary."

"Might it be Amy?"

"Ah, speak not of poor Amy."

"Speak not of her indeed! Poor soul, I pity her. She happens to be your wife."

"I spoke of a Queen," he said. "I spoke of the only one in the world whom I could ever love, but who, I fear, is far beyond my reach."

"What name has she?"

"Elizabeth."

"The same as mine!"

"You mock me!"

"Robert, you are a philanderer, as many know to their cost."

"If that is so, might it not be because, knowing I can never reach my love, I seek desperately to find others who remind me of her?"

"So these others . . . these country girls . . . remind you of her?"

113

"In some small way, mayhap. Perhaps one has blue eyes; another has hair—not the same colour, for how could that perfection be matched?—but perhaps when the sun shines in a certain way that hair has a faint resemblance to Elizabeth's. Perhaps one has white and slender fingers, lacking the perfection, it is true, but they serve to remind."

"Robert Dudley," she challenged, "a woman would be a fool to put her trust in you."

"*One* would not. But who am I to hope she would dare look my way?"

"You are under sentence of death," she said quietly.

"I am almost glad of it. Because of it I am reckless. I say to the one I love that which, in other circumstances, I would not dare to say."

"Say on," she murmured.

"I love you . . . no one but you. There would be no place in my life except by your side. It is well that soon they will come for me and that I shall walk out to the scaffold, for, loving one so far above me, how could I hope for that love to be returned?"

"A man is a fool who gives up hope."

"Is that so then?"

"Hope is what we live by . . . such as we are."

"What could I hope for?"

"For life."

"But what would life be worth if it held not love?"

"Then hope for life *and* love."

"Elizabeth . . . my love!"

"It is true," she admitted, "that I have a fondness for you."

"I am the happiest man alive."

"It is a marvellous thing, Robert, that you can say so at such a time."

"Would I could be there beside you on the grass."

"I fancy that you would be over-bold, which might mean that I should have to be cold to you."

"I would break through your coldness."

"Yes. I have heard that you have melting powers."

"You have heard much of me. I am flattered again that you lent your ears so often to news of me . . . even when it went against me."

"I did not forget you. You were such an arrogant boy."

"You remember how we danced together . . . how our hands touched?"

"Do not talk of the past. Talk of the future."

"What has the future for me?"

"Or for me?"

"You! There will be a great future for you. You will be a Queen."

"Shall I, Robert?"

"A Queen! And your husband will be a foreign prince of great power and riches. Your ministers will choose him for you."

"If I am ever Queen I shall choose my own husband."

Such words set his hopes rising. Such hopes were absurd, he told himself. But were they? She was so proud, so brave, so determined. She was her father's daughter; he had heard it said many times. Her father had married outside royalty. It was true that two of his wives had lost their heads; but Robert was sure of his powers.

"If ever I come out of here alive . . ." he began.

"Yes, Robert?" she prompted.

"I shall dedicate my life to your service."

"Others have promised that."

"I shall serve you with the love of a subject and . . . a man."

"Subject?"

"When you are Queen . . ."

"You talk treason. If any heard, that would, without delay, cost you your head."

"My heart is so deeply involved that my head seems of little importance."

"I dare stay no longer."

Yet how she wanted to do so! What a pleasant game it was that she played outside the walls of the Beauchamp Tower.

It was one of the children who broke the enchantment.

Little Susannah came to her one day as she walked in the gardens.

Susannah had found some keys, and these she had brought to the Princess. The little girl had listened to the conversations of her elders and had thought how she would like to do something for the sweet young lady. Young Will took her flowers, and those pleased her so much. What could Susannah do?

Then Susannah thought of something better than flowers. The Princess was a prisoner, was she not? Flowers were pretty to look at, but keys were so much more useful. So purposefully Susannah took the keys to the Princess, holding them out in her small chubby hand.

"These are for you, Mistress. Now you can unlock the gates and go home."

Elizabeth bent over the child, but her guards had come forward.

116

"Your Grace will understand," said one of the guards, "that I must take these keys, and that it will be necessary for me to report what has happened."

"You may do as you please," said Elizabeth. "This innocent child but plays a game."

Susannah cried: "But the keys are for the lady. They are so that she may open the gates and go home."

Elizabeth stooped to comfort the child. "It was good of you to bring me the keys, Susannah," she said. "But you see, my dear little one, they will not let me have them."

Susannah began to whimper: "Have I done wrong then, Mistress?"

"Nay. You thought to please me. That was not wrong."

"But they are angry now."

"Nay. They have taken the keys because I am their prisoner and that is how they wish to keep me."

"But I would help you to escape."

"I know, my little one. But that is not to be. You must be of good cheer. I am happy because you brought me the keys—not so that I might escape for I could not go until they say I may—but because it shows you love me."

Susannah was comforted.

But now the officials of the Tower were conferring together.

"A child . . . to take keys to the Princess! That is very dangerous. Important keys could be smuggled into her apartments in this way."

"The keys which the child took to her were useless keys. They had been thrown away."

"That is so. But keys! And what is this about flowers?"

"Only that one of the warders' boys takes her a bunch of flowers now and then. He picks them from his garden and takes them to his favourite prisoner."

"Messages . . . notes . . . could be concealed in a bunch of flowers. We have here an important state prisoner. If she should escape it might cost us our heads."

The result of this conference was that young Will found himself standing before a committee of impressive gentlemen, among them the awe-inspiring Lieutenant of the Tower himself.

Will was a little afraid, because he sensed the trepidation of his father, who waited outside while Will stood before a table about which sat the gentlemen.

There was one thought in the little boy's mind: He must not betray the fact that he had carried a note in the bunch of flowers. Lord Robert had been most insistent about that. That was why they were angry, but he would not tell them. He must remember that Lord Robert did not wish it, and he did not care how angry the gentlemen were so long as he did what Lord Robert wished.

He stood there, his feet wide apart, his face firm and set, remembering that he was Lord Robert's friend.

"Now, my boy, you took flowers to the Princess, did you not?"

"Yes, sir."

"Where did you get these flowers?"

"From our garden." That was true; the flowers had come from the garden.

"Now listen, my boy. Did any of the prisoners give

you anything to put among the flowers?"

"No, sir." That was true too. Lord Robert himself had put the notes among the flowers.

"Think very hard. You are sure no one gave you a letter to take to the Princess?"

"I *am* thinking hard," said the boy. "Nobody gave me a letter, sir."

The men looked at each other.

"Has he ever visited Courtenay's apartments?" asked the Lieutenant.

"We will have his father in and ask him."

Will's father entered.

"Has the boy ever accompanied you to the apartments of the Duke of Devonshire?"

"No, sir. I have never been there myself."

"Have you ever visited any of the prisoners who have recently been brought to the Tower . . . those concerned in the Wyatt rebellion?"

"No, sir."

The men again looked at each other and at the small boy who presented such a picture of bewildered innocence. It was said that the Princess was fond of children and they of her; it was probable that there was nothing in this matter but pure friendship between the Princess and the child. So far no harm had been done. Elizabeth was still their prisoner.

"I will double the Princess's guards," said the Lieutenant. "We will curtail her freedom. She shall walk only for a short time in the gardens and not where she willed as heretofore. And, warder, your son is to take no more flowers to prisoners. Is that clear?"

"Yes, sir."

"And you, my boy, you understand? You must take

no more flowers to the Princess."

The boy nodded miserably.

When he next saw the Princess she was walking in her little garden, and the gates were locked so that he could not reach her. But he called to her through the railings.

She did not come near because her guards surrounded her; but she waved and smiled at him.

"I can bring you no more flowers, Mistress," he called sadly.

The Queen fell ill and there was consternation among those who had persecuted Elizabeth. The chief of these was Stephen Gardiner, the Bishop of Winchester—he who was the most formidable of the Princess's enemies. He had a clear picture of what would happen to him if Mary died and Elizabeth became Queen.

He was the Queen's favourite Bishop and statesman; he could take liberties; and it seemed to him that unless he took a very great one now, he could not expect to outlive Queen Mary by more than a week or two. So he decided to act with extreme boldness.

He wrote a death warrant and had a special messenger take it to Bridges in the Tower. The sentence was to be carried out on the Princess Elizabeth without delay.

When Bridges received the warrant he was bewildered.

Nothing had been proved against Elizabeth, although she was under constant suspicion. Was she to be executed without trial? That did not appeal to the fair-minded Bridges. He was proud of his office; he wanted justice to prevail in his domain. Moreover he was not insensible to the charm of the Princess. She was so young and her good spirits and bravery in captivity had made a marked impression on him; he was also not unmindful of what the future might bring.

A death warrant! Instructions to hurry on with the execution, to keep it secret and hustle the Princess from her prison to the scaffold in the early morning, to behead her while the country was ignorant of what was happening!

"I like that not!" murmured Bridges.

The Queen was not by nature a cruel woman, and the Princess had implied that she was very willing to accept the Catholic Faith. Bridges did not believe that the Queen would wish to take the life of her sister except on religious grounds, or of course, if treason were proved against her—which was not the case.

He examined the death warrant once more. That was not the Queen's signature. He looked closely. Yes, Gardiner had signed for the Queen during her indisposition.

Bridges made up his mind. He would rather risk Gardiner's displeasure than send a young girl to her death.

He took up his pen and wrote to Gardiner:

"I see that this warrant does not bear Her Majesty's signature, and I should consider I was not acting within the bounds of my duty if I allowed to take place an execution of so important a state prisoner without special instructions from Her Majesty the Queen."

Gardiner was furious when he received the letter and realized that his plan had miscarried. He pondered the matter for a few days, wondering whether to command Bridges to carry out his wishes. But in the meantime the Queen had recovered, and when she heard what had happened she was horrified.

All her sentimental feelings came to the surface. She remembered the baby Elizabeth who had won her affection. Elizabeth was misguided; she had been brought up in the wrong religion; and it was true that she must be looking with ambition towards the throne; but nothing had been proved against her—and she was Mary's own sister.

She did not reprimand Gardiner; she had too high an opinion of him. She knew that he was a staunch Catholic and that in itself endeared him to her. It was Elizabeth, the heretic, whom he wished to persecute; and she was not sure that he was not right in that.

As for herself she saw Elizabeth as her sister—heretic though she might be. Elizabeth was young; she had not been proved a traitor; therefore it was the Queen's duty to save her from heresy.

Mary called to her a man whom she trusted completely; this was her old friend Sir Henry Bedingfeld.

"I have a task for you," she told him, "which I would entrust no other."

"I shall execute it with all the strength at my disposal, Your Majesty."

"I know it, dear Bedingfeld. That is why I give it to you. I know you will watch over her and that you will be just, both to her and to me. I speak of my sister."

Bedingfeld was dismayed.

"Yes, my dear friend," went on the Queen, "I have decided to put the Princess in your charge. You will watch over her night and day. Every action of hers will be noted and, if need be, reported to me. This is a difficult task I have set you, but, my lord, I do so because I know you to be one of the few about me whom I can trust."

"I am your Majesty's obedient and humble servant."

But he showed himself to be perplexed, and Mary marvelled that a man as courageous as Bedingfeld should be so disturbed at the prospect of guarding a young girl.

Elizabeth heard the approach of Sir Henry Bedingfeld with a hundred men-at-arms. From a window she saw them and when she knew that they were all about her apartments she feared this could mean only one thing, and her terrors returned. She clung to her favourite attendant, Isabella Markham, and cried: "Isabella, this is the end. I did not think I should greatly mind, but I do. My sister has sent Bedingfeld to see her orders carried out. Tell me . . . is the Lady Jane's scaffold still in its place?"

"Hush, dearest Princess. I beg of you be calm as you always have been. Wait and learn what this means before you believe the worst."

"Bedingfeld is my sister's trusted knight. She has sent him to destroy me. I feared as soon as I entered this place of gloom that I should never leave it." She cried out hysterically: "It shall not be an axe for me! I shall have a sword from Calais!"

Her ladies, knowing that she thought of her tragic mother, bent their heads and wept.

But it was not Elizabeth's way to mourn for long.

Very soon she became the imperious Princess. She cried: "Send for Bridges. Command him to come to me at once."

When he came she demanded haughtily: "What means this? Have you not guards enough that you must send to my sister for more?"

"Your Grace refers to Sir Henry Bedingfeld and his company?"

"I do indeed."

"Your Grace, this is not a matter for alarm, but for rejoicing. Sir Henry will soon present himself to you and tell you of his instructions. You are to leave the Tower."

"To be freed?"

"You will be in the charge of Sir Henry, but no longer a prisoner in the Tower."

Elizabeth was relieved. She was to change one captivity for another, but the Tower was a place of ill omen. But after a while she was conscious of some regret, for the Tower still held Robert Dudley.

The barge carried her from Tower Wharf to the Palace of Richmond, a strong company of guards accompanying her.

Her sister sent for her when she arrived at the Palace.

Mary, so recently recovered from what many believed would be a fatal illness, looked exhausted. She was nervously awaiting the coming of her bridegroom, with feelings which alternated between eagerness for him and apprehension as to what he would think of her.

The sight of her young sister—so healthful in spite

of her recent imprisonment—filled her with melancholy and envy. What would Philip think when he saw this sister? Would he wish that she were the Queen of England and his bride?

But it was absurd to envy Elizabeth whose life was in the utmost danger; and if Mary were wise, according to Gardiner and Renard, she would not hesitate to send that young lady to the block.

"So you are recently come from the Tower?" said Mary coldly.

"Yes, Your Majesty. By your great clemency, I come hither."

"Many have spoken against you," said the Queen.

"They lied who spoke against me," said Elizabeth. "But Your Majesty is wise and recognizes the lies of a liar—as she does the poor babblings of those under torture—for what they are worth."

"I am not convinced of your loyalty."

Elizabeth opened her blue eyes very wide. "Your Majesty cannot mean that!"

"I am not in the habit of saying what I do not mean. Now, sister, I know you well. Remember we have spent many years together. When there was trouble in your nursery, as I well remember, you had little difficulty in proving your innocence."

"Your Majesty, it should be an easy matter for the innocent to prove their innocence. It is only the guilty who face an impossible task."

The Queen waved a hand impatiently. "I have a husband for you."

Elizabeth grew pale. She was tense, waiting.

"It is Philibert Emmanuel, the Duke of Savoy."

"The Duke of Savoy!" echoed Elizabeth blankly.

She had expected death and had been offered a duke. To die would be the end of life, but to marry a foreign duke and leave England would mean abandoning all that she had hoped for. Only now did she fully realize how she had always longed to be the Queen of England. To resign her hopes would be as bad as death.

She said firmly: "Your Majesty, I could never agree to the match."

"*You* could not agree!"

"*I* could not agree, Your Majesty."

The Queen bent forward and said coldly: "What right have you to object to the husband I have chosen for you?"

Elizabeth was thinking of Robert Dudley as she had seen him through the bars of his cell—tall, dark, handsome . . . and those passionate daring eyes. If it were Robert . . . she thought. No, not for him would she abandon her dream. But she was not being offered Robert. She was offered a foreign prince whom the Queen favoured because he was a vassal of Spain; and all things connected with Spain were good in the Queen's eyes since she had taken a look at the picture of a short, trim young man who was destined to be her husband.

"There is only one reason why I could object to your choice, Your Majesty, and that is because I feel within myself that the married state is not for me."

Mary looked cynically at her sister. "You . . . to be a spinster! When did you make up your mind to this?"

"I think Your Majesty, that it is something I have always known."

"I have not noticed that you have shown much

126

maidenliness towards the opposite sex."

"Your Majesty, it is because I have always felt thus that I have perhaps at times appeared to be unguarded."

"Do you feel then that there is no need to guard that which you have determined at all costs to preserve?"

"Your Majesty, it is only necessary to put a guard on that which one is in danger of losing. My inclination for virginity being what it is, I had no need to restrain myself as have some maidens."

"I would not have you come to me in frivolous mood."

"Your Majesty, I was never more serious."

"Then we shall contract you to the Duke of Savoy."

Elizabeth folded her hands on her breast. "Your Majesty, I am of such mind that I prefer death to marriage."

"I should not talk too readily of death. It could be reckless talk."

"Your Majesty, I *am* reckless. I prefer death to betrothal to the Duke of Savoy."

"We shall see," said Mary.

She summoned the guard, and Elizabeth was taken back to her apartments, believing that her end was at hand.

She lay on her bed staring up at the tester. Her ladies were weeping quietly. She had come back from her interview with the Queen and had told them: "I think I am to die."

Did she really prefer death to marriage with the Duke of Savoy?

For so many years she had dreamed that she would

wear the crown. How many times had Kat Ashley read it in the cards? She could not give up that dream. But would she in truth rather die?

Once during the night she half rose. She thought: Tomorrow I will go to the Queen. I will accept Savoy. I am a fool to go meekly to death.

Wait, said her common sense. Has there not always been safety in waiting?

The next day she left the Palace, but not for the Tower. The Queen was undecided what to do with her sister, and finally she resorted to the old method. Elizabeth should go back to Woodstock, where she would remain a captive, although living in the state her rank demanded. The people would be appeased if the Princess was in one of her country houses; they had been restive while she was in the Tower. Elizabeth, sly and cunning, appeared to them young and pathetic; and she had the people on her side as always.

Even when she sailed up the river the people lined the banks to watch her pass. They called cheering words to her; they had gifts for her. At Wycombe cakes were brought to her, and so numerous were these that she could not accept them all. She thanked the people prettily, and all along the river their cries resounded: "God bless the Princess. God save Her Grace."

She felt happy now. She had done the right thing in refusing Savoy. Time would always be her ally, for she was young and the Queen was old.

She arrived at Woodstock, yet even there she was not given the royal apartments but taken to the gatehouse. This was surrounded by guards, and Sir Henry Bedingfeld told her that his instructions were that she was to be kept under strict surveillance.

She wept a little. "Like a sheep to the slaughter I am led," she said, as her ladies helped her to retire.

As she lay in her bed unable to sleep, the door of her room was quietly opened; the curtains of her bed were suddenly divided, and she found herself held tightly in a pair of loving arms.

"Kat!" she sobbed in relief. "How did you get here?"

"Hush, my love! Hush, my little lady! I am free once more. This prisoner is released, so what did she do? When she heard her lady was on the way she arrived before her. I reached the house before Master Bedingfeld and his merry men. And what do we care, sweetheart, since we are together!"

"What do we care!" said Elizabeth and began to laugh.

Kat lay beside her on the bed; and through the night they talked of what had happened.

Elizabeth said suddenly: "And, Kat, what do you think? I had an adventure when I was in the Tower. You remember Robert Dudley?"

"Remember him! Who could forget him! The loveliest man I ever saw . . . except one."

"Except none!" said Elizabeth.

And they pulled the bed coverings over their heads that they might gossip and laugh together without being overheard.

Elizabeth's captivity at Woodstock passed merrily enough. Kat was with her, and Sir Henry Bedingfeld did not think it necessary to report this matter to the Queen. Perhaps he knew that if he did so Kat would be removed and that removal would mortally offend the

Princess Elizabeth. He could see no harm in Kat's being with her.

So they were together as they had been in the old days. There was laughter and gossip and talk which if overheard might have been called treason.

When they were alone Kat whispered: "Your Majesty!" and that was sweet music to Elizabeth. Kat read the cards with that flattering skill which provoked much laughter.

"Here is that dark, handsome man again! See how close he is to your little Majesty. We shall hear more of him, I doubt not."

It was like the old days when Kat had seen another handsome man in the cards. They had recognized him as Thomas Seymour. Kat reminded Elizabeth that she had been wont to say there would never be one like him, never one so charming.

"But then," said Elizabeth, "I did not really know Robert Dudley."

IV

When the Princess Elizabeth was taken from the Tower, Robert fell into deep melancholy. There were times when he felt he would go mad if he were left much longer in his dismal cell. He would look through the bars at the grass on which she used to walk, and he would remember others who had spent a lifetime in the Tower. Shall I be here until I am old and grey? he would wonder. But he did not really believe that could happen to Robert Dudley.

There was nothing to do but brood. If Elizabeth were Queen . . . ah, if Elizabeth were Queen, she would not suffer him to stay long in the Tower.

But at length change came.

It was June, and he had heard from the jailors and his servants that preparations were going forward for the reception of the Prince of Spain who was already on his way to England.

The Queen was not yet forty; she would marry Philip and if there were children of the marriage, there was small hope of Robert Dudley's regaining his freedom.

"My lord," said his jailor one day, "prepare to leave this cell. You are to be taken to the Bell Tower, there to share a room with your brother the Earl of Warwick."

131

He felt elated. He might have known that Fortune would not allow him to continue gloomy. It would be good to be with brother John.

The brothers embraced warmly. Imprisonment had left a deeper mark on John, Earl of Warwick, than on Robert; John had had no charming adventure with which to while away the time. He brightened with the coming of Robert, although they were very sorrowful recalling their father and Guildford.

"It might have been you . . . or I," they reminded each other. "Mere chance made it poor Guildford."

"Yet," said John, "how do we know we shall not meet a like fate?"

"Nay!" cried Robert. "If they intended that, the deed would have been done ere now. If we stay here quietly and nothing happens to call attention to us, we shall, ere long, be free."

John smiled. "That is like you, Robert. You always believed that something miraculous was reserved for you."

"How can you know that it is not!"

"What . . . for a poor prisoner in the Tower!"

"Other poor prisoners have survived and risen to greatness."

"You are indeed a Dudley," said John, not without a trace of sadness in his smile.

Fortune was turning in their favour. They were to be allowed to have visitors. Their wives might come and see them in their cells; their mother might also come.

Jane came first, and bravely she smiled at her two sons. John looked ill, she thought; Robert had scarcely changed at all.

"My darling," she cried. "Why, John . . . how thin

you are! And you . . . you are still my Robin, I see."

"Still the same, dear Mother."

"You keep your spirits up, my dearest son."

"And mine too," put in John. "He refuses to believe that we are unfortunate. We are certain of a great future, he says."

"Come," said Robert, "it is not the first time the Dudley fortunes have been in the dust."

"Do not speak thus," begged Jane. "That was how your father talked."

"But Father was a great man. Think of all he did."

Jane said bitterly: "All he did! He led his son to the scaffold, that with him he might shed his blood in the cause of ambition."

But Robert laid his arm about her shoulders. "Dear Mother, that is the way of the world."

"It shall not be your way, Robert."

"Nay, do not fret. The axe is not for us. See how they keep us here. They leave us in peace. We are well fed, and now we may have visitors. Soon the day of our release will come."

"I pray for it each night," said Jane fervently.

She wished to know how they were fed, how their servants behaved.

"We are allowed more than two pounds each week for food," said Robert, "and more for wood and candles. So you see, Mother, if we do not live like kings, we do not live like beggars."

"I rejoice to hear it. But there is an evil odour here."

"It comes from the river."

"We dread the hot days," said John.

"I will speak to the servants. They must take great care to keep the apartments sweet. This is not a good

133

place to be in . . . especially during the summer."

Robert was determined to drive away gloom. He was sure, he told her, that soon they would be free. He guessed it. He knew it. He had a way of knowing such things.

She could smile as she listened to Robert.

"How glad I am, dear John, that your brother is with you."

"It has been merrier since he came," said John.

And when Jane left them she felt happier than she had since she had lost them. That was due to her darling.

He can charm away even my miseries, she was thinking.

Amy came to see Robert. John asked that he should be taken to another cell, that husband and wife might be alone together.

Amy clung to Robert, covering his face with kisses. He returned her embrace and for a short while he was ready to make love to her. It was so long since they had met.

"Robert," she insisted, "you still love me?"

"Have I not made that clear?"

"I have been so unhappy . . ."

"And what have I been, do you think?"

"But it has been so *miserable* without you. I thought that you would *die*."

"Nay. I have many years before me."

"Yes, Robert, yes. Do you think you will soon be free?"

He shrugged his shoulders.

"But you do not seem to *care*."

134

He was thoughtful for a second or so. He was thinking of freedom, the return to the life in Norfolk, farming, riding, making love to Amy. Was freedom so desirable? How foolish Amy was! He had a fancy for a different woman—a sharper-tongued, subtler woman, with flaming red hair and an imperious manner. He wanted a Princess, not a country girl.

"Of what do you think?" she asked suspiciously.

Had she sensed his desire for another woman? he wondered. Had she more discernment than he gave her credit for?

He said: "I have been thinking that if I had not married you I might not be here now."

"Where would you be then?"

"In my grave."

She stared at him for a moment, then she threw her arms about him. "Why, Robert, I am some use to you then."

He laughed aloud because the sun was shining outside and it was good to be alive. He lifted her and kissed her with that sudden abandonment which was a way of his.

Now he was the passionate lover as he had been in the beginning, and when he was thus he was quite irresistible.

Amy was happy. She was with him again. He loved her; he was glad they had married.

She did not know that the memory of a Princess was constantly with him and that his thoughts of her filled him with a delightful blend of excitement, desire and ambition.

The days were hot and sultry. The smell of the

befouled river pervaded the cell. The sweating sickness had come to London, and the most dangerous place in the City was the Tower.

Day after day the corpses were taken out, but the place was still overcrowded, as it had been since the Wyatt rebellion. The heat hung over the river and the prisoners lay languid.

One morning John complained of feeling very sick indeed. Robert looked anxiously at his brother. The Earl's face was a sickly yellow colour and, to his horror, Robert saw the drops of sweat forming on his brow.

John had contracted the dreaded sweating sickness.

Five of Robert's brothers and sisters had died of this terrible disease. He wondered: Is John to be another?

But he determined that it should not be so. He would not lose John that way. Here was something to be done after weeks of inactivity, and he was glad of it.

He called to their two servants. They came running in.

"The Earl is sick," he said; and he saw the terrible fear in their faces. He felt reckless; in spite of his anxiety for his brother he almost laughed. He was not afraid. He knew that he would not die miserably in prison of the sweat. He would do his utmost to save his brother; he would be the one who was constantly with him, ministering to him, because he felt himself to be immune from infection. For greatness, he was sure, awaited Robert Dudley.

It was a glorious feeling to be unafraid among the fearful.

He said coolly: "Go at once to my mother. Tell her what has happened. Ask her to send some of her simples to me. Tell her she is not to come visiting until I send the word. Be very sure of that."

"Yes, my lord."

Already they were looking at him as though he were a god.

He returned to his brother and, lifting him in his arms, he carried him to his bed and covered him up. He sat beside him and, when the palliatives arrived from his mother, he himself administered them.

He talked to John, trying to arouse him. It was said that if the patient did not come out of his coma during the first twenty-four hours he would die.

Robert often wondered afterwards how he lived through that day and night; he himself must have been almost delirious.

He found he was speaking his thoughts aloud. "The Princess Elizabeth is in love with me. Bars separated us and I could not approach her, yet was I assured of her love. If ever she becomes Queen, greatness awaits me . . . greatness such as our father never knew . . . the greatness he would have had for Guildford if all had gone as our father wished. I think of our grandfather—humble lawyer, a farmer's son who rose to sit in the Council chamber of a King. I think of our father who became Protector of England—almost the King he wished Guildford to be. In two generations from obscurity to greatness . . . only to die on the scaffold. I am of the third generation. I shall learn from the mistakes of others. Perhaps in the third generation a Dudley shall be a king."

Yes, he must be almost delirious to speak such thoughts aloud.

John opened his eyes suddenly and said: "Brother, is that you?"

Then Robert knew that he had successfully nursed

137

John through the sweating sickness, and he was certain that the sickness could not touch him. He was as certain of this as he was of the glorious future which awaited him.

There were many Spaniards at the Court that summer. None could find so much favour with the Queen as a Spaniard. Her bridegroom had come and she doted on him.

Jane Dudley—although she could not go to Court, was often found outside the palaces in which the Queen was residing.

She pleaded with old friends. She gave gifts to the Spanish ladies. She would tell them of the fate of her sons. Would not this kind lady, that kind gentleman, seek a moment, when the Queen was in a soft mood, to speak a word for poor Jane Dudley?

There were many who felt pity for her; and so those words were eventually spoken to the Queen.

Mary loved her husband, and love had softened her.

"Poor Jane Dudley," she said, "what has she done to suffer so?"

Jane was a heartbroken mother, and now that Mary soon hoped to be a mother, she understood maternal hopes and griefs. Jane's sons had risen against the crown, but they had obeyed their father in this. Mary in love was a kindly Mary.

As the hot summer gave place to autumn she decided she would pardon the Dudleys. They would still be attainted of high treason, of course, which meant that their lands and goods would not be restored to them; but they should have a free pardon.

Jane was almost delirious with delight.

At last her sons were to be free. Land and riches? What did they want with those? Let them live quietly, humbly; let them abandon their ambition which had proved so fatal to the family.

But Jane's joy was clouded. His imprisonment in the Tower had changed her eldest son John from a strong man to a weakling. He died a few days after his release.

Of Jane's thirteen children only five were left to her. Yet even while she wept for John she thanked God that Ambrose and Robert (and in particular Robert, for even the fondest mothers must have their favourites) had come safely through the ordeal.

As Robert rode with Amy from London to Norfolk, all that elation which had come to him when the gates of the Tower had shut behind him, left him. He was conscious of a nagging frustration.

His brother, whom he had nursed through sickness, was dead. His mother had Death written on her face. He realized how deeply she had suffered—far more deeply than any of them; and he knew that having spent her energies on working for their freedom, she would not live long to enjoy the result of her labours.

And if he was a free man, what was left to him? Amy and life in Norfolk! It had been made clear that although the Queen had graciously granted him his liberty, he must expect no further concessions. He, Lord Robert, son of a man who had been ruler of England, was now nothing but a penniless youth, married to the daughter of a country squire on whose bounty he was dependent.

When he looked at Amy he almost wished that she were not so faithful, or that he was less attractive.

He said, almost hopefully: "I have been away a long time, Amy. You are young and pretty. Come, you have not been faithful to me all the time, I am sure."

She was indignant. "But, of course I have. How can you say such things?" Tears welled into her eyes. She went on: "Do you think that I could ever meet any to compare with you?"

She gazed at him through her tears. He had grown a little older during his imprisonment, but he was no less attractive for that. If his mouth were more stern, that but added to his strength; and if the events of the last months had set a little sadness in his face, that but made his smile the more intriguing. Beneath the sadness there was still that gaiety and vitality which told any woman who looked at him that he found life exciting, and that to be with him meant sharing in that excitement.

He smiled at her, but there was a hint of impatience in his smile. He knew she spoke the truth. The women of the Court had always smiled on him; and poor Amy, tucked away in the country, had not their opportunities.

His father-in-law greeted him with pleasure. He believed that if Lord Robert was unfortunately placed at this time, he would not always be so.

"Welcome home, Robert. Right glad we are to see you. It will be good to have the house made brighter by your presence and poor Amy happy again. The girl has been moping about the place, driving us all to share her melancholy."

And so to the simple life. But how could the gay Lord Robert fit into that? Wistfully he thought of the Court and all the splendours he had once taken for granted. Robert the squire! Robert the farmer! It was too ironical. His great-grandfather had been a farmer. Had he, Robert, then completed the circle?

He would ride about the estate, watching the labourers at their work as they threshed the corn in the barns. Sometimes he would take one of the long staves with the short club attached and help flail the corn because it gave him some satisfaction to hit something. He would take the fan-shaped basket in which the grain was winnowed and shake it in the wind. And these things he did with a fierce resentment. He, Lord Robert, deprived of his lands and riches, was now nothing but a farmer.

He took part in the November killing of livestock and the salting for the winter; he gathered holly and ivy and decorated the great hall with it; he sang carols; he drank heartily, ate ravenously of the simple fare. He danced the country dances; he made love to the local women, among them the wife of a neighbouring squire, and a dairy maid. It mattered not who they were, they were all Lord Robert's if he willed it.

But this could bring only temporary satisfaction.

In January Jane Dudley died and was buried in Chelsea. She left the little she had to her children and expressed the hope that soon their full inheritance would be restored to them.

After the burial Robert did not immediately return to the country. He walked the streets with his brothers and sometimes saw members of the Court from which he was now shut out. He saw the Queen and her husband; he heard the sullen muttering against the Spanish marriage; he observed how ill the Queen looked, and rejoiced.

In Smithfield Square they were now lighting the fires at the feet of Protestants. Robert sniffed the acrid smell, listened to the cries of martyrs.

Ambrose and Henry were with him one day when they had been to see the terrible sights of Smithfield. They walked, shuddering, away and lay on the bank of the river, all silent, yet with angry thoughts in the minds of each.

Robert was the first to speak. "The people are displeased. Why should he be allowed to bring his Spanish customs here!"

"The people would rise against him if they had a leader," suggested Ambrose.

"As Wyatt did?" said Henry.

"Wyatt failed," put in Ambrose, "but he might not have failed."

"Such matters," said Robert, "would need much thought, much planning and preparation between trusted friends. Do not forget the damp cell and the odour of the river, the tolling bell. Remember our father. Remember Guildford. And John was killed in the Tower, though he in fact died afterwards. He would be alive now, but for his imprisonment."

"Is this Robert speaking?" cried Ambrose. "It sounds unlike him."

Robert laughed. He was thinking of April in the Tower of London and the passion expressed in words which were spoken between the bars of a cell. "One day," he said, "you will see what Robert will do."

"You are making plans down there in Norfolk? Have a care, brother."

"My plans are safe. I share them with none. That is the way to make plans."

142

Two men passed them. They looked over their shoulders and said: "Good day to you, my lords."

The brothers were on their feet. "We know you not," said Robert.

"But all know the lords of Dudley."

"Would you have speech with us?" asked Robert.

"We served your noble father, my lord," said one of the men. "We forget not those days. May good fortune return to your family. My lords, the people like not the Spanish marriage."

"That is the Queen's affair," said Ambrose.

"My lord, you think so? Others think a Queen's marriage is the affair of her countrymen. Those who think thus meet in St. Paul's churchyard. They welcome among them those whose nostrils are offended by the smell of Smithfield smoke."

The men bowed and walked on, and the three brothers looked at each other.

Henry said: "Let us not meddle. Have we not learned our lesson?"

But Robert was not attending. He was thinking of the monotony of life in Norfolk. Here was the place for him—if not at Court, then among the agitators of St. Paul's.

The excitement of the meetings stimulated Robert. There were plots to be made in the precincts of St. Paul's, plots to depose the Queen and put the Princess Elizabeth on the throne. Once she was there, the dull life would be ended. He would present himself to her and remind her that he had sworn to be her slave. It might not be long before she was his slave. What woman who had loved him had ever been able to escape from him? That masculine charm was irresistible to duchess and dairymaid; so should it be to Princess and Queen.

Amy was fretful for him. Why did he stay so long in London? If he did not return she would die of melancholy. She would travel to London to see what detained him; she was longing for her Robert.

He tried to soothe her with loving messages and with brief visits to Siderstern. He explained some of his plans. "You see, Amy, at Siderstern I am more or less dependent on your father. I like that not. I would wish to recover my inheritance."

"You will be in trouble again," she said. "You will be sent to the Tower and I shall die."

Then he would be his gay self, enchanting her as he knew so well how to; he would play the passionate lover. "How could I tear myself away from you unless it were necessary! But this is important. We shall be rich again. We shall have power. I shall take you to Court with me, and your beauty will startle them all."

She believed him; and she longed to go to Court as Robert's wife.

When he left her he would leave her with happy dreams. She would see herself dancing at the Court balls, clad in velvet, stiff with jewels. She would lie on her couch eating the sweetmeats which she loved so well, lazily planning the future.

Pinto would shake her head, and while she warned her mistress that she would grow very fat if she ate so many sweetmeats, she would be thinking that Robert was visiting a woman in London. Poor Pinto! She did not understand Robert. He was very ambitious, but he was content with his wife. Amy remembered the passion between them. But he had another love, it was true; the love of power, the longing to see his riches restored; and was that not natural in one so proud?

But Pinto went on sorrowfully wondering. If Amy could not hold him when he was a simple country gentleman, how would she when he became the great man he intended to become?

He came riding home from London one summer's day. Amy saw him from her window, coming into the courtyard with his servants about him. Her heart fluttered. She was wearing an old muslin and she called frantically to Pinto.

"Pinto, my lord is come. Quick . . . quick . . ."

Pinto helped her to pull off the old muslin, but before she was in her cherry velvet he was in the room. He stood looking from her to Pinto.

"Robert!" cried Amy.

Pinto scarcely turned, because Pinto always pretended to be unaware of him. She would say: He may be the gay Lord Robert to others; they may tremble at the sight of him; but not Pinto. To Pinto he is just a man—no different from any other.

Amy's cheeks were first red then white; she was almost swooning at the sight of him. "Pinto . . . Pinto . . . look!"

And he cried, his words mingling with his merry laughter: "Pinto, look! Lord Robert is here!"

"A merry good day to you, my lord," said Pinto, turning her head very slightly and making do with a nod instead of a curtsey.

He strode towards them; he caught them both in his

arms. He lifted them and kissed first Amy, then Pinto. Amy was blushing with pleasure; Pinto was prim with disapproval.

"Now, Pinto," he said, "get you gone, and leave a wife to her lawful husband."

"I'll first see my mistress dressed," said Pinto.

"You'll not!" he retorted. "For I like her best as she is." And he took the cherry velvet and threw it to the other side of the room.

Amy squealed in delight, and Pinto went sedately to the dress and, without looking round, picked it up and walked out of the room.

Robert, laughing, began to kiss and caress Amy.

"Robert!" she gasped. "No warning! You should have let me know."

"What! And give you time to send your secret lover packing?"

Amy clung to him. Pinto often said that his constant references to Amy's secret lovers worried her. It was as though, said Pinto, he would put bad thoughts into the head of an innocent girl. But Pinto was against him. Poor Pinto! Poor simple countrywoman, she had never really known a Court gallant; and such a man as Robert must seem to her full of a sinister strangeness.

But why think of Pinto when Robert was here, glad to be home and full of passionate longing for his wife?

But his high spirits did not endure.

He and his brothers had been warned, he told her, that if they did not keep away from London, they would find themselves under arrest. The Queen's agents had most seriously warned them that they must not forget that although they had been pardoned and had eluded the death penalty they still stood attainted of high treason. One false step, and they would again find themselves the prisoners of the Queen; and if they were once more in trouble, it was hardly likely that they could hope for their former good fortune to be repeated.

Robert was thinking—as he often did—of the Princess who had so much to win, so much to lose, and who had survived most miraculously by waiting. He and she were young, and the Queen had played out her ridiculous farce of false pregnancy; it was clear that there would be no royal offspring.

He longed to see Elizabeth. He made plans for breaking into her house either at Woodstock or Hatfield and presenting himself to her as her constant knight, her desperate lover who was ready to risk his life for a glimpse of her. But he quickly realized the folly of doing any such thing. He must wait, and waiting meant that he must endure the simple life and a return to the woman who was fast losing any power she had once had to attract him.

He was exasperated often and there were quarrels which reached their climax in her peevish reproaches. But always he could sweeten her when he wished to do the sweetening. Often he wished that she were not so madly in love with him. Even when he was harsh with her, when he took her clinging hands from about his neck and put her from him, even when he cried out that he had been a fool to marry her, still she came back whimpering for more love or more rough treatment. There was about him—whatever his mood—that ever-present fascination which could not fade. His power was in his person—the tall slim figure, the powerful shoulders, the haughty set of his well-shaped head, the strong features, the flashing eyes, the air of extreme masculinity, the curling moustaches and pointed beard, the blue-black hair, the arrogant, careless charm; and above all perhaps the certain assurance that there was only one thing on Earth which Robert Dudley could not do, and that was make women cease to love him.

Amy had to accept his carelessness, his philandering; all she asked was that he should stay with her and give her some of his attention.

But he was, of course, impatient to leave her; he was longing for adventure and excitement, and when, after two and a half years of this unsatisfactory existence, Philip of Spain persuaded Mary to join in war against France, Robert seized the opportunity as heaven-sent.

When St. Quentin fell to the English and Spanish soldiers under Philip, Henry Dudley met his death. Robert was complimented on his bravery which was so marked that Philip himself sent for him to thank him and tell him that he had played no small part in the victory.

In the King's quarters on the French battlefield the two men faced each other—the trim little Spaniard with the fair hair and the blue eyes, and the powerfully built black-haired Englishman.

Robert could not resist the thought which occurred to him: If strangers had come into the tent and were asked which was the King and which the commoner, it was not difficult to guess what their answer would be. Kings should tower above their subjects as great Henry had over his.

But the mild young man, who was heir to more than

half the world, had a kindly smile for the handsome beggar.

"Your Majesty," said Robert kneeling, "you sent for me."

"Rise, my lord," said Philip. "I know of your circumstances. Now that the battle is won you have my leave to return to England if you wish to go."

"Retire, Sire! With the French in flight and Paris open to your Majesty's armies!"

Philip shook his head. "I have seen sights this day which have sickened me of war. We shall stay here. It would be unsafe to go on to Paris."

Robert said nothing. A wise man did not argue with Kings. Not to seize the opportunity of marching on Paris would surely be the biggest mistake that had ever been made; but it was not for a penniless lord to tell a commander that.

Philip said: "You have displeased the Queen."

"Your Majesty, I am the son of my father. I obeyed my father, as it seemed to me a son should."

Philip nodded. "You were right in that."

"And now, your Majesty, it is my earnest wish to serve the Queen."

"I believe you," said Philip. "And because you have proved this by your conduct on the battlefield, I will give you a letter which you may take to the Queen from me. In it I am telling her of your conduct."

Robert fell on to his knees and kissed Philip's hand.

"I have asked her to be kind to you," said Philip. "You may prepare at once to leave for England."

Robert remained kneeling while he expressed his gratitude and his desire to serve with his life the titular King of England.

Philip smiled wanly and dismissed him; and Robert lost no time in setting out; and while he urged his horse onwards, while he waited for the boat which would carry him to England, he was filled with joy because the first step was taken.

There was much excitement at the Manor of Hatfield. The Queen was very sick and it was many months since her husband had visited her.

Elizabeth now had some of her old servants with her besides Kat Ashley and Parry; she was still guarded although she was allowed to hunt the buck in Enfield Forest. Spies surrounded her; and she knew that all her actions were reported to the Queen's ministers.

Gardiner was dead, and that was the greatest relief she had had for a long time. Her hopes had never been so high. Already ladies and gentlemen were coming to her and asking for a place in her household, for they knew now that the Queen would never bear the child she longed for. But after Philip's second visit she had declared herself to be again pregnant.

Then Elizabeth shut herself up with Kat and demanded that the cards be read. Kat declared that the cards told her there was no child in the Queen's body; there was nothing but the delusions in her head. Elizabeth had commanded that certain astrologers be brought to her; and they came in the guise of servants, and much trouble that had caused, the gentlemen eventually being taken and tortured in the Tower, and the Princess herself put into great danger which might have cost her her head but for the calm answers she gave.

The weeks would have been tedious without Kat's

gossip. Elizabeth liked to talk of the Queen's husband and how his eyes gleamed when they rested on *her*, and how she was sure that he had wished she were the Queen.

"Mayhap one day," said the frivolous Kat, "we shall have the King of Spain asking for your hand in marriage."

"What! Marry my sister's widower! Never. Remember the trouble my father had through marrying his brother's widow."

"Well, the King of Spain is not so handsome as some gentlemen. There is one in particular. . . . I was thinking of that dark young gentleman who haunts our cards, my lady."

Then Elizabeth would talk of the days she had spent in the Tower, embellishing her adventures as Kat loved to garnish her stories. It was like putting the flavour into a tansy pudding, Kat always said when caught in an exaggeration; and what would tansy pudding be without its flavour?

Marriages were proposed for the Princess. Philibert's name came up again. Philip wished her to marry that man. Then there was Prince Eric of Sweden whose father was eager for the match with his son.

Elizabeth resisted: "Never, never, never! To leave England? Never would I be guilty of such folly."

"And why should King Philip, being so enamoured of your fair person, so passionately wish for your marriage with Philibert?" demanded Kat slyly.

"Stupid Kat! Do you not understand his cunning? Philibert is his vassal. Philip does not know how sick Mary is. He cannot wait for me. He wants me near him—as I should be if I went to Savoy."

"He seemed such a cold, passionless man."

"You did not see him when he was with me."

She always had an answer ready; and if she was often frivolous and coquettish, when danger approached she was as alert as a jungle animal.

But now the dangers were less acute. Even the Queen could no longer believe in her second false pregnancy. Philip, it was said, would never come back to her; and her days were numbered. Never had hopes at Hatfield been as high as they were that summer and autumn.

One day a young man came to Hatfield and asked for an audience of the Princess; and when her attendants asked his name he answered; "Lord Robert Dudley."

When Elizabeth heard that he had come, her eyes sparkled and she demanded that a mirror at once be brought to her.

"Bid him wait awhile," she told her women. "Tell him I have some business to attend to before I grant him an interview."

And the business was to be alone with Kat, for only Kat must see the excitement which possessed her.

"Kat . . . my emeralds! How do I look?"

"Never more beautiful, Your Grace."

"I cannot receive him in this gown."

"Why not?" said Kat artfully. "He is only a lord recently free from the taint of treason."

"Not treason to me, Kat. And I speak of dresses. Let us have the one with the green thread work. Hurry. He is a most impatient man."

"As impatient to see you as you are to see him, my lady."

"I am not so impatient that I cannot pause to change my dress."

"Now have a care, my lady. Have a care. You are not yet Queen of England, and the man's an adventurer."

"I am an adventuress, Kat, and adventurers are the men for me. My coif."

"You are beautiful, dearest, but 'tis not the emeralds nor the gown nor the coif that make you so. 'Tis the joy bubbling within you. Have a care. Remember Thomas Seymour."

"I'm older now, Kat. I'm almost a Queen now. And he is not Thomas. Tell them to send him to me."

He came and knelt before her, keeping her hand in his while he raised his ardent eyes to her face.

She is not Queen yet, thought Kat; but you believe she will be, my lord. Oh, my love, take care. He is too handsome, this man. There is too much fascination there. Even I go weak to contemplate it.

"It is good of you to come to see me, my Lord Robert," said Elizabeth with cool dignity.

"Good!" His voice had a ringing tone, and all the confidence in the world. "The goodness comes from Your Grace because you have permitted me to wait upon you."

She laughed. "Many people wait upon me now, Lord Robert. A short while ago they did not come to Hatfield."

"Might it not be that they stayed away for fear of putting a fair and gracious lady into danger?"

"Or themselves?" she suggested. "But I hear you have recently returned from France, in which land you did splendid service to our country; so we could not accuse you of cowardice, eh?"

"Yet it was fear that kept me from Hatfield ere this—fear of what an impulsive action might mean to one whose safety is of greater account to me than my own. Could I have speech with your Grace alone?"

"My lord, indeed not! Could I, a young and unmarried woman, be left alone with a man of . . . forgive me, my lord, but these tales reach us . . . a man of your reputation with my sex? Kat Ashley will stay. She is my very good servant and friend."

Robert appeared uneasy. Kat Ashley was not noted for her discretion. But the Queen was on the point of death and Elizabeth was all but on the throne; he need not be too concerned about the gossiping Ashley. Moreover he knew that his lot was cast with the Princess. Her failure would be his; as would her triumph. There comes a time in the life of an ambitious man when he must openly show which side he is on. But if only he could be alone with her, what weapons would be his! How far might he not go at one meeting! Did she know this? Was she, the young woman who had faced Gardiner and his like with calm courage, afraid of Robert Dudley's potent charm?

He said almost sullenly: "It seems my fate never to be near Your Grace."

She liked such sullenness. It was manna to her. He was comparing Kat with the prison bars. Elizabeth felt dizzy with pleasure. Yes, she must keep herself aloof until she grew accustomed to such intoxication.

"You forget my position, my Lord Robert," she said, taking refuge from her feelings behind her royalty. "Now tell me why you have come to see me."

He lifted hurt and angry eyes to her face. "Your Grace must have known that I would present myself at the earliest possible moment."

"Is this the earliest possible moment? How should I know that?"

"I had believed there was a deep and lasting friendship between myself and Your Grace."

"Ah yes. We have both suffered, have we not? Come, cheer up, my lord. I know you for my friend."

"I have brought proof of that friendship."

He laid two bags at her feet.

"What are these, my lord?"

"Gold. You say I may speak freely. Well, I will do so. Many, you say, come to pay you homage. Since the Queen has grown so sick, the roads to Hatfield are becoming congested. Dear Lady, if the Queen should recover, the roads back to London will become even more congested, and if aught should go wrong Hatfield might again become a lonely prison."

"Aught go wrong?"

"It is a dangerous world in which we live."

"You know of plots against me?"

"I know of no plots. Do you think that any would confide them to me . . . the most staunch supporter Your Majesty . . . Your Grace ever had!"

"My lord!"

"Aye," he cried, "I have made that clear, have I not?"

He had risen and taken a step towards her. The impetuous man! she thought with tender emotion.

But her eyes flashed. Do not forget, they said, that I am about to be your Queen. But a caressing smile accompanied the warning.

"I trust you, Lord Robert," she said. "What are these bags you bring me?"

"They are full of gold. I bring them as a token. More

155

awaits you . . . if you should need it. I have sold lands and will sell more. The end of a reign is not always followed by peaceful succession. I wish Your Grace to know that if you should need me . . . in any capacity . . . I am yours to command. My recently restored fortune I place at your feet. These bags are but a symbol. These arms are yours, this heart, this body, this man."

She was deeply affected. She held out her hand for him to kiss, but he did not take it. He muttered: "Your Grace, I cannot. You are so beautiful . . . I could not trust myself . . ."

These words pleased her as much as the bags of gold. She was not only a Princess about to become a Queen, he was telling her; she was the most desirable woman, who could make him forget all else because he loved her so madly.

"Go now," she said softly. "We shall meet again."

He knelt before her; he did not touch her; and as he rose he said: "When Your Grace is Queen of England I shall be the first to come to pay you homage and to offer myself in your service. I swear it."

When he had gone, Kat picked up the bags.

"He has bewitched you," she said.

"I know, Kat. And might it not be that I have bewitched him?"

"Bewitching is second nature to him."

"Mayhap it is to me."

"It is easier to be sick of love for a Queen than for a gentleman of fortune. Do not forget, when your hour comes, that you have other friends. Remember William Cecil who has served you well all these years at your sister's Court, writing to you, advising you."

"Why should I forget William Cecil? Have I not said that he is my very good friend?"

"Nay, you have not! But *he* does not possess a pair of flashing black eyes that look at you as though they would devour you. *He* does not tell you that your beauty goes to his head, that he dares not touch your hand for fear of seducing you here and now in front of your good servant, Kat Ashley."

"Shame on you, Kat! Did Lord Robert say any such thing?"

"He did, my lady."

"Then I did not hear it."

"But you saw . . . and I saw . . . as he meant it to be seen. He is an adventurer."

"Well, what should I want—a sit-by-the-fire? A dwarf? A pock-marked ninny?"

"So you want this man?"

"You are dismissed, Kat Ashley. I'll have no more of your insolence."

"You have my love, and love such as mine is indifferent to the anger it may cause. It seeks to serve even if the serving sometimes gives displeasure."

Then Elizabeth turned and embraced Kat. "I know it, Kat. I know it. But don't provoke me." She smiled. "So he looked at me as though he would devour me? I confess 'twas so. But as long as he but *looks*, what matters it? Have no fear, Kat; I shall not allow myself to be devoured. Let us take a look at the cards. Let us see what they have to tell us of our tall dark man now."

"Beware of him! That is what they will say."

"I? Beware? Let him beware of me!"

"No, my lady, it is you who are a-tremble. Have a care. He is no ordinary man."

"There you speak truth," said Elizabeth beginning to laugh in anticipation of a passionate friendship. "He is indeed no ordinary man."

November came. The house at Hatfield was the scene of much activity. The Princess had become more haughty; she was regal yet gay, arrogant and more quick-tempered than ever.

The Count of Feria called upon her, and this caused fresh excitement, for all were aware what this meant.

Feria, on behalf of his master, Philip of Spain, had come to ingratiate himself with Elizabeth.

The Count bowed low—lower, Elizabeth was quick to notice, than he had on their last meeting. Such behaviour made her want to laugh aloud. She thought: So your master will give his support to me whom he suspects of heresy, rather than allow his old enemy the King of France to put Mary of Scotland on the English throne.

It was good to know that she was to receive the support of mighty Philip, and to know that whatever she did would not alter that. She could be cold to Feria, if she wished; or she could be warm, and neither attitude would alter his master's decision. She was the lesser of two evils as far as Spain was concerned, and so she would continue to be.

"I am honoured, my lord Count," she told him, "that you should lighten my humble house with your presence."

"It is I who am honoured," said the solemn Spaniard.

Elizabeth looked at him appraisingly and wondered what had made Jane Dormer fall in love with him. He was handsome in his way—but a Spaniard! Give her a good hearty Englishman. Always her thoughts returned to Robert Dudley.

She bade Feria sup with her.

"It gives me great pleasure to know that you come to assure me of your master's friendship," she told him as they sat at table.

"It has always been my master's endeavour to show friendship to Your Grace," he answered. "You know that the Queen is very sick indeed?"

"I have heard it."

"Your Grace, this is a momentous time for you," went on Feria. "You will be named as the Queen's successor. That is the wish of my master. You know of his influence with the Queen, and it is due to him that this will come to pass."

The light sandy brows shot up; the tilt of the head was haughty in the extreme. "Your master is my very good friend, I doubt not," she said, "but I cannot see that he—or any—can give me that which is mine by right of inheritance. None has any power of bestowing on me that which is my right; nor can I, with justice, be deprived of it."

"It is the custom in England that a monarch shall name his or her successor, is it not?"

"It is the custom in England, my lord, that the succession goes to the next of kin."

"There were some difficulties with regard to the marriage of Your Grace's father and mother."

"I am my father's daughter," she said. "Any, who knew him and knows me, doubts it not."

"You speak truth and it is the Queen's delight—at the suggestion of His Majesty, my master—to make you her successor. I would have you know that His Most Catholic Majesty is your friend."

She put her head on one side. Feria could scarcely believe that this haughty young woman was the demure eager-to-please Princess of a few years ago. She knew her position was secure; she knew that the Queen was on her death-bed; she knew that it was but a matter of weeks—or possibly days—before she would be Queen of England. She behaved as though that honour were already hers, thought the exasperated Spaniard.

"There will be conditions," he said. "You will be expected to discharge Her Majesty's debts."

"I should deem it my duty to do so."

"She wishes that you shall not change her privy councillors."

Elizabeth lifted her shoulders gracefully. "I should believe myself to be at liberty to choose my councillors, as she was to choose hers."

The Count was silent for a few moments. She was being truculent and he saw trouble ahead. He continued, "And, what is most important of all, she would require you to make no alteration in the religion of the country."

She bowed her head and spoke with reverent dignity. "I would not change it, providing only that it could be proved by the word of God, which shall be the only foundation of my religion."

Feria was too exasperated to hide his feelings. What troubles lay ahead for his master, for Spain, with such a woman on the throne? What could he make of her? She was all coquetry when he admired her dress and jewels, so that it would seem he had a foolish simpering girl with whom to deal; then unexpectedly he found himself confronted by a cunning statesman.

He was anxious for the future and he fervently hoped that he would be recalled to Spain before he had to serve in a country governed by such a woman.

Jane Dormer, the betrothed of Feria, called at Hatfield. Her visit gave rise to much speculation, for next to Mistress Clarencius she was the favourite lady-in-waiting to the Queen.

Elizabeth received Jane with reserve. She looked at her speculatively—this lovely young girl, this fanatical Catholic who was about to become a Spaniard . . . and a spy, doubtless for that lover of hers.

Elizabeth trusted Jane Dormer slightly less than she trusted all those of the Queen's Court who had not proved themselves to be her friends.

Jane knelt and told the Princess that as the Queen's health was fast failing she had, on Mary's request, brought the crown jewels to Elizabeth.

"Your Grace, I bring three requests from Her Majesty. They are that you shall be good to her servants, repay her debts and leave the Church as it is—re-established by Her Majesty."

"Thank you, Mistress Dormer," said Elizabeth. "You may rise. Her Majesty may rest assured that I shall be good to her servants and pay her debts. As to religion, as I have already said, that is a matter concerning which I rely on no other than God."

Jane said: "I bring also a casket of jewels from the King."

Elizabeth was pleasantly excited. She was fond of jewels, and jewels presented by Philip—who she felt was already beginning to woo her—were doubly attractive.

"He says they are to be presented to you as he knows

161

you will admire them and they will become you."

"So those were his words?" said Elizabeth.

Jane assured her that they were; and Elizabeth, well pleased, treated Jane to a show of affection.

When she had dismissed her, the Princess became thoughtful. It was clear that Mary must be very near to death. She remembered Robert's warning and the gold he had brought. Had she been too firm over this matter of religion? Had she been too haughty with Feria? What if Spain should withdraw support after all? What if the French King should have set in motion some plot for putting Mary Queen of Scots on the throne?

She sent for a man whom she knew to be one of her ardent admirers, and whom she could trust. Nicholas Throgmorton had been concerned in the Wyatt rebellion but acquitted on account of insufficient evidence against him.

"Go with all speed to the palace," she said. "Enter with as little fuss as possible and make a point of conversing with the ladies of the bedchamber. Most of them are willing to serve me—with the exception of Jane Dormer and old Clarencius. The Queen always wears a black enamelled ring which was given to her by her husband at the time of their marriage. It is unmistakably a Spanish ring. Send that ring to me so that I may be sure the Queen no longer lives. I remember when my brother died, guards were placed about the palace and the news was not allowed to leak out. I must know immediately. Send me the ring with all speed."

Sir Nicholas departed; but before he had time to reach London there was another visitor to Hatfield. He came hurrying into the house, demanding audience with the Princess, and when it was granted he fell on his knees before her and cried: "God save Your Majesty! God save Queen Elizabeth!"

He stood up, towering above her, and she was filled with delight in him.

"You know this to be true?"

"I was determined to be the first with the news. I swore it."

Overcome with emotion she turned aside. She was Queen of England at last; and the man who had occupied her thoughts for so long and so pleasantly stood before her offering himself in her service.

Then she sank to her knees and cried: "This is the Lord's doing and it is marvellous in our eyes."

For a short while she gave herself up to solemn contemplation of her destiny. Then she rose and turning to him said: "Now I am indeed your Queen."

He bowed his head and murmured: "Your Majesty . . . your most beautiful and beloved Majesty!"

"My friend," she said, extending her hand to him, "my very good friend, you shall not regret the day you rode to the Queen with such news."

She drew back as he stepped towards her. He said: "I hear others coming. The news is out."

In a few seconds this intimacy would be over. She allowed herself to give him a caressing smile.

"Lord Robert Dudley," she said, "from this moment you are Master of the Queen's Horse."

"My humble thanks, Your Majesty."

She noted the heightened colour in his cheeks. The post in itself would bring him fifteen hundred pounds a year. She thought: Never did a Queen have a more handsome Master of her Horse than Robert Dudley.

"You are well suited for the post," she said; "and it means that you will be in constant attendance upon me."

He said passionately: "Your Master of Horse shall be all that Your Majesty requires of him."

The intimacy was broken. Others were coming to proclaim Elizabeth the Queen.

V

The Queen began her triumphant journey to London, and as she rode through the countryside she was smiling at the cheering people who lined her way.

"God bless the Queen!" they cried. "Long may Elizabeth reign over us!"

She was young and fair; she had always shown a fondness for the people, and they loved her. Now, they promised themselves, there would be an end to the terrible fires which had been burning, not only in Smithfield Square but in many other parts of the country. This was the end of persecution. Bloody Mary was dead and England would be merry again.

At Highgate the Bishops were waiting to receive her. She was gracious to them, although making an exception of Bonner who had been persecutor-in-chief since the death of Gardiner. Would that old enemy was here! she brooded. It would have been pleasant to have had Master Gardiner trembling before her. The people noticed her cold manner to Bonner and they cheered afresh.

She rode on for her traditional entry to the Tower, and there was great rejoicing as she passed through the City's gates.

Now she sat in a splendid chariot which was drawn

165

along Barbican to Cripplegate that she might be received by the Lord Mayor and the City dignitaries. When she had received their homage she remounted her horse, and magnificent she looked in her purple velvet. There was no need now to wear sombre clothes; she had no rival now. *She* was the Queen.

She was continually aware of her Master of Horse who rode beside her. What attention he aroused! Some of the women looked at him instead of their Queen. He glittered with jewels—a dazzling figure.

"That is Lord Robert Dudley," people whispered, "who came so near to losing his head in the last reign. Did you ever see such a man!"

"They say he compares with His Majesty King Henry the Eighth in the days of his glowing youth."

Let him win their approval, meditated the Queen. Let them all see him as she saw him. She was not sure what role she had in store for him; and she wanted the people to retain a picture of him—magnificent, towering above all others.

Music filled the air; gay tapestry banners hung from the windows. As she reached the Church of Blanch Chapleton on the corner of Mart Lane she heard the Tower guns begin to boom. Through Tower Street she went, and she paused to listen to the children of St. Paul's singing her praises, remembering—it seemed long ago now—how they had sung her sister's.

She prayed: "Oh God, help me in this task. Help me to play my part nobly and honourably."

She was filled with emotion. Her greatest desire had been granted; she must prepare herself to fulfil her duty and be worthy of the role. She was even glad of her misfortunes for she had come safely through them, and they had taught her more than easy living would have done.

All these people who cheered her now should be her first consideration. She would not be foolish as her sister Mary had been. Mary too had ridden into London to the cheers of her people; but these same people now called her Bloody Mary; they reviled her for making a Spanish marriage and bringing foreigners among them; they blamed her for the loss of Calais; they rejoiced that she was dead.

It should not be so with Elizabeth. They should love her, these common people, all the days of her life. They were her strength; she would sacrifice anything rather than their devotion. She must never forget that they were the pillars which supported the throne.

At this sacred time she was oblivious of the picture she made in her purple velvet; she had forgotten her Master of Horse; she was only a Queen, determined to rule wisely, determined to make her country great.

It was a solemn moment when she entered the Tower.

All the officials were waiting to make obeisance to her. She dismounted. All about her were the nobility of England; and she was conscious only of a deep humility.

The words she spoke were spontaneous. "Some," she said, "have fallen from Princes in this land, to be prisoners in this place; I am raised from being a prisoner in this place to be a Prince of this land. That dejection was a work of God's justice; this advancement is a work of His mercy. As they were to yield patience for the one, so I must bear myself to God thankful, and to men merciful for the other."

She turned then to the Lieutenant of the Tower.

"Conduct me now to those apartments which I occupied when I was a prisoner here."

This was done, and she went into them wonderingly; and in great emotion she fell once more upon her knees and thanked God for her deliverance. "For," she said, "like Daniel I have come safely out of the lions' den, and I shall never forget His Mercy."

There was no sign of the frivolous girl on that memorable day when Elizabeth came to the Tower of London as Queen.

Mary was buried with great pomp, and the Queen attended the burial. Dr. White, the Bishop of Winchester, preached the funeral sermon, and that day he proved himself to be a bold man.

He spoke of the late Queen, sighing over her many virtues, and he spoke with vehement regret. She had been a wise woman, a great Queen; she had renounced Church Supremacy; she had declared that St. Paul forbade women to speak in Church and that it was not therefore fitting for the Church to have a dumb head.

How dared he speak thus! brooded the young Queen, as she sat quietly before him. How dared he, the old greybeard! He doubtless saw only a young woman sitting before him; he would have to learn something of the spirit within that youthful body.

Fortunately the sermon was in Latin and there were few who understood as Elizabeth did.

He wept when he talked of Mary, declaring that their greatly lamented Queen had left a sister who was a worthy lady whom they were all obliged to obey. This they must do perforce. *Melior est canis vivus leone mortuo.*

The blue eyes were burning points of fire. She a live dog and Mary a dead lion! He should learn something of the lion heart beneath these glittering queenly jewels. The insolent man clearly did not understand the nature of his Queen. A live dog indeed!

As Dr. White left the pulpit, the Queen rose. She cried to her guards: "Arrest that man."

The Bishop lifted a hand to hold off the guards who had immediately sprung forward to carry out the Queen's orders.

"Your Majesty," he said, "it is in my power to excommunicate you unless you insist that your subjects adhere to Rome."

Her father would have sent him to his death. But she was not yet as strong as her father, although in one way she was stronger. The years of danger had taught her to curb her anger when it was necessary to do so. She could see in the Bishop's eyes what she believed to be a fervent desire for martyrdom. She would not let him indulge it. The people had hated persecutions. She had stopped them, and men such as this Bishop should not goad her into restarting them.

Calmly she watched her orders being carried out. Let him cool his fanaticism in prison. Time would show her how to act, for Time was as important to a Queen as it had been to a captive Princess.

The Queen gathered together her Privy Council. William Cecil was at her right hand, and she gave the Great Seal to Nicholas Bacon; and of the late Queen's

Council, Lord William Howard, with Arundel and Sackville, were allowed to remain in office.

So far none had noticed the tender looks which she bestowed on her Master of Horse. His office meant that he must necessarily be in constant attendance; and the fact that he had been chosen for the post aroused no comment. His knowledge of equestrian matters was undoubtedly great; and all agreed that no one looked quite so magnificent on a horse as the handsome Dudley.

But during those first weeks of queenship, Elizabeth's thoughts were more of state matters than of love. Each morning she awakened to a sense of power and excitement, but never did she forget those lessons she had learned during the days of adversity.

Her first task was to break away from the Pope, and this she must do without offending her Catholic subjects, for they were many. Therefore there should be no overt break. The change should be gradual, so that she might feel the temper of the people as she made it.

The Mass was still celebrated in all churches, and Elizabeth attended regularly; but on Christmas Day she left the church after the service and just as the Bishop was preparing to conduct High Mass.

She had taken a firm step in the direction which she intended to follow, but not another step should be taken until she knew the effect her conduct would have on the people.

There was no doubt about the verdict on her conduct. Too many remembered the Smithfield fire. England was not made for fanaticism; the English loved Justice too much to have any regard for its natural enemy, Persecution. Only a few deplored her action and those—considering the case of Dr. White who might so easily have become a martyr for his public abuse of her—did not believe that she would persecute them as her sister had persecuted the Protestants.

Elizabeth knew then that it was safe to take the next step, and on another great occasion—that of New Year's day—she proclaimed that the church services were to be held in English.

Thoughts of her Coronation occupied her mind. She looked forward to it with great eagerness; it had figured largely in her dreams; and now she wished to discuss it with one whose triumph was her triumph and who should have his prominent part to play in its ceremonies.

What a joy it was to be in his company during those days of preparation! It seemed the more exciting to her because they were never alone together. Always surrounding her were her Councillors of state or the ladies of her bedchamber. Poor Robert! She knew he was at times incensed, for how could he say what he wished in the presence of these people! He must keep his distance, address her as his Queen; he must play the subject, never the lover. Her royalty was between them now as once his prison walls had been. Yet each day she knew that she was more deeply in love with him, for if she did not see him she was fretful and disappointed. She could not continually demand to know where he was. She was trying to exercise her usual caution. She would not wish to tell the Court that she was in love with her Master of Horse.

I verily believe, she thought, that I would marry him.

But he has a wife. Does he forget that, the sinful man!

She should be grateful to that woman. What was her name? Annie? Amy? She pretended not to remember. Stupid little country wench! What had she had to attract him in the first place?

There was nothing she liked so much as to escape from her councillors and sit among her courtiers—if Robert were with them—and talk of pleasure: masques, balls and all the ceremonies which must attend her coronation.

"I doubt not," she said one day, "that the Lord Mayor and his fellows will give me as good a Coronation as they gave my sister. Would I knew which would be the most propitious day. What do you think, my Lord Dudley?"

"The day would be unimportant, Your Majesty."

"How so?"

"The very fact of its being your Majesty's Coronation day would make it the greatest any of us had ever lived through."

"What means the man? Do you know, Mistress Ashley?"

"I think he means that the greatest boon this country has ever received was your Majesty's accession to the throne," said Kat.

"Mistress Ashley has explained my meaning, Madam," said Robert.

She looked from him to the lady who was sitting beside him—a dark, and sparkling-eyed beauty. The sight did not please the Queen.

"I pray you, do not shout at me from such a distance, Master Dudley. Come here and sit beside me."

Willingly he came, his eyes adoring, pleading: Why cannot I see you alone? Why must there always be these people between us?

She wanted to answer: Because I am the Queen and you were foolish enough to marry a country girl. If you had been a wiser man, who knows what I might not have done for you!

Was he too familiar? Now he looked a little sullen. Was he a little too certain of her favour? She could not reprove him before her ladies and gentlemen. If she did, he might absent himself from her presence, and that would be as much punishment for her as for him.

She fancied those about her were smiling slyly. Had they noticed her preference? Her reign was too young for her to make any false steps.

Kat said to her later: "Your Majesty, they are beginning to notice. There are whispers."

"Of what do you speak, woman?"

"Of our dark and handsome gentleman, Madam. It is noticed that your eyes are often upon him, and that you like not to see him laughing with other ladies."

"I'll not endure such insolence. Who are these gossips?"

"The whole Court, Your Majesty. And 'tis true, you know. You give away your feelings. You could not show them more plainly if you put your arms about his neck and kissed him before them all."

Elizabeth so far forgot her queenly dignity as to box Kat's ears. But Kat knew that her warning had gone home.

Elizabeth was perturbed.

At the next assembly she said: "I wish for advice of Dr. Dee on my Coronation. You will go to him, my

173

Lord Dudley, and ascertain from him which day would be more suited to that event."

"When does Your Majesty expect me to leave?"

"At once . . . at once."

He looked at her reproachfully. Even if it were only for a short time, he was being sent away from Court. He was hurt and angry. But so was she.

She watched him leave, with such longing in her eyes that Kat felt she merely betrayed herself the more.

When Robert left the Court for his visit to the Queen's favourite astrologer, Dr. Dee, he was in an exalted frame of mind.

Elizabeth had not hidden her feelings from him. He knew enough of his powers to recognize in her the same longings he had so often encountered in others. Very soon, he was sure, that longing would grow to such magnitude that not all her pride nor all her royalty would be allowed to stand in its way.

He contemplated the future with complacence. No member of his family had risen as he would rise. But there was one obstacle—Amy.

The very thought of her angered him. He compared her with Elizabeth. The Queen attracted him apart from her royalty. Had she not been the daughter of Henry the Eighth she would have been his mistress ere this, he was sure. But she was doubly desirable; not only could she give him erotic satisfaction but that crown which his father had intended for Guildford.

He would be King of the realm, for no woman had yet refused him what he demanded; and Elizabeth had shown quite clearly that she was essentially a woman.

He could not ignore Amy. She was becoming

174

restive; she wanted to come to Court and share in her husband's good fortune. She wrote asking if he were in love with some lady of the Court who was demanding all his attention. Amy had discovered the truth. Elizabeth certainly demanded constant thought, constant attention.

Dr. Dee welcomed him warmly at his country residence and, on consulting his charts, decided that the 15th of January would be a very good day for the crowning of the Queen.

When he left the astrologer, as he was not far from Siderstern, he felt that it would be a good opportunity of seeing Amy and making some attempt to stifle her desires to share his life at Court. He was afraid that if he did not visit her, she might decide to come to Court to see him. He did not think the Queen would be very pleased to see Amy at Court.

When he reached the house it was early afternoon and all was quiet. He sent his servants to the stables with the horses and went into the house to find Amy.

The hall was deserted; he went quickly up the staircase and along the gallery to the bedroom which he shared with Amy when he lived in the house.

Someone was in the room, bending over a press. It was Pinto.

"So . . . Pinto!" he said.

She straightened and bobbed a curtsey. She was embarrassed, he saw. "Lord Robert! We were not expecting you."

"I know it. And your mistress?"

"She is riding with her father, my lord."

"Is anything wrong, Pinto?" he asked.

"Wrong, my lord! No . . . no. All will be well for my

lady now that you are here."

Lightly he wondered why Pinto interested him; but he knew almost at once. She was not ill-favoured; and she was deeply conscious of him. In her case it was not love but dislike which he engendered. What a strange woman Pinto must be!

She was preparing to hurry from the room, but he felt in a mischievous mood.

"Do not let me disturb you, Pinto. Do not hurry away."

"I was merely putting away my lady's things."

"Then I pray you continue to do so."

"But I have finished, my lord."

He came towards her slowly, aware that her agitation was increasing. "What is it, Pinto?" He caught her chin in his hands and looked into her eyes. "I like it not that you should mistrust me. I like it not that you should run away when I appear, and cast those fearful glances at me when you think I do not see."

"But, my lord . . ."

He bent his head swiftly and kissed her. He was almost as astonished as she was, and for a moment he sensed a deep pleasure.

She twisted free and ran from the room. He was smiling as he watched her. How foolish he had been to think that she hated him. She was after all a woman.

Poor Pinto! She covered her feelings for him under a veil of mistrust and suspicion. There was no need for her to fear. Her virtue was safe from him.

When Amy came riding home and found him there she was almost hysterical with delight.

"But Robert, why did you not send a message!" she

cried, throwing herself at him. "I've missed hours of your company, and you will be running away ere long, I doubt not."

He was charming as he knew so well how to be. "It is wonderful to be home," he said, "away from the garish Court."

"You speak as though you do not like it there."

"How can I when it keeps me from you . . . and home?"

She could not keep her hands from caressing him. She pouted and said that she had heard rumours.

"Rumours of what?"

"It is said that the Queen greatly favours you."

"The Queen is just. She remembers those who were her friends in adversity."

"Yes. But they say you are a special favourite."

"It is just talk."

Later he rode with her through the estates; he must see the new lambs and watch the sowing of the oats and beans; he feigned delight in these things and congratulated himself that he had escaped from them for ever.

He could not keep the knowledge from her that this was a flying visit.

"No . . . no, no!" she protested.

He thought her a pampered girl. It was due to her being her father's heiress and living with grown-up half-brothers and half-sisters—the pet of them all. He must have been mad to marry her.

"Alas, my love, I am on a mission for the Queen. I must go back and prepare myself for the ordeal of the Coronation."

"Why cannot I go, Robert?"

"It is impossible."

"But other lords have their wives at Court."

"Only if they have posts in the Queen's household."

"Could I not be a lady-in-waiting?"

"That will come, Amy. But give me time. The Queen has scarce been on the throne a month, and even if she does favour me now as you have heard, I cannot ask too much of her."

"Would it be asking too much of her to give your wife a place at Court?"

He could smile ironically at that. "I am sure it would, Amy."

"But, Robert, something will have to be done. I cannot stay here for months and months while you are away from me."

"I will come to see you, Amy, whenever it is possible. You may depend on that. My duties as Master of the Queen's Horse keep me occupied. I think I may earn the Queen's displeasure for absenting myself so long."

"I am afraid of the Queen, Robert."

"You are wise to be so. She would be angry if she knew you were detaining me here."

"And mayhap send you to the Tower! Oh, Robert, shall I ever be able to come to Court?"

He soothed her with gentle words and caresses and plans for the future. Yet how glad he was when he could ride away from Norfolk to London and the Queen!

The day before her Coronation Elizabeth rode through the City that she might receive the loving greetings of her people.

She had gone by water from Westminster Palace to the Tower several days before that Saturday fixed for the ceremonial parade; and she left the Tower on the Saturday in her chariot—a beautiful and regal figure in her crimson velvet. She was not quite twenty-six years of age, yet she looked younger than she had when she had made the journey along the Thames for the Tower on that mournful Palm Sunday four years before.

There were, for her delight, pageants and ceremonies similar to those which had been prepared for her sister Mary, yet how different was the feeling of the crowd! London had welcomed Mary, but Mary was coldly formal. Not so Elizabeth. She was certainly a dazzling sight in velvet and jewels, but she belonged to the people as Mary never could. All during that day she was anxious to show them that she thought of them as they thought of her, that her one wish was to please them as they wished to honour her.

"God save Your Grace!" they cried.

And she replied: "May God save you all!"

Even the poor brought flowers to her. Those about her would have held them back, but Elizabeth would not allow this to be done. She must smile on all; she must speak to them, however humble they were; and the flowers of her poorer subjects were those which she insisted on keeping in her chariot.

She knew that she had the people with her. She, though so young, was wise; and her greatest delight was in the outward signs of her people's love.

She smiled as she passed the Spread Eagle in Gracechurch Street, for across that street was an arch on which was depicted a pageant concerning the

179

Queen's ancestors: Her grandparents, Elizabeth of York and Henry the Seventh; her father, Henry the Eighth; and there was a picture of a beautiful and spritely lady to whom no reference had been made for many years: the Queen's mother, Anne Boleyn. Nothing could have pleased Elizabeth more.

Then there were pageants in Cornhill and the Chepe; and Elizabeth had some apt remarks to make concerning each of them. She would have the citizens know that she was no mere spectator; she was one of them. Her smiles were for all—for the aldermen and the members of the City's guilds; for the governors and scholars of Christ's Hospital, one of whom made a speech to which she listened with grave attention.

Most significant of all was her encounter with the two old men who sat at the Little Conduit in Cheapside, one with his scythe and his hour-glass, representing Time. Time was her friend; she had always said so. And the other represented Truth; he gave her a Bible in English; and all those about her noticed with what fervency she took this holy book and kissed it.

She listened to the singing of the song which told her of her subjects' wishes:

"... our hope is sure
That into error's place thou wilt the truth restore..."

And as she listened she held the Bible against her breast and raised her eyes; and when the people cheered and called blessings on her, she cried: "Be ye assured that I will stand your good Queen!"

180

And so she went to Whitehall; and the next day to the Abbey for the crowning. The dream had come true. Hers was the anointing; in her hands were placed the orb and the sceptre; and the voices echoed about her: "Yea, yea, yea. God save Queen Elizabeth!"

There was one duty which, Elizabeth was assured by her councillors, she must not evade. The country would not be completely happy until there was a royal nursery at the palace and the son of Elizabeth was born.

"Marry!" was the urgent advice. "And the sooner the better."

In spite of a coquettishly expressed love of the virgin state, Elizabeth was by no means unwilling to consider suitors; and as there was no better *partie* in the world than the Queen of England, there were many to compete for her hand.

In the meantime she was making her future policy clearer.

She had discreetly declared to the Protestant countries her desire to return England to the Reformed Faith; and at the same time, as she had no desire to offend France and Spain, she let it be known that she intended to allow her subjects freedom of thought in religious matters.

The Pope was enraged. He declared that he was unable to understand what right a woman, who had been born out of wedlock, had to the throne; and furthermore, in his opinion, Mary Queen of Scots was the rightful heir. He did not understand how this new doctrine of liberty of conscience could be successful. He feared its consequences.

The Queen, secure in her own country, could snap her fingers at the Pope; she felt that was what most of her subjects wished her to do. She recalled her ambassador from Rome, but he, threatened with excommunication if he obeyed her, stayed where he was. The Queen was indifferent. England was with her; so what did she care for the rest of the world? The Catholic peers had kissed her cheek and sworn to give her their allegiance. She had the common people firmly behind her, for the brief return to Rome under Mary, which had brought with it misery and persecution, seemed to them an evil thing.

She continued magnanimous towards her old enemies; and they, finding they had nothing to fear from her, as she had guessed they would be, were ready to serve her.

She had laughed at their terrors. "We are of the nature of a lion," she said. "We cannot descend to the destruction of mice."

The country had emerged from the reign of Mary in a poor condition; but hopes were high under the new young Queen. Now all looked confidently to her to marry; it was believed by all her statesmen that, although she had shown some wisdom, being a woman, she needed a firm masculine hand to help her rule.

That made Elizabeth smile. She intended to show them that a lioness was as fitted as a lion to defend her own. But that would come. In such matters she must never abandon her caution.

Her subtlety soon began to surprise those about her; and none realized this more fully than the Spanish ambassador, the Count of Feria. The hopes of Feria rested on the Catholic peers who, he was certain, had gone over to Elizabeth's side only for expediency's sake. He advised his master that these men could easily be won to the service of Spain, providing the bribes which were offered them were attractive enough. Philip saw reason in this, and was prepared to spend a great deal of Spanish money on his Catholic friends in England.

The Count considered the most likely "pensioner" to be Lord William Howard, a Catholic, whom the Queen had made her Chamberlain; and he quickly discovered that Howard was amenable to bribes. But before the first payment was made Howard appeared reluctant to accept the money. Feria was disconsolate; he had hoped for much from the Chamberlain. Then to the Count's consternation, a few days after Howard had refused to accept the bribe, he came to Feria and told him: "I could not accept your magnificent offer until I knew the Queen's pleasure." Feria was astounded; he had naturally discussed the matter of payment to Howard with the utmost delicacy, but it had never occurred to him that the man had not clearly understood for what purposes the money was to be paid. Then came the most astonishing revelation. "I have now the Queen's consent to accept the money and shall be glad if you will send me the first payment."

Philip and Feria were exasperated beyond endurance. They had learned yet another lesson regarding the sharp wits of the Queen.

Nor did Elizabeth allow the matter to rest there. She blithely told Feria that she was delighted to hear of his generosity. She added coyly: "I hope his Most Catholic Majesty will not be offended if *I* employ some of the servants he has here among my courtiers."

He wrote to his master that he would go no further in this matter of bribes. He had hoped to lure Cecil, Bacon, Robert Dudley, and Parry to work for Spain. Cecil however, was possessed of a large fortune and would not be interested in money; Bacon was his close friend and a brother-in-law of Cecil's, for they had each married a daughter of Sir Anthony Cooke—two very learned women and tiresome bluestockings; there was not much hope in that direction. Thomas Parry, who had long been her cofferer and whom she had now knighted, might be amenable. His real name was Vaughan, but because his father's name was Harry and he came from Wales he had been called, after the fashion there, Thomas ap Harry, which had become Parry. This man was a gossip, but so attached to the Queen was he that Feria would not hasten to approach him with offers of money. As for Lord Robert Dudley—that handsome young man about the Queen's own age—Elizabeth appeared to dote on him, and indeed her conduct was giving rise to rumours. In the opinion of the Spanish ambassador it was not easy to know who could be trusted to work for Spain.

The Queen suddenly put an end to such trains of thought by declaring that there must be an end to all "pensions" from Spain.

She was now ready to consider her suitors, a project which gave her much pleasure.

The first and most important was her brother-in-law, Philip, the King of Spain himself.

How she enjoyed herself, alternately gay and serious, tormenting the solemn Feria, refusing to see him, then having him sit beside her and making much of him. She did not think, she declared, that such a marriage would be successful; she was reminded again and again of all her father had suffered when he went through a form of marriage with his brother's widow.

Feria assured her that the Pope would give his dispensation. She pointed out that the Pope had shown himself to be no friend of hers. The Pope, Feria said coldly, could be persuaded by his master; and if the marriage took place Elizabeth would have no need to fear Papal enmity.

That was true, she admitted; but as she was in no fear of the Pope whatsoever, she had little to gain in that direction.

There were other suitors. There were Eric of Sweden and Archduke Charles, son of Emperor Ferdinand. It gave her great pleasure to consider each and discuss them in turn, to blow hot and cold, to raise objections and then pretend to be favourably inclined. There were many conferences and entertainments to honour the ambassadors of her suitors; but none of the courtships progressed.

She told the ambassadors that she could not forget the unpopularity of her sister's marriage. The English, she believed, would wish to see their Queen married to an English husband.

Such statements set wild hopes soaring in the minds of certain noblemen. There was the Earl of Arundel who had offered his hand to Elizabeth before she was Queen. Elizabeth pretended to consider him—not only because she was delighted with any man who declared his wish to marry her, but mainly because she wished for the support of all men of influence at this stage of her reign.

Another was Sir William Pickering; he was forty-three, but handsome, and it was said that he had lived merrily. The Queen showed special favour to such as Pickering, and as, it was remembered, from the days of his youth he had been very successful with women, a match between himself and the Queen, although unlikely, was not impossible.

There were many quarrels between Pickering and Arundel; and the Court amused itself by laying bets on their chances.

Cecil regarded all this frivolity without a great deal of tolerance. He was against the matches with Spain, Austria and Sweden, favouring alliance with the Earl of Arran who had been chosen for Elizabeth in her childhood. Such an alliance, Cecil declared, would unite England and Scotland and much trouble between those two countries might thereby be avoided.

Elizabeth listened to her ministers, went on discussing matrimony, studied the pictures of her suitors—and looked with longing eyes at her Master of Horse.

Cecil would remonstrate with her. He was not a man to mince his words, and often aroused her anger; but she was clever enough to appreciate him, and was always prepared to give him her ready smile after a difference between them; and what was even more important, she invariably took his advice.

She gave as much attention to matters of feminine vanity as to state affairs, yet the latter did not suffer for that.

While she was considering an answer to Philip of Spain, her silk woman, Mistress Montague, brought her a New Year's present—a pair of knit silk stockings; and these stockings seemed to delight her far more than

186

a brilliant marriage with His Most Catholic Majesty could have done.

She would lift her skirts to show them to her women. Mistress Montague proudly declared that, seeing Her Majesty looked so well in the stockings, she would without delay set about making more.

"Indeed, I like them!" cried the Queen. "There shall be no more cloth stockings for me. I shall wear only silk."

Thus, when Cecil came to talk of state affairs, was she occupied with her silk woman. And while she amused herself with her suitors, her fine clothes, and her great position, she kept one man beside her. Her delight in him did not diminish; in fact, it grew so great that it became apparent to all.

The Queen, so quick in other matters, was slow to realize this. Cecil, that blunt and fearless man, brought it home to her on the occasion of the misalliance of the Duchess of Suffolk with an equerry in her service.

The Queen laughed aloud when she heard the story. "So she has married her horsekeeper, that proud Madam!"

Cecil answered: "Yes, Madam; it is true that she has married her horsekeeper, but she might retort that Your Majesty wishes you could do the same!"

The Queen stared at her minister.

Now she knew. She had betrayed her passion for Robert.

There was little opportunity for seeing him alone, and while this did not disturb her greatly—for it seemed enough to her that she often had him in her presence and could give him soft looks and receive passionate and daring ones from him—he was by no means satisfied. He would show his dissatisfaction by being coldly deferential, by being attentive to others; he would absent himself from her apartments now and then; and while he continued to perform his duties with care, she could not reprove him for this. She loved him for his independence—she could not tolerate meekness in men—yet in his case it distressed her.

She told Kat when they were alone together that he must be brought to her with as little ceremony as possible.

"You would have me bring him here alone . . . to your apartment!"

"Why not? Why not?"

"Dearest Majesty, it could not be kept secret."

"You mean *you* could not keep it a secret."

"Nay! I would rather die than divulge it."

"If it is divulged, I shall blame you, Kat."

"Sweetest Majesty, have a care. He is a bold man."

"I know it," said Elizabeth smiling. "But do not forget that if I am a Queen, I am also a woman who knows how to take care of herself."

"He's no ordinary man."

"Am I an ordinary woman?"

"Nay! That is why I fear. You both tower above all others."

"Go and bring him to me, Kat."

"Dearest, is it wise . . . ?"

"Go, I say, and do not meddle, woman."

So Kat brought him to her and left them together. Kat was right when she had said he was bold. The Queen held out her hand for him to kiss, but he would have none of that. He would have her know that he only tolerated ceremony for the sake of others. He would not kiss her hand but her mouth.

"Robert," she protested breathlessly, "you forget . . ."

"I have remembered too long."

"I did not send for you to do this."

But her assumed reluctance was unavailing. He was too experienced, altogether too fascinating. He was, in fact, irresistible, and he knew it.

He lifted her in his arms and strode with her to the chair of state—that chair in which she alone should sit.

There he sat, still holding her. Have done with queenship, he implied. You are a woman now. There has been too much teasing. It is finished.

She was excited. This was *lese-majeste*; yet that was how she would have it, for she loved his boldness. She herself was weak with love. She wondered how she could stand out against him, as she must. This was a battle between them; never must she forget that. He wished to seduce the Queen that he might be the master; she wished to keep him desiring to seduce, that she might remain the mistress. It was a battle she knew well how to fight; she had fought it with Seymour and had come through victorious, and she had been but a girl then. But she knew that this battle would be the fiercest she had ever fought.

She laughed as she lay in his arms. "Have you forgotten, sir, that it is the Queen you hold? Have you no respect for the crown?"

"I have nothing . . . nothing but my love for Elizabeth. I care not if she be Queen or drab. She is mine, and I'll wait no longer."

"How dare you!" she cried; and in her voice was the

189

trill of excitement, since his words pleased her more than any profession of loyalty could have done.

"How dare you torment me so?" was his answer.

"I?"

But there were kisses now—given and returned—and words were impossible.

At length he said: "I wonder I did not do this before them all."

"Arundel would have run his sword through you. I should not have wished that to happen."

"Arundel! Pickering! You demean yourself!"

"Yes, I demean myself . . . because you only are worthy to mate with me. At least that is what *you* think."

"And you?"

"How could I think that, when you have a wife, and could have none but dishonourable intentions regarding me?"

"There is one thing I must know," he said earnestly.

"You *must* know? You are very bold, Lord Robert."

"And intend to be bolder."

She shrieked with assumed dismay.

His lips were on her throat, and he said between kisses: "Would you marry me . . . if I were free to marry you?"

"Would I marry you?" she gasped. "You . . . you . . . the son of a traitor! You . . . a Dudley! Do you think the Queen could marry with such!"

"Yes, I do. Am I a fool? Am I blind? Elizabeth . . . nay, I'll not call you Your Majesty. To me you are Elizabeth, the only woman in the world who will do for me . . . who maketh all others of no account so that they tire me and make me run from them to dream, alas, but to dream—of her who torments me and denies with words the love that shines from her eyes. You *would* marry me, would you not . . . would you not?"

She answered hesitatingly: "I . . . do not know."

"Is it because you do not know, that you will give no answers to these suitors of yours?"

"It might be."

"Because you are in love with a man who cannot marry you since he has a wife already? I will have the truth. I demand the truth."

She looked into his brilliant eyes and said: "I shall never forgive you for this. I have never been so treated . . ."

"You have never been loved as I love you."

"Am I so unattractive that you think no one has the least regard for me?"

"No one has ever loved you as I love you. You would marry me, would you not, if I were free?"

Looking into his face, marvelling at his beauty, she told the truth: "I believe I should be greatly tempted to do so."

She saw his triumph, and that sobered her a little; but she was still under the spell of enchantment. She put her arms about his neck and stroked the soft curling hair, as she had longed to do so many times.

He said: "Mayhap one day we shall marry. Oh, happy day! And while we wait . . ."

She raised her eyebrows daring him to go on. She did not yet know how daring he could be.

"We could be lovers," he said, "as surely we were meant to be."

Now she sensed danger, and the Queen immediately

took command. Her voice was suddenly colder. "You are a fool, Lord Robert."

He was startled. He had become the subject once more.

She went on quickly: "If there were any hope of our marrying . . ."

He interrupted: "There is hope."

Her sudden happiness could not be hidden; it shone from her eyes and she was the woman again.

"How so?"

"My wife is a sick woman. She cannot live long."

"You . . . speak truth, Robert?"

"She suffers from a growth in the breast. It will prove fatal."

"Robert . . . how long?"

"A year perhaps. You will wait, my love, my dearest Queen? A year . . . and you and I . . . together for the rest of our lives."

"Why did you not tell me this before?" she demanded sharply.

"I dared not hope."

"You . . . dared not! You would dare anything."

He kissed her. "Only since I knew how you loved me."

She would not allow the embrace to continue. He was too insistent, too clever, too *practised*. He knew exactly how to play upon her feelings. The Queen must command the woman not to act like any village drab—or perhaps any normal woman in the hands of Lord Robert.

"It is true?" she asked.

"I swear she will not live long."

"The people . . ."

"The people would be delighted if you married an Englishman."

"Yes . . . but one of noble family."

"You forget. My father was Lord Protector of England when you were called a bastard."

"He went to Tower Hill as a traitor. I was born a Princess, and a Princess I remained."

"Let us not bother with such matters. They are unimportant, for you have said you would marry me if I were free."

"I said I believed I might."

"My darling, I am no foreign ambassador pleading for his master. I am flesh and blood . . . warm and loving . . . here . . . your lover."

"Not that . . . yet."

"But soon to be!"

She freed herself and walked up and down the room. She said after a pause: "It is not often that we may meet thus, and you waste time, my lord. If, as you say, there may come a time when I might marry you, there should be no scandal concerning us beforehand. The people would not like that. Continue to be my Master of Horse, my loyal subject, until such a time as I may find it possible—and in my heart—to elevate you to a higher rank. But leave me, Robert. Leave me now. If you stay longer it will be known. The gossips will be busy with us."

She gave him her hand and he took it, but his lips did not stay on her fingers. He clasped her in his arms again.

"Robin," she said, "my sweet Robin, how I have longed for this!"

But Kat was already at the door with the news that

William Cecil was on his way to see the Queen.

But how could she keep this overwhelming love a secret? It obsessed her. She could think of little else. If he were absent, nothing pleased her; but the Master of the Horse only had to put in an appearance and she was all gaiety.

She wanted to show her love and her power at the same time. She gave him the Dairy House at Kew, and that was a lovely old mansion; nor was that all. He must, she decided, be rich beyond all her courtiers; she liked to see him clad in fine clothes and jewels, for who else could show them off as he did? There were some monastery lands which must go to my Lord Dudley; and as many merchants in England had grown rich through the export of wool, he should have a licence to export that commodity, and lands and riches with which to develop the industry. As if this was not enough, she must invest him with the Order of the Garter. There was no gainsaying her. Let any man come to her and say that my Lord Dudley was unworthy of such honours and she would make him feel the full force of her displeasure.

She was fiercely in love. Thus had her father, King Henry, been when he had become enamoured of her mother. The main topic of conversation throughout the Court was the Queen's passion for Robert Dudley.

She arranged special pageants at which much time was devoted to jousting, for none could joust like Robert Dudley. She would sit watching him, her eyes soft, then kindling with applause, for he was always the victor, his skill being so much greater than that of any other man.

She talked of him at every opportunity; when she was with her women she would bring the conversation back to him again and again. She liked to have him compared with other men that she might point out how greatly he excelled them all. She even encouraged her courtiers to criticize him so that she might have opportunities of enlarging upon his perfections.

She was in love and she did not seem to care who knew it. On one occasion when he was competing in a shooting match, she disguised herself as a serving girl and entered the enclosure that she might be near him. But when he had beaten his opponent she could not resist calling out: "Look, my lord, who has passed the pikes for your sake."

The Earl of Sussex remarked that it might be a goodly conclusion to the matter of her marriage, if Lord Robert Dudley were free for her, for he was sure that a woman so full of desire for a man as the Queen was for Dudley, could not fail to get children.

Cecil had the courage to warn her. It might, he told her in his blunt way, be impossible for her to marry elsewhere, if rumours concerning herself and Dudley persisted.

But she did not heed him. Headstrong as her father, she would show her favour where she wished; and if that favour fell upon "the most virtuous and perfect man" she had ever known, it was only right and natural that this should be so.

"Favour!" cried Cecil. "But what favour, Madam? It is said that you would marry this man if it were possible for you to do so."

"I like a *man*, Master Cecil," she said. "And the man I will marry will be no sit-in-the-cinders kind of man.

He will be a man of many perfections, worthy to marry the Queen."

Cecil sighed and had to content himself with urging caution.

But the rumours were spreading beyond the Court. "The Queen plays *legerdemain* with my lord Robert Dudley," it was said in the hamlets and villages. And from that it was an easy step to: "Have you heard then? The Queen is with child by Lord Robert Dudley. What next, eh? What next?"

Great news was expected. There was tension throughout the country. Even those who did not believe the Queen was pregnant, believed that Robert was her lover.

Cecil inwardly raged while the Court whispered. But for the existence of poor unwanted Amy Dudley, there was no doubt who the Queen's husband would be.

Kat, as usual, had her ear to the ground. She was worried, for these scandals rivalled those which had been circulated when Seymour had been reputed to be Elizabeth's lover.

She came to the Queen and said; "Dearest Majesty, I beg of you to take care. Terrible things are said of you."

"Who dares?" cried Elizabeth.

"The whole country. Mayhap the whole world!"

"They shall suffer for their lewdness."

"Dearest Majesty, I fear it will be you who suffers. You must consider these rumours. You must remember you are a Queen, and a Queen of England."

"What rumours are these?"

"They say that you live in dishonour with Lord

Dudley . . . That you are his mistress."

The Queen laughed shortly. "Yet all those about me know such rumours to be false. Look at me! Look at the people who are always about me. My councillors, my statesmen, my ladies of the bedchamber, my gentlemen of this and that . . ." She spoke almost regretfully: "What chance have *I*, Katharine Ashley, to lead a dishonourable life!" Her eyes flashed. "But if ever I had the wish to do so—but God I know will preserve me from this—I know of no one who could forbid me!"

Kat was dismissed; and she went out shaking her head, wondering what would happen next.

Robert did not enjoy the same popularity with his own sex as he did with the other. Envious eyes followed the Queen's favourite. Robert knew that there was nothing that could produce hatred so surely as success, and that therefore he must have inspired much enmity. His great desire was to marry the Queen but he wished to do this with the full support of her ministers. He and Elizabeth had been foolish to expose their feelings to the public gaze. Robert sought—with the Queen's consent—to remedy this.

The Archduke Charles—the son of the Emperor —was now seeking to marry the Queen. Robert called his sister Mary to him. Mary Sidney had, through her brother's influence, a high post in the Queen's bedchamber. Elizabeth was fond of Mary. Was she not the sister of Robert, and was it not pleasant to talk to one who loved him in such a sisterly way? Mary Sidney very quickly had the confidence of the Queen.

"Mary," he said, "there is much gossip concerning the Queen's marriage."

"Robert . . . is there any news of you . . . and the Queen?"

"What news could there be while Amy lives?"

Mary's eyes expressed her anxiety. "But, Robert, Amy will continue to live. She is so young."

"Yes, yes," he said impatiently, "so it would seem. But . . . because I have married her and because of the rumours regarding myself and the Queen, many are speaking against me. I would remedy this, and I want you to help me."

"You have done so much for us all. There is nothing we would not do for you, Robert."

"My dear Mary, I trust I shall always be your very good brother. Now the Queen is with me in this: Archduke Charles is eager to marry her; and although she is by no means eager to marry him . . ."

"Being eager to marry only one man," interrupted Mary with an affectionate smile.

He nodded. "She and I would have it believed that she is contemplating this match, which, as you know, would greatly please the Catholic peers. I want you to seek an opportunity of telling the Spanish ambassador that the Queen has hinted to me that if she could see and approve of the Archduke Charles, she might marry him."

"Robert, this means . . ."

"It means one thing. I wish to put an end to these rumours which do none of us any good. I wish the Court and the country to believe that the Queen has discussed her marriage plans with me, and that she and I, knowing a marriage between us is impossible, have

198

agreed that it would be wise of her to take the Archduke."

"I will do this, Robert; and, of course, I understand your meaning."

After Mary's words to the Spanish ambassador there was great excitement among the Catholic peers; Norfolk, in particular, was delighted. Who, they asked each other, could know the Queen's mind better than the Dudleys? The Queen was too wise a woman, and Robert Dudley too wise a man, to believe for a moment that they could marry each other. Robert would have to divorce his wife to do so, and the people would not be pleased at such procedure.

Amy meanwhile had heard the rumours regarding her husband and the Queen. It was impossible for them to be kept from her, for Robert had become the most talked-of man in the country.

At first she had been proud of him; she had heard of his exploits at Court; how at Greenwich he had held the lists against all comers; how the Queen favoured him and had presented him with lands and honours.

Then she began to understand the cause of the Queen's favour.

"So," she said to Pinto, "it is because she is in love with him! Oh, Pinto, it is a frightening thought: The Queen is in love with my husband!"

Pinto said grimly: "You and she are not the only two ready to make fools of themselves for his lordship's sake."

"You should not hate him so, Pinto. You should try to understand him."

"Have I any reason to love him when he makes you so unhappy?"

"You seem a little strange when I speak of him. Do you think he will try to divorce me?"

"It would not surprise me."

"I will never let him go. How can I? How could I want to live if I were no longer Robert's wife?"

"It would be a happier state for you if you were not his wife, Mistress."

"But I would rather have his brief visits than no visits at all."

"Little mistress, you are a fool."

"No, Pinto. I am in love with him. That is all. But perhaps love makes fools of us and you are right when you say that I am one. I only know that I must continue to be one, because I love him now that he no longer cares for me, just as I did in the first days of our marriage."

"Then you show little sense."

"Does anyone in love show sense?"

"Perhaps they do not."

"I wish he would come here that I might ask him what these rumours really mean. I would ask him whether, if I were no longer here, he would marry the Queen."

Pinto was angry. She hated to talk of Robert, Amy knew. Yet to whom else could she speak of him as she wished to speak?

"We are very rich now, Pinto," said Amy. "I should have a grand house. I shall ask Robert why I do not. During the season we could entertain the nobility. Is that not what is due to the wife of a man in Robert's position?"

"No man was ever before in his position," said Pinto.

"I will not stay here in my father's house," said Amy. "I shall travel a little. Why should I not? Let us leave the day after tomorrow for Denchworth. The Hydes will be glad to have me."

"Everybody would be glad to have Lord Robert's wife," said Pinto.

"They would indeed. You see, Pinto, why I could never give him up. I would never consent to a divorce. Would you, Pinto? *Would* you?"

"How can I say? How could I know?"

"Ah! You would wish for a divorce. You would be only too glad. But then, you do not love him. You do not know how different he is from all others."

"Let us go to the Hydes, Mistress. The change will be good for you."

Pinto sat stitching her mistress's new gown in preparation for the visit to Denchworth.

She was thinking of the messenger who had come to the house three days ago. He had brought money and gifts from Robert for Amy. Pinto was a little afraid of Robert's gifts. She had grown alert.

This messenger was unlike the previous messengers. He was gentle in manner, softly smiling, eager to ingratiate himself with the household, and in particular with Amy's personal maid. He must have recently joined Robert's service for Pinto had never seen him before.

She chanced then to look out of the window and she saw this very messenger sauntering in the gardens. On impulse she put aside her work and went downstairs. She did not go to him; she let him see her and come to her, as she guessed he would, for she believed from his manner that he had hopes of learning something from her.

They walked together in the rose garden.

"I should imagine that you have a good position here with Lady Dudley, Mistress Pinto," he said.

"Very good indeed."

"It is clear that her ladyship is fond of you."

"I have been long with her."

"I doubt not that you know all her secrets. She is a beautiful young lady. Many must admire her."

Was he trying to make her disclose some story of indiscretion? wondered Pinto. Was he hoping to discover something which would enable Lord Robert to put her from him?

She said: "I know not who admires my lady. I know only that she has no admiration for any man but her lord."

"That is clear, Mistress Pinto. What sort of health has my lady? She looks blooming, but one can never tell."

"Health! Lady Dudley's health is of the best."

"Come, come, you may trust me. I have heard that she suffers from some growth which is gradually sapping her strength."

"It is not true!" cried Pinto.

"Are you sure it is not true . . . ?"

"I swear it. I am in her confidence. She could not keep such a thing from me."

The man nodded; and Pinto had a feeling that his mission was completed. He made an excuse to go back to the house. She accompanied him.

She was trembling when she returned to her needlework. A terrible thought had come to her.

202

Rumours regarding her mistress's health had been set afloat. And who would be likely to start such rumours? To what could they lead? Did it mean that one day Pinto would find her mistress dead of some strange malady?

Was this poisonous gossip the forerunner of more deadly poison?

William Cecil and Nicholas Bacon were with the Queen. Cecil was explaining that he could not send for the Archduke Charles unless the Queen would give him a direct Yes or No. She must not forget the position of the Archduke; to ask him to show himself on approval would be an insult. If the Queen would give her definite answer and tell them that she was prepared to marry the Archduke, nothing would delight them more than to send for this suitor.

"Yes or no, Your Majesty. You understand this is imperative."

"Oh, come," said Elizabeth, "I could not give a direct answer until I see him. I might hate him, and how could I marry a man whom I hated!"

"But Your Majesty has already expressed your deep interest in this match."

Elizabeth looked haughtily at her chief ministers. "How can you know my feelings?" she demanded. "Have I told you I am ready to marry Charles?"

"Your Majesty, Lord Dudley and his sister Lady Mary Sidney have made it quite clear what is in Your Majesty's mind."

"How should they know what is in my mind?"

"Madam," said Cecil, "it is believed that they, more than any in your realm, have your confidence."

"They have misunderstood me this time," said Elizabeth.

"Then we are to understand that Your Majesty has come to no decision with regard to the Archduke?"

"Your understanding is not at fault. I am no more inclined to Charles than to any other."

Cecil and Bacon were annoyed by this, but Norfolk was furious.

The Duke angrily sought out Robert and demanded to know what right he had to spread rumours which were without truth.

"I! Spread rumours?" cried Robert.

"You and your sister! Did you not imply that the Queen had chosen her husband?"

"I am sorry you are disappointed," said Dudley.

"Have a care, my lord!" cried Norfolk. "You go too far. Much is spoken against you."

Robert's hand went to his sword hilt. "You place yourself in danger, my lord Duke," he said. "The Queen would not consider you a good Englishman and a loyal subject since you wish her to marry outside the realm. You would bring foreigners among us. Her Majesty would not like that . . . she would not like that at all."

Norfolk stared at Robert. How would he represent this encounter to the Queen? Was it not a fact that she would be inclined to believe anything that Robert told her, since she was as infatuated with him as ever? Norfolk retired, seeing his mistake.

The victory was Robert's. But he had not added to the number of his friends.

The news came to England that Philip of Spain was

to marry Elisabeth de Valois, daughter of Henri Deux. A blow to England this, for it meant the union of her two enemies against her. Queen Elizabeth seemed unperturbed. She refused to look at the marriage politically. She merely pouted on hearing of the withdrawal of so powerful a suitor.

"What inconstancy!" she cried to Philip's ambassador. "Could he not wait a few short months? Who knows, I might have changed my mind. And there he will be . . . married to a French Princess when he might have married the Queen of England."

But no one took her seriously. They knew that she was waiting and hoping for something, and that Robert Dudley was concerned in those hopes.

The French King had died unexpectedly during a joust, when a splinter from a lance had entered his eye. His young son, Francois, was now King of France, and Mary Stuart the Queen. She styled herself Queen of France and England—an insult Elizabeth determined to hold against her.

But she was not seriously annoyed, it seemed to those about her. She would smile to herself and continue in great humour while Lord Robert was beside her.

The Spanish ambassador, furious at the trick which had been played on him by the Dudleys (for he had written to his master and told him that it was certain the Queen would take Archduke Charles) now wrote bluntly to Philip telling him of the rumours which were circulating throughout England, and which, he assured Philip, seemed to have firm foundation.

"The Queen," he wrote, "gives much time and attention to Robert Dudley still; and it is the opinion of many who are close to her that she hesitates to marry only to gain time. She is waiting for Lord Robert to dispose of his wife, which many think he will attempt to do by means of poison. He has circulated rumours that she is slowly dying of a fatal disease, and this has proved to be untrue. He wishes, of course, that when she dies, there will be little surprise, and it will be believed that her death was the natural outcome of her malady. The Queen's plan is to engage us with words until the wicked deed is done. Then it is thought she will marry Lord Robert."

And all through the spring and summer the rumours multiplied.

Amy so enjoyed her stay with the Hydes at Denchworth that she prolonged her visit; and the Hydes were pleased to have her company. Amy quickly formed a friendship with Mistress Odingsells, Mr. Hyde's widowed sister, and this lady became her constant companion.

They all petted Amy. It was the delight of the cook to make her favourite sweetmeats. Nothing could please Amy more for she had a fondness for all sweet things; while she was at Denchworth, bowls of sweetmeats were kept in her room; and the kitchen maids took pleasure in making new flavours for her delight. They could not do enough for Amy. Although she was the wife of the most talked-of man in the country, they were sorry for her. The Hydes urged her to stay on; and Amy, feeling that the atmosphere of the house was rather as her own had been in the days when her mother was alive and her half-brothers and half-sisters had made a pet of her, could not resist the invitation.

Pinto was glad that they stayed at Denchworth. She too liked the atmosphere of the house. Here, reflected Pinto, she felt *safe*.

Often she thought of Lord Robert and wondered of what he talked with the Queen. Did they discuss marriage? What a King he would make! There was that about him which must conquer all—even one as proudly royal as the Queen of England, even one as determined to hate him as humble Pinto.

As long as she lived she would remember the moment when he had come upon her as she bent over the press. What had made him kiss her? What had made him notice her for the first time? Had she betrayed her feelings for him? He would have forgotten the kisses, for he would have given so many. Often she thought how different life would have been if Lord Robert had never come to Norfolk, if little Amy had married a pleasant gentleman like Mr. Hyde.

"Oh God, let us stay at Denchworth where it is quiet and safe!" she prayed.

At Denchworth all wondered what was happening in the gay world of London and the Queen's Court. It was being said now that the Queen would marry the Archduke Charles and that he was coming to London for the betrothal.

"Even so," said Amy to Pinto, "we shall see little of Robert. I doubt not that he will continue to be occupied at Court."

"It may be that the Queen's husband will not wish to have him there."

Amy agreed that might be so. "Then perhaps he will be banished to me as he was before. Do you remember, Pinto, how happy I was during those two years when he could not go to Court? That was before this Queen was Queen and when there were so many rumours that she would lose her head. How did she feel, I wonder, to be so near death as she must have been?" Amy's eyes had grown wild.

Then she has heard the rumours! thought Pinto. Oh, my poor little mistress. God preserve her!

"Do you know, Pinto," went on Amy, "I believe that to be near death would make a woman feel that she must live every minute of her life to the full because life is, after all, so precious. Bring me my new purple velvet gown. I will put it on. I think it needs a little alteration. I should like to know that it was ready . . ."

Ready? thought Pinto. Ready to wear for the husband who so rarely comes?

But at least, here at Denchworth, they must be safe.

They did not stay at Denchworth. It was while Amy was trying on the velvet dress that Anthony Forster and his wife arrived.

Amy, hearing their arrival and hoping it might be Robert, went down clad in her velvet. It hurt Pinto, who followed her, to see her disappointment.

Anthony Forster, whom Lord Robert had made his treasurer, had come for a purpose, Pinto surmised.

"My lord thinks," he told Amy, "that you should not stay so long the guest of Mr. and Mistress Hyde. He would like you to remove to your own house; and as you so like this district he says you may go to Cumnor Place which, as you know, is not such a great distance from here. There you can live in state and entertain Lord Robert and his friends when they come to you."

Amy, always eager for excitement, accepted the plan with enthusiasm. The idea of Robert's bringing his friends for her to entertain had always attracted her. There would be something to do besides lie on her bed, eating sweetmeats, chattering to Pinto and trying on her dresses.

Cumnor Place! Why, of course. It was a lovely old house, and Robert had leased it a few years ago from the Owens. It had been a monastery at one time, and had been given to the present Mr. Owen's father by King Henry the Eighth for good services as the King's physician. It was only a few miles from Denchworth, and about three or four from Abingdon.

She would prepare to go there at once; and when there she could entertain the Hydes as they had entertained her; then she would prepare for grander company—all the ladies and gentlemen whom Robert would bring from the Court.

Pinto seemed disturbed when she told her of the plans.

"Cumnor Place. You remember it, Pinto?"

Pinto did remember it. A lonely house, surrounded by trees, a tall house with views of the downs from the top windows. Pinto did not let her mistress see the shiver which ran through her.

"I remember it," said Pinto.

"You do not seem to be eager to leave here. Have you become attached to Denchworth?"

"Mayhap I have. Who will go with us to Cumnor Place?"

"Mr. Anthony Forster and his wife will be there for a while to prepare for my husband. And I think that Mistress Owen will be there. She is much attached to the place, and Robert allowed her to stay. We shall not be lonely, you see."

209

"And my lord . . . suggested this move?"

Why did suspicions leap to her mind? wondered Pinto. Cumnor Place was so lonely. His servants would be there—men and women who would not hesitate to do anything the future King of England demanded of them.

"Yes. It is my belief that he wishes to entertain his friends there. Oh, Pinto, the lonely days will be over. We shall have many guests to fill the house. I must have some new dresses."

Pinto said on impulse: "Mistress Odingsells is very fond of you. Why not take her with us? She would be a pleasant companion for you, and you know how you hate to be alone. When you have not me to talk to, you will have her. And it will be doing her a good turn. Take her as your companion."

"Why, I like that idea, Pinto. Yes. I shall take her as a companion."

Pinto was glad. She could not get out of her mind the thought that it would be good for Amy to have as many friends as possible in lonely Cumnor Place.

The Queen was worried. She was wondering how much longer she could stave off a decision. It seemed that unless she acted quickly she would be forced into a position which she was determined not to accept.

There was war in Scotland. The Scottish Protestants were in revolt against the French, who, under the Dowager Queen of Scotland, Mary of Guise—mother of Mary Queen of Scots who was now Queen of France—were taking too prominent a part in Scottish affairs. They determined to rid themselves of their Gallic masters, and in this Elizabeth must help them, for if the French gained possession of Scotland she would have a very powerful enemy on her borders.

Her ministers advised war, and she saw the wisdom of this. Philip of Spain was watching and hesitating according to his custom, not caring to throw in his lot with the French, yet, stern Catholic as he was, finding it impossible to aid the Protestants.

But when he saw how well the war was going for the Protestants, he ordered his ambassador to deliver an ultimatum. Unless the peace was made and kept, he declared, he must send aid to the Catholics. The Queen was in a panic. Philip must be held off at all costs, so she placated him by the only means at her disposal: she promised she would marry the man he wished her to—Archduke Charles.

Philip was well pleased, for if Charles should be King of England he foresaw the return of England to the Catholic fold; but he was beginning to know Elizabeth, and he would not be put off as he had previously been.

Plans, he commanded, should be made at once for the coming of the Archduke to England.

Robert and Elizabeth met secretly and alone.

"I am afraid of what may happen," she told him. "With Charles here my hand may be forced."

Robert exulted. Never before had he realized how completely she needed him. She was appealing to him now. Something drastic must be done.

The question they were asking each other was: What?

Robert knew that he had many deadly enemies. The Queen was popular enough to withstand the scandal their relationship had set in motion; but the people did not like to think that their Queen was conducting a dishonourable association with a married man. They therefore blamed Robert.

In the streets harsh things were said of the Dudleys, and in particular of Lord Robert. Who is this upstart? it was asked. It is true that he is the son of a Duke, the brother of a King and the grandson of a Knight; but his great-grandfather was a farmer, and he was the only one who died in his bed an honest man. Let Lord Robert get back to his farm, and sowing his crops reap the family honesty.

Would they accept such a man as their King? And what would their reaction be if he divorced his wife in order to marry the Queen?

Elizabeth looked at him, seeing in him all the manly vigour of his twenty-eight years. She yearned for him; but even as she yearned, she cried out angrily: "Why did it have to be you . . . you with your blood tainted with treason, with your father, grandfather and brother all dying by the axe . . . you, a married man with a wife between us!"

Robert gripped her arms, and her heart beat faster as she felt the strength and power of him.

"My beloved," he said, "something shall be done . . . and soon." She looked at him expectantly and he went on: "If I were free to marry and we married, our troubles would be over. All will be reconciled to our marriage when our son is born."

She nodded, still keeping her fearful eyes upon his face.

"Nothing must stand between us," he said, "Nothing!"

"But, Robert . . . "

"I know . . . I know what you think. We cannot thrust this aside just because it seems impossible. It is the most important thing in the world that we should be together . . . important for us and England. None but I shall give you your sons."

She said faintly: "That is how I would have it, my sweet Robin. But how can it come about?"

"It *shall* come about . . . and speedily."

She saw the set of his mouth and she understood.

The days of Amy Dudley were numbered.

She told him to leave her, for she felt she could bear no more. After he had gone she sank on to a stool and sat there in silence. What was one death in a great destiny? she asked herself. How many times had she come near to losing her own life? She was a Queen, and any who stood between her and the sons she would bear, must surely die.

William Cecil returned from Edinburgh where he had signed a treaty with the French. He was triumphant. England had come satisfactorily out of the affair. Now he would receive the gratitude of the Queen, which he hoped would take a practical form, for his family was growing and he was a family man who looked to the future.

Cecil was the cleverest man in England; he had come successfully through the difficult years. Although he had served Protector Somerset he had not fallen with him, but had transferred his allegiance to Northumberland; and when Northumberland had ceased to be a power in the land he had worked for Mary, never forgetting that he must remain the friend of Elizabeth. And because he was both calm and bold and never hesitated to set forth what he believed would be the best policy for the country, he continued successful; and Elizabeth—more than any who had gone before her—appreciated his qualities.

So now he came to Court to receive the Queen's most grateful thanks.

Elizabeth's twenty-seventh birthday was on the seventh of September and the Court had gone to Windsor Castle that the important event might be celebrated there.

So to Windsor came Cecil, for it was necessary to discuss with Elizabeth the arrangements for the coming of the Archduke Charles.

Cecil was pleased. The war was satisfactorily ended and Elizabeth was committed to the marriage. He believed that, once his mistress had a husband to guide her, the management of affairs would be easier, for when the Queen began to bear children she would be ready to leave affairs of state to her husband. Charles would steady the friendship with Spain and, in view of the French claims through Mary Queen of Scots, there was safety in Spain's friendship.

He was therefore feeling very satisfied when he was shown into the royal apartments.

He knelt before the Queen, but even as he did so he was aware that all was not well. She looked older and there were signs of strain on her features. She did not congratulate him on his clever statesmanship in the arrangement of the treaty, which was the least she might have done. He told her that the Spanish ambassador had accompanied him to Windsor and was awaiting audience that the arrangements for her marriage might be discussed.

"There is too much haste concerning these arrangements," she said sharply.

"Too much haste, Your Majesty! You will forgive me if I say that the Archduke has shown the utmost patience in this matter."

She snapped: "I am in no mood to see the ambassador."

"Your Majesty, if you fail to make these arrangements you will incur the wrath of the King of Spain."

"What care I for that man! His feelings seem of little importance to me."

"Madam, they are of the utmost importance to England."

She stamped her foot. "Have done! Have done! Are we vassals of His Most Catholic Majesty as we were in my sister's time?"

Cecil knew then that the state of affairs had not changed in the least. She had the look of a woman deep in desperate love; and that meant she still hankered after Lord Robert and was determined to have him or none other.

Cecil could see ahead quite clearly. This was what came of having a woman on the throne. Her personal feelings, her personal emotions were to put the country into jeopardy. If she were a King she would take a mistress and none think the worse. But she was a Queen, and the scandals concerning herself and Dudley were rampant.

Would that man were dead! thought Cecil.

Then he made a decision. His success was due to his consistent frankness. If he had served Protestant and Catholic irrespective of religion, he had never failed to serve his country. As he saw it, England's relationship with foreign powers was all-important, and at the moment the most powerful ally England could have was Spain, and Philip must not be offended.

"Madam," he said coldly, "I see you are so far gone in love for Lord Robert Dudley that you are neglecting your business, which is to rule this realm; and if you continue in your neglect you will ruin this country."

Elizabeth gasped. Her impulse was to order Cecil to the Tower; but she quickly saw the folly of that. What would she do without Cecil? She honoured him; and such was her nature that, even in that moment of anger, she knew that he was speaking the truth and that he was the one man—even more than Robert whom she loved passionately—to whom she wished to entrust her affairs.

"You overreach yourself, Master Cecil," she said, with a coldness that matched his. "None could prevent my marrying where I wished."

"You are wrong, Madam," said Cecil wryly. "Lord Robert's wife prevents you."

"Nothing else?" she said, and her words were a question. "Nothing but that?"

"Madam," said Cecil, "if Lord Robert were in a position to be Your Majesty's husband, your ministers would doubtless have no objection since your heart is set on this, and the country needs an heir."

A slow smile spread across her face. "Your insolence is overlooked on this occasion. I think that soon we shall reach a settlement of these matters. Lady Dudley will not live long."

"Madam," said Cecil aghast, "I see trouble ahead."

"Go now," she said, "and rest. You have had a long journey."

He bowed and retired.

His thoughts were in a turmoil. Did he understand aright? Were they planning to rid themselves of Lady Dudley? But what a scandal that would be! Did they not see that? Even Queens—young and popular Queens—cannot with impunity connive at murder.

As he was leaving the Queen's apartment, he met Alvaro de Quadra, the Spanish ambassador who had replaced Feria. De Quadra, spy for his master, ever on the alert, noticed the strained look on the face of the Secretary of State.

Falling into step beside Cecil, de Quadra asked: "And when may I have audience of Her Majesty? There is much to discuss concerning the marriage."

Cecil was silent for a few moments, then he burst out: "Do not ask these questions of me. I am thinking of leaving my office. I see great troubles ahead. Your Excellency, if you are a friend of England's, advise Her Majesty not to neglect her duty as she does. Would to God Lord Robert Dudley had lost his head with his brother. That would have been a good thing for England."

"Lord Dudley?" said de Quadra. "So the Queen still frets for him then?"

"Frets for him? She thinks of nothing else. I know this, and it fills me with dread: They are scheming to murder his wife, that marriage between them will be possible. They say she is suffering from a malady which will shortly rob her of life, but I have discovered this to be untrue. Poor woman! Doubtless she is taking good

217

care not to be poisoned, since she has lived so long."

The Spanish ambassador could scarcely believe that he had heard correctly. Was this calm Cecil, the wily statesman, the man whose custom it was to consider his lightest remark before uttering it! And to speak thus before the Spanish ambassador, well known to be a spy for his own country!

Cecil recovered his poise; he grasped de Quadra's arm and said earnestly: "I beg of Your Excellency to say nothing of this. This is the Queen's secret matter."

The ambassador gave his word, but immediately retired to his own apartments that he might write despatches which on this occasion, he was sure, would prove of the utmost interest to his royal master.

A September haze hung in the air. Pinto was in one of the attics looking out over the countryside. How quiet it seemed! Yesterday she had watched the Fair people riding by on their way to Abingdon for the Fair. The servants were talking of it now. She was glad of that. When they were discussing the Fair they ceased to talk of Lord Robert and the Queen.

Poor Amy! She was desperately afraid—afraid of every footfall, afraid even of her fear, for she did not speak of it even to Pinto. She had reason to be afraid. She stood between Lord Robert and his marriage with the Queen.

A woman of Brentford, so they had heard, had been arrested for saying that the Queen was to have Lord Robert's child. Had she spoken the truth?

Pinto was afraid in this house.

The grounds were beautiful and extensive, but the house itself was shut in by many trees; and it was only by climbing to the top that it was possible to see the open country.

Some of the rooms were large, but those which had been cells, were very small. There were two staircases. One of these, which led from the kitchen quarters, was a narrow spiral one; that which swept up and round the old hall, which had been the monks' common room, was wide with elaborately carved banisters. This staircase was not enclosed, so that it was possible to look down into the "well" from any point.

It was a house full of shadows, full of echoes from the past. Pinto did not like the thoughts which had come to her while she had been living in this house.

Only last week a very disturbing incident had occurred.

Amy had fallen ill and Pinto, fearing that already she was being poisoned, had been frantic with anxiety.

Her fears had been so great that she had persuaded Amy to call a physician—not one of Lord Robert's but a friend of the Hydes.

And the man had refused to come.

Lord Robert had his own physicians, he had said. It was their place to look after the health of Lord Robert's wife.

There was something so alarming about such behaviour that even Amy could not shut her eyes to it. The man would not come because he suspected Amy was being poisoned and wished to have no part in it. If Amy died suddenly and there was an autopsy, and her death were proved to be due to poison, it would be necessary for persons in high places to find a scapegoat; this man was clearly intimating that he had no intention of being that scapegoat. If Amy wanted a physician she must have one of her husband's.

"Nay," said Amy, "I do not think I need a doctor after all. I was just feeling a little melancholy. It is nothing more."

But how frightening was this life!

There was one thing of which Pinto felt sure: Amy's life was threatened. It was clear from the doctor's attitude that the whole country was expecting her to die by poison, for that would mean that her death could be said to be due to a fatal disease. Rumours had already gone forth that she suffered from a cancer of the breast.

Since everyone was talking of poison, it was obvious that Lord Robert would be aware of this; therefore it seemed almost certain that Amy would not die by poison. Die she must if she were to be removed from Robert's path towards ambition, but her death would have to seem accidental or the whole country would cry: Murder. What could Pinto do? Where could she turn? She could only keep near her mistress, hoping to guard her. But they were two defenceless women against a relentless enemy.

She went downstairs, and in the hall she found Forster talking with Mistress Owen who, living apart from her husband, had asked leave to stay on in the house. Amy, being fond of company, had been glad to have her.

Forster said pleasantly as Pinto came down the stairs: "I doubt not you'll be asking your mistress's leave to go to the Fair."

"That may be," said Pinto.

"A messenger has just come from Windsor. He brings letters for my lady. He tells us that tomorrow or the next day Master Thomas Blount will be riding here

from Windsor with special gifts and letters from my
lord for her ladyship."

"My lady will be pleased to hear from Lord Robert,"
said Pinto.

She passed on.

Master Thomas Blount! He was a kinsman of Lord
Robert's, a man whose fortune was bound up in that of
his master; a man who would be ready to follow Lord
Robert's instructions . . . even if they were to murder
his wife.

He sends letters, he sends gifts, thought Pinto; and
he longs to put her out of the way.

It seemed to Pinto that danger was moving nearer.

It was night. Amy lay still, the curtains pulled about
her bed. She had awakened with a start, aware that
someone was in her room.

She sat up, pressing her hands to her heart. What
fear was this which possessed her, which made her start
at every sound? There was terror all about her.

She knelt on her bed and opened the curtains. Pinto
was standing there, a lighted candle in her hands.

"Pinto!" cried Amy in great relief.

"Oh, Mistress . . . are you awake then?"

"You frightened me so."

"Mistress, I had to come to talk to you."

"At this hour?"

"It would not wait . . . or so it seemed. I have to say
it now. Perhaps I could not say it by day. Mistress,
before your marriage, I used to come to your bed and
sleep with you at night when you had dreams. Do you
remember?"

"Yes, Pinto. I have indeed bad dreams now. Come you in beside me."

Pinto blew out the candle and climbed into the bed.

"You're trembling, Pinto."

"You tremble, Mistress."

"What is it, Pinto? What is it?"

"We are afraid, Mistress. Both of us are afraid of something, and we are afraid to speak of it by daylight. That is why I come to you at night. Mistress, we must speak of this thing."

"Yes, Pinto, we must."

"They seek to put you away, Mistress."

"It's true, Pinto. It's .rue." Amy's teeth were chattering.

"You see," said Pinto, "he is an ambitious man, and all he desires would be ready for him to take but for you. I am frightened. Never eat anything unless I prepare it for you."

"They are trying to poison me, Pinto?"

"I do not think they will."

"Why not?"

"Too many have talked of poison."

"Pinto, what can I do? What can I do?"

Pinto's eyes were wet. It was as though Amy were a child again, coming to Pinto for help. No! It was quite different. This was no childish problem. This was a matter of death.

"I have thought of something, Mistress. We will go away from here."

"Where could we go?"

"I have thought that we could go to your brother John. He loves you dearly. We could live in his house secretly . . . as serving maids mayhap. I have not thought beyond that. He is wise. He will advise us. First we must get to his house."

"Should we be allowed to go like that, Pinto?"

"Nay, we should not. We should have to go in secret. Oh, Mistress, I have thought and thought until my thoughts are in a whirl. Master Blount will be here late tomorrow or the next day. Mistress, I greatly fear that man."

"You think . . . he comes . . . to kill me . . .?"

Pinto did not answer that. "I would wish that we were away before he comes."

"How, Pinto?"

"Listen carefully, dearest Mistress. Tomorrow is Sunday. Send all the servants to the Fair. Send even Mistress Odingsells, for she is talkative and inquisitive, and I fear that if she were here she might blunder about us and make it impossible for us to leave. Keep Mistress Owen for company; and the Forsters will be here, I doubt not. But let all the rest of the household go to the Fair. I shall go with them and, as soon as I can without attracting attention, I shall return to the house. Rest until I come, that you may be ready for a tedious journey. I will come quietly into the house and together we will slip out to the stables. This will be your last night in this house."

Amy clung to Pinto. "Oh, how glad that makes me. I am afraid of this house. We will do that, Pinto. We will go to my brother."

"You must insist that all go to the Fair. We must run no risk of being seen as we leave. Stay in your room until I return. But be all ready to leave . . ."

"But, Pinto, how shall we go . . . two women . . . alone from here to Norfolk?"

"I do not know. But we must. We can go quickly to an inn, rest there and perhaps engage more servants to accompany us. None should know who you are. I have not thought of that very clearly. There is one thing which occupies my thoughts. We must get away from this house before Master Blount enters it."

"Yes, Pinto, yes. But I have thought of something. It is Sunday tomorrow. Only the lowest and most vulgar go to the Fair on Sundays."

"It is a pity. But they must go. You must insist on that. How do we know who among them spies on us?"

"They shall go. And you will come back soon, that we may start on our journey."

"As soon as I can safely do so."

"Oh, Pinto . . . it is such a wild . . . wild plan. There are dangers to women on the roads."

"There is no danger so great as that which lurks in this house."

"I know . . . Pinto. I feel it . . . all around me."

"Let us try to sleep now, Mistress. We shall need all our strength for tomorrow."

"Yes, Pinto."

They lay still and occasionally they spoke to each other. It was not until the dawn was in the sky that they could sleep.

Sunday morning came.

Amy felt happier now, because the sun was shining brightly and this was to be the last day she would spend in this frightening house.

She called the servants to her and told them that, as it was a fine day, they all had her permission to go to the Fair in Abingdon.

They had hoped to go on Monday and were not too pleased; but they dared not refuse to do as the mistress bid.

Amy turned to Mistress Odingsells, who had acted as her companion ever since they came to Cumnor Place, and asked her to go too.

"I . . . go on a Sunday!" cried Mistress Odingsells, who was very conscious of her dependent state. She was indignant. She . . . a lady . . . to be sent to the Fair with the vulgar on a Sunday!

"It is a pleasant day," murmured Amy.

But Mistress Odingsells was greatly put out. She would certainly not go to the Fair on a Sunday.

"You shall go at your own pleasure," said Amy quickly, "but all my servants shall go . . . every one of them."

"And who will keep you company?" asked Mistress Forster.

"You and your husband will be here. And Mistress Odingsells it seems, with Mistress Owen. There will be plenty to keep me company if I wish for company. But I am a little tired, and I shall go to my room to rest for a few hours, I think."

Mistress Odingsells said she would retire to *her* room for, since her company was not desired, she would be sure not to impose it upon anyone. Amy did not try to soothe her. Mistress Owen thought Amy seemed a little distraught—nay, more, quite hysterical, so determined was she that all should go to the Fair. It was strange because usually she liked to have plenty of people about her.

Amy went to the top of the house to watch them set out. Pinto was with them. She turned and waved her hand to her mistress who she knew would be watching.

Pray God, thought Amy, she comes back quickly.

She stayed at the window for some minutes looking out over the country. Could it really be true that Robert was planning to kill her? She could not believe it. She thought of him in the days of their courtship, so eager, so passionate, and so determined to marry her whether his father granted permission or not. She remembered the first days of their marriage. Of course there were rumours about a man like Robert. He was so dazzlingly handsome, the most successful man at Court. Of course the Queen was fond of him.

But what was the use? She knew Robert was planning to murder her.

Now the quietness of the house was frightening her again. She had an impulse to run out of it, to run after the servants, to go to the Fair with them. That was foolish. Pinto was a wise woman. Her plan seemed wild, and wild it certainly was; but it was the only way of escape from a dangerous situation.

"Go to your room and try to sleep," Pinto had said.

She would do that.

Just as she was turning from the window she saw a man on horseback coming towards the house. For a moment she was terrified, thinking that Thomas Blount had arrived. But it was only Sir Richard Verney who had ridden over to do some official business with Forster.

She saw Forster go out and greet him, and the two men finally walked away from the house. Forster was taking Verney to some trees which she believed were to be cut down.

She turned away from the window and went to her room, and lying on her bed pulled the curtains. She must try to sleep. She must remember that she was safe until Thomas Blount arrived.

There was a dish of sweetmeats lying on the bed where she had left them last night. Her maid must have replenished the dish before she went to the Fair. She saw that some of her favourites were there; she could never resist them, and almost mechanically she began to eat them. They were delicious.

Before she had finished she began to feel very tired. She fell asleep in the act of reaching for another.

It was less than an hour later later when the door of Amy's room was quietly opened. Two men came in. Very quietly one of them pulled aside the bed-curtains.

"What if she wakes?" asked one.

"Impossible," said the other, looking at the dish.

He was smiling. It had been too good an opportunity to miss. All the servants—almost the entire household—at the Fair! This was the time when an accident must happen.

"Come," said the other. "Let us get it done with."

One placed his hands beneath her shoulders; the other took her feet; and, carrying Amy between them, they went quietly out of the room.

It was not easy to slip away. Pinto was anxiously awaiting the favourable moment.

And when it came there was the long walk back to Cumnor Place.

Could her plan succeed? What would happen if they

227

were seen? Would she be murdered with her mistress? Then he would have two deaths on his hands.

She must not blame him. He was different from other men. He must not be judged by their standards. It would seem to him only right that Fortune should deny him nothing. Pinto understood.

But she would not give him Amy's life. She would fight for that even at the cost of her own, even if by doing so she made him a double murderer.

They would creep out of the house. They would go to the stables. They would ride fast . . . and before nightfall they must be well away from Cumnor Place and where none knew them. They must find the right inn. They must succeed.

She would not visualize failure. She saw them arriving at the home of John Appleyard. John would do anything for his sister, she knew. He loved Amy dearly.

She had reached Cumnor Place.

Now she must creep quietly in and by way of the main staircase hurry along to Amy's room. If she met the Forsters or Mistress Odingsells or Mistress Owen she must say that she had lost sight of the other servants and had deemed it wise to return to the house. But she *must* not meet them; she must meet no one.

How quiet the house seemed. But she must be thankful for the quietness.

She came into the great hall which was flooded with sunlight. As she was about to hurry forward she stopped short, staring at the figure lying at the foot of the staircase.

Her limbs were numbed. She could not move. She could only stand there staring before her while horror,

228

such as she had never before known in the whole of her life, possessed her.

She knew that she was too late.

Amy Dudley was dead. She had been found on the floor of the hall at Cumnor Place, her neck broken, after what was obviously a fall down the staircase. The Court and the countryside could talk of nothing else; there was one explanation and that was murder. It was not necessary to look far for the murderer.

The Queen sent for Robert, declaring that she must see him alone. Elizabeth was afraid—not only on his behalf but on her own. She knew that this was one of the most dangerous situations she had ever faced. She knew that Royalty must be in command, bidding Love take second place.

But when she saw him, she knew that whatever came between them she would always love him. Her affection for him would remain even when she looked back with horror at the hysterical woman it had made of her. She loved him no less because he had committed murder. Had he not murdered for her sake? She herself had faced death too many times to hold the lives of others dearly.

But she had to save him and herself.

"What now?" she said, as soon as they were alone. "What now, Robert?"

"She fell from the stairs," he said. "It was an accident."

She laughed mirthlessly. "An accident! At such a time!"

"That is what it seems. What it *must* seem."

"Do you not see how foolish we have been, you and

I? We have shown feelings to the world which we should have been wise to hide. Such an accident to the wife of an obscure courtier would have aroused no comment. But to *your* wife . . . at such a time . . . when the whole world knows of the love between us . . . Robert, no one will believe in this accident."

"You are the Queen," he said.

"Yes, yes. But there is one thing I have known all my life: A Queen or King must be loved and respected by the people. They murmur against me. They say lewd things. They say I am to bear your child. Now they will say that this had to be, that our child might be born in wedlock . . . the legitimate heir to the throne. And they will whisper about me. They will call me a lewd woman."

He said: "Your father married six wives. Two of them lost their heads; two he put from him when he tired of them; one all but lost her head, and only his death, some say, saved her. You talk of this scandal. How can it compare with your father's senary adventure in matrimony!"

"A Queen is not a King. A King may love where he will, but a Queen who is to bear the heir to the throne must be above reproach."

He came to her and put his arms about her; and she was moved temporarily by his masculine charm.

"All will be well," he said. "We shall come through this storm. And remember, there is nothing now to keep us apart."

She was silent. She was not the woman whom he had known. She was older, wiser; the old habit of learning her lessons had not been lost. Thus she had been when she had stood before Lady Tyrwhit at the time they had beheaded Thomas Seymour. She had deceived them all then.

Never again must she allow herself to be overwhelmed by her love for a man. She must for evermore be Queen first, a woman second.

She must not forget that she was in danger now, and she must learn her lesson quickly. When she had extricated herself from the result of her folly, never must she err in that respect again.

"Robert," she said, releasing herself from his arms, "there is only one thing to be done. I must put you under arrest until this matter is cleared up. It is the only way. Think of the future, my love, and do as I say. Go to Kew under arrest by orders of the Queen."

He hesitated, but he was wise enough to see that the Queen was in control of the woman.

"You are right," he said. "You must not be involved in this. Our mistake has been to show the world that we love each other. Once this has blown over . . ."

She nodded, and throwing herself into his arms, kissed him fiercely.

"Go now, my dearest. All will be well. No harm shall come to you. But we have to learn from the mistakes we have made. There must be no more. Her death has to be an accident. You and I must not even have wished it to happen. Because you are her husband you will, of necessity, be suspected; and the Queen's orders are that you stay in your house at Kew . . . under arrest. Go now, and soon all will be well."

"All will be well," he said, returning her kisses with a fierceness which outstripped her own. "Soon you and I shall be husband and wife."

"If all goes well," said the Queen soberly.

This was the greatest scandal that had shocked and entertained the world since Elizabeth's father had played out his tragic farce with six wives.

If justice were to be done, said the world, the Queen should take her place with her lover on trial for murder.

Robert was frantic. Confined to his house at Kew he was in desperate and urgent correspondence with his faithful servant and kinsman Thomas Blount, commanding him to sound opinion at Court and in the countryside, particularly in the region of Cumnor Place. Thomas Blount was to question the servants, bully them, browbeat them into admitting that Amy's death had been an accident. He, Dudley, was still an influential man; he would get into touch with the foreman of the jury and see that the "right" verdict was declared. When he was King of England he would not forget those who had helped him to his place, any more than he would forget those who had tried to impede him.

Cecil had recovered his balance. He was the calm minister once more. He saw the country threatened with a crisis which could do much harm. Confidence in the Queen must be restored. He must remain her chief minister, for if he retired he might find himself in the Tower; besides, how could he bear to give up his ambition?

He was beside the Queen now, supporting her when she needed his support. She had the utmost confidence in him; and he was too good a minister to fail her.

He remembered that, in his agitation during a weak moment, he had spoken incautiously to the Spanish ambassador, and that his words would doubtless have been reported to Philip of Spain. What had he said? That he saw troubles ahead, that his mistress and her lover were planning the murder of Amy Dudley! That was a terrible mistake to have made, because he had said those words only a few hours before Amy had been found in Cumnor Place lying at the foot of a staircase with her neck broken. Could such a coincidence be accepted? It must be. The only way to keep the people loyal to the Queen was to have a verdict of accidental death brought in. The Queen might commit political murders, but she must not be implicated in the murder of a woman whose husband she wished to marry. That was something the country would not accept. Royal murder was permissible. But the charge of personal murder—murder for passion, love, lust, whatever the people called it, must be laughed to scorn.

This Queen's whole future was at stake. There was Jane Grey's sister, Catharine, who would find ready supporters. There was Mary Queen of Scots who was now the Queen of France. Clearly if Elizabeth was to stay on the throne she must not be implicated in murder. Therefore there must have been no murder; for if murder had been committed, the Queen would seem as guilty as her lover.

Cecil accordingly decided that his course of action must be to laugh at the suggestion of murder.

This attitude would give the lie to the words the Spanish ambassador had already written to his master. Even Philip might doubt the veracity of de Quadra, if Cecil treated the scandal with scorn and contempt.

Cecil went ostentatiously to Kew to visit his dear

friend Lord Robert Dudley, and to assure him of his belief in his innocence.

The Queen was pleased with Cecil; she knew that she and he could always rely upon each other.

But the country was demanding justice. Several preachers in various parts were asking that a full enquiry be made into the death of Lady Dudley, and grievous suspicions disposed of.

And all knew that in this there was not only a threat to Lord Robert, but to the Queen herself.

Thomas Blount worked assiduously in the service of his master.

He went to Cumnor Place with the express purpose of proving Amy's death an accident.

He questioned Mistress Odingsells, Mistress Owen and the Forsters. Mr. Forster told him that Amy seemed a little absent-minded on that fatal Sunday morning. It would not surprise him if she had fallen down as she was descending the stairs. But the Forsters were suspect, as any servants of Lord Robert's at Cumnor Place must be; for if the task of murder had to be entrusted to one of them, it would be to a man in Forster's position.

A jury, deciding that it dared not offend the man who might be King, and at the same time the Queen herself, would not bring in a verdict of murder; but this was not only a matter for a court jury; in this case the whole of England was the self-appointed judge and jury; and the whole of England could neither be bribed nor threatened.

It seemed strange and mysterious that Amy, who had always insisted on having people about her, should have tried to send the entire household to the Fair on that Sunday morning.

Blount was puzzled. He must carefully question every person in the household in an endeavour to understand Amy's strange action.

At length he came to Amy's personal maid, the woman who, he had heard, was devoted to her mistress.

Pinto had lived in a daze since the tragedy.

It was all so clear to her. Someone—she suspected Forster—had been awaiting the opportunity; and it was her actions, her schemes which had given him what he sought.

She knew of the murmuring throughout the country. She knew that people were saying: "Robert Dudley is a murderer. His grandfather and his father died on the block. Let him die on the block, for he deserves death even as they did."

What if he were to die for this? She could not call to a halt that procession of tableaux which haunted her. She thought of a hundred pictures from those two and a half years when he and she had lived under the same roof. Often she had watched him when he did not know he was watched. He had not noticed her except for one moment, and then it had been her apparent indifference to him that had so briefly attracted him.

Yet she knew that during the whole of her life she would never forget him.

One of the maids came to her and said that Master Blount wished to question her as he was questioning the whole household.

The maid's face was alive with eagerness. She whispered: "He is trying to prove it was an accident.

235

Lord Robert has sent him to do so. But . . . how can they prove that . . . and what will happen now to my lord?"

What would happen to him now?

Pinto was excited suddenly because she felt that there was within her a power to decide what should happen to him.

She could tell the truth; she could tell of the plan she had made with Amy. That would not help Lord Robert. But there was one explanation which was not incredible. No one would believe Amy's death was due to an accident; but might they not believe in that one alternative to murder: suicide?

That would not endear Lord Robert to the people; he would still have his detractors; but at the same time a man who neglected his wife to serve his sovereign was not on that account a criminal.

She stood before Thomas Blount, who studied her intently. A personable creature of her kind, he thought; and one whose grief showed her to have had a real affection for the dead woman.

"Mistress Pinto, you loved your mistress dearly."

"Yes, sir."

"What do you think of her death? Was it an accident or was it caused through villainy?"

Pinto hesitated briefly. It seemed as though he were there beside her. He was mad for distinction. She was making excuses for him. He had been tempted and, weakly, he had been unable to resist. It seemed to her that he was pleading for her help, he who had never asked her for anything. What woman had ever been able to resist him? And it was in her power to give him more than any had ever given him before.

236

Her mind was made up. She couched her answer in carefully chosen words.

"Sir, it was an accident. I am sure it was an accident. She would not have done such a thing herself. Never!"

Eagerly he seized on her words. This was the first suggestion of suicide. Here was a way out that he had not foreseen.

"Tell me," he said, gently, "why should you think she might have done it herself, Mistress Pinto?"

"Oh, but I do not!" Pinto stared at him wildly, like a woman who has betrayed that which she had planned to hide. "She was a good woman. She prayed to God to save her from the consequences of desperation. She would have committed no such sin as taking her own life."

"Had she some idea in her mind of destroying herself?"

"Nay, nay! It is true that there were times when she was so wretched that . . ."

"She was sick was she not?"

"She had troubles."

"Troubles of the body as well as of the mind?"

"Lord Robert came so rarely to see her."

They watched each other—he and Pinto, both alert.

He was thinking: Suicide! The next best thing to accident. He was framing his story. "Amy Dudley was suffering from a disease of the breast which she knew was killing her. It was painful, and she decided she would endure it no more. She sent her servants to the Fair so that, on that Sunday morning, she might end her life. A strange way in which to kill oneself? A fall from a staircase might not have meant death? Oh, but Amy's state was one of hysteria. She would hardly have

237

been aware of what she was doing. She longed for the company of her husband, but owing to his duties at Court he could not visit her as often as he would have wished. So, poor hysterical woman, she had sent her servants to the Fair that she might have a quiet house in which to kill herself."

A sad story, but one which could cast no reflection on Lord Robert and the Queen.

Pinto was conscious of the triumph of a woman who loves and serves the loved one—even though she does so in secret.

On a warm Sunday morning, two weeks after she had died, Amy's body was carried to the Church of St. Mary the Virgin in Oxford. The funeral was a grand one. It was as though Robert was determined to make up for his neglect of her during her lifetime by lavish display now that she was dead. There was a procession of several hundred people; and Amy's half-brother, John Appleyard, as he walked with other relations of hers and the students from the University, was filled with bitter thoughts. He had loved his young sister dearly, and he deeply resented her death; for nothing would convince him that it had not been arranged by her husband.

While the bell tolled, while the funeral sermon was being preached, John Appleyard's heart was filled with hatred towards Robert Dudley.

There were others at the funeral who felt as John did.

There were many who would have wished to see Robert Dudley hanged for what he had done to an innocent woman who had had the misfortune to marry him and stand between him and his illicit passion for the Queen.

So Amy was laid to rest.

But although the jury had brought in a verdict of Death by Accident, all over the country people were talking of the mysterious death of Amy Dudley, and asking one another what part her husband and the Queen had played in it.

Robert was hopeful and expectant. Surely the Queen must marry him now that he was free.

As for the Queen, she wanted to marry him. This terrible thing which had happened had not altered her love. She was defiantly proud, exulting in the fact that he had put himself in such jeopardy for love of her. He was a strong man and there was in him all that she looked for. He was ready to marry her and face their critics; he was defiant and unafraid.

But her experiences had made her cautious. She wanted him, but she had no intention of losing her crown.

She could snap her fingers at Cecil, at Bacon, at Norfolk and Philip of Spain; but she must always consider the people of England.

Reports from all quarters were alarming. The French were saying that she could not continue to reign. How could she—a Queen who permitted a subject to kill his wife in order to marry her! The throne was tottering, said the French. They may have been beaten in Scotland, but soon it would be Elizabeth who suffered defeat. A people as proud as the English would never allow a murderess and an adulteress to reign over them.

When she rode out, her subjects were no longer spontaneous in their greetings.

All over the world there was gossip concerning the Queen and her paramour; lewd jokes were bandied about as once they had been with regard to the Princess Elizabeth and Thomas Seymour; stories were invented of the children she had borne her lover; she was spoken of as though she were a harlot instead of the Queen of a great country.

She was perplexed and undecided. There were times when she longed to turn to Robert and say "Let us marry and take the consequences." At others she was reluctant to take any further risk. Always she seemed to hear the cries of the people when she had ridden through the streets of London at her Coronation: "God save Queen Elizabeth!"

She kept Robert at her side; she shared state secrets with him. The Court looked on. It was said that it could not be long before she made him her husband.

But she wanted time to think, time to grow away from the emotional weeks which had culminated in Amy's death. Time had always been her friend.

"Why do we wait?" asked Robert. "Cannot you see that while we hesitate we are in the hands of our enemies? Act boldly and end this dangerous suspense."

She looked at him and fully realized his arrogance; she recognized the Dudley fire, the Dudley temperament which had raised two generations from the lowest state to the highest. This man whom she loved saw himself as King, the master of all those about him, *her* master. There was one thing he had forgotten; she too had her pride; she too had risen from despondency to exultation, from a prison in the Tower to greatness—in her case a throne. She might take a lover, but she would never accept a master.

Cecil decided that matters must not be allowed to remain as they were. It was imperative that the Queen should marry. Let her marry the man for whom she clearly had an inordinate desire; let there be an heir to the throne. That was the quickest way to make the people settle down and forget. When they were celebrating the birth of a Prince, they would forget how Amy Dudley had died.

The wedding could be secret. The people need not know of it until an heir was on the way.

Such procedure would be irregular, but Amy's death was very unpleasant. It had to be forgotten. Much which this Queen's father had done was unpleasant, but that King had kept his hold on the people's affections.

Robert was delighted with Cecil's change of opinion. He was triumphant, believing he had won; but he had reckoned without the Queen.

She had come to know her lover well, and those very qualities which she admired so much in him and which had made her love him, helped her now to make the decision that she would not marry him . . . for a while.

She knew that during those difficult weeks she had learned another lesson . . . a lesson as important to her as that which she had learned through Thomas Seymour . . . as important and as painful.

She was Queen of England and she alone would rule. Robert should remain her lover, for all knew that lovers were more devoted, amusing and interesting than husbands who could become arrogant—especially if they were arrogant by nature.

She would win back the people's love as she had after the Seymour scandals. Moreover, if she did not marry Robert, how could it be said that she had urged him to kill his wife?

Her mind was made up. She could not marry Robert now, for to do so would be tantamount to admitting she had schemed with him to murder Amy. Therefore she would stand supreme. She would keep her lover and remain the Queen.

VI

As the months passed, Elizabeth began to regain her hold on the people, and she knew that she had acted wisely. All the world thought that Robert had murdered his wife; but how could they believe that Elizabeth had had a part in that murder when she showed as little eagerness to marry her favourite as she did one of her royal suitors?

The Archduke Charles was spoken of once more. She also pretended to consider Eric, who had now become King of Sweden. She was sure of herself now, and determined never again to be the prey of her emotions.

This did not mean that she loved Robert any the less. She was unhappy when he was not with her and she was gay in his company; she liked to keep him at Court, guessing whether or not she would marry him.

She could not hide her affection. She believed she would never know another man who could stir her emotions as Robert did. Steadfast affection was one of her qualities, as Kat Ashley and Parry had seen; they had betrayed her once, but she understood and forgave them; once she loved, she did not easily cast that love from her.

And Robert's charm had by no means diminished.

To him their life together might seem unfulfilled; not so to her. She had all she wanted from him—his company, his admiration, his passionate love, which must always be kept at fever heat. She could almost be grateful to Amy for preventing their marriage—first as his wife by her existence, and then as his victim by her mysterious death.

The Queen was gay during those months, enjoying the festivals which were prepared for her, delighting to honour those who pleased her—and none did that as much as Robert. They did not understand her, these people about her; when Robert knelt to her and she so far lost her dignity before a company of statesmen, courtiers and ambassadors, as to stretch out a hand and stroke the curling hair at his neck and even call attention to his well-shaped head, they thought she was so much in love with him that she would surely marry him. They did not understand her desires; and it was her delight, as well as her necessity, to keep her secrets.

There were quarrels. He was the most arrogant of men, raging to be the master. Well, she would ask herself, how could I love a ninny? How could I love a man who was afraid to cross me for fear of losing my favours? A man must be a man, and never was there such a man as Lord Robert Dudley. She showered gifts upon him, it was true; but she wished them to be the rewards of the statesman not the lover. He was indeed becoming a statesman, taking a great interest in affairs of a political nature, preparing himself for the role of King of England. She would watch him, strutting a little. And why should he not? Was it not for men to strut? Why should he not show insolence to my lord of Norfolk who thought himself more royal than the

Queen herself? A pox on Norfolk! A pox on the whole Howard breed! Her father had had to lower their pride; nor would she hesitate to do the same. They thought too much of their birth; they worried too much whether a man's ancestors were lords or farmers. They should take care, for my Lord Robert would stomach none of *their* insolence; and, by God, she thought, I'll make him an Earl . . . the mightiest Earl in the Kingdom, one day.

But although it gave her great pleasure to see him in his manly arrogance, she too enjoyed teasing him. At times she would stamp her foot, slap his face, and would herself remind him of his humble origins. "Do not dare show your arrogance to me, my lord. Remember it is to me you owe your position here at Court." She would pretend that he had offended her over some lack of courtesy to the Queen when in truth they both knew that her outburst was due to her having caught him smiling a little too tenderly at one of her women.

She implied that she expected fidelity from him; but in reality she did not. He must be essentially masculine; and he was. Men, she believed, were not noted for their fidelity. Not for her some sighing love-sick fool. She must have a rampaging lover, impatient, angry sometimes, wayward perhaps. Robert had all these characteristics; and he provided all the joy in her life.

He longed for rank that he might flaunt it in the faces of such as Norfolk. He wanted to take first place, not only through the Queen's love, but in his own right of nobility.

He would come familiarly into her bedchamber, startling her ladies; and once, after he had kissed her hand, he had the temerity to kiss her cheek . . . before them all.

"My lord!" she reproved him with mock dignity, but her eyes sparkled and he was in no mood to be moved by her assumed anger.

"I have kissed you before them all," he said. "So would I serve you careless of others . . . all through the day . . . all through the night . . . all through my life."

"Listen to him!" she cried. "What if the whole Court came in to kiss me good morning!"

"They should never enter this chamber. My sword would prevent them."

She looked at her women, commanding them to admire him. She knew there were several among them whose thoughts were occupied unduly with Lord Robert Dudley.

He had dared to take her shift from the hands of the woman who held it; but Kat had snatched it away from him, declaring that it was not meet for a man to know the Queen wore such a garment.

How Elizabeth loved such games! She sat there imperiously, aware of his desires, protected by her women.

"Don't dare leave me with Lord Robert! I fear this man!" she cried.

And his answer came: "If I read your Majesty's meaning, you have need to fear him . . . though he would protect your life with his."

"I know it," she said tenderly. "But I forbid you to come thus into my chamber . . . ever again."

But he heeded not the warning; he knew that she would be disappointed if he did not come. Kat said it was as it had been with my lord Admiral. Did Her Majesty remember? It seemed that these big and handsome men found great delight in storming her chamber.

Kat's face was slapped affectionately; and Elizabeth was very gay that morning.

When she next saw him she reproved him, whispering to him under cover of the music which was played in the gallery.

"My lord, you go too far."

"Nay," he said, "not far enough!"

"In my bedchamber! And daring to hand me my garments!"

"Ere long I trust I shall be with you all through the days and nights."

"Ah . . . if that might only be!"

He showed his exasperation, which set a frown between his well-shaped brows. "It could be . . . quite simply."

"No, Robert, not yet."

"Not yet!" he cried hopefully; and he would have seized her hand but she prevented him.

"Have a care, foolish one. Do you want the whole Court to start its scandals once more?"

"They have never stopped."

"How dare you suggest there are scandals concerning me? You forget I am your Queen."

"Would I could forget it! Would it were not so. . . . Then . . ."

"Then you would have no need of me?"

"If you were a dairymaid I would have need of you."

She laughed and retorted with the Tudor frankness: "Yes, for five minutes under a hedge."

"Five minutes under a hedge *and* for the rest of my life."

"Robert, when you look at me thus I believe that to

be true. But we are too far apart."

"That could be remedied."

"It shall be, my darling."

But later, when the papers which would have made Robert an Earl and restored the Earldom of Warwick to his brother Ambrose were put before her, she was in a perverse mood.

He was with her at the time; she looked from him to the papers. If he were an Earl—and the Earldom she would grant him would be one which hitherto had been granted to none but persons of royal blood—she knew that she would be very close to marriage with him. She could not help noticing the gleam in his eyes; she remembered how she herself had coveted the crown. She pictured herself relenting—for indeed there were times when, for all her resolutions, she felt herself weak in his company. She hardly ever granted him an interview with herself alone. She was strong, but so was he. To her he was the perfect man and as such would necessarily be triumphant, and how could he be unless she surrendered? It was only because she was a Queen that she could resist him.

He should not have his Earldom yet. He should remain her gay Lord Robert. So she frowned and, to the astonishment of all, asked that a knife be brought to her. When this was done she drew it across the papers, cutting them through.

"How can I heap honours on these Dudleys!" she cried. "Have they not been traitors to the Crown for three generations!"

Robert faced her, his eyes blazing. How she loved him! What a man he was! He cared for nothing.

"Madam," he said, "I understand you not. How, pray, have the Dudleys failed to serve *you*?"

"What excitement is this?" she asked as she smiled at him. "How can I, my lord, grant honours to the Dudleys? Do you forget that my great father had good cause to send your grandfather to the block? Do you deny that your father rose against the Crown and tried to make your brother King?"

"If my service to Your Majesty is considered treachery . . ."

She lifted her hand and gave his cheek a light slap—the most affectionate of slaps—denoting familiarity and indulgence.

Those present smiled. This was nothing but a lovers' quarrel.

She is as much in love with him as ever, they thought; but he has offended her of late because his eyes have been straying to a fair young lady of the Queen's bedchamber. The Queen is merely telling him that there must be only one love affair in the life of Robert Dudley.

All the same he continued to be plain Lord Robert.

The Queen was tormented by thoughts of those who she feared might be deemed to have a greater claim than herself to the throne. Nobles of royal blood always haunted, like grim shadows, the lives of the Tudors. Henry, her father, had solved his problems by murder; he liked to know that those who might have ousted him were dead. That was a wise policy, Elizabeth often thought; but times had changed, and she was not the absolute monarch that her father had been; she was more dependent on her ministers. After the persecutions of the Marian reign, the people looked to Elizabeth for clemency.

There were three women who gave her cause for

anxiety; two of these were the sisters of Lady Jane Grey—Lady Catharine and Lady Mary. She knew that there were some who still considered her to be a bastard and usurper; these people would like to make the Lady Catharine Queen. The grandmother of the Grey girls had been Henry VIII's sister and there was no doubt of their legitimacy.

Elizabeth was continually afraid that there would be a rising against her. Indeed that had been her great fear at the time of Amy's death. The Grey sisters had been carefully brought up and their conduct was not likely to give rise to scandal. There had never been any admirals in their lives to burst into their bedchambers and slap and tickle them while they were in bed. There had never been a handsome man so in love with them that he was suspected of murdering his wife. The characters of Lady Catharine and Lady Mary were quite different from that of Elizabeth. They were quiet, learned, and good Protestants. Many remembered that Elizabeth had been ready to change her religion when she deemed it expedient to do so. The Greys were gentle, pliable; Elizabeth was full of feminine vagaries. Many people in this land might think Lady Catharine or Lady Mary would make a more suitable Queen than this red-headed virago who had a *penchant* for goading men to scandalous behaviour.

There was another, even more formidable—Mary Queen of Scots. She was a greater rival, and she was far away, so that Elizabeth could not keep a watchful eye upon her. She would have been happy to have Mary in England, nominally as an honoured guest but in reality a prisoner. That was why, when Mary had left France recently on the death of her husband, Francois Deux, Elizabeth had refused her a safe passage. What a prize a captured Mary would have been!

Mary had said—so Elizabeth had been told—when the death of Amy had been reported to her: "Ah, now the Queen of England will be able to marry her horse-master!"

"Insolence!" muttered Elizabeth. "Could she but see my 'horse-master', I doubt not she would throw at him some of the languishing glances which we hear are so fascinating."

That was another quality of Mary's which exasperated her. Mary was reputed to be very beautiful, and it was mortifying to be reminded that she was nine years younger than Elizabeth herself. At least there was nothing of the meekness of the Grey sisters in Mary's character.

There were many Catholics who looked on Mary as the real Queen of England.

Such thoughts of her rivals often made Elizabeth fretful; she would lose control of her temper, and many of those about her would be chastised, and not only with words. But her rages were short-lived and would give place to pleasant smiles; and when she felt that she had been unjust she would always seek to make up to her victim in some way.

One day when she was riding to the hunt she noticed that Lady Catharine Grey was not in the company. On enquiring the reason she was told that the lady was sick and had stayed in her apartments. She tried to forget the trifling incident and, if it had been any other she would not have given it a further thought.

During the hunt she lost her temper, and as Robert was riding beside her he felt the full force of her annoyance.

She said to him quite suddenly: "I have decided that

I cannot put off my marriage. I shall invite the King of Sweden to come to England without delay, that the preparations may go ahead."

Robert was astounded. "The King of Sweden!" he cried. "That man! He is nothing more than an imbecile."

"How dare you speak thus of your betters?"

"Not being an imbecile, Your Majesty, I do not consider that man to be even my equal."

"Master Dudley, you give yourself airs."

His temper was as hot as hers. Their natures were similar; therein lay the great understanding between them. Each was quick to anger and quick to forget it; both were proud of their positions yet perpetually aware of humble ancestors.

He answered: "Madam, I speak the truth—which is what I believe you have said you wished from me."

"I would thank you to look to your own affairs."

"Your Majesty's marriage is my affair."

"I do not think so."

"Madam . . ."

"I command you to keep your nose out of my affairs."

"And I insist that your marriage *is* my affair—mine as much as yours."

"So you think I will marry you, do you?"

"You have led me to believe that it is not an impossibility."

"Then you are a fool to hold such hopes. You . . . a Dudley . . . to marry with a Queen! Do you think I could so far forget my royal rank as to marry such as you!"

"Does Your Majesty mean that?"

"We do mean it."

"Then have I Your Majesty's permission to leave Court? I wish to go abroad."

"Go! Go by all means. Nothing could please us more. It is with the greatest pleasure that we give you leave to go."

He was silent. She watched him covertly. There, Master Robert, she thought, what now? That will show you who is in command.

He performed his duty with great care and detached perfection during the hunt. She was almost restored to good humour by the time they returned to the palace; but she waited in vain for him to ask her pardon.

For a whole day he absented himself from Court, since there was no particular duty to keep him there. The Queen's ministers were alert. They had heard of the quarrel. Was this the beginning of a coolness between them?

The following day Cecil said to her: "Since Your Majesty has decided on a match with the King of Sweden, it would be as well to invite him here without delay."

She was furious suddenly: "I decide on a match with the King of Sweden! I have heard he is nothing more than an imbecile!"

"Your Majesty, he is a King and would make a worthy husband."

"I am the best judge of who shall be my husband."

"Then Your Majesty has no intention of proceeding with this match?"

"I have no such intention."

Cecil retired exasperated. So her statement, during the hunt, which had been reported to him by those who

253

worked for him, had been made with no other purpose than to anger Robert.

She waited for Robert to hear of her remarks. He would, she felt, return humbly and she would meet him half way; there would be one of those reconciliations which delighted her. She needed such consolation after a whole day without him, for other men seemed stupid and witless when compared with him.

But he did not come; and at length, when she commanded his presence, diffidently he came.

"Why is it that you have absented yourself from Court?" she demanded.

"Because I have been making preparations to leave the country, and I thought by so doing I was obeying Your Majesty's orders."

She became woeful and helpless. Her eyes pleaded: So you would desert me! You would leave me to the mercy of my stern ministers. Is that all your love is worth! Do all your protestations mean nothing?

"My lord," she said despondently, "is it your wish to leave the country? If that is what you desire, so great is our wish for your contentment that we will grant you the permission to go, even though it is against our wishes to do so."

He was smiling as he kissed her hand with ardour. "How could I ever find contentment but in the service of Your Majesty?"

"Then all is well," she said gaily.

"And the King of Sweden?"

She "pupped" with her lips, which was a habit of hers; then she began to laugh, and he laughed with her.

"Come," she said, "sit beside me and give me the benefit of your conversation. I declare the Court has been a dull place these last hours."

And when the French and Spanish ambassadors were with her, and one expressed his surprise that Robert Dudley was still at Court, as he had heard his lordship had Her Majesty's permission to go abroad, she laughed lightly.

"I cannot live if I do not see him every day," she said.

Then, because she fancied Robert's smile was too complacent she added quickly: "He is as my lap-dog."

That brought an angry look to his face and she put out a hand to him with a very tender smile. "Nay," she went on, "'tis true that I will not be without him, and where this Dudley is, there you may be sure to find Elizabeth."

Then the whole Court knew that she was as much in love with him as she had ever been; and they did not believe—nor did Robert—that their marriage would be long delayed.

Time passed pleasantly at Windsor. Elizabeth walked often on the terrace which had been built for her before the castle on the north side. She was fond of walking and was often seen at the head of a little procession of ladies and gentlemen, with Lord Robert beside her, holding an umbrella over her if it rained.

Often she hunted in the park or the forest, for she was as fond of the hunt as her father had been. Bullbaiting and cock-fighting delighted her. She had a stage put in the castle that she might indulge her taste for the drama, and many strolling players had come to Court in the hope of pleasing her and making their fortunes. There were places too for musicians; and in the

Windsor Castle orchestra were players of many instruments including lutes and bagpipes, flutes and rebecks.

But she did not forget that it was a Queen's duty to show herself to her people, and so she set out on a progress through Essex and Suffolk, staying at various houses which belonged to those ladies and gentlemen who were wealthy enough and worthy enough to entertain her.

Whilst they were staying at Ipswich, Lady Catharine Grey attracted the Queen's attention.

It was during the robing—always an important ceremony, for there were so many dresses from which to choose, so many jewels which must be tried on only to be discarded. Eventually Elizabeth decided on a gown of black velvet and a caul that went with it set with pearls and emeralds; there was a black velvet hat spangled with gold and adorned with a drooping feather which hung over the shoulder.

While the Lady Catharine was adjusting the jewelled girdle she fell into a faint at her mistress's feet.

For a few seconds Elizabeth stood still, looking down at the girl, who was very beautiful and in that moment astonishingly like her sister, the tragic Lady Jane.

"See to the girl," said Elizabeth.

It was Kat who came forward and unlaced Lady Catharine's gown.

"It is but a faint, Your Majesty."

"Lift her up," said the Queen. "Get her to a couch. She looks a little better now. She is too tightly laced, I doubt not."

While the women were putting Lady Catharine on a

couch, Elizabeth drew Kat aside.

"What do you think, Kat?"

Kat's eyes were alert. When a young lady fainted, one could always suspect a certain reason.

Elizabeth's eyes were steely. "I know what you are thinking, you evil-minded creature."

"Your Majesty, I may be wrong, but I have wondered about the lady of late."

"You have wondered?"

"It is a look in the eyes, Madam. I just cannot explain."

"You said nothing to me."

"Madam, how could I be sure, and how could I voice such suspicions unless I was sure?"

"It would seem you have learned discretion in your old age. This is a matter of some moment. She is not a mere serving wench, you must know. I have a duty towards my kinsfolk and those in my personal service. If your suspicions are justified . . ."

"My dearest lady, do not be harsh with her. She is young and so pretty, and Your Majesty knows how easy it is for these things to happen."

"Easy!" cried the Queen. Had she not fought *her* temptations? Had she not almost succumbed? Did she not long to be in the condition which might well have overtaken Lady Catharine? "Easy for harlots it may well be!" she snapped. "But this is Lady Catharine Grey—one of three sisters of whose virtue we hear so much."

She could not control her wrath and jealousy. She thought of the pleasure she might have enjoyed; and being Elizabeth Tudor she was whipping her indignation to fury because the sly Catharine Grey was a possible rival for the throne.

She strode over to the group of women who were clustered about the couch.

"Well?" she demanded. "Well? Well? What is the meaning of this? Why does the girl faint in my presence? Have you discovered yet?"

"No, Your Majesty."

"Then why not?" She bent over the Lady Catharine, who looked at her with frightened eyes. "Your Ladyship has often absented herself from duty," went on the Queen. "Why? Answer me, girl. Have you been meeting a lover? Why do you lie there looking so frightened? What have you to fear if your conduct has been above reproach? But has it been above reproach? Come . . . let us see for ourselves!" Elizabeth pulled at the gold thread which laced Catharine's bodice; she seized Catharine's skirts.

Catharine scrambled up and fell on her knees crying: "Your Majesty, it is true that I am to have a child."

Elizabeth's cheeks were scarlet, her eyes blazing. "You . . . you harlot! You dare tell me that!"

"Your Majesty, it is not as you think. We were married before Christmas and . . ."

"Married! So your crime is even greater than I thought. What right have you to marry without our consent?"

"Your Majesty, we feared that it might not be granted and we could not endure to be parted . . . without . . ."

"Stop! Who is this man?"

"It is Lord Hertford. He is in France, as Your Majesty knows; but he is my lawful husband."

"We will bring him back from France to answer for his sins. As for you, you will go to your apartment and there you will stay . . . my prisoner."

"Your Majesty . . ." The girl had flung her arms about the Queen's knees. "I beg of you, have pity on me. Do not blame him. It was not our fault . . ."

"So you were forced to marry against your wills, I suppose?"

"We acted so, Your Majesty, because we truly loved."

"Take her away," said Elizabeth. "I am covered with shame that this should happen in my Court. I do not believe there was a marriage. The girl's a slut, and she talks thus to throw dust in our eyes. Take her away at once. She offends us."

She gave Catharine a push with her foot, and the girl fell backwards. Two ladies-in-waiting came and helped her to her feet; they led her away weeping.

"See that she is well guarded," said Elizabeth.

And as she turned away, she was smiling. The Lady Catharine Grey had put herself into the Queen's power, and Elizabeth was too shrewd a statesman to miss the opportunity which was offered.

Lord Robert came to the apartment of the Lady Catharine Grey. He was uneasy, for there would be trouble if the Queen heard of this visit; yet he could not ignore such an appeal as he had received.

She had sent a note to him, imploring him to come and see her. Robert was ruthless; he was self-seeking; but, beneath the shell which had been made by ambition, he had a kind heart. He was generous by nature, and it was his pleasure to help those who begged favours of him. He did not wish to bring trouble to any except those people who stood in his way or had slighted him. The Lady Catharine had never done him any harm; she was a beautiful young woman and he liked beautiful young women. Therefore, at the risk of Elizabeth's displeasure, he could not ignore Catharine's plea.

With great secrecy he was let into her apartment where he found her melancholy in her distress.

"My lord, it is good of you to come," she cried.

"I am distressed on account of your plight."

"Could you not speak for my husband with the Queen? It is for that reason I begged you to come. I so fear what will happen to him when he returns."

Robert was silent. The young fool Hertford could lose his head for marrying a lady of royal blood without the sovereign's consent, and he should have known it.

"The Queen is incensed that you should have married in secret."

"I know, but what harm will it do her?"

What harm indeed! thought Robert. You who have a claim to the throne, some think, and about to produce an heir! Poor foolish girl! But so charming, so helpless, and looking to the powerful Lord Robert with such appealing and most beautiful eyes.

But he had not come to talk politics with the girl.

"You may rest assured that I will speak to the Queen on your behalf."

She seized his hand and kissed it.

"But," he went on, "this is a serious offence for a lady of your rank to have committed."

"I ask nothing . . . only to live quietly with my

husband and child. We will go away from the Court. We will live in the country. It is what we both wish.".

Poor innocent young woman! Would the Queen allow her to go from Court into the country where she might plot against the Crown, where she might ferment trouble? What an unfortunate family the Greys were! Would Catharine suffer as had her sister Jane?

"My dear sister," said Robert, "I beg of you, do not hope for much leniency. I will choose a propitious moment to speak with the Queen. I will ask her not to be too harsh with your husband."

"Robert, my dear brother, I have been so frightened. I have dreamed of late . . . about Jane. Poor Jane! She did not wish to make trouble. Did Guildford, I wonder? *My* sister and *your* brother. They were so young, were they not? Perhaps they only wanted to be happy, as we do. Is it our fault that we were born near to the throne?"

Robert comforted her and as soon as possible took his leave. He dared not stay long. As he went away he thought how ironical life was. The Greys had been born royal, and two of them at least wished this had not been the case. Yet he, who had been born far from royalty, longed to share it.

He did speak to Elizabeth about the Lady Catharine who, by that time, had become a prisoner in the Tower.

Kat was present at their interview, but he was accustomed to her being there and he spoke frankly before her.

"What will you do with that poor girl?" he asked.

"I am enraged," said the Queen. "She . . . my own kinswoman . . . so to behave!"

He said boldly: "Your Majesty is envious of the child she will bear."

"I . . . envious of a bastard!"

"Not a bastard. The marriage was lawful."

"Without the Queen's consent!"

"The marriage is lawful enough, Your Majesty. You would not be envious now if you were to bear a child."

"How can you say such things to me!"

"Because from one who loves you as no other loves you, you must expect the truth. Elizabeth, we are wasting our time. Let us marry. Let us have children, as surely we were meant to."

She put her hand in his and exultation leaped within him. "Would that it could be so," she said.

"But why not?"

She shook her head but her eyes were brilliant.

"Dearest Elizabeth, do we not always see matters in the same light? We are one. We were meant for each other."

"We see the world in the same light," she said. "You are my eyes, dear Robin. Yes, you are right. I long for a child."

"It is your duty. These perfections should not be allowed to pass away. They must be perpetuated."

"I know of none who speaks to me so elegantly. What arts you have, Robert!"

"Nay! 'Tis love, not art, that puts these words into my mouth, the love inspired by the greatest lady in the world."

She smiled and leaned against him.

Kat, watching, sighed. Why does she refuse him? wondered Kat. How can she refuse such a man? He does not lose his graces. He has murdered his wife for her. Dearest and most perverse, most strong and most frail Mistress, what more do you ask of a man?

But Elizabeth drew away from her lover. "Why should you plead for that girl? Is it because she has a fair face?"

"Is it fair? I had not noticed. I remember I have rarely seen her but in your presence."

"She is pretty enough."

"A pale moon compared with the blazing sun. When I plead for her, I think of you. That is why I say deal leniently with her. It is what the people would expect."

"Robert, there are some who would make her Queen. My father would have chosen this moment to send her to the block."

"But you have wisdom as well as beauty."

"Was my father not a wise man, then?"

"Not always."

"I think that could be called treason."

"Nay, call it love . . . love for you, my dearest Queen. The people would not like to see you murder your rivals as your father did his. It is unworthy of you. You are stronger than that. A lioness does not slay mice."

"What! Should I pardon her! Should I leave her and her husband to raise a brood of children to menace the throne!"

"Not so. Keep her prisoner and keep Hertford prisoner, but do not take their lives."

She tapped his cheek in her affectionate way. "Did you think I should take their lives? Nay! I would not have her blood upon my hands. I shall keep her prisoner in the Tower, and Hertford shall be my prisoner. There I shall know that she is harmless. I would not hurt her silly head. Let her live . . . my prisoner."

He kissed her hand fervently. "You are the wisest as well as the most beautiful of women."

"Enough of Madam Catharine. Let us talk of more interesting matters."

"Of Madam Elizabeth perhaps?"

"And Master Robert."

"Then let us talk of the days when they met in the Tower, and of how he in his lonely cell dreamed of the future."

"Well, that will make pleasant talk, I doubt not. I'll send for a musician to charm us with his lute while we talk."

He looked reproachful; but she felt too soft towards him to trust herself alone with him.

The Queen was pleased that the Lady Catharine Grey should be her prisoner. Lord Hertford was now in the Tower on a charge of treason. They should spend the rest of their lives there, decided the Queen. None should accuse her of having their blood on her hands.

She thought continually of that other and greater menace to her peace of mind. The very mention of Mary Queen of Scots could send her into a black mood.

If she had the Queen of Scots—and the Lady Mary Grey—in prison, she would be a happier woman. But there was another who had come to her notice; this was Margaret, Countess of Lennox. This lady was not very far removed from the throne, since she was the daughter of Margaret Tudor, Henry the Eighth's sister. The Countess needed careful watching, for she had a son, Lord Henry Darnley; and women with sons could be very ambitious.

Prying into the affairs of the Countess of Lennox, the Queen's spies soon discovered that she had been corresponding with Mary Queen of Scots.

Elizabeth laughed when the news was brought to her. " 'Tis clear to me what she would wish. She would marry that boy of hers to the Queen of Scotland, and then plot to give him England as well."

Robert agreed with her that this was doubtless in the lady's mind.

"I wonder if Mary would take him," mused Elizabeth. "But I doubt it. Madam Lennox sees him with a mother's eyes. I see a beardless boy—more like a girl than a man."

"Your Majesty's Eyes sees him in the same way."

She laughed at her "Eyes"—her new pet name for him. "What else do my Eyes see?" she asked tenderly.

"That the woman may well be a danger to my beloved one."

"We'll put her into the Tower. That's where she should be."

It was not difficult to find an excuse. The Countess's apartments were searched, and some charts of the stars were found. Her servants, under torture, confessed that she had employed astrologers to discover how long Elizabeth would live, and they had foretold that she would die during the next year.

Here, beyond dispute, was high treason.

The Countess of Lennox became the Queen's prisoner in the Tower.

Now she had two dangerous women behind bars; but her thoughts were still of Scotland.

That autumn Elizabeth fell ill of the smallpox.

All the country believed that she would die and that the prophecy of the Countess's astrologers was to be fulfilled.

There was tension throughout the country. Two brothers of the Pole family, who had Plantagenet blood in their veins, tried with their followers to march on London. The plot was discovered and the brothers taken prisoner. They insisted that they had not meant to depose the Queen but merely to demand that the succession should be fixed on Queen Mary. Cecil and his ministers forcefully declared that there would be trouble until the Queen married and produced an heir.

Meanwhile the Queen had become so ill that she believed death was near. She opened her eyes and seeing Robert at her bedside she smiled feebly and held out her hand to him. "Robert," she said, "so you are here with me. That is where you should be. You . . . of all others. Had I not been a Queen I should have been your wife."

Those who heard those words were sure that if she recovered she would marry him.

She was filled with remorse because she had not treated Robert with fairness. She loved Robert; she would never love any as she loved him; and if she died, what would become of him? He had many enemies, and he had nothing but her favour. She could have given him the highest position in the land, and she had given him nothing . . . nothing but lands and riches, not even the earldom he had so ardently desired. Such nobles as Norfolk would deride him, taunt him with his lowly birth; he had no place in the Privy Council; she had delighted in having him by her side, and she had made a lap-dog of the most perfect man in her kingdom.

She sent for her ministers and gathered her strength to address them. "There is one thing I would ask of you, my lords. It is my dying wish, and I beg of you not to ignore the wish of a dying woman. When I die I wish Lord Robert Dudley to be Protector of this Realm. I wish you to swear to me that you will obey him, respect and honour him, for, my friends, he is a great and good man; he is the most perfect and virtuous gentleman it has ever been my lot to know."

And when they had left her, having sworn to do as she asked, she lay back on her pillows and imagined him—Lord Protector as his father had been. She pictured him in all his manly beauty, his dignity and power; and she thought: How can I bear to leave a world that contains him? For what happiness could there be elsewhere compared with that of being near him?

She was not going to die! Life was too good while she had a crown which she had long coveted, and Robert Dudley was at her side.

She began to recover; and a few days later she again called her ministers to her. Robert Dudley was immediately to be made a member of the Privy Council. He was no longer to be a lap-dog. He was to be the Queen's passionate and devoted friend, the statesman who must always be beside her to give her his advice, her Eyes, her companion, the man who must never cease to hope to be her husband.

In a happy mood she pardoned the two Pole brothers, providing they were exiled from the country;

and each day her health improved and, with Lord Robert beside her, she planned entertainments to celebrate her recovery.

The Queen was fully restored to health when there came news from Scotland which infuriated her.

The Archduke Charles, who had for so long been her suitor, had now turned his attention elsewhere; and to none other than the Queen's hated rival, that other Queen, Mary of Scotland.

The Queen sent for Cecil and declared herself to be insulted; she assured him she would never consent to Mary's marriage with that philanderer of Austria.

As the Archduke had shown the utmost tolerance, patience and courtesy, Cecil shrugged his shoulders and wrote to the Emperor requesting that his son's advances should be made once more to the Queen of England. Elizabeth meantime wrote to Mary telling her that she would never give her consent to a marriage which could not fail to cause enmity between them; and as Mary's heirs might succeed to the English crown she would be ill-advised to marry without the consent of the English Queen.

But the courtship of the Queen of England was beginning to be looked upon as one of history's farces, and the Emperor wrote to Cecil that he could not have his son exposed to insult a second time. Cecil was perturbed. Eric of Sweden was now out of the marriage market. He had romantically married a beautiful girl whom he had seen selling nuts not far from his palace. So struck had he been with the grace and charm of Kate the nut seller, that he had defied all opposition and married her.

The Queen had laughed with great heartiness when she had heard of this, although she was piqued, as always, to lose a suitor. But now the news of the retirement of the Archduke from the field was disturbing.

The Queen must marry, and in Cecil's opinion, if she now married Dudley the people would be ready to believe that she at all events was innocent of the unsavoury suspicions connected with Amy's death.

Perhaps, thought Cecil, when Mary had married the Archduke, Elizabeth would so intensely wish to be married that she would follow the example of the Queen of Scots. But Mary was ambitious. She wanted the throne of England for the son she hoped to have, and therefore she had no intention of offending Elizabeth.

She wrote humbly to the Queen saying that she would decline the Archduke, and was very willing to listen to any good advice on the matter of matrimony which her good sister of England would deign to give her.

So Elizabeth began to look for a suitable consort for Mary Queen of Scots.

Elizabeth was spending a good deal of time in the company of Sir James Melville, the Scottish ambassador.

The man amused her; he was so dour, so unlike the rest of her courtiers who had come to understand that one of their indispensable duties was to make love, conversationally, to the Queen, for the more accomplished they were in this, the more likely were they to succeed at Court. None, of course, had the elegant looks, the magnificent figure, the exuberant charm and the manner of paying a compliment which were Robert Dudley's; but many of them were beginning to learn these arts, and almost to rival him.

Therefore it amused the Queen, while she plotted in her cautious way against Mary, to entertain this man who seemed somewhat uncouth. She would have him sit beside her, very close; she would tap his cheek affectionately; she enjoyed shocking him by the magnificence of her clothes, with the love-making of her courtiers to which she so archly responded; she would have music played while they talked, for she knew that he believed any sensuous pleasures to be sinful.

She insisted on his talking of that woman who was hardly ever out of her thoughts and for whom she felt an overwhelming jealousy.

"They tell me your mistress is a very fair woman, Master Melville," she said.

"Aye, 'tis so."

"And do *you* think so, Master Melville? Do you admire her as we hear all men do?"

"She is my mistress. How could I do aught else?"

"As a Queen and your mistress, yes. But then such a righteous man as you would admire a hump-backed one-eyed witch. Now tell me, how doth she look?"

"Her Majesty the Queen of Scots is neither hump-backed nor one-eyed."

"You tease me, sir. Tell me of her clothes. Which does she favour? She has lived long in France, and they say that the French fashions are more becoming than the English. What do you say, Master Melville?"

"I know little of fashions, Madam."

"But you must know which she likes. I myself favour the Italian caul and the bonnet. Do you know what is said of my preference? They say that I like it because it does not hide my hair, and I am very proud of my hair, of its colour and curl. It is this redness which makes them say that."

Melville was uncomfortable. It seemed an odd thing that the Queen should consider it part of his duty to discuss fashions and the colour of hair.

He shifted in his seat, but she would not let him go.

"Whose hair is the better colour—the Queen of England's or the Queen of Scots'?"

"I beg Your Majesty to excuse me. I know nothing of such matters."

"I believe that you do not remember what colour hair your mistress has. It cannot have struck you very forcibly, you treacherous man."

"Madam, I serve my mistress faithfully . . ."

She tapped his arm and laughed, for she was in a very frivolous mood; and it was as though her secret thoughts were so amusing that she could not refrain from laughter.

"I know it, I know it," she cried. "You have not noticed your mistress' hair, because it is so like other ladies' hair that it has passed your notice. Now here is a simpler question: Who is the more beautiful, the Queen of England or the Queen of Scotland?"

Melville answered: "You are the fairest . . ." She smiled graciously at him, but he continued: ". . . in England. Our Queen is the fairest in Scotland."

She pouted. "Come, come! That will not do."

"Nay, Your Majesty pokes fun at this poor ambassador."

"I am in earnest. I wish to know. I greatly regret that I have not my dear sister here in England. I would remedy the lack. I wish to know exactly how she looks."

"Your Majesty, you and she are the fairest ladies in your Courts."

"I am fairer of skin and lighter of hair, am I not?" she persisted.

"That is so, Your Majesty, but . . ."

"But what, sir?"

"Our Queen is very beautiful."

"We have heard that said. We would we had her here that we might prove the truth of it. Who is the taller, she or I?"

"Our Queen is taller, Your Majesty."

"Then she is too tall!" said Elizabeth. "For it is said that I am neither too tall nor too low."

She was a little annoyed, and talked no more of appearances. This man was certainly uncouth; he did not even know how to compliment a Queen. She thought of the charming things Robert would have said to reassure her.

"How does your Queen pass the time?"

"She hunts."

"Does she read?"

"She does, Your Majesty. She reads good books—the histories of countries."

"And does she love music?"

"Very much, Your Majesty."

"What instruments does she play?"

"The lute and the virginals."

"Does she play well?"

"Reasonably well, Your Majesty . . . for a Queen."

Then the Queen must play for the Scottish ambassador; she did so, and he had to admit that, on the virginals, she excelled her rival.

Then she must arrange for dances to be performed before him that she might show him how she danced. The inevitable question was asked: "Who is the better dancer, the Queen of England or the Queen of Scotland?"

He was frank: "My Queen dances not so high nor so disposedly as Your Majesty."

She was inclined to be amused at the reply, but she answered tartly that she held the dance to be an expression of joy and high spirits, not so much a matter of elegance as she believed the French and the Spaniards looked upon it.

"Ah, that I might see your Queen!" she sighed. "You cannot guess how I yearn for a meeting. Would you could bring her to me."

"I would willingly convey Your Majesty to Scotland. Our King James the Fifth went in disguise to France in order to inspect the Duke of Vendome's sister who was proposed for his bride. He was dressed as a page. What if Your Majesty so disguised herself?"

"Ah, that it could be so!" she sighed.

Then she said those words which set the whole world laughing and raised the high indignation of Scotland. "I have found a husband for your mistress."

"Your Majesty?"

"Yes. I will give her the only man in the world whom I consider worthy to mate with her. This is the most virtuous, the most perfect of men, one whom I would have married myself had my mind not been given to the virgin state. You have guessed? But surely you have.

There is only one man who could fit such praises. I refer to my Lord Robert Dudley."

The ambassador was at a loss for words.

She smiled at him pleasantly. "Ah, you feel his rank is not high enough? That is easily remedied. I shall do for him that which I have long promised. I shall make him the first Earl in the country. Now, my dear Melville, to your chamber, and write to your mistress that she may no longer remain in ignorance of the great good I would do her."

Robert was furious.

He demanded instant audience and she, nothing loth, granted it.

"My lord, what ails you? See how I have your good at heart!"

"You would make a laughing-stock of me, Madam."

"What! In offering you one of the most sought-after of brides?"

"There is only one bride I would have."

"You are too ambitious, Robert."

"I do not understand you."

"You do not seem to understand that you speak with your Queen."

"But you have led me to believe you would marry me."

"Time and time again I have told you that I would never forsake the virgin state. Why, Robert, she is the fairest of women."

She waited and of course it came: "That is untrue. *You* are the fairest of women."

"Master Melville does not seem to think so, and he has seen us both."

"The man is an uncouth ruffian from a land of barbarians."

"I believe you are right, Robert."

"Then put an end to this farce."

"Come here, my love. Kat . . . a cushion for my lord. I would have him kneel at my feet. Nay, woman, the best of my cushions, for only the best is good enough for him. Hath he not said so?" He took her hand and kissed it. "Robert," she said, "my fool Robert, do you think I would let you go to her!"

"Do you think I would ever leave you?"

"I'd send you to the block if you tried."

"Then we see this matter through the same eyes as always?"

"Yes, my dearest Eyes, we do. But the woman is an arrogant creature. She will be angry when she knows I offer you, and she'll not dare refuse you. But she will be angrier still when you refuse her. It will be as though you choose between us—marriage with her or the hope of marriage with me. And Robert, you are a man whom any woman would delight in having for her husband."

"Except one who torments and teases and will not decide."

"It is the Queen who is uncertain. The woman would take you this moment."

"My beloved . . . my Queen . . ."

"Hush! That sly Kat listens. My dear one, now I shall show my love for you. I shall make you an Earl . . . the Earl of Leicester and Baron of Denbigh, that title which has only been used until now by royal persons; and I shall give you the Castle of Kenilworth and Astel-Grove. Now, you see, my darling, why I have seemed harsh to you to whom I could not be harsh. I did not grant you this state before, for I did not wish our enemies to call you my lap-dog. Now a great title will be yours; you will be the richest man in England—almost a King—and that is what I wish you to be. This I can do now, and none dare say me nay; for to marry with the Queen of Scots you must indeed be Earl of Leicester. And if you do not marry the Queen of Scots, you will still be with your own Elizabeth and you will be none the worse—the Earl of Leicester instead of plain Lord Robert."

He was kissing her hands, her throat and her lips.

Robert was created Earl of Leicester with great pomp and ceremony at Westminster.

The Queen had insisted that, before he departed for Scotland, Sir James Melville must witness the ceremony, that he might report to his mistress in what high esteem the Queen held the man she was offering to her dear sister of Scotland.

She would allow none but herself to help him put on his robes. He was very solemn and dignified, and never had he looked quite so handsome as he did in his robes of state.

All those present noted the tender looks the Queen bestowed upon him; and, as he knelt before her and bent his head, she could not resist tickling his neck, there before them all.

She turned to the Scottish ambassador and, her face shining with love and pride, said: "How do you like him?"

"He is doubtless a worthy subject," said Melville. "He is happy to serve a Queen who discerns and rewards good service."

She smiled and her eyes fell on young Darnley who, as Prince of the Blood Royal, was standing near her. She knew that the sly ambassador was in touch—as he thought, in secret—with that young man, and that he hoped to make him, instead of the Earl of Leicester, the husband of Mary Queen of Scots.

She pointed to Darnley and said, imitating the Scottish accent: "Yet you like better yon lang lad."

He was sly, that man. He did not know how much she had learned of his secret plotting. He whispered, thinking to please her: "No woman of spirit, Your Majesty, would make choice of such a man—for although he is very lusty, so I have heard, he is beardless and has the face of a lady."

The Queen signified that she was well pleased with this answer, and her eyes went back with admiration to the newly made Earl.

Later at the banquet to celebrate the occasion she kept the Scot beside her.

She reminded him of the great affection she had for Mary.

"To no other would I offer Robert Dudley, the Earl of Leicester. You must tell your mistress that in so doing I offer her the greatest compliment I could offer any. I am giving her the man I would have married myself were I not determined to live and die in the virgin state."

"Madam," he said, "ye need not to tell me that, for I know your stately stomach. You think that if you married you would be but Queen of England, and now you are both King and Queen. You will not suffer a commander."

She looked at him shrewdly. He was no fool, this dour Scotsman.

Very soon after Robert was made Earl of Leicester, the Archduke Charles, having been rejected by Mary, began again to sue for Elizabeth's hand. Catherine de' Medici was trying to get the Queen for her son, King Charles; and failing him, for his brother, the Duke of Anjou.

Elizabeth meanwhile feigned to consider these suggestions with rapt attention. She allowed Darnley, against the advice of Cecil and her Council, to leave for Scotland.

It seemed that as soon as the Queen of Scots saw the beardless boy with the lady's face, she fell in love with him and decided to dispense with the consent of the Queen of England. She married him.

It was not until after the ceremony that Elizabeth heard of the marriage.

She received the information calmly, and laughed merrily over it with the newly-made Earl of Leicester.

VII

It was now eight years since Elizabeth had become Queen, and still she was unmarried, and still Robert continued to urge their union; but he was less hopeful than he had been.

He was now in his thirties—a little less handsome but not less attractive to women; and if the Queen could not make up her mind whether she would marry him or not, there were many ladies who would not have hesitated for a minute if he had offered himself to them.

He was one of the richest men in England now; he was the most powerful. But he had paid for these honours, and Robert was beginning to think that he had paid dearly.

He had always been attracted by children; the little boy who had served him so nobly during his imprisonment was no exceptional case. Children's eyes followed him; they liked his magnificence, his great stature, his handsome face. His manner towards them was all that children desired it to be; he treated them with an easy nonchalance; he made them feel not that he was stooping to their level, but that miraculously he had lifted them to his.

He now began to examine his dissatisfaction. He believed that above all things he had wished for marriage with the Queen; perhaps he still did. But he also felt a great desire to have children—sons—and they must be legitimate; yet what chance had he of getting legitimate sons while he must go on awaiting the Queen's pleasure? Naturally he would prefer his first-born to be heir to the throne; but had Elizabeth decided to wait until they were too old to have children?

He had heard the words of the Scottish ambassador: "Madam, I know your stately stomach. You would be King *and* Queen."

There was truth in those words, and it might well be that she, who would tolerate none equal with herself, had secretly made up her mind never to marry.

He had not, of course, been faithful to the Queen; but his love-affairs had had to be secret. He could never so much as look for long at any one of the Court beauties, for if the Queen's jealous eyes did not detect a Court peccadillo, her spies would; and they were everywhere. He had powerful enemies who were hoping for his overthrow; Cecil was one of them, and since he had been made Earl of Leicester and Cecil had received no similar honour, the Queen's chief minister must certainly be envious. Norfolk, Sussex, Arundel—those most powerful men—were only a few of his enemies. He knew that they were secretly working against his marriage with the Queen, and that the friendship they feigned to express was merely a sign that they feared Elizabeth might one day marry him. He suspected that Cecil had put into Elizabeth's head the idea of marrying him to Mary Stuart, and although he had come well out of that matter as the Earl of

Leicester, he could not help feeling that he had been exposed to a certain amount of ridicule.

Such thoughts as these were in his mind when he first noticed Lettice.

Lettice was one of the Queen's ladies, and in appearance not unlike the Queen herself, for she was the daughter of Sir Francis Knollys, a cousin of Elizabeth's.

The Queen had greatly favoured Sir Francis and a good match had been made for his daughter Lettice with Lord Hereford.

Although Lettice bore a family likeness to the Queen, all who were impartial would agree that Lady Hereford had real beauty; indeed she was secretly voted the most beautiful lady of the Court. The perfect oval of her face was enhanced by her ruff; her hair was not red as was the Queen's, but yellow-gold; her large eyes were brown, her features clear-cut, her teeth white, and she was tall and most graceful.

She was a bold woman and by no means afraid of provoking a situation which, if it came to the Queen's knowledge, might end in disaster for herself and Robert. For her, the moment's enjoyment was all-important. She was married to a man whom she did not love, and she was by no means displeased when she saw the eyes of Robert Dudley on herself. William Devereux, Lord Hereford, was some years younger than Robert and he seemed callow and dull when compared with the Queen's favourite—the man who was acknowledged to be the most handsome and desirable at Court.

It seemed natural to Lettice that she and Robert

281

should fall in love, and she proceeded to give him that encouragement which made him ready to put aside caution.

They met daily in the presence of others, but that was good enough for neither. Notes were exchanged; he must see her in private.

Could they meet in the pond garden? A meeting by night was arranged. A full moon shone that night on Hampton Court Palace.

This was recklessness. Robert knew it. But he was tired of waiting for the Queen's decision; he was tired of village girls. He was even wondering what the Queen's reaction would be if he told her he had decided to marry Lettice Knollys. It was true that Lettice had a husband, but husbands and wives could be dismissed in special circumstances. There was divorce. But he remembered Amy and the trouble she had caused. He had no real intention of marrying anyone but the Queen. Who knew, if he told her of his affection for Lettice, Elizabeth might realize that she was putting too great a strain upon him and, since he was sure she would never allow him to marry anyone else, marry him herself?

His thoughts were a little incoherent, but he was safe with a married woman; and why should he not enjoy a love affair which might bring him closer to marriage with the Queen?

Was this recklessness after all? Or was it sound good sense?

He went down to the pond garden to wait.

But Lettice did not come.

Nor came the storm for which Robert waited, for he knew that Elizabeth had discovered his philandering.

Elizabeth was not merely a jealous woman; she did not forget that she was also the Queen. The affair had not surprised her and she was not so displeased as Robert imagined her to be. The death of Amy had taught her a good deal. Love of power was in future to be the big brother in charge of her wayward affections; they should march together.

Her ministers were becoming alarmed at her failure to choose a husband, for suitors were not so eager to make a bid for her hand as they had once been. All the world believed that she was the mistress of Robert Dudley, and that as soon as she considered it expedient to do so, she was going to marry him. It was believed that only the scandals which still clung to her favourite, and which must touch herself, were preventing her.

She had been over-fond of Robert. Now she would show the world that he was not the only handsome man at her Court, and that fond as she was of him, she had affection to spare for others.

She was cleverer than Robert; he was merely a man, with a man's appetites, while she was a Queen who knew the meaning of power, the absolute joy which that power alone could give her; and she intended never to forget it, never to place it in jeopardy if she could help it.

She admitted that Lettice was beautiful. She would have been furious if he had chosen any but a beautiful woman. Lettice was also married and that meant he could not become too involved with her. The gossips were busy. Robert should flirt with Lettice while the

Queen showed the world that Robert was merely one of the young men whom she liked to have about her. She had already singled out a charming gentleman who was married to one of her ladies: Sir Thomas Heneage, a gentleman of the bedchamber. He was already wondering why favours such as those heaped upon Leicester should not fall on other handsome shoulders.

Very well, let the world see her affection straying from Robert. Then the suitors would re-appear and Master Cecil and his men would be satisfied because they could dabble in foreign politics to their hearts' content. The Queen did not like to think that she had frightened away her suitors; one of the most amusing pastimes of her reign had been to consider marriage with one or other of them.

But moonlight meetings in the pond garden she would not allow. Robert's love affair with Lettice must not go beyond a few languishing glances and whispered words. Let Robert wait in suspense. Let him, if he dare, make another assignation with Lettice. He should never keep it. Meanwhile the Court might whisper that the Queen seemed less fond of Leicester and was keeping at her side a most handsome gentleman of her bedchamber.

Negotiations with Austria were renewed, for the Emperor had died and Charles's brother had taken the Imperial crown. The Queen was now thirty-three years old, and her ministers were restive. How could they hope for an heir if she did not marry soon?

She was alarmed, she told Cecil, concerning the religion of the Archduke. "Remember," she said, "the marriage of my sister. The people were against it, and it brought no good to England. And, Master Cecil, if you would say that I might marry an Englishman, I would ask you to turn your eyes to what has happened to my sister of Scotland."

She was clever. She knew what she was talking about. The Queen of Scots had found in her husband, Darnley, a weak and dissolute youth who was no good to her. The murder of David Rizzio before the Queen's eyes had just taken place, and the world was still shocked by it. The Queen of Scots was six months pregnant, and there were many who said that the child she carried was Rizzio's.

Here was a pretty scandal, Elizabeth could point out to her ministers, a scandal such as—in spite of the evil gossip of lewd people—no one had been able to lay at her door. Here was a fine example of marriage; and she would say to them all that it made her cling more eagerly than ever to the single state.

Let her ministers contemplate affairs in Scotland before they urged her to set out on the perilous journey which the Scottish Queen was undertaking with such dire results.

Her ministers quailed before her; in a battle of words she could always confound them. They were called upon to face her feminine illogicality to which they could find no answer in their masculine logic; and when they were exasperated almost beyond endurance, and when they were ready to retire from office rather than serve such a woman, she would turn about and present them with an irrefutable truth which would astound them, since for all their clear thinking, they had missed it.

She kept her eyes on Scotland; she dreamed of having the Queen of Scots in her power. Catharine

Grey was still her prisoner; Catharine's sister, Mary, had obligingly made a love match without the Queen's consent, and now Mary and her husband with Catharine and Hertford were in the Tower. Darnley's mother, the Countess of Lennox, who had had to be released since the sorcery charges could not be proved, had been sent back to the Tower on the marriage of Darnley with Mary of Scotland, for Elizabeth accused her of having arranged the marriage, knowing it would be against the wishes of the English Parliament.

Quietly, and for reasons other than the apparent ones, she had collected her dangerous enemies and was keeping them under lock and key. Cecil, Norfolk, Bacon, Leicester, Sussex and Arundel watched her with amazement; they had thought themselves wily statesmen until they tried to pit themselves against this woman of thirty-three.

Cecil, who knew her a little better than did most people, did not now turn from Leicester as Norfolk and Sussex had. Cecil believed that she still kept a fond eye on her beloved Earl, that her seeming indifference to him was not to be taken too seriously and that it would be folly to seek the friendship of young Heneage whom she was using, partly to show Leicester that he must not turn to other women of the Court and partly to deceive the foreign ambassadors.

It was typical of her that she should get the utmost amusement out of the situation.

She ordered that Robert be brought before her. She would not see him alone, and there before her ladies and some of the gentlemen of the bedchamber, she warned him that she did not care to see philandering in her Court between widowers—however eligible—and

286

married women. It shocked her profoundly and she would not tolerate it.

Robert wanted to retort that she herself set a poor example. Was she not casting coquettish glances on a gentleman of the bedchamber who was married to one of her women? But he saw the cold light in her eyes which told him clearly that this was Elizabeth the Queen who was reprimanding him.

He was profoundly shaken. He feared that if he showed any more interest in Lettice he would be banished from the Court.

Elizabeth was triumphant. She had established a new relationship between them. She wished him to stay at Court. He was *a* favourite—one of many.

This change did not go unnoticed.

Leicester's reign is over, it was whispered. The Queen has fallen out of love. What of this new man, Heneage? Is he to take the favourite's place? What had he that Robert had not? It was true that he was a little younger, but in everything else he was inferior.

Heneage was with the Queen on that day at Greenwich when, after supper, the whole Court was dancing in the great hall, and Cecil came to the Queen to tell her that the Scottish ambassador was without and wished to see her.

There was news from Scotland, and when Cecil had whispered this news into the Queen's ear, she no longer had any heart for dancing. She sat down, putting her hand to her head, unable to hide her deep feeling. She said in a mournful voice to her women who had gathered about her: "The Queen of Scots is lighter of a fair son, and I am but a barren stock."

Cecil waved away the women and, bending over her,

whispered: "Madame, I know your feelings; but it would not be well for Melville to see you in this state. You must let him see you rejoice in the Prince's birth."

She grasped his arm and said: "You are right, as you generally are, my friend. Now bring in Melville."

She was up and dancing when he came. She pirouetted merrily at the sight of him.

"This is good news you bring us," she cried. "I have not felt so well for many weeks as I do on contemplating the birth of this fair son to my sister."

Melville knelt before her and kissed her hand.

He said with emotion: "My Queen knows that of all her friends Your Majesty will be the gladdest of this news. Albeit her son has been dear bought with peril of her life. She has been so sorely handled in the meantime that she wishes she had never married."

Elizabeth was pleased with this remark which the wily Scot had clearly added for her pleasure.

"You will be gossip to the baby Prince, Your Majesty?" asked Melville.

Elizabeth said that she would be pleased to stand godmother to the child.

But when she dismissed the ambassador and there was no longer need to play a part, she remembered with some disquiet that here was another claimant to the English throne who could not lightly be dismissed.

There was now no doubt that the Earl of Leicester had lost much of the Queen's favour. Norfolk and Sussex came out in the open and showed their dislike on every occasion. Only Cecil, being wiser, kept aloof from the feud between them.

For the Twelfth Night Festivities the Queen

astonished all by proclaiming Sir Thomas Heneage King of the Bean—a role which normally would have fallen to Robert Dudley, for none had the wit, the charm and the gaiety to play the part as he had always played it.

Robert was secretly furious but he could do nothing. It was impossible for him to have private audience with the Queen, and he wished to speak to her in a way which he could not use before others.

Elizabeth appeared to be completely diverted by the new favourite. Norfolk and Sussex tittered together, and some of their followers were involved in quarrels with Robert's men.

It was an intolerable position for Robert. Cecil was outwardly his friend, but Robert knew that he was merely following his cautious course; one word from the Queen that her indifference had turned to dislike, and Robert would have hardly a friend at Court. As for the people, he had never been popular with them; they had blamed him for all the scandal which had touched the Queen.

He was wondering whether he would support the marriage with the Archduke. But he could not do that; it would be to deny all that he had hoped for. He had ceased to look at Lettice, and was greatly disturbed because the Queen did not seem to be interested, while she herself continued to smile at Heneage. He had believed in the first place that when he dropped Lettice, she would drop Heneage; but she was clearly showing him that he and she were no longer on the old terms. If he were to continue at Court he would, like everyone else, have to obey the Queen.

He felt desolate and melancholy; and the Twelfth

Night Festivities seemed to him the climax of his suffering, for during them Heneage was deliberately insulting. He ordered Leicester to ask the Queen a question, which was: "Which is the more difficult to erase from the mind, an evil opinion created by a wicked informer, or jealousy?"

This was a significant question, made doubly so since the man Elizabeth had once so evidently loved must ask it of her.

With the nonchalance to be expected of him, Robert put the question to the Queen, who smiling, pretended to consider deeply before answering: "My lord, it is my opinion that both are hard to be rid of, but jealousy is the harder."

After the revels Robert, in a fury, sent one of his men to Heneage's apartments with a warning that he should prepare himself for the arrival of the Earl of Leicester, who was about to set out with a stick with which he would administer a beating to Thomas Heneage.

Heneage's reply was that the Earl of Leicester was welcome, but if he should come with a stick he would find a sword waiting for him.

Robert was baffled. He dared not provoke a duel, for duels had been forbidden by the Queen herself.

When the Queen heard of this she dismissed from Court the gentleman who had dared to take Robert's message to Heneage. Duelling was forbidden by her command, and any man who took part in any attempt to provoke one should be punished.

She sent for Robert.

"As for you, my lord Leicester," she said, without looking at him, "I beg of you, retire to your apartments." She stamped her foot suddenly, crying out: "God's Death, my lord! I have wished you well, but my favour is not so locked up in you, that others shall not participate thereof, for I have many servants, unto whom I have and will, at my pleasure, confer my favour; and if you think to rule here, I will have to teach you otherwise. There is one mistress here and no master. Those who by my favour become impudent, must be reformed. They should remember that as I have raised them up, so could I lower them."

Robert bowed and without a word retired.

In the utmost dejection he kept to his apartments for four days. But at the end of that time Elizabeth cried in pretended surprise: "Where is my lord of Leicester? It seems some time since I saw him."

He presented himself, and although she was gracious to him, she was no more than that.

Leicester is in decline, said his enemies gleefully.

Yet again she acted as though he meant no more to her than any other courtier.

Sussex openly flouted him while the Queen looked on.

Antagonisms flared up. Robert insisted that his followers wore blue stripes or laces that he might know them immediately and recognize any stranger among them. Norfolk put his followers into yellow laces. Quarrels were continually breaking out between the two factions; and the Queen's reprimand was as harsh for Robert as it was for Norfolk.

In despair Robert asked permission to leave Court, and to his even greater despair it was granted.

He went to Kenilworth, asking himself if his dream

were over. Not only did he fear that she would never marry him, but it seemed she had taken a violent dislike to him.

He tried to interest himself in enlarging the castle and extending its parks. When Kenilworth had come to him it had been a small estate, but he had spent thousands of pounds enlarging and beautifying it; and now it was one of the most magnificent places in the country.

Robert soon found that more trouble lay ahead, when his kinsman and servant, Thomas Blount, came riding to Kenilworth Castle. He had brought news that a man had sworn to Norfolk and Sussex that he had, for the sake of the Earl of Leicester, covered up a crime which the Earl had committed some time since; this concerned the death of Leicester's wife which without doubt had been a case of murder.

The man who was thus attacking him, said Blount, was Amy's half-brother, John Appleyard.

"He has been talking in Norfolk, my lord, and this having come to the ears of those noble lords, they have lost no time in seeking out Appleyard and promising him rewards if he will say in a Court of Justice in London what he has been saying to his rustic friends."

Robert laughed wryly. He said: "To think I have rewarded that man. Much land and possessions he owes to me. In the last years he has asked me now and then for help, but since I left Court I have not responded to his requests as readily as I did, so he must seek to be revenged on me."

"My lord," said Blount, "you must deny this charge. You have done so before. You will do so again."

Robert shrugged his shoulders. "Once," he said, "I

292

was the Queen's friend. Now I no longer enjoy that privilege. I see now that but for her I should not have escaped my enemies when Amy died."

"But for her, Amy would not have died!" said Blount fiercely.

"The verdict was accidental death!" retorted Robert.

But he was listless. For the first time in his life a woman had turned against him and, no longer desiring his company, wished to be rid of him.

He was growing old. He was not the man he had been. Some of his ardour for living had deserted him.

Kat was alone with her mistress and, said Kat, this was like the old days before her dearest Majesty was called Her Majesty in public, and only in private by those who loved her.

"I remember it, Kat," said Elizabeth.

"And the cards, dearest lady?"

"Aye, and the cards."

"And now we have Master Cornelius Lanoy working for us to produce his elixir, you no longer have need of poor old Kat Ashley to look into the cards for you."

"Will he produce it, think you, Kat?"

"If he should do what he says he will, dearest, he will find an elixir which will give eternal life and youth! Make sure that none but your own darling lips drink of it, for if it becomes common property that will do us little good. With everyone perpetually living and perpetually young, it would be as though Time stood still."

"Nay," said the Queen, "it shall only be Elizabeth who drinks of Lanoy's mixture; but perhaps I'll let my dear old Kat have a sip for old times' sake."

"Just a sip, Madam!"

"Mayhap two sips, for where should I be without you? If I am to live for ever I must have Kat with me."

"The man is a fraud, Madam."

"Is it so then, Kat? Perhaps you are right."

"You believe in him because Your Majesty believes that all the good you hope for will come to pass. Mayhap therein lies the secret of greatness. Others say 'It cannot be.' Great Bess says 'It shall be!' And because she is a witch and a goddess, there is good chance that she will be right."

"You talk like a courtier, Kat."

"Why, my love, you've lost another aglet from your gown. 'Tis the ruby and diamond, I'll swear. And I wanted to fix it on the cloth of gold you'll be wearing this night. And do I talk like a courtier then? But courtiers no longer talk as they once did."

"What means that?"

"That one, who talked better than any and whose words pleased Your Majesty more than any I know of, is no longer with us."

Elizabeth was silent.

"He is sad, I trow, to be away from Court," said Kat.

"Doubtless he amuses himself with the women round Kenilworth!" snapped Elizabeth.

"You should not be jealous of Lettice Knollys, my darling."

Elizabeth swung round, her eyes blazing and shining with tears; she slapped Kat sharply. Kat put her hand to her cheek and grimaced.

Then she said: " 'Tis a pity. That ruby and diamond aglet will be lost, I swear; and it makes the pair."

"Oh, be silent!"

Kat obeyed, and after a while Elizabeth burst out: "Why do you stand there sulking? Why do you not speak of him if you wish to?"

"Have I your gracious permission to speak of the man, Your Majesty?"

"What is it you have to say of him?"

"That it is sad to see Your Majesty fretting for him."

"I fret for him! Leave fretting to that she-wolf!"

"To whom, Your Majesty?"

"That harlot, that lewd woman, that Lettice . . . or whatever her name is. She married some man . . . Hereford, was it? I pity him! I pity him!"

"Ah!" sighed Kat. "It is a sorry thing to see a man, once proud, fall low. The dogs are at his throat now, my lady. They'll drag him to death and disgrace, if I mistake not."

"Dogs! What dogs?"

Kat whispered: "His great and mighty Grace of Norfolk. My lord of Sussex. My lord of Arundel. They are the dogs who will tear our pretty gentleman to pieces. Does Your Majesty not know that they have taken John Appleyard and put the man to question? He swears that he helped to cover up the murder of his half-sister for the sake of Robert Dudley."

Elizabeth was staring straight ahead. It must not be. Old scandal must not be revived. Amy Robsart must not be dragged from her grave to smirch the Queen's honour.

"So," went on Kat, "I say it is a sad thing to see a great man brought low. Why, those are tears in your sweet eyes, my darling. There! There! It matters not that your Kat sees them. Do you think you deceived her? You love him, and you think he loves Lettice better . . . or would if she were the Queen."

Elizabeth laid her head suddenly on Kat's shoulder. She murmured with a catch in her voice: "The Court is so dull without him, Kat. These . . . these others . . ."

"They are not the same, my love."

"No one is the same, Kat. We were together in the Tower, were we not. Can I forget him?"

"Of course you cannot."

"Heneage . . ."

Kat blew contempt in imitation of her royal mistress.

"A pretty man," she said, "nothing more. The lioness amuses herself with a pretty puppy. But they'll have the people against my lord of Leicester, dearest Majesty. The dogs are at his throat. They'll say; 'The lioness has left him to his fate, and he is wounded . . .' "

Elizabeth stood up. Her eyes were shining, for she felt it to be good when inclination and common sense could march together. "We'll have him back at Court," she said. "I'll recall him. I'll not let the dogs get him, Kat. You shall see how they go slinking away. As for Master Appleyard, he shall wish he had never left his orchards! Kat, there must be no more scandal, though. He must have done with his arrogance. I'll not brook that."

"Shall I look at the cards?" suggested Kat.

"Nay, not now. He shall just return to Court as a gentleman we have missed. It is merely because he has so many enemies that I shall have him back. I would not wish it to be thought that I forgot those I once loved."

"And still love?" said Kat quietly.

So he came back to Court and his enemies retreated.

John Appleyard confessed that he had been offered a reward to speak against Robert; he admitted that his brother-in-law had been very generous to him in the past, and that it was since he had fallen into disfavor that his gifts had ceased. Had John Appleyard whispered against the Earl of Leicester when he had been accepting those gifts? He had not. So it was only when he did not receive them that he thought unkindly of his generous brother-in-law? John Appleyard was glad to slip back into obscurity.

The affair of Amy's death was not to be revived.

Rumour started up again. Was the Queen contemplating marriage with Leicester? She had dropped Heneage now, and appeared to have no special favourite. She must marry someone soon. Did she think that because she was a Queen she could defy the passing of time?

When Parliamant was opened and the Queen asked for certain monies which she needed for her exchequer, she was met by stern opposition from the House of Commons.

It was pointed out to her that she was still unmarried and that the country needed an heir. The Commons refused to discuss the money bill unless the Queen would give her word to marry without further delay. There was an alternative; if she was set against marriage so strongly that she would not undertake it, she must name her successor. There was a great deal of argument; blows were exchanged in the House. The Commons, in an ugly mood, finally approached the Lords, demanding that they join them in their stand against the Queen; and this the Lords, after some hesitation, decided to do.

Elizabeth might accept what she called insults from the Commons, but she would not from the Lords.

Robert, understanding now that it would be wise for him—as there was no hope of marrying her himself—to support the marriage with the Archduke Charles, allied himself with the Lords and Commons. He knew that, if he did not, he would stand alone, and he was no longer sure of the Queen. During his exile, he had discovered the power of his enemies. He surmised that this was really what she wished him to do, for his exile had been partly due to her wish to show foreign powers that she had no intention of marrying him. He had been greatly heartened by her summons to return to Court, and it had been wonderful to realize that when he appeared to be deserted and his enemies ready to attack, she should have come to his aid. Yet she herself had been involved in the scandal attached to Amy's death, and her motive in recalling him might not have been entirely due to her wish to see him back at Court. He must play her game, which was, after all, out of necessity, his own. So now he ranged himself with those who were urging her either to marry, or name her successor.

She turned on them angrily. She dismissed Pembroke as a swaggering soldier. Let him get back to the battlefield, for it was all that he was fit for. As for Norfolk—he was a little too proud. It would be well for him to remember how her father had dealt with some of his family. Then she turned to Robert.

"And you, my lord of Leicester, you too have abandoned me! If all the world did that, I should not have expected it from you."

Robert knelt before her and tried to take her hand.

"Madam," he said, "I would die for you this minute if you were to command it."

She pushed him away with her foot. "Much good would that do me!" she cried. "And it has nothing to do with the matter."

Her eyes went to the Marquis of Northampton who was recently divorced and had married a new young wife.

"It is a marvellous thing, my lord, that you dare talk to me of marriage with your mincing mumping words. As if I did not know that you have just most scandalously divorced one wife and taken another."

And with that she turned and left them all staring after her.

Uncertain how to act, the Lords and Commons began to concoct a petition. They were determined that the Queen should either marry or fix the succession; but when Elizabeth heard that they were doing this, she summoned certain leaders from both Houses to appear before her. There she harangued them with fury.

"You and your accomplices tell me you are Englishmen and bound to your country, which you think will perish unless the succession is fixed. We have heard the Bishops make their long speeches telling us what we did not know before!" Her eyes flashed scorn at them and she said with an air of great wisdom: "That when my breath fails me I shall be dead!" She laughed. "That would be a danger to the state, they think. It is easy for me to see their object. It is to take up some cause against me.

"Was I not born in this realm? And were not my parents born in this realm? Is not my Kingdom here?

Whom have I oppressed? Whom have I enriched to other's harm? What turmoil have I made in this commonwealth that I should be suspected of having no regard for the same? How have I governed since my reign? I will be tried by envy itself! I need not use too many words, for my deeds do try me."

She glared at them and continued: "This petition you prepare is, I understand, to consist of two points: my marriage and the succession. My marriage you noble lords put first—for manners' sake! I have said I will marry. I hope to have children, otherwise I would never marry. I suspect you will be as ready to mislike my husband as you are now ready to urge me to marriage; and then it will appear that you never meant it at all. Well, there never was so great a treason but might be covered under as fair a pretence.

"You prate of succession, my lords. None of you has been a second person in this realm as I have and tasted of the practices against my sister. Would to God she were alive! When friends fall out the truth appears; there are some gentlemen in the Commons now who, in my sister's reign, tried to involve me in conspiracy. I would never place my successor in the position I once endured. The succession is a baffling question, full of peril to the country, though, my lords, in your simplicity you imagine the matter must needs go very trim and pleasantly. I would honour as angels any who, when they were second in this realm, did not seek to be first, and when third, second.

"As for myself, I care nothing for death, for all men are mortal, and though I be a woman, yet I have as good a courage as ever my father had. I am your anointed Queen. I will never be by violence constrained to do anything. I thank God I am endued with such qualities that if I were turned out of my realm in my petticoat, I were able to live in any place in Christendom."

She was invincible at such times, in every respect a ruler. Those who had spoken with her were for stopping the petition, but other members of the Commons insisted that they should proceed with it.

Elizabeth recklessly forbade them to discuss the matter. Then members of the Commons talked of privilege. There were now three questions demanding discussion instead of two: the Queen's marriage, the succession, and the privilege of the House.

Elizabeth knew when she had gone too far. Cautious Cecil was at her elbow advising her, and once again she recognized his wisdom. She lifted the veto on free discussion. She could be gracious when she knew herself at fault. Not only were they at liberty to discuss, she said, but she had decided to remit a third of the money for which she had first asked. Thus she came safely through a difficult situation; but the questions of her marriage and the succession were still open. She had given her word to marry, and she would marry the Archduke, she said, if she could be assured that he was not ill-formed, and ugly of person.

Exasperation filled the minds of those about her. Such feminine views should be suppressed. But it was well known that she could not endure ugly people near her. Only a few days earlier a lackey had been taken from her immediate service because he had lost a front tooth.

The Archduke was the best match available, she was reminded. The Earl of Sussex was sent to Austria to report on him, and sent back the news that his personal appearance left nothing to be desired, and that even his hands and feet were well-shaped.

"There is," said Elizabeth, "the question of religion."

The statesmen about her had now divided into two parties—one under the Duke of Norfolk, the other under Leicester. They could not agree as to the proposed marriage. Norfolk and his followers were for it. Robert, sensing her reluctance, which meant a rebirth of his own hopes, was against it. The Queen was still cool to him, but he knew her well enough to realize that she was not eager to marry the Archduke, and wished for this division between her statesmen.

It was characteristic of her that while she worried about her suitor's personal appearance, while she became again coquettish and entirely feminine, she suddenly should put the matter so clearly before them that they were astounded by her insight and the truth of what she said.

"You talk of my marriage!" she cried. "You talk of the succession. My friends, look at France. There the succession is happily fixed, you would say. Yet that country has been torn by civil war. Look at Scotland! There is a Queen who married as you, my lords, would have wished. She has produced a fine son and that, my lords, is what you would say is a good thing. And here, in this country, there rules a barren woman. Yet, my lords, in this poor country under this poor woman, you have enjoyed peace and growing prosperity. What this country—what any country needs—is not an heir to the crown, but peace . . . peace from wars which torment it and suck away its riches. A week ago a man

302

went to an altar while the service was in progress and he cast down the candlesticks and stamped upon them. There are many to support that man. In this country religious differences have not made wars. But what if your King were of the Catholic Faith, my lords? What if he wished to lead your Church back to Rome? We should have troubles such as you now see in France between Catholic and Huguenot. Nay! It is not a husband for your Queen that you need. It is not even an heir to your crown. It is peace. Think of my sister who made a foreign marriage. Think of these things, gentlemen, and see whether I am wrong to hesitate."

As before, she had made them pause. She had shown them the statesman hidden behind the frivolous woman.

Now the coolness between them was over. She could not hide her pleasure in having him beside her. He was not to be arrogant, she wished him to understand; he was not to think her favour was exclusively his. He was never so far to forget his respect for her as to go courting another lady of her household. He was her servant, her courtier, but a very favourite one.

Who knew, in time, she might even marry him!

He was her "Eyes" once more. No one could amuse her as he could. She doubted not that if he would remember all she asked of him, he would rekindle that old affection which had seemed to die.

He was cautious now; he was wiser; he was not content merely to be the courtier. He would be the statesman also. He stood with Cecil to govern the country.

It became clear to those about him that they would

be wise not to ignore him in the future. He might have his differences with the Queen; but he was still her favourite man.

When he fell ill, she was herself filled with anxiety. She visited him in his apartments on the lower floor of the palace and, examining them, declared that she feared they were damp and not good for his health. He should be moved to better quarters immediately, for she could not allow her Eyes to run such risks.

The quarters she chose for him were immediately adjoining her own.

A gasp of astonishment greeted this decision. It was an indiscretion which might have been committed in the days of her early passion for the man.

It became clear that, although there might be differences between them, those differences would be as ephemeral as lovers' tiffs, provoked rather for the enjoyment of ultimate reconciliation than through anger or by a lessening of their love.

VIII

As time passed, Robert was constantly with the Queen, but their relationship had become a more sober one. He was still her favourite, but they were like a married couple who have passed through stages of passion to trust and friendship, which was, in its way, more satisfying than the earlier relationship had been.

All eyes were now watching events in Scotland, and the matrimonial adventures of Queen Mary were leading all England to think that, in remaining unmarried, Elizabeth was again showing her sagacity.

After the murder of Rizzio, the Queen's husband—Darnley—had met a violent death in which many believed Mary to have played a part.

Elizabeth was alert. She thought of Mary in that wild and barbaric land, a dainty woman, brought up at the intellectual but immoral Court of France, a passionate and lustful woman who had a power to attract men which was apart from her crown.

Mary was weak in those characteristics which were the strength of Elizabeth. She would be impetuous where Elizabeth would always employ the greatest caution. Yet Elizabeth knew that there were some in the country—and this applied particularly to those staunch Catholics, the Northern Peers such as the Percys and the Nevilles—who would like to see Mary on the throne of England. Therefore, everything that Mary did was of the utmost importance to England.

But Mary was a fool in some matters, whereas Elizabeth was the wiliest woman in the world.

Elizabeth thought often of all that had happened to Mary. Had she, wondered Elizabeth, planned the murder of Darnley with that ruffian Bothwell? She knew that the barbaric chief—which was how she thought of Bothwell—had had to divorce his wife in order that he might marry Mary. Was it true that he had raped and abducted the Queen of Scots?

Mary was a fool to give great power to a man like Bothwell. Mary forgot that which Elizabeth would never forget—the dignity of queenship.

Cecil came to her with fresh news.

"Madam, the lords of Scotland have risen against Bothwell and the Queen. They accuse them of the murder of Darnley. Bothwell has escaped to Denmark and the Queen of Scots has been brought captive to Edinburgh."

"A prisoner . . . in her own capital city!" cried the Queen.

"The people of Edinburgh have abused her as she passed through their streets. They cry out that she should be burned alive. They say she is an adulteress and a murderess, and should not be allowed to live."

"How dare they!" cried Elizabeth. "And she a Queen!"

Cecil looked at her. His eyes were steady. He was telling her without words that if the people of Edinburgh should take it upon themselves to do what they would call justice to the Queen of Scotland, Elizabeth would be without a powerful rival. Perhaps his thoughts ran on as hers did. If they could have the baby Prince brought to England and put in charge of the Queen's Parliament, much trouble might be saved.

Mary's disaster was Elizabeth's opportunity—as Cecil saw it.

But Elizabeth could not get out of her mind the picture of Mary, a captive, riding through the streets of Edinburgh, while the mob shouted at her. All other emotions were submerged by the horror of that picture, for Mary, like Elizabeth, was a Queen. How could one Queen rejoice in the insults thrown at another? Elizabeth might be jealous of Mary; she might even hate Mary; but she would never approve of insults being thrown at an anointed Queen, for no such evil precedent must be set.

Cecil, watching her, marvelled at her yet again. The woman and the Queen! He could never be sure with which of them he had to deal.

When the little coffer of silver and gilt was brought to England, feelings ran high against Mary, for the coffer contained those letters—always known as the Casket Letters—which Bothwell was reputed to have left behind him in his flight. These letters—if they were not forgeries—damned the Queen, labelling her as Bothwell's accomplice in the murder of Darnley.

Still Elizabeth would defend her. And when Mary escaped from her captors, raised men to fight for her, was defeated and threw herself once more on Elizabeth's mercy, though there were many to urge the execution of this dangerous woman, still Elizabeth continued to remember that Mary was a Queen. Elizabeth must uphold the status of royalty. Kings and Queens might err, but the common people must see them as the chosen of God, and the peers must never be allowed to judge them. Mary was certainly a foolish woman; there was little doubt that she was a murderess; there was still less that she was an adulteress; but she was a Queen.

"The lords have no warrant nor authority by the law of God or man," said Elizabeth, "to be superiors, judges or vindicators over their Prince and Sovereign, howsoever they do gather and conceive matters of disorder against her."

That was the Queen's verdict, and she did not forget that Mary and Bothwell stood in relationship to Darnley as once she and Robert had to Amy Robsart.

She would have a dangerous enemy to contend with, but that enemy was merely a woman and a foolish one; she had the Catholics to consider; but these matters were tangible. A subtle canker growing in the minds of the people was an entirely different matter; for that grew unseen and unchecked; it could undermine all thrones, all royalty.

She offered Mary asylum in England, first in the Castle at Carlisle, then, as she felt that to be too near the borders of England and Scotland, in the Castle of Bolton at Wensleydale. Let her stay there while the Queen of England waited on her old friend Time.

Mary was tempestuous, arrogant and wilful. She had expected to be received at Elizabeth's Court. She had not come as a prisoner, she complained, but as a visiting Queen.

Elizabeth could deal with that matter. Mary, she

answered, was being given protection, for her position was a dangerous one. The Queen of England would be remorseful to the end of her days if aught happened to her dear sister while she was in her care. And as for coming to the Court, Mary would readily see that the Queen—as an unmarried woman so closely related to Lord Darnley—could not, in propriety, receive Mary at her Court while she was still under suspicion of Darnley's murder.

Her dear sister of Scotland must understand that nothing would delight her more than to hear that the truth had been discovered and Mary proclaimed innocent of her husband's murder.

So Mary had to be content with her captive state; and the Queen waited, ever watchful of her dear sister, yet determined to show the people that Queens were above reproach, no matter what charges were brought against them.

This was necessary, for Amy Robsart had a disturbing habit of rising from the grave now and then. The people must not be allowed to make unhappy comparisons.

It was at this time that the rift with Spain became too wide to be ignored.

To England the Queen was a symbol. She gathered handsome and chivalrous men about her; they must be gallant and adventurous. She wished to be to them a fair ideal, the mistress they all wished to serve because they were in love with her perfections; yet she was the mother, and their welfare was the dearest concern of her life. She was Woman, warm and human, yet because she was an anointed Queen, she was invulnerable and unassailable. She wanted her men to be bold, to perform feats of courage and adventure for her sake; these she rewarded with her smiles and favours. She was a spiritual mistress; they must be faithful to her; they must perpetually seek to please her; their words to her, their thoughts of her, must be the words and thoughts of lovers. They must all be in love with her; to them she must be the perfect woman. But they must never forget that she was mistress of them all. And while to her handsome and gallant courtiers, to her statesmen and soldiers, she was the queenly mistress and beloved woman, they must constantly remember that to her people she was Mother—the all-embracing Mother—and her thoughts and her energies were directed towards the good of her people. She wished England to be a happy home for her people—a prosperous home—and as, to her belief no home could be happy and prosperous unless it were peaceful, she abhorred war.

Often she would say to her ministers when she reproved them for urging her to some action, of which she did not approve, against a foreign power: "My father squandered great wealth in war. I have studied the histories of many countries, and I have never yet seen any good come out of war. There is a great waste of a nation's substance and its man-power; there is poverty, famine, pain and heartbreak but never good. I am not a King to seek military glory. That has no charm for me. I am a Queen—not the father but the mother of my people; and I wish to see them content in their home. I know this contentment can be brought about by our prosperous merchants, by good harvests. My people would love me less if I wrung taxes from them to pay for wars, as others have done before me. And I am a mother who wishes to keep her children's love."

So did she hate the thought of war that she would grow angry if any spoke of it; and often during a meeting of the Council she would slap a statesman's face or take off her slipper and throw it at him, because she believed he was urging his fellows towards a war-like policy.

But at the same time she longed to make England great; and England was beginning to be aware of her sea power. John Hawkins had begun the slave trade, which was proving profitable for England; he was taking cargoes of men and women from West Africa to Central America and the West Indies for the local planters. His young cousin, Francis Drake, had given up dreaming dreams on Plymouth Hoe and had joined Hawkins. These two intrepid seamen of the West Country had already come into stormy contact with the Spaniards on the high seas and off the coasts of Mexico and Peru. Martin Frobisher was wondering why the sea and the new lands should be left a prey to Spain and Portugal. Were not the English as bold—if not bolder—than the Spaniards! If English ships lacked the elegance of Spanish galleons, the bravery of English seamen made up for that. Moreover, did they not serve a Queen before whom they wished to show their mettle!

She applauded them, but silently. She was the mistress before whom they might strut, at whose feet they must lay their treasures. But it was to be clearly understood that they must bring no harm to her family. If these adventurers looked upon the Spaniards on the high seas as their natural enemies, if they took on the role of pirates and stole the plunder which the Spaniards had already stolen before them—that was all well and good; but her family must remain safe. She would not go to war on behalf of her pirates. What they did was their own affair. They must finance their own adventures; she would not tax her children to provide the funds. Let them show themselves true men—men who believed in their ventures; she would love them all the better for that.

Thus she secretly encouraged her adventurers while openly she washed her hands of them. Spain looked on in puzzled irritation. What could be done against such a woman? She made her own rules. She was perversely feminine when it suited her to be.

She had always had the common touch, but during these years the affection of the people deepened for her. They accepted her at her own valuation—as someone more than human. Yet she was continually showing them how human she was, continually discarding formality, which she said was made for her, not the Queen for it. She had pet names for those who served her. First, of course, was her beloved Eyes; and now a new young man, Christopher Hatton, had won her favour. Handsome, charming, capable of making flowery speeches, he was also the most excellent dancer she had ever known. She called him her "Lids." Meanwhile Cecil had become her "Spirit."

The trouble with Spain had increased with the dismissal of her ambassador, Dr. Mann, from Madrid. Elizabeth bridled. The Queen would not, she said, lightly forget this insult from Spain. She added that Philip had never forgiven her for refusing to marry him, and that was why he had sent that odious de Spes as ambassador to replace his charming predecessor. De Spes did not compliment her nor flatter her, and she disliked him intensely; she was sure he was determined to misrepresent her to his master.

She was in this mood when four Spanish ships on the way to Flanders were chased by French pirates and forced to take refuge in Southampton, Falmouth and Plymouth.

When Cecil and Robert brought the news to her she smiled complacently.

"And what do these ships contain?" she asked.

"Bullion," Cecil told her. "It comes from Genoese merchants, and is a loan on the way to Alba in Flanders."

"And Your Majesty knows well for whom that money is intended," said Robert.

"I do. It is to pay those soldiers of his who are making it possible for him to stay in that wretched land and torture its people."

"I fear so, Your Majesty," said Cecil.

"It makes me sad to think of those poor souls," she said, "at the mercy of Alba and his Inquisition."

"Many of those who have escaped have found refuge in this land," Robert reminded her. "They will bless Your Majesty until they die."

"Poor men! Poor men! And this bullion is to pay those wretches . . . those soldiers who serve such tyrants. What think you, my dear Eyes? What think you, Sir Spirit, would His Most Catholic Majesty do if that bullion never reached his tyrant Duke?"

"He would say that of Your Majesty which *I* would not dare utter," said Robert.

"I did not ask what he would say, Robert. I asked what he could *do*."

Cecil said: "His hands are tied. He could do nothing. His forces are not at his disposal. He has too much territory to guard. If the bullion did not reach Alba it is possible that his soldiers would mutiny."

She gave her high laugh and her eyes sparkled. "Then, my dear lords, the bullion must not reach Alba. Have not the French pirates attempted to attack the ships in my ports? Let the bullion be brought to London for safe keeping. It is private property, is it not? It is the property of Genoese merchants. I cannot see that it belongs to His Most Catholic Majesty any more than to me. We could use a loan, could we not? And here it is on our very shores."

Cecil was silent. Robert was gleeful.

"God's Death!" he cried, using one of her oaths. "Why should we not crush this Catholic domination? Why should Your Majesty not be supreme head of the Protestant world?"

"There speaks the soldier," she said, giving him a sharp tap on the cheek. "Let us have war that my lord of Leicester may distinguish himself and bring great glory to his name! Nay, Robert, the good things are won in peace. Is that not so, Master Cecil?"

"At this time, Madam, it would be daring enough to confiscate the bullion."

"What reprisals could be taken by our little saint in his Escorial?"

"I do not think he is in a position to do overmuch. But there is the wool trade to consider and, as Your Majesty is well aware, our best customers are the Low

Countries. Alba could seize our merchants' goods there."

"Well, we could seize the goods of the Netherlanders in England, which I believe are greater. Think of the riches these Netherlanders have built up in our country. Why, if we seized their goods and property here they would make such an outcry that the Spaniards would be forced to come to a peaceful settlement. Nay, my dear lords, no harm will come of this. We shall have the bullion as our loan; and this will teach these Spaniards to have more respect for Englishmen on the high seas. Hawkins was treated maliciously by those Spanish Dons in Mexico. Shall I allow my subjects to be treated thus?"

"But Hawkins gave as good as he got, Your Majesty," said Robert.

"As good as he got? Nay, better, which is what I would expect of an Englishman."

And in such good mood was she that Robert dared show his jealousy of her newest favourite.

"This Hatton man," he said, when Cecil had left them. "Your Majesty cannot truly be so delighted with his company as it would seem."

"But I am, Robert. I am. I declare my Lids are as necessary to me as my Eyes . . . or nearly so."

"How can you say that?" he demanded passionately.

"Because it is true, dear Eyes.'

"Your Majesty seeks to torment me."

"And why should I do that?"

"Because I have loved you long and you grow tired of such enduring devotion."

"God's Body!" she cried. "Never would I tire of

fidelity. It is to my way of thinking the most endearing quality."

"And Your Majesty doubts mine?"

"I doubt it not, dear Robin. Doubt not mine for you."

He kissed her hand, wondering whether he might speak to her of marriage, but he was more cautious than he had been in the days before that spell of disfavour. She smiled at the frown between his brows, and she thought: Dear Robin, he grows older. He loses those handsome looks.

There were streaks of white in the once black hair; the skin beneath the eyes was a little pouchy, the fine line of the jaw a little flabby. A tenderness came over her. She would not tell him so, but she loved him no less than she had in the days when she had so often thought of him as a husband. If her thoughts were calmer now, they were no less affectionate.

She was still the coquette; but she had made her wishes clear. She was to be eternally young, even though Lanoy had failed to find his elixir. All handsome men, whatever their ages, must be in love with her. It was part of the homage she demanded as their Queen.

She was ready to tease Robert a little about Hatton, that greedy man, who had been bold enough to ask for part of the Bishop of Ely's garden. Hatton had received his garden—twenty acres of fertile land between Holborn Hill and Ely Place—although Bishop Cox had protested most bitterly.

"Methinks, Robert," she said, "you are more than my Eyes. I read your thoughts. I have given a garden to Hatton. But think, my dear friend, what I have given to you. And I doubt not that, ere you and I leave this Earth, I shall give you much more. Yet in return what do I ask? Your affection, your loyalty to the Queen and your fidelity to Elizabeth."

"They are yours, my beloved."

She smiled at him, and although the smile was tender it held a warning. She had heard that two sisters at Court were madly in love with him; and that there was continually strife between them because of this. One was Lady Sheffield and the other was Frances Howard. He must so far have remembered the pain of his exile, which had started with a flirtation with Lettice Knollys, for Elizabeth had not heard that he had given either of these sisters the slightest encouragement.

And, she thought grimly, it would be wiser for him not to do so. She could not tolerate any of her favourites' marrying, but that her first favourite should have a love affair at Court was more than she could bear. It seemed to her that her life and Robert's life were closely bound; she had always been attracted to him—first in the nursery, then in the Tower and later at Court; she knew now that she would always love him beyond all others whatever befell. She felt a similar affection for Kat Ashley. She might quarrel with her and with Robert, but she would love them until she died. And whereas Kat was the friend, Robert was the lover.

He made one more attempt, and she enjoyed his making it because it was the symbol of his jealousy.

"What is it you admire so much in the popinjay?"

"Come, Robert, do not show your jealousy of a man because he is younger and more agile on his feet than you. Have you seen the fellow in the dance?"

"The dance!" said Robert. "I will bring Your Ma-

317

jesty a dancing master who will perform more gracefully before your eyes than Master Christopher Hatton."

"Pish!" said the Queen. "I'll not see your man. It is his trade to dance."

She laughed at his discomfiture. She was pleased, thinking of her love for Robert, of the bullion which would shortly lie in her coffers, and of the pique and embarrassment of that pale man of Spain who had had the bad taste, after seeking to marry her, not to wait for more than a few months before marrying a French Princess.

In the Castle which was now her prison, Mary Queen of Scots heard of the tension between Spain and England. Tempestuous and impulsive herself, she was certain that this would mean war between the two countries. She did not understand the characters of Philip and Elizabeth; neither was of a nature to plunge into war. Mary, alas for herself, knew no such caution. Now she had wild hopes. If there were war, and Spain were victorious, she would not only be restored to her throne, but given that of England as well, providing she was ready to return the country to the Catholic Faith; and this she would be most happy to do.

The Casket Letters were causing a great deal of scandal, and many were asking themselves and each other how such a woman as Mary, obviously unfitted to govern her country, could possibly be restored to her throne. A solution was suggested: Why should she not marry an English husband chosen for her by the English Parliament, and one whom she could marry with Elizabeth's consent? Then she might be considered next in succession if Elizabeth died childless. If her husband were an Englishman, England could be sure of peace with Scotland. There was one man very suitable for the position of Mary's husband; this man was the first peer of England, Thomas Howard, Duke of Norfolk.

This opinion was put forward by the Catholic peers of the North, for although Norfolk professed himself to be of the Anglican Faith, he was at heart a Catholic.

Leicester, with Sussex and Throckmorton, decided that, providing Norfolk and Mary became good Anglicans and took the rites of the Church of England to Scotland, this match could not fail to be beneficial to England.

Ambition made Norfolk eager for the marriage, but he was a little shaken by the revelation of the Casket Letters.

The Queen, hearing of the plan, sent for Norfolk. "So, my lord, you make great plans?" she said. "You would marry the Queen of Scots and change your rank of Duke for King?"

"Nay, Your Majesty. Why should I seek to marry so wicked a woman, such a notorious adulteress and one who had committed murder? I love to sleep on a safe pillow."

"There are some who might consider a crown worth such risks."

The old Norfolk pride showed itself. "Your Majesty, I count myself, by your favour, as good a Prince at home in my bowling alley in Norfolk as she is in the heart of Scotland."

The Queen nodded. Those were not idle words. Norfolk, first peer of England, the country's only

Duke, was one of its richest men.

"And, Your Majesty," went on Norfolk, "I could not marry with her, knowing that she pretends a title to the present possession of Your Majesty's crown. If I did so, Your Majesty might justly charge me with seeking the crown of England."

"I well might do so," said the Queen grimly.

Norfolk felt that he had come well out of a difficult interview, but the thought of a crown, even though it was but the crown of Scotland, could not lightly be dismissed. Mary was a dangerous woman, but she was a fascinating one.

He discussed the matter with Robert, who felt that he could not oppose the marriage while the succession was still not fixed. Elizabeth was strong and healthy, but often people died suddenly. If Mary became Queen of England, Elizabeth's favourite would have little to hope for unless he showed himself, during the lifetime of Elizabeth, not unfriendly to Mary. Robert's love and loyalty were for Elizabeth; but he did not see how this marriage of Mary with Norfolk could affect that.

"I will do my best," said Robert, "to show the Queen the advantages of this marriage. The tormenting problem of the succession must be fixed in some way, and how better than this?"

Norfolk looked at his old enemy. They had never liked each other. Norfolk still regarded Robert as an upstart; Robert did not forget old insults.

Robert arranged that Norfolk should sup with the Queen and put his case before her; but Elizabeth was suspicious, and before he had a chance of speaking of the marriage, she leaned towards him and, taking his ear between her thumb and forefinger, nipped it hard.

320

"I would wish you, my lord," she said, "to take good heed to your pillow."

That was a sly reference to his own remark. The pillow could mean that which he shared with Mary, or another one of wood on which he might lay his head before the axe descended.

Norfolk rose from the supper table at which they sat and, throwing himself upon his knees before her, assured her that his one wish was to serve *her*, and that he had no intention of making any marriage which should not be in accordance with her wishes.

He left, relieved that he had emerged from a difficult situation with safety. But the matter did not end there. Mary began to write letters to him; and into those letters it seemed that she infused some of that charm of which he had heard so much. She was an adulteress, he believed; he suspected her of murder; but he became more and more fascinated, not only by Scotland's crown, but by Scotland's Queen.

In spite of Elizabeth's objections, the lords would not abandon the idea of the marriage, for it seemed to them the only means of avoiding war with the great Catholic countries, France and Spain, who were ever watching, seeking an opportunity to overthrow Protestant England. The Netherlands were in a sorry state and, once they were completely subdued by the iron hand of Alba and the Inquisition, it might be that Alba's next task in the establishment of the Catholic Faith throughout the world would be to subdue England. There was one way of holding off that calamity: Promise the succession to Mary Queen of Scots and, to ensure her good behavior, give her a good English husband, a man who could be trusted as they believed they could trust the Duke of Norfolk. The project was the hope of the Catholics in England, and of these there were many.

These peers believed that if they could get rid of Cecil and his party they could achieve this object, for Cecil was upholding the Queen in her objections to the match.

A conspiracy was set on foot to depose Cecil and, because many remembered what had happened to Thomas Cromwell in the days of the Queen's father, they had the axe in mind for Cecil.

Robert, who had somewhat half-heartedly thrown in his lot with the opponents of Cecil, was chosen as the man to lay the proposition before the Queen. He chose a meeting of the Council to do this; and he pointed out to her that it was the considered opinion of those of her ministers who were not of Cecil's party, that his policy was leading England towards danger. This policy had, it was felt, so far alienated England from France and Spain, that the only way in which the damage might be remedied was to offer Cecil as a sacrifice to Catholic opinion abroad.

Never had Robert seen the Queen in such a rage.

"These are not my father's days!" she cried. "I do not send my ministers to the block to make way for others who fancy their rewards! If Cecil is against the marriage of Mary of Scotland to Norfolk, then so is Cecil's mistress! And you, my lords, should look to your own ways, for it may well be that you will find yourselves in the sort of trouble you plan for Cecil. As for the Queen of Scots, she had better have a care or she may find some of her friends shorter by a head!"

It was clear that the enraged lioness was going to protect her cub Cecil, and that if the lords were to go on with their project, they must do so in secret.

Shortly after that meeting there was a plan to arrest Cecil out of hand, but Robert, who knew of their plans, was alarmed. He was aware of the Queen's nature; he knew how furious she would be if her ministers acted against her orders and her well-known wishes. He knew that she was a woman who, having once given her loyalty, was not lightly to be turned from it. Cecil had been her good friend; if he had failed in his policy—and the Queen would not admit that he had—he had served her faithfully.

Robert therefore disengaged himself from the plotters and warned them that, unless they desisted, he would have no alternative but to tell the Queen what they intended to do. Cecil himself came to the rescue by offering to modify his attitude; he declared that if the Queen consented to the marriage he would not stand against it.

The Queen of Scots was a born schemer. She could not wait for the propitious moment. She was binding Norfolk more closely to her. Robert saw what was happening. He knew that if there was a rising—and he believed that Norfolk, under the influence of Mary, might be foolish enough to attempt one—civil war would sweep the land; and he, having sided with those who were for the marriage, might be perilously involved.

Elizabeth was his Queen and his love; he would never work with any against her. He felt his position to be dangerous, however, and that it was necessary for him to have an immediate audience with the Queen.

Even so, if he put his case frankly before her, he could not be sure that Elizabeth would entirely acquit him of mischievous dabbling. He knew his Queen better than any one else did; so he retired to his bed in his manor at Tichfield.

It was not necessary to feign sickness, for he was sick with anxiety. He sent a messenger to the Queen, telling her that he thought he was dying and that he must see her before he left this world.

Then he lay back on his pillows, rehearsing his apologies while he waited for the coming of the Queen.

Elizabeth was with her women when the message was brought to her. She rose, and they noticed how she swayed a little. Robert dying! It was impossible. She would not allow it. Her sweet Robin, her Eyes, the man she would love until she died! They were too young to part. There must be many years left for them to be together.

Kat was beside her. "Bad news, Your Majesty?"

"We must leave at once for Tichfield."

"My lord of Leicester?"

"He is ill . . . asking for me."

Kat turned pale. She more than any knew of her mistress's feelings for that man. It would break Elizabeth's heart if aught happened to him.

"Do not stand staring!" cried the Queen. "We will set out at once. We will take doctors and simples . . . elixirs which *must* bring him back to health."

As she rode to Tichfield, she thought of all he had meant to her. She could not get out of her mind the memory of his face behind the prison bars in the Beauchamp Tower.

She hurried to his bedchamber. The sight of him in his bed, wan and exhausted, hurt her profoundly. She knelt by his bed and, taking his limp hand, covered it with kisses.

"Leave me," she said to Kat and those who had accompanied her. "I would be alone with my lord."

"Robert," she said when they had all gone. "My dearest Eyes, what ails you, my sweet Robin?"

He murmured: "Your Majesty, it was good of you to come to sweeten my going."

"Do not speak of it. It shall not be. I'll not allow it. You shall be nursed back to health. I myself will nurse you."

"I, your humble servant, have called you to my bedside . . ."

"God's Body!" she cried. "My humble servant indeed! You are my Robert, are you not? There are times when *I* seem to be the humble servant."

"Dearest lady, I must not waste the time that is left to me. I must talk with you. There is a plot afoot and I do not hold myself guiltless. I believed that it would be good for England if Norfolk married Mary. Dearest, I feared your life to be in danger while the succession was unsettled."

"Have done with the succession. It is a bogey that haunts you."

"Nay, 'tis not so. I fear now that Your Majesty may be in danger. Norfolk makes plans, I fear, in secret with the Queen of Scots. Many of your lords are involved in this . . . as I myself have been. They meant no treason. They fear Your Majesty to be in danger. Their plan is no more than to restore Mary to Scotland with a good friend of England as her husband, and to

325

satisfy France and Spain by proclaiming Mary your successor."

"I see, I see," she said.

"Then I am forgiven for the part I played in this—though I was thinking only of my dearest lady's safety? Then I am to die happy?"

She bent over him and kissed him. "If there was aught to forgive, my darling, it is forgiven. '

"Now I shall die happy."

"You'll do no such thing!"

He smiled at her wanly. "I know, dear lioness, that it is forbidden to speak of death in your presence. There again I crave your pardon. You are strong. You are impatient of death. You are immortal."

"Come," she said, with a "pup" of her lips, "we are going to get you well. I myself shall see to that."

Then she called to her women. She would try her physician's new medicine. It should cure my lord of Leicester. She commanded him to be cured.

"Already," said Kat, "he seems miraculously recovered. He looks almost himself."

"Her Majesty's presence at my bedside is more health-giving than any elixir," he murmured.

Elizabeth set about restoring him to health; but meanwhile she sent a messenger to Norfolk bidding him return to Court.

Norfolk was now in the Tower.

Elizabeth's ministers were of the opinion that Norfolk was loyal to her, but had been led astray, and that he might be released with a warning not to dabble in treasonable matters again.

But the Queen was unsure. She insisted that they

wait awhile, keeping him a prisoner while they waited.

Norfolk had many friends at Court, and some of these smuggled messages to him concealed in bottles of wine. This trick was discovered, and the Queen, declaring that Norfolk was guilty of treason, summoned Cecil to her.

"Now, Master Cecil," she said, "we have proof of his treason."

"How so, Madam?" asked Cecil.

"These letters which have been sent to him in bottles. What better proof?"

"They prove nothing except that he received messages in bottles, Your Majesty."

The Queen merely glared at her minister.

"Madam, I will send you the statute of Edward III in which there is clear statement of what does and what does not constitute treason."

"So you are all for letting Norfolk go that he may plot my downfall?"

"Why not marry Norfolk to someone else, Your Majesty? That would be the best way to put an end to this plan for marriage with Mary."

She smiled at him. She could trust Cecil. His mind worked in the same way as her own. "I think, Sir Spirit, that you have a good plan there."

But even as he was leaving her presence a messenger arrived, with the news that all through the North of England the bells were ringing backwards. The men of the North, those ardent Catholics who had risen against her father in the Pilgrimage of Grace, were now ready to rise again; and they looked on Mary Queen of Scots as their leader. The Queen was aghast. War she dreaded more than anything; and here was war in her own country, the most hated of all wars: civil war.

Cecil said: "They will try to reach Mary, and our first task must be to remove her from Tutbury. I will send men there at once. We will send her with the utmost speed to Coventry."

The Queen nodded her approval.

Civil war! Her own people rising against her. The thought made her wretchedly depressed until her anger replaced such feelings. Mary had caused this. Wherever Mary was, there would trouble be. Mary was her hated rival whom she longed to put to death, but for the sake of royalty—that divine right of Kings—she dared not.

The rebellion was speedily quelled. Poor and simple men from the hamlets and the villages were hanging from the gibbets for all to see what happened to those who rebelled against the Queen.

In her wrath, men said, she is as terrible as her father was.

Six hundred men who had followed their leaders were now lifeless hanging corpses, and the North was plunged into mourning.

They must learn, said Elizabeth; they must understand the rewards of treason to the throne.

But Mary she merely kept more closely guarded, while Norfolk lived on in the Tower.

Norfolk had learned his lesson, said the Queen; and she was not entirely sure that he was responsible for the rising. As for Mary, adulteress, murderess and fomenter of plots that she might be, as a Queen she was apart from ordinary mortals.

Elizabeth's ministers shook their heads in sorrow

and anger. They assured her that she risked her life while Mary lived; she also risked the safety of England.

Elizabeth knew she was risking much, but she felt that in tampering with the privileges of royalty, she risked more.

Mary could not learn her lessons and it was not long before she was plotting again. This time the services of a Florentine banker, named Ridolfi, were employed. Ridolfi lived in London where he had a branch of his business, but he travelled freely about the Continent, and for this reason he was chosen to carry messages between the Pope, the Spanish ambassador and the Catholic peers in England.

Norfolk, now home at his county seat, was still under some restraint since his release from the Tower. He was approached by Ridolfi, and, weakling that he was, under the spell of Mary to whom he had been sending money and gifts, found himself once more drawn into mischief and danger.

This time the danger was unmistakable, for messages had come from Alba himself, who promised that if Norfolk would start a revolt, he would send an Army to England to consolidate any success.

The Queen, snapping her fingers at Cecil's detractors, had created him Lord Burghley; and Burghley was not a man to forget that Norfolk was under grave suspicion, although no longer a prisoner. A messenger from Ridolfi was captured as he landed in England from the Continent, where the Florentine now was. The message was vague and merely indicated that all was going well; but Burghley and his spies were on the scent; and when Norfolk's servants were put to severe questioning, it was discovered that a plot was in train, involving Norfolk, Mary, the Catholic peers and—most disturbing—the Pope, Philip and his commander Alba.

Burghley's spies were busy and, when letters were smuggled in to Mary, they were intercepted; so the plot was discovered before it had fully matured.

Burghley could restrain his impatience no longer; he presented his evidence to the Queen, with the result that Norfolk was arrested and the Spanish ambassador sent back to his own country.

Now the Queen's ministers were calling for the blood—not only of Norfolk but of Mary. Elizabeth was calm, as always in moments of danger.

Strangely enough she was still reluctant to execute either Norfolk or Mary. The truth was that she hated strife; she hated executions. Her father and sister had left a bloody trail behind them, and she did not wish to rule as they had—by fear. She had given her consent to the execution of the six hundred at the time of the rebellion, but that, she assured herself, had had to be, for royalty must be maintained and men must learn that it was a cardinal sin to rise against their ruler. Yet, Burghley would reason with her, had not Norfolk rebelled? Was not the Queen of Scots more worthy of death than those six hundred men?

What he said was true. But Mary was a Queen, and Norfolk was the first peer in the land.

She faced her ministers; she listened to their railings against Mary and Norfolk.

"This error has crept into the heads of a number," said one man, "that there is a person in this land which no law can touch. Warning has already been given her.

Therefore the axe must give the next warning."

"Shall we say," said another, "that our law is not able to provide for such mischief? If this is so it is defective in a high degree. Mercy was shown my lord of Norfolk but no good followed."

Then came the great cry from all: "To the scaffold with that monstrous dragon, that adulteress and murderess. And to the scaffold with the roaring lion of Norfolk."

She temporized as she knew so well how to do. She gave them Norfolk, and on a hot June day he walked out to the scaffold on Tower Hill; but she would not give them Mary.

IX

During these politically troublous times, Robert's private life was providing complications.

Robert, as he himself admitted, was a frail man where women were concerned; yet the Queen did not seem to understand how frail he was in this respect; she did not seem to understand the strain she put upon him. He longed for children. He had two charming nephews of whom he was very fond—Philip and Robert Sidney; they were to him as sons; but he was not a man to be content with his sister's sons.

Burghley had a son of his own. It was true that Robert Cecil was a puny creature, had been hard to rear and had inherited his humped back from his studious mother. Only Robert Dudley, the most virile, the most handsome at Court, was without legitimate children.

His first and most cursed marriage had been a childless one; he knew that was due to Amy and not to himself; he had proved that. But illegitimate children were not what he wanted; to them he could give his affection, but not the Dudley name.

For some years he had been having a very pleasant love affair with Douglass, Lady Sheffield. This was highly dangerous, but his passion for Douglass had been so strong that, to satisfy it, he had been ready to risk discovery and the Queen's displeasure.

He remembered well the beginning of their love affair. The Queen had been on one of her summer pilgrimages which she had insisted should take place every year. A great procession would set out from Greenwich, Hampton or Westminster—the Queen usually on horseback but sometimes in a litter followed by numerous carts containing furnishings and baggage. All must show a gusto to equal her own in these journeys.

The people would come for miles to see her pass, and stage entertainments for her. She loved the easy manners of the people who, she declared, though they might lack the grace of her courtiers, loved her no less than they did.

As to the route which should be followed, she changed her mind again and again. One farmer, having heard that she was to go one way, and then had decided against it before finally taking the road she first intended, shouted beneath the window of the inn where she was staying that night: "Now I know the Queen is but a woman; and she is very like my wife, for neither can make up their minds." Her ladies were shocked. How dared the man thus talk of the Queen? But Elizabeth put her head out of the window and cried to her guards: "Give that man money to shut his mouth."

One man called to the royal coachman to "Stay the cart that I may speak with the Queen!" And the Queen smiling graciously, commanded that the cart be brought to a full stop; and not only did she speak to the man but she gave him her hand to kiss.

These familiarities endeared her to the people.

When she stayed at humble inns, she would insist that the good innkeeper did not beggar himself to entertain her; but when she stayed at noble houses she expected lavish display.

On the occasion of which Robert was thinking, the party rested at Belvoir Castle, the estate of the Earl of Rutland; and among those noblemen who came from the surrounding country to pay homage to the Queen was Lord Sheffield.

The most beautiful woman in that assembly was Douglass, Lady Sheffield. She was of high birth, being a Howard of the Effingham branch; she was young and impressionable.

She had heard of the great Dudley who had recently been created Earl of Leicester and offered as husband to Mary Queen of Scots. Circulating about the country were stories in which the Queen figured largely; the whole of England had gossiped about the love affair, the murder of Amy, the children they had had, and of the Queen's passionate jealousy regarding him. It seemed to Douglass that this Earl of Leicester was not so much a man as a god—often a malignant god, but an intensely fascinating one.

And when she saw him, magnificently attired and sitting his horse as no other sat his, she thought—as others had thought before her—that nowhere in the world and at no time had a man lived to equal the physical perfection of this Robert Dudley.

When Douglass knelt before the Queen, Leicester was beside Her Majesty; and for a moment Douglass saw his eyes upon her. She shivered. This was the man who had planned the murder of his wife for the sake of the Queen. This was the man who some said was the wickedest in England. He was aware of her look. He smiled, and she felt that was one of the most important moments of her life.

There was a banquet and ball that night in Belvoir Castle. The Queen was flirting in her lively fashion with her new favourite, Hatton, and inclined to be tart with Robert. It might have been that she had noticed his glance at the beautiful Lady Sheffield.

Thinking of Douglass, Robert knew, out of his experience, that in her case there would be quick surrender, and felt a sullen anger towards the Queen rising within him. What a life he might have had! What if he had married a woman such as the charming Lady Sheffield? What children they might have had—sons like Philip and Robert Sidney. If he had married the Queen, their son would have been heir to a kingdom. But she was perverse and would rule alone. Amy had died in vain and he had an evil reputation. He had suffered much on account of this, and yet he might have remained married to Amy all these years, for all the difference it had made.

In the dance he found himself next to Douglass.

She was not bold, as Lettice Knollys had been. Lettice had been attracted because of his reputation, Douglass in spite of it. But he was excited by this young woman. Let Elizabeth flirt with her dancing master.

He bent close to Douglass and said: "Fate brings us together."

She started, and he went on: "You have heard evil tales of me. Do not believe them, I beg of you."

"My lord," she began, but he interrupted with: "Come. 'Tis true. Much evil has been spoken against me."

335

She recovered her composure. "We know you here for the great Earl . . . the greatest Earl . . ."

"The wickedest Earl!" he put in. "That saddens me. I would like an opportunity of proving to you that it is not true."

"I . . . I did not believe it," she said.

But the dance had taken her from him. He thought of the pleasure which would be his when she became his mistress. He pictured happy meetings, riding away from Court to meet her at one of his houses; perhaps even arranging that the Sheffields should come to Court. It would be dangerous, but he was in the mood for recklessness.

The dance had brought him to the Queen.

"I have been watching you at the dance, my lord." Her eyes challenged him.

He answered ironically, excited by Douglass who was so young and charming: "I am honoured by Your Majesty's attention. I did not believe that in the dance your Eyes could interest you as do your Lids."

She gave his arm a nip. "You must not be jealous, Robert. There are some who excel at one thing, others at another; some are born dancers, some lovers of women."

"And some fortunate ones, both, Your Majesty."

She gave him her hand and he pressed it fervently. He saw that she was satisfied, and that was what he wished; he wanted no interference with his new experience.

Yet for all his arts and wiles it was not until the last day of his stay at Belvoir Castle that Douglass became his mistress. She feared her husband; he feared the Queen; therefore a meeting was not easy to arrange.

But he was expert at such arrangements. He managed to lure her away from the others during a hunt; he knew of an inn nearby where they might stay awhile to refresh themselves. He was so fascinating, so debonair that he could conduct such matters with skill and charm. To Douglass it seemed that he was all-powerful; and in any case he was quite irresistible.

Yet such an important personage could not absent himself even for a few hours without attracting some attention. Mercifully the Queen did not notice his absence, but there were others to smile behind their hands and to whisper together of my lord's latest amorous adventure.

When the royal party left Belvoir, promises were exchanged between the lovers.

That had happened some time ago, yet Robert had never lost interest in Douglass. She was so charming, so well-bred, being one of the Howards of Effingham; she displayed none of the Tudor tantrums.

Two or three years after their first meeting, Lord Sheffield had unfortunately died. Robert regretted this because Douglass had changed when she became a widow. She was by nature a virtuous woman, and only the great fascination which Robert was able to exert could have made her break her marriage vows; consequently she had suffered much remorse, and she longed for a regular union. Whilst her husband lived, that, happily for Robert, was out of the question; but when he died and a suitable period had elapsed, she began pleading for marriage. She was even more in love with him than she had been during those ecstatic days at Belvoir Castle. It would be the happiest day of her life, she told him, when she could enjoy their union

337

and feel herself to be free from sin.

It was at this time that a new danger presented itself. Douglass came to Court; and her sister, Frances Howard, who was also at Court, became enamoured of Robert. The two sisters were jealous of each other and their jealousy became a subject for gossip.

And as if this were not enough, Douglass continued to plead for marriage.

Robert was charmingly regretful. "But, my dear Douglass, you know my position at Court. You know what I owe to the Queen's favour. I doubt not that I should lose all that I have gained if there was a marriage between us."

"What of a secret marriage, Robert?"

"Do you think such a matter could long be kept secret from the Queen? She has her spies everywhere. And I have my enemies."

"But our love has been a secret."

He smiled wryly at her. If only it had been so, he would have felt much easier in his mind.

"Do you know," he asked her, "what I have risked for your sake?"

"Oh, Robert, if I should bring disaster to you I should never forgive myself."

He would consider it worth while, he told her; but it would be senseless to run unnecessarily into danger.

Then the troublous times had come. The rebellion and the execution of Norfolk had given him other matters with which to occupy his mind. There was a new personality at Court—Sir Francis Walsingham—a protege of Burghley's and a man of great astuteness. He had been ambassador to the Court of France and, when he returned to England, had become a member of the Privy Council. Robert had recognized the dynamic qualities of this dark-skinned man and was trying to win him over to his side, that, if need be, they might stand together against Burghley. These matters took his thoughts from Douglass until it was necessary for her to leave Court because she was to have a child.

Now Douglass was alternately joyful and despairing. She wanted the child but could not bear that it should be born a bastard. How could she explain its existence, she wanted to know. It was some years since her husband had died. Robert *must* marry her now.

Robert himself was torn with indecision. What if the child should be a boy? Had he not always longed for a son? And yet . . . what of the Queen?

Frantically he searched for a solution.

Douglass, retiring though she was, was by no means a calm woman; she was given to bouts of melancholy and hysteria; and Robert was afraid that in her pregnancy these weaknesses might be intensified. He had many enemies, but he also had his supporters. There was his own family; his brothers and sisters and all those connected with the Dudley family looked to him as their leader; if he fell, they would fall too. He had his followers and they were dependent on him, so he could trust their loyalty. He was without doubt a powerful man, but because his power had come to him through his personal qualities rather than his achievements, he regarded it more lightly than a man would have done who had earned it by careful, constant effort. Robert had had much success; he believed he could succeed in what others dared not attempt.

So at last he agreed to go through a form of marriage with Douglass very quietly at Esher, with only a few of his trusted servants as witnesses.

This seemed to him a master-stroke, for he felt sure that the Queen's anger would not be lasting if he were not properly married; and at the same time, as a result of this mock marriage, Douglass could call herself—in secret—the Countess of Leicester, and soothe her qualms.

She was soothed and thought of nothing but preparing for the child.

It was a boy, and they called him Robert.

But their enemies were already whispering one with another that the Earl of Leicester had secretly married, and that it was well known how he and the lady had been lovers before the death of Lord Sheffield.

The *death* of Lord Sheffield! Now how had Lord Sheffield died? Of a catarrh, it was said. Might it not have been an artificial catarrh which stopped his breath?

They only had to cast their minds back to another death. Had they forgotten the poor lady who had been found with her neck broken at the foot of a staircase at Cumnor Place! That was when Lord Robert had thought he might marry the Queen. And now that the Earl of Leicester wished to marry another lady, that lady's husband had most conveniently died.

Such rumours there would always be concerning one so prominent, one who had known such spectacular good fortune.

Robert must make sure these rumours did not reach the ears of the Queen.

News of one of the most horrible massacres the world had ever known came to England.

On the Eve of St. Bartholomew's Day, King Charles with his mother, Catherine de' Medici, and the Duke of Guise had incited the Catholics of Paris to murder thousands of Huguenots assembled in the capital for the wedding of Catherine's daughter, Marguerite, to Henry of Navarre.

The whole Protestant world was shocked and scandalized by the bestial cruelties which had been let loose. The streets of Paris, it was said, were running with the blood of martyrs. Two thousand, it was reported, had been slain in Paris alone; and in Lyons, Orleans and many other cities the horror had been repeated. The noble Coligny himself—known throughout the world as the most honourable of men—was one of the victims; his son-in-law Teligny had followed him, as had many other gentlemen of high reputation.

The little boats were crossing the Channel and thousands of men and women were seeking refuge in England; the whole of the Protestant world was ready to take arms against the Catholics.

Preachers thundered from pulpits; letters of warning were sent to the Queen and her Council, "Death to all Catholics!" cried the people. "Make a treaty of friendship with Germany, with the Netherlands and with Scotland. Stand together against the bloodthirsty idolators. And take that dangerous traitress, the pestilence of Christendom, the adulteress and murderess, Mary of Scotland, without delay to the block. Was it not her relations, the Guises, who had been behind the massacre! The Duke of Guise had conceived the murderous plan in conjunction with that Jezebel, the Italian Catherine de' Medici. The Queen of England was in danger. Let her not bring rape, robbery, violence and murder into the land for the sake of her miserable mercy to a horrible woman who carried the wrath of God with her wherever she went."

Elizabeth was shaken. Like everyone else she daily expected war. She believed that the massacre was a preliminary move in a full campaign of the Catholics against the Protestants. She had all the ports manned; the ships of England were ready. She allowed Burghley and Leicester to persuade her to take some action with regard to Mary; but she would not agree to her execution. Mary was to be sent back to Scotland where she would doubtless be tried for Darnley's murder and executed. Thus Mary would die and Elizabeth be said to have had no hand in her death.

But the months passed and there was no attack by the Catholics. Mary was still detained in England; but Elizabeth and her ministers knew that as long as there were Catholics and Protestants in the world there would be strife in one form or another between them.

Even as she looked at those ministers about her, Elizabeth sensed their irritation with her actions regarding Mary.

Burghley was a stern Protestant. Robert, though not religious, was giving himself to the Protestant cause. Only the Queen remained luke-warm. She would not admit it, but she favoured neither sect. Both provoked bloodshed, and that fact prevented her from approving of either. How could it matter, she would ask herself in secret, whether a man believed the bread of the sacrament to be the body of Christ or blessed bread! What mattered was that she should continue to reign over her people, that her people loved her, and that her country should come to greatness through that peaceful prosperity which only tolerance could bring.

Life flowed more easily in England, although the Queen and her ministers were watching events abroad with an even keener interest than they had before the massacre.

The Dutch, under the Prince of Orange, were rebelling against the Spaniards who, with their relentless Inquisition, had inflicted such cruelty upon them.

Later the Queen issued a law against the wearing of over-sumptuous apparel among the common people, although her own wardrobe had never been so magnificent. There was trouble in Ireland and, to subdue it, Elizabeth had sent over the Earl of Essex who had been Lord Hereford and the husband of Lettice—the central figure in Robert's escapade of some years before.

The King of France died, and Elizabeth, who had considered the Duke of Anjou, who was now Henri Trois of France, as one of her suitors, pretended to be annoyed because he had married unexpectedly.

Wheat was scarce and the price rose to six shillings a bushel. This was disquieting; the people began to murmur.

Then came the threat of war. The Prince of Orange and the Provinces of Zeeland and Holland suggested to Elizabeth that she should become their Queen, but she was stout in her refusal. Her ministers begged and implored. "What!" she cried. "Plunge my people into war with Spain!"

In vain did they protest and point out that she would become the head of the Protestant world. She wanted no part in the wars of religion, she told them. Let others fight such wars. She would remain aloof. She believed that those who stood aside and looked on at the wars of others were the real victors.

That summer she took her usual trip through the countryside. Robert had gone on ahead of the royal party, for the route that year passed through Kenilworth and Robert was to be the Queen's host for twelve days of July. He was determined to prepare such pageants and entertainments as had never before been seen.

He was uneasy as he rode North. He could not help wondering whether she had heard the rumours concerning Lord Sheffield s death; he wondered whether any had dared face her wrath by telling her that Douglass believed herself to be married to him and that he and Douglass had a son.

Elizabeth had been haughty with him recently and it was this that had started those uneasy thoughts. She was more devoted to her old Mutton and Bellwether—her new names for Hatton. She was very fond of her Moor; this was Walsingham, who was swarthy enough to merit the name. Therefore, thought Robert, he must plan such diversions as had never been known, even in the days of Cardinal Wolsey and her father.

Kenilworth Castle was surrounded by nearly twenty miles of rich estates. Robert had spent thousands of pounds beautifying the place and cultivating the land. He was a proud man as he rode through his estates. He wished that his father—who had always been his model—were alive to see him. This year alone the Queen had already seen that fifty thousand pounds had come his way—and that was in addition to the income he received from his many activities.

He no longer hoped for marriage with the Queen, for he now believed that she would never marry. She was a strange woman, not to be judged by ordinary standards. Many rumours circulated concerning her. Some said that she would not marry, knowing herself, on account of an obstruction, to be incapable of sexual intercourse. He knew the Queen better than any living person. He knew that love, for her, was a matter of flattery, compliments, kisses and fond embraces. Her eyes would glisten at the sight of a handsome man; she could not refrain from caressing him. She was indeed a strange woman. She was fond of men, but she was perpetually in love with power. And . . . she wished to linger in romantic lanes, never reaching any definite journey's end.

When arrived at the Castle, a shock awaited him, for Douglass was there, and the child was with her. He was astounded. She should be at one of his manor houses awaiting the day when he could visit her. Although these people who were with him were his friends, he was not entirely sure that he could trust their discretion for ever.

She had evidently decided not to embarrass him. "My dear friend," she said, "I was passing nearby and, hearing of your great plans, called in to give you my help. You will have much to do here and I fancy I can be of some service to you."

Were there amused smiles among the spectators? Was that a frown of anxiety between Philip Sidney's eyes? Robert's nephew loved him as did no other man, and Philip was wise. He scented danger.

Robert's quick wits asserted themselves. "You are good indeed, Lady Sheffield," he said. "I doubt not that I owe much to your kindness."

But he was thinking: What when the Queen is here! And his delight was turned to apprehension.

Elizabeth was very gay as she set out on her journey. With her were all the ladies of the Court, forty earls and more than sixty lords and knights. She was looking forward with pleasure to her arrival at Kenilworth, to see Robert surrounded by that magnificence which he owed to her.

Dear Robert! He was not so young now. To tell the truth the figure which had once been lithe and slender was no longer so; the dark curling hair which she had loved to fondle was thinning and turning grey, and there were pouches under the beautiful eyes. She, who loved him, saw him clearly; all his faults she saw, but they mattered not, for they could not alter her affection. He had not the clever mind of her Sir Spirit or her dear exasperating Moor; yet he had twice their ambition. He was—she would confess to herself—a little too careful of his health; he loved taking a physic; she often smiled to hear the earnestness with which he discussed a new cure with another such as himself. She herself defied pain; she would never admit she had any. She defied death and old age.

She could scarcely take her mind off the pleasures in

store and give attention to serious matters.

Peters and Turwert, the two anabaptists from Holland, were to be burnt at the stake while she was out of her capital. She had had many letters concerning these men. Bishop Foxe, whose chief concern was with martyrs, had written to her begging her not to sully her name, her reign and the Reformed Church by emulating the Catholics. Bishop Foxe and those who agreed with him did not understand. She must not come into the open as a supporter of anabaptists. Philip of Spain was watching. If only her people knew how she dreaded that man, how in her heart she knew that he, with that fanatical fervour she had once glimpsed in his eyes, was waiting for the day when he and the Catholic community would dominate the world, and all men would go in fear of the Inquisition!

She did not concern herself overmuch with these two Dutchmen. She was, like her father, not given to brooding over torture inflicted on others.

There was another matter which offered more pleasing reflection.

Catherine de' Medici—now that her beloved son Henri was King of France and a married man—was hoping that Elizabeth might reconsider as a suitor her younger son, he who had been Alencon and, since his brother had become King, taken his brother's title of Duke of Anjou.

Elizabeth found it amusing to play at courtship again.

The little man was quite ugly, she had been told; but the French ambassador—that most charming La Mothe Fenelon—was loud in his praises. The little Duke, he intimated, was beside himself with love for the English Queen; and if she were older than he was, he liked her for that. He was no callow youth to enjoy mere girls. Elizabeth had also heard that he was a little pock-marked, which she had said, made her hesitate. Catherine de' Medici wrote to Elizabeth saying that she knew of an excellent remedy which, it was claimed, would remove all trace of the pox and make the skin smooth again. Elizabeth replied that this was excellent news; and they must at once have the remedy applied to the face of the Duke.

And now . . . to Kenilworth.

It was July and very warm when the procession arrived at Long Ichington, which was six or seven miles from the Castle. Here Robert had erected a tent in which a banquet was prepared.

The Queen, in good humour and most affectionate, would have Robert sit beside her; and when the banquet was over, Robert had a fat boy, six years old, brought to her—the fattest she had ever seen, but so foolish as to be unable to understand that she was his Queen. After the fat boy, she was invited to inspect an enormous sheep: the biggest of their kind, these two, and both bred on Roberts territory. The Queen laughed immoderately, and this was a good beginning.

They left the tent and followed the chase which was to lead them to Kenilworth Castle.

The Queen, at the head of the chase, kept Robert beside her, and while he pointed out with pride all the beauties and richness of the scene, he said: "I owe all this to my dearest mistress. May I die the moment I forget it!"

She was pleased, and as she was reluctant to give up

the hunt, there was little daylight left when they reached the gates of Kenilworth Park.

In the Park, pageants greeted her. Smiling, she acknowledged the greetings of all; and when she reached the castle itself, there at the entrance stood a man of immense stature, carrying a club and keys. As she approached he expressed surprise at the magnificence of the company, until, affecting to see the Queen for the first time, he went on with great wonder:

"Oh, God, a priceless pearl!
No worldly wight, I doubt—some sovereign goddess sure!
In face, in hand, in eye, in other features all,
Yes, beauty, grace and cheer—yea, port and majesty,
Shew all some heavenly peer with virtues all beset.
Come, come, most perfect paragon, pass on with joy and bliss:
Have here, have here, both club and keys, myself, my ward, I yield.
E'en gates and all, my lord himself, submit and seek your shield."

The Queen smiled happily; she loved such eulogies; and she loved this particularly because it had been designed by her Robert.

As the company passed through the castle gates, Robert saw, for the first time, one in that company who made his heart leap with sudden pleasure.

Lettice Knollys had come to Kenilworth.

349

Robert conducted the Queen to her chamber. Through the windows she could see the fireworks which made a good display in the Park, a sign to the countryside that the Queen had come to Kenilworth. At intervals the guns boomed forth. It was as though a King entertained a Queen. And that was how Elizabeth would have it.

"Robert," she said, "you are a lavish spender."

"Who could spend too lavishly in the entertainment of Your Majesty?"

She gave him the familiar tap on the cheek, thinking: Age cannot take his charm from him. It is there just as it was in the days of his flaming youth; and now he is a subtler man, and I doubt not many would love him still; yet he has remained unmarried for my sake.

"I shall remember my stay in Kenilworth to the end of my days," she said. Then, to hide her emotion, added: "The clock there has stopped."

He smiled. "All clocks in the Castle were stopped the moment Your Majesty entered.'

She "pupped" her lips and raised her eyebrows.

"Time stands still for goddesses," he said.

That was a nice touch and typical of Robert.

He took her hand and kissed it. "You have promised to rest here for twelve days. During that time we will forget clocks. We will forget all but the entertaining of Your Majesty."

"There was never one like you . . . never!" she said tenderly.

"Madam," he answered, "a goddess might lose her Mutton and her Bellwether, her attendant Moor, and even her Spirit; but her Eyes do her better service than any of these."

"Mayhap there's truth in that," she said. "Now leave me, Robin. I am tired with the day's journey."

He bowed over her hand and raised it to his lips.

She was smiling affectionately after he had gone.

In a corridor he came face to face with Lettice, and he knew that she had waylaid him. She was more beautiful than she had been in those days when he had first attracted her. She was no longer Lady Hereford, for her husband had been made Earl of Essex. She seemed bolder, and because of that faint resemblance to the Queen which came from her grandmother, Mary Boleyn, she reminded him of the young Elizabeth whom he had known in the Tower of London.

"A merry day to you, my lord," she said.

"I knew not that you would come."

"You remember me?"

"Remember! I do indeed."

"I am honoured. So the great Earl of Leicester forgets me not! The most honoured man in the realm—by the Queen if not by the people—does not forget a humble woman on whom he once looked without disfavor." Her eyes flashed angrily. She was reminding him that he had dropped her while their affair had still promised much enjoyment to them both.

"How could a man look with disfavour on one so beautiful?" he asked.

"He might if his mistress commanded him to do so . . . if he were so much her creature that he dared do no other."

"I am no one's creature!" he retorted haughtily.

She came nearer and lifted her brown eyes to his face. "Then you have changed, my lord," she mocked.

Robert was never at a loss. He could not with any credit to himself explain his neglect in words, so he embraced her and kissed her. Such kisses were more adequate than any words could have been.

Douglass came to his apartment, bringing her boy with her. Poor Douglass! She felt that their son might appeal to his affections, even if she could not.

He dismissed his servants, trusting he could rely on their loyalty.

"It was foolish of you to come here," he burst out when they were alone.

"But, Robert, it is so long since I saw you. The boy so longed to see you."

He lifted the boy in his arms. It seemed to him dangerously obvious that this little Robert had the Dudley looks. The child smiled and put his arms about Robert's neck. He loved this handsome glittering man, although he did not know that he was his father.

"Well, my boy. What have you to say to me?"

"This is a big castle," said the boy.

"And you like it, eh?"

The boy nodded, staring in fascination at his father's face.

"Mamma says that it is Kenilworth."

Had she said: "You are the rightful heir to Kenilworth!" No! she would not dare.

He held the boy against him. For the sake of this child he was almost ready to acknowledge Douglass as his wife. He would have been proud to have taken young Robert by the hand and introduce him to the company. "Behold my son!" What consternation those words would cause.

The Queen would never forgive him; and indeed, he was weary of this boy's mother. Her meek compliance and her suppressed hysteria reminded him uncomfortably of Amy. Why could not these women fall out of love as easily as he could?

Lettice was a different kind of woman; and Lettice too had a fine son. She had called him Robert. Was that in memory of Robert Dudley? This boy of hers, now eight years old, was of outstanding beauty. Why should Lettice not give him sons?

He thought of their embrace in the corridor. They were two experienced people, he and Lettice; she could give him much that he had hoped for all his life, and which, because of the Queen, he had missed: pleasure, children and family life.

Lettice had a husband. Robert shrugged his shoulders. Then he looked at Douglass, who was watching him closely, and it seemed to him that he heard the mocking laughter of Amy Robsart in that room.

He said angrily: "Have a care! This is a great indiscretion. If the Queen should discover aught, this might not only be the end of me but of you."

She fell down on to her knees and covered her face with her hands. "Oh, Robert, I will take care. I promise you . . . she shall not know."

"You should never have come here," he reproved her.

But the boy, seeing his mother's distress, began to cry, and, picking him up to comfort him, Robert thought: If his mother were another woman—not one of whom I am heartily tired—if she were Lettice, I believe I would marry her for the sake of this boy.

The next day, being a Sunday, all the company went to church; and later in the day there was a banquet more splendid than that of the previous day; there was dancing and music, and as soon as darkness came, the sky was illumined with greater and better displays of fireworks; and the guns boomed once more.

During that day three women thought often of their host, each longingly, each in her own way in love with him.

There was Douglass—apprehensive and nervous —knowing that he no longer loved her and that, but for the child, he would have wished he had never loved her; it seemed to her that throughout the Castle of Kenilworth there was an air of foreboding, of warning perhaps from another woman who had been Robert's wife and whom he had found an encumbrance.

The Queen thought of him tenderly—the best loved of all men in her life. Even Thomas Seymour had never excited her as Robert did; she doubted whether, had Thomas lived, he could have held her affection as did this man. For all Robert's weaknesses she loved him now as once she had loved him for his strength. In those glorious days of youth when he had been the hero of the tiltyard, she had loved him as the most perfect and virtuous man she knew. Now she knew him to be neither perfect nor virtuous, yet she loved him still. She was the very contented guest at Kenilworth.

Lettice's thoughts were all of him. She wanted Robert for her lover, but she was no Douglass to be taken up and cast aside. If Robert Dudley became her lover she must become the Countess of Leicester. She brooded and smiled, for she was a woman who, when she wanted something badly, had found that it invariably fell into her hands.

The days were hot and sultry. The Queen kept within the castle until five in the evening, when she would ride forth with a great company of ladies and gentlemen to hunt in the surrounding country. There was always a pageant to greet her on her return to Kenilworth Park, and each day's pageant strove to be more grand, more splendid than the last.

But the first day's pleasure was clouded as the days passed. Perhaps she was tired of listening to speeches concerning her own virtues. Robert was preoccupied, and she had an uneasy feeling that this was not only due to the vast pains he was taking to entertain her. He was looking worn and strained.

She brought her horse close to his and asked: "Are you not sleeping well, my lord?"

He started, and such a look of guilt came into his face that her fears were increased. She suspected an entanglement with a woman. She knew Robert's nature. It was to his eternal credit that he had remained outwardly faithful to her; but surely at such a time he would not dare to think of another woman.

"You start!" she said harshly. "Is it a crime then, not to sleep?"

"It should be a crime to be laid at my door, Your Majesty, if *you* did not sleep whilst under my roof."

"We were not discussing my rest, but yours."

"I feared that Your Majesty had been put in mind of the matter because of your own ill rest. I beg of you to tell me if your chamber be not to your liking. We will have it changed. We will have an apartment refurnished for you."

She tapped him sharply on the arm. "A plain question demands a plain answer, my lord; and it should be given its reward . . . unless it is feared that the giving might not please."

"My dearest lady, I would not wish to trouble you with my ailments."

"So you are sick again?"

"It is naught but an internal humour."

She laughed aloud in her relief. "You eat too much, my lord."

"I could not expect Your Majesty to do full justice to my table unless I did so also. You might think I disdained that which had been prepared for your royal palate."

"Then 'tis just a sickness of the body. I feared it might be an indisposition of the mind that kept you awake at night."

Sensing her suspicion, he said: "Your Majesty shall know the truth. It is a woman."

He saw her quick intake of breath and he turned to her with all the passionate fervour of which he was capable. "Knowing that she whom I love lies beneath my roof," he said, "how could I sleep at night unless she lay with me."

The Queen whipped her horse and galloped ahead; but he had seen the pleased smile on her face.

"My lord," she said over her shoulder, "you are

offensive. Pray do not ride beside me. I do not wish to scold my host, yet so great is my anger that I fear I shall do so."

Nevertheless he kept beside her. "Your Majesty . . . nay . . . Elizabeth, sweetest Elizabeth as you were to me in the Tower . . . you have forgotten, but I shall remember till I die. You put too great a strain upon me."

She spurred on her horse; and she did not speak to him again, but all her good humour was restored; and when the hart was caught alive in a pool, she cried: "Do not kill him. I am in a merciful mood. I will grant him his life, on condition that he loses his ears for a ransom."

And she herself cut off the poor creature's ears, and smiling, watched him rush bewildered away with the blood dripping from his head. Then she called out: "Where is mine host? Why is he not beside me?"

Robert came to her and they rode side by side back to Kenilworth.

"I trust, my lord," she said primly, "that you will not so far forget yourself again. I might not be so lenient if you were to do so."

"I would not swear it," he answered. "I am but a man, and perchance must take the consequences of my rash speech."

And while he complimented her he was thinking of Lettice and the many passionate meetings between them, the delight they found in each other, the sudden surrender of both which would not be checked, the knowledge that nothing on earth could keep them apart, nor stem the violent passion which they each had for the other.

And if Elizabeth discovered this? He kept thinking of the trapped animal with the haunted look in his eyes as she had stood over him with the knife; he thought of the blood-lust of the huntress which showed in her face; and he thought of the poor creature, running from them. That was the Queen's mercy.

In the Park a pageant was awaiting her. A tall man, dressed as the god Sylvanus, stood before her and recited a eulogy of her charms. But she tired of his oration before he reached the end and, turning her horse, rode on. But the young poet, not to be outdone, and determined to serve his master in the praise of Her Majesty, ran beside her horse, declaiming her virtues; and she, with a wry smile, pulled up, for he was clearly suffering from loss of breath.

He bowed before her. "Your Majesty," he said, "if it is your wish to proceed, pray do so. If my rude speech doth not offend your royal ears, I can run and speak for twenty miles or so. I would rather run as Your Majesty's footman than be a god on horseback in heaven."

She rewarded the man with a smile and gracious words, for she liked that tribute better than his verses. "I like," she said, "that which comes from the heart better than that learned by it."

But when Sylvanus had finished his speech, he broke the branch he was carrying, and threw it from him. Unfortunately it fell near the Queen's horse which reared violently.

There was immediate consternation, but the Queen, controlling her horse, cried out: "No hurt! No hurt!" Then she turned to console Sylvanus who was beside himself with grief.

Robert brought his horse close to the Queen's. "Your Majesty," he said, "I pray you let us go into the castle. I feel your precious person will be safer there."

He was apprehensive as they entered the castle.

It had been an exciting day with the bears. Ban dogs, which had been kept locked away were suddenly let loose on thirteen of them. The noise, the shrieks, the growls and the tearing of flesh had set the Queen's eyes sparkling.

The sun was hot and the Queen and some of her ladies were sitting in the shade of the trees on one of the lawns when a small boy made his way towards them.

He stood still and stared at the Queen. He was such a handsome little boy and the Queen, being fond of all handsome people, including children, called to him: "What is it, my little man? Have you come to see the Queen?"

"Yes," said the boy.

"Then come closer that the Queen may see you."

He came, his eyes wide. He laid his hands on her knees and looked up into her face. "You *are* a beautiful lady," he said.

Nothing could have delighted her more.

"You are handsome enough yourself," she answered. "You know who I am. Now tell me who you are."

"I am Robert," said the child.

She laughed. "That is my favourite name."

He smiled and touched one of the aglets on her gown; as he bent his little head to study it she noticed how the dark hair curled about his neck. Involuntarily she put out a hand to touch it.

"What do you here, my child?"

He looked at her in astonishment.

"Who brought you?" she asked.

"My Mamma."

"And who is your Mamma?"

"My Mamma!" he said with surprise.

"Of a certainty. How foolish of your Queen!" she beckoned to one of her women. "Whose boy is this, do you know?"

"My lady Sheffield's, Your Majesty."

The Queen frowned. "Sheffield died some time ago, did he not? I thought it long ago. How old are you, little one?"

"Three."

Robert, seeing from afar that his son was with the Queen, felt dismayed and angry that this should be so. Who was responsible for this? He hesitated, wondering how much damage had been done, and whether it would be wiser now or later to face anything that had to be faced. He decided to go straight to the Queen and discover the worst.

He quickly realized that this was a mistake for, as soon as the child saw him, he deserted the Queen and running to Robert caught him about the knees and looked up at him with an expression which clearly indicated that this was not their first meeting.

With perfect naturalness Robert picked him up and said: "And what is this, and what do you here?"

The boy laughed and pulled at Robert's beard.

"The young man seems very familiar with the Earl of Leicester," said the Queen; and Robert fancied he heard the sharp note of suspicion in her voice.

"Who would not be friends with a boy like this?" he said lightly. He put down the boy and came to kneel before the Queen; he took her hand and asked if his humble entertainment left anything to be desired.

"We are being well entertained," said Elizabeth with a trace of tartness.

The boy again trotted up.

"Whose son is this?" asked the Queen, looking at Robert.

"Lady Sheffield's."

"She is not of the Court now."

"You remember Sheffield, Your Majesty. He was a friend of mine. His widow, with the boy, her friends and servants, has been resting here at Kenilworth while I was at Court. Then, Your Majesty, they expressed such a desire to see you that I could not turn them away."

"We do not remember having seen *them*. Why have they not been presented?"

"Lady Sheffield has been indisposed."

"I will see her at once."

"I will myself inform her of Your Majesty's pleasure."

"Let a servant go to her and command her to come to me."

Robert turned in order to see if there was any servant, whom he could trust, within reach. He saw such a man and called to him.

"Her Majesty wishes Lady Sheffield to come to her. Pray bring her here."

"I will, my lord."

"And," added Robert, "take the boy with you. Doubtless his nurse will be looking for him."

The servant went away with young Robert, while his father fervently hoped that Douglass would do what was expected of her.

The Queen talked of the bears, and how she had enjoyed the spectacle. But all the time Robert sensed that she was watching him closely.

To his great relief the servant came back alone.

"Lady Sheffield sends her thanks to Your Most Gracious Majesty. Lady Sheffield is distraught because she is so unwell that she cannot leave her bed. She begs that Your Majesty, with your well-known clemency, will excuse her for this occasion."

"We will," said the Queen. "Yet will we see her before we leave. We will visit her in her bedchamber if need be. But tell her now that we excuse her for this day."

Robert felt almost gay.

"I seem to have seen that boy before," said the Queen.

"I am fond of him," said Robert, "and I have a reason for being so."

She was alert.

"He reminds me of a boy I knew long ago . . . in the Tower of London. I was a desolate prisoner and he took flowers from me to a goddess whom I adored from the moment I saw her."

Such flattery was food and drink to Elizabeth. She remembered too.

"He was a pleasant child," she said, "but methinks he lacked the good looks of this young Robert."

Robert went on: "I remember the day you came by, and I looked through my prison bars. I firmly believe that I have never been happier in the whole of my life than I was then."

"A poor life has been yours, my lord, if your best moments were those of a poor prisoner. Is that the way for a proud man to talk?"

"It is indeed, gracious Majesty, for then I had hopes . . . great hopes. I dreamed of love . . . of a perfect being. But alas, my dreams were only partly fulfilled. I had high hopes once."

"A man should never give up hope, my lord. Surely you know that. Never as long as he lives."

"But, Madam, what is a man to do when he finds the woman he loves is a goddess, above all earthly desires and needs?"

"He might become a god. Gods may mate with goddesses."

So did he delight her with this flattering conversation, luring her away from a train of thought which, started by a handsome boy named Robert who had something of the Dudley looks, might have led to grave disaster.

Robert and Lettice met in a quiet chamber of the castle. Their meetings must be brief for they must not both be missed at the same time; and Robert was expected to be in constant attendance upon the Queen.

Meetings were very precious. Lettice might have urged him to recklessness, but she was looking far ahead. Once she had lost him through the Queen, and she was determined not to do so again.

She said to him as they lay behind locked doors in that small room: "And what afterwards?"

"We must see each other," he said, "and often."

"How so?"

"Doubtless it can be arranged."

"The Queen watches you as a dog watches a rabbit.

And what when my husband returns from Ireland?"

"Essex must not return from Ireland."

"How can that be prevented when his task is completed?"

"There will be a way."

"There may be a way. But *we* shall not meet. There is too much to prevent our doing so."

"We shall," he insisted. "We must."

"I would that we might marry. I long for that. To live graciously . . . without these secret meetings . . . to have sons like my own Robert, but your sons."

"You cannot know how fervently I wish that."

"Will you spend the rest of your days behaving like the Queen's lap-dog, yapping at her heels, cowering from her anger, being taken up and set down at the whim of a moment?"

"Nay!" he said passionately.

She strained herself against him. "Should we not mould our own lives, Robert? Were we not meant to marry, to have children?"

"You are right. We were meant to. But," he added, "there is Essex."

She was silent for a while, then she said: "Mean you, my lord, that only Essex stands between our marriage . . . not the Queen?"

"But for Essex we would marry. We could keep that secret from the Queen."

She said quietly: "It would have to be a true marriage. My family would insist on that. My sons would be your heirs . . . nothing less."

"Nothing less," he repeated.

"And only Essex is between us and that?"

"Only Essex."

He thought of the boy whom she had borne Essex—young Robert Devereux—one of the tallest and most beautiful children he had ever seen. Such would his sons be if he married Lettice. He loved Douglass' boy, but not enough to make Douglass his true wife.

Her next words startled him: "How much do you love me?"

He answered: "Infinitely."

He knew then that she was thinking of Amy Robsart; and next day, during the water pageant he had planned for the Queen's delight, he also was thinking of Amy.

Douglass knelt before the Queen. She had never been so frightened in the whole of her life. She had scarcely seen Robert since the Queen had come to Kenilworth. He had paid one visit to her to tell her how she must conduct herself before the Queen. He had been cold, and she had sensed his deep anger; and that anger she knew was directed against herself.

She knew too that he was in love with the Countess of Essex. She had heard it whispered. They could not keep it secret as they would wish; it showed in their faces when they looked at each other. Pray God the Queen did not notice. No one would tell her, for she would not thank the one who did, and that person would gain the eternal enmity of the Earl of Leicester.

And now who knew what questions the Queen would ask of Douglass whose mind was not quick and clever. She prayed that she might find the right answers.

The Queen was in a mellow mood. She bade

Douglass rise while she studied her closely. Douglass had been a beautiful woman, but the days and nights of strain had left their mark upon her face in dark shadows under her eyes; and an air of drooping melancholy could not be hidden from the Queen.

He may have loved her once, mused Elizabeth, but he no longer does.

"Come, Lady Sheffield, sit beside us. We hear you have been indisposed, and we are sorry."

"Your Majesty is most gracious."

"It is a pity indeed that you have missed those pageants which have been prepared for our delight. Our host has surpassed even himself, and we have rarely been so entertained. We hear you had some hand in the arrangements."

"Oh, no, Your Majesty. My husband was a friend of the Earl's who graciously gave me permission to rest here whilst he was at Court. And so did I. I confess that a desire to see Your Majesty made me delay my departure."

"Well, you have seen me now. I trust you are pleased with the sight. Have I changed since you served at Court?"

"Your Majesty performs the miracle of growing more beautiful with the passing years."

"You have a charming son."

"Yes, Your Majesty."

"Named Robert, eh?"

"Yes, Your Majesty."

"The Earl seems fond of him."

"The Earl, like Your Majesty, has a fondness for children."

"That's so. And the boy is three years old, I hear."

"Yes, Your Majesty."

"I remember your husband . . . Sheffield."

Elizabeth had the pleasure of watching the flush spread from Douglass' neck to her brow, and the circumstances seemed clear to her. But she was sure the affair was over, so she was only mildly annoyed; her wicked Robert, she told herself, must be given a little licence.

But she must be sure that the affair was over. She would keep the woman where she might see how she behaved in the future.

She said: "Lady Sheffield, I like your manners. You shall join us in our journeyings, and when we return to Court there will be a place for you in the bedchamber."

Douglass fell to her knees in gratitude. Her joy shone from her eyes. If she were at Court, she would see Robert constantly.

A few days after that interview the royal procession left Kenilworth.

The Queen was thrown into a flutter of excitement by the arrival at Court of Monsieur Simiers, for this energetic little Frenchman came on a romantic mission; he came on behalf of his master, the Duke of Anjou, to ask for the Queen's hand in marriage.

Elizabeth, certain now that Douglass' child was also Robert's, felt the need for a little courtship, and she welcomed Monsieur Simiers graciously.

Very soon the young man became her Monkey (because of his name, she told him, but his features did suggest the name) and he was seen walking with her, riding with her, sitting beside her; in fact he seemed scarcely ever out of her presence. He was practised in all the arts at which the French excelled—dancing, paying compliments, adoring her with his eyes, hinting that he would barter twenty years of his life if he might be her lover in reality and not as proxy for another.

She bestowed upon him all the favours which she was wont to bestow on others; and his was the cheek which was affectionately tapped, his the arm on which she leaned, his the lips which kissed her hands. Her Monkey put her Eyes, her Lids and her old Bellwether into the shade.

It was all a little ridiculous for, although she was well over forty, she was behaving like a girl of sixteen—and a frivolous lovesick one at that.

So absorbed was she with her Monkey that she scarcely noticed that the Earl of Essex was back in England and that there seemed to be burning within him a smouldering anger.

When Robert informed her that Essex's work was not completed in Ireland and that he must therefore be sent back at once, she gave her consent and the Earl went most reluctantly.

Essex had been back in Ireland little more than a month when the news came that he had died of a flux; and there were rumours that his death was not a natural one.

Elizabeth snatched a few moments from the society of her Monkey to discuss this matter with Robert.

"What think you?" she asked. "Doubtless the man had his enemies. I like not these rumours."

Robert answered: "Rumour must be quashed. There shall be an inquest, and my brother-in-law Sidney, as the Deputy of Ireland, will see that it is carried out in a fitting manner."

"Let that be done then."

And it was, for Sir Henry Sidney was able to report that the death of the Earl of Essex was due to natural causes.

Shortly afterwards a man who had been closely connected with Essex died similarly. This man had uttered wild words; he had said that a very notable person in England had so urgently wished for the death of my lord of Essex that he had sent his professional poisoners to Ireland to despatch him; and as those in charge of the inquest had been very near to that notable person, and their fortunes wrapped in his, the matter was not sifted as it might otherwise have been.

But this man was of no standing, and his death did not call for the investigation which had followed that of the Earl of Essex.

Kat, hearing the rumours, was frightened.

The gossip in her longed to disclose to the Queen all she had heard. But Kat loved her royal mistress even more than she loved gossip. The murder of Essex could mean only one thing: Leicester must this time be so deeply in love that he was considering marriage. It was all very well for Elizabeth to flirt with her Monkey, to speak of the charms of her dear Bellwether. Lightly she loved these men; but there was one whom she truly loved.

If she had married him, reasoned Kat, she would have been happier than she was without him. She would still have been the Queen and he would have had to obey her. She had chosen the wrong man if she expected him meekly to accept a position which was well-nigh intolerable.

She said to Elizabeth when they were alone:

"Dearest Majesty, this Monkey and his master . . . you are not serious?"

"I am."

"Would you then marry a man so much younger than yourself?"

"Am I so old then? Am I so ugly?"

"You are the youngest lady in the world—but that is in spirit, sweetheart. You are the most beautiful; but he is small and puny; and his skin is pock-marked."

"How do you know?"

"We have heard it; and even his mother admits he has not the stature of his brother."

"You meddle, Kat."

" 'Tis because of my love."

"I know that. But I want no meddling."

"Darling, why did you not marry him whom you truly love?"

"I know not whom you mean."

"Ah yes, you do, darling. You have loved him long and he has loved you . . . and he is the one for you, and you for him."

"Leicester!" she snapped; and her face hardened.

Was she thinking of Lady Sheffield and her child? wondered Kat. Or had she heard of the greater menace that was to come from the Countess of Essex?

Kat did not know and dared not ask; but she believed that it must be of Lady Sheffield that the Queen was thinking, for she would be less composed if she knew of his liaison with Lettice.

"What!" she cried. "Shall I so far forget myself as to prefer a poor servant of my own making to the first Prince in Christendom?"

Kat shook her head and was filled with sorrow.

"God preserve your Majesty from all unhappiness," she murmured.

And Elizabeth lifted a hand to pat Kat's arm affectionately.

Robert was on his way to a meeting with Douglass. He had asked her to come that day to the Close Arbour in the grounds about Greenwich Palace.

He was worried concerning Douglass who was becoming hysterical now that she guessed something of his plans regarding Lettice. Douglass had a post in the Queen's bedchamber and that was a highly dangerous situation, since it brought her into close contact with the Queen.

He had made up his mind.

He had heard of Elizabeth's words to Kat Ashley; and he was sure now that, for many years, she had had no intention of marrying. Perhaps if he had never married Amy, if he had been free when they were both young, there would have been a different story to tell. But it was too late to think of that. He wanted children. He thought often of all the fine young men about the Court today who were the sons of his contemporaries. There were boys like Philip and Robert Sidney, and Bacon's son Francis; there was Lettice's own son Robert Devereux, since his father's death, the Earl of Essex; and even Burghley's son, young Robert Cecil, though humpbacked and far from prepossessing, was a son. The Queen was fond of him in spite of his lack of beauty, and this was not only because he was his father's son; his keen wits and alert intelligence made him a son of whom to be proud; even the Queen, who could not tolerate ugliness, had a fondness for him and had christened him her Pigmy. And he, Robert, had no legitimate son! Come what may, he had decided to marry Lettice.

Accompanying him to this tryst with Douglass were a few of his trusted servants, those whose fortunes were so closely bound with his own that they dared not betray him even if they wished to do so.

Douglass was waiting for him.

He posted several of his men outside the Close Arbour that he might be warned of the approach of any whom he would not wish to witness this meeting between himself and Douglass.

She was pale and trembling.

He smiled kindly at her and, laying his hand on her shoulder said: "You must not be afraid, Douglass. As you know, I have long both loved and liked you. I have always found that earnest and faithful affection in you which has bound me greatly to you. Douglass, that still exists, does it not?"

"It does," she answered.

"But I made clear, did I not; on my first coming to you, in what sort my good will should and must always remain to you? It seemed to me that you were fully disposed to accept this."

"It was before the child was born," she said.

"But I had made my meaning clear ere that time. Had I not told you that I was not free to marry, that if I did and the Queen should hear of it, I were undone, disgraced and cast out of favour for ever?"

"Yes, but that was before the child came . . . and we were married."

"It was no true marriage, Douglass. It was entered into for the sake of your peace of mind. You have no claim on me, but I will give you seven hundred pounds a year if you will disclaim that false ceremony and forget that it happened."

"I could not do it."

"You must," he insisted.

"I must think of my son. Shall he face the world as a bastard?"

"We must all face the world as we are, my dear. Have no fear as to his future. I will watch him as carefully and with as much love and affection as though he were my legitimate son."

"I cannot. I cannot. I believe he is your legitimate son. He is your heir."

"Think over what I have said. Take the money I offer. Accept my good services for your son; for if you do not, what good can come to yourself and to him? I should never see you again and you would have no money from me. But take this income; admit there was no marriage; and all will go well with you and with him."

She shook her head and began to weep as he took his leave of her.

Douglass lay on her bed. Her women stood round her. She had long lain staring at the tester, and those about her feared for her sanity.

One of her maids, who had been with her since she was a child, had wept bitterly when she had witnessed her mistress's infatuation for the Earl of Leicester.

Now this good servant dismissed the women and sat by her mistress's bed, quietly watching her; and when she saw that the tears had started to flow down Douglass's cheeks she came nearer and said quietly:

"Dearest mistress, do as he asks. It is the only way. Remember Amy Robsart . . . and remember what has recently befallen a gentleman in Ireland."

Douglass did not answer her but asked that her child be brought to her.

The boy knelt on the bed and asked her why she was so sad; but she merely shook her head and said: "It will pass."

"I know of one who could make you happy," he said. "I will find him and bring him to you."

Wearily she shook her head.

"But you are always happy when the great Earl comes to see you . . . and so am I!"

She looked at him sadly and, drawing him to her, she kissed him.

"You and I will be happy together, my darling," she said at last.

But she seemed to hear a voice warning her: "Be wise. Remember Amy Robsart!"

Robert and Lettice were married at Kenilworth that summer. They were reckless, both of them; yet they strove to keep their secret from the Queen.

Lettice's family heard what had happened, and insisted that the ceremony be repeated under their auspices at their house in Wanstead. They were not going to see their daughter in the position of poor Douglass Howard.

The Knollys family had been greatly disturbed when they heard of their daughter's infatuation, and at the lengths to which it had carried her and the Earl. No one in the kingdom believed Robert guiltless of the murder of his first wife, and now the name of Essex was added to his victims. Rumours concerning him had multiplied, and yet, oddly enough, the news of the marriage had so far not reached the Queen.

But when Lettices family had assured themselves that Robert could not repudiate the marriage even if he wished to do so, and when they considered his power and his Protestant leanings, they realized the great advantages which could accrue from a connexion between their house and his.

Philip of Spain had carried his persecution too far when he had set up the Inquisition in the Netherlands. William the Silent was leading his people against the tyranny and fanatical cruelties of the Spaniards. It was more than a local struggle. It was a world-wide struggle between Protestants and Catholics; and the Knollys's—that great Protestant family—wished to see England join in the struggle; they held, as did many statesmen, that the Queen's aversion from war might lead the country to disaster, and that refusal to join the smaller conflict with friends might leave her to face a greater one alone. If Spain were victorious in the Netherlands, undoubtedly Philip's savage fanaticism would be turned against the greatest stronghold of Protestantism in the world, which was England.

The Protestant Party must stand firm and strengthen itself in every way possible; and, in marrying a daughter of the foremost Protestant house, it was considered that Robert had abandoned his lukewarm profession of Protestantism and was now its staunch ally. Robert's nephew, Philip Sidney, had married the daughter of another great Protestant, Sir Francis Walsingham. So now, as one of the greatest statesmen of the day, by his marriage with Lettice Robert found himself looked upon as the leader of the Protestant Party. And the Protestant Party opposed the Queen's marriage with the Duke of Anjou.

Meanwhile Elizabeth continued to flirt with her Monkey, who was becoming more and more impatient with the passing of every day.

Would not Her Majesty allow him to bring her the marriage contracts? he was continually asking. His master was well-nigh sick with love of her.

She became perverse, as she always was when matters were being driven towards a conclusion.

"Dear Monkey," she said, "I could not decide on marrying a man whom I have not seen."

"Madame, I assure you he is the most handsome Prince in Christendom."

"We have heard views to the contrary."

"If he lacks a little in stature, he makes up for it in the bigness of his heart, Your Majesty."

"But those pock-marks! I think of them often."

"Now that his beard has grown, they are scarcely visible."

"And the French are such deceivers. I think of his father who kept a mistress to whom he did more honour than to his wife."

"He is more enamoured of Your Majesty than any man ever was—even of his mistress."

"As for his grandfather, I am too modest to speak of his conduct."

"Ah! The Duke comes from a family of great lovers."

"Lovers of women who were not their wives!"

"Those Kings loved incomparable women. King Francois loved above all others Madame de

376

Chateaubriand and Madame d'Etampes; but these, Madame, were goddesses, not women. And my master's father, great Henri Deux, loved throughout his life Diane de Poitiers. She too was a goddess. But there is one goddess incomparably beyond all others, a hundred times more beautiful, a thousand times more fascinating. She wears the crown of England; and I swear on my life that when my master sees her he will never think of another woman."

"All the same I should wish to see a man before I married him!"

"Then, Your Majesty, allow me to bring him to you."

"I am but a woman, dear Monkey. My ministers command me. They speak against the marriage."

"The greatest Queen on Earth in fear of her ministers!"

"And my people . . . they murmur against the marriage."

"Are you not their ruler, Madame?"

"In the long run rulers rule only by the will of their people."

Simiers was growing angry. Always there was hope and then this perpetual frustration. Sometimes he felt it was all more than he could endure.

He knew who his enemies were. He realized that he was being outwitted by the Protestant Party, and at the head of that Party was the man who had on more than one occasion prevented the Queen's marrying a French suitor.

The climax came when the Queen invited Monsieur Simiers to accompany her in her barge from Hampton to Greenwich. Elizabeth had been in conversation with

Simiers and, as soon as the Frenchman took his leave of her, a shot rang out. It had been fired from a nearby boat.

There was great consternation, and in the confusion, the marksman, in his boat, made off. One of the Queen's bargemen lay on the deck of the royal barge, shot through the arm.

The Queen was calmer than those about her, in spite of the fact that she believed this to have been an attempt on her life. She unwound her scarf and bound up the man's wound herself.

"Be of good cheer," she comforted him. "I shall see that you never want. That bullet was meant for your Queen, and you took it in her stead."

But the bullet had passed very close to Monsieur Simiers, and he had his own ideas about the intended target.

Back in his apartments he paced up and down in angry exasperation.

"Now," he said to the members of his suite, "they are attempting to take my life. What can I do? How can I bring about a match between Monsieur and such a woman? They are barbarians, these people. And I know who is the instigator of this plot. It is Leicester. Would to God some of his enemies would take it into their heads to kill him. If that could be done, much trouble might be saved."

"He still hopes," said one of Simiers' men, "to marry the Queen himself."

"I do not see how that can be," said another, "for I heard news of my lord of Leicester only the other day and, if it is true, he must have lost all hope of marrying Her Majesty."

"What story is this?"

"It is said that he has married the Countess of Essex."

Simiers threw back his head and laughed aloud. Then he became serious. "Did not the Earl of Essex die mysteriously in Ireland some time ago?"

"That is so."

"And there was an enquiry into his death conducted by Leicester's brother-in-law! Come, this is the best news I have heard since I first set foot in this land. We have played Monsieur Leicester's game too long. Now he shall play ours."

Simiers presented himself to the Queen.

"Your Majesty blooms like a rose . . . and that after your mishap on the river!"

" 'Twas nothing, Monsieur Monkey. A Queen must be prepared for any possibility."

"She needs a strong arm to protect her."

"Do not fear, Monsieur; she is strong enough to protect herself."

"She needs the affection of a husband. Will you not sign this document which I have prepared? It is a summons to my master to appear before you. Once he sees this he will come with all speed. Then you will see for yourself how he adores you; and, Your Majesty, so handsome is he, that I doubt not you will find him the most irresistible man you have ever set eyes upon."

She pretended to consider this. How could she send for him? Did she want trouble with France? To send for him and refuse him would be an insult they would never overlook. One did not inspect Princes as one did a horse.

"Ah, would it were in my power, dear Monkey. These ministers of mine . . ."

"Your Majesty should marry. Is not marriage in the air? Those about you enjoy its blessings. Will Your Majesty remain aloof from them?"

"Those about me? You mean . . . some of my ladies?"

"Nay, Your Majesty; I was referring to my lord of Leicester and his recent marriage to the beautiful Countess of Essex."

She put out a hand as though to steady herself. He snatched it and put it to his lips.

She did not see his ugly face. She only saw those two together: Lettice, who was not unlike herself, but younger and more beautiful, and Robert her favourite whom she loved as she would never love another person.

She could not doubt the words of this man. She wondered why she had not guessed what had happened. She remembered now the change in Robert and the mincing complacency of that she-wolf. There had been secret looks among her ladies and gentlemen.

Now she was possessed by such rage as she had never felt before.

"Where is this document, man?" she cried harshly.

"Here . . . here, Your Majesty." Simiers turned from her to hide the triumph in his eyes. He spread the papers on a table and handed her a pen.

Even her signature was an angry one.

"Your Majesty, my master will be enraptured. This will be the happiest day of his life . . ."

"Leave me now," she said.

Sly and knowledgeable, hiding his delight, he bowed

low and hurried away before she could change her mind.

Now there was no longer need for restraint. "Where are my women?" she shouted. "Why do they not attend me? Kat . . . you sly devil, where are you? What have you been doing all these weeks?"

They came running in and stood before her, trembling.

"What news of Leicester?" she spat out at them.

They were silent, each waiting for another to speak first.

She stamped her foot. "What of that snake?" she screamed. "What of Leicester?" She took the woman nearest her and shook her until she begged for mercy.

The Queen's hair had broken loose from her headress; her eyes grew wilder and purple colour flamed into her face.

No one dared speak until at last Kat said: "Dearest Majesty . . . dearest . . . dearest . . ."

"Did you not hear me?" shouted the Queen. "I said: 'What of that snake who calls himself a man?' So he has married that sly animal, has he? He has married that low creature, that she-wolf?"

"Majesty," said Kat, "it is true. They married . . ."

"They married!" cried Elizabeth. "Did they ask my consent? Did they keep it secret? Did you? Did you . . . and you?" Each "you" was accompanied by a stinging blow on the cheek for all those nearest. "And you . . . and you and . . . you . . . knew this, and thought it meet to keep it from me?"

"Dearest, dearest!" begged Kat. And in an agonized whisper she added: "Remember . . . remember . . . do not betray your feelings thus."

Elizabeth was swaying vertiginously with the intensity of her emotion.

"Quick!" cried Kat. "Help me unlace Her Majesty's bodice. There, my love. Kat has you. Come, lie on your couch, darling. You'll feel better then. Kat's here beside you."

With great presence of mind Kat dismissed all the women; she knelt by the couch, chafing the Queen's hands while the tears ran down Kat's cheeks and words babbled from her lips. "Oh, my darling, I would have given my life to spare you this. But, dearest, you would not marry him. You must not blame him . . ."

"Blame him!" flared Elizabeth. "By God's Body, I'll blame him! He shall pay for all the pleasure he has had with her."

"Darling, it was only natural. You see, he has been so long unmarried."

"Have I not been long unmarried?"

"But it was my darling's royal wish."

"They shall lose their heads for this, and I'll see the deed done."

"Be calm, my sweeting. Be quiet, my sweet Bess. Let me get you a little wine."

"You know I do not like wine."

"I'll mix water with it. It will revive you, dearest. There . . . there . . . that's better."

"It is not better, Kat. It will never be better. You know how I loved him."

"But you did not marry him, dearest."

"Stop all this talk of marriage. You do it but to torment me."

"Dearest Majesty, remember you are the Queen. You must not show your jealousy like this. You are above such things."

"I am indeed. I am above them all, and I'll have obedience. They shall go to the Tower at once . . . both of them."

"Yes, yes, my love. They shall go to the Tower."

"If you try to soothe me, Madam, and continue to talk to me as though I am four years old, you shall accompany them to the Tower."

"Yes, darling, so I shall."

"Oh Kat! What a deceiver! What a scoundrel!"

"He is the worst man in the world," said Kat.

"How dare you say it! You know he is not. It is all her fault. Ha! Little does he know the woman he has married. Let him discover."

She stood up suddenly. Kat watched her fearfully as she strode to the door.

She said to the guards there: "The Earl of Leicester is here at Greenwich, is he not?"

"He is, Your Majesty."

"Then go to his apartments with a party of the strongest guards. Place him under close arrest, and tell him he may expect to leave shortly for the Tower."

She came back to her couch and, flinging herself upon it, gave way to bitter weeping.

All England was talking about the "Mounseer." He had come to England, and he had come without ceremony, and in disguise had appeared suddenly at Greenwich with only two servants, asking to be taken to Her Majesty that he might throw himself at her feet.

He was very small and far from handsome; his face was dark and pock-marked; but he could murmur the kind of compliment that delighted the Queen as none of her courtiers—not even Robert—had been able to do. His clothes were exquisite; he could foot a measure with such grace as to make Christopher Hatton appear clumsy; he displayed French graces of such elegance that Elizabeth, smarting under what she privately called Leicester's betrayal, declared that she was charmed with him.

Robert and Lettice were under arrest, and Elizabeth had the satisfaction of knowing that they could not meet. She had not sent Robert to the Tower as she had at first intended; Burghley with Sussex had begged her not to do so and thereby expose her jealousy and passion to the world. To keep him a prisoner at Greenwich until her anger cooled was one thing; to make him a state prisoner in the Tower quite another, they cautioned her.

She saw the wisdom of this advice, and kept Robert prisoner at Greenwich in his own apartments, while she amused herself with Monsieur.

And how she seemed to enjoy herself! At least it was some balm to her misery. Kat, who loved her so tenderly, in dismay watched her caressing the little Prince in public. She had quickly nick-named him her Frog, and continually wore on her bosom a jewelled ornament in the shape of a frog.

But the country was not pleased with the suitor. The marriage would be a ridiculous one, it was said, since the Queen was forty-six and Anjou twenty-three. Was it possible for the Queen to have a child at her age? it was asked. And what other reason could there be for the marriage?

A man named Stubbs published a pamphlet he had written denouncing the match.

"This man," he wrote, "is the son of King Henry, whose family ever since he married with Catherine of

Italy is fatal as it were to resist the gospel and have been, every one after the other, as a Domitian after a Nero."

Stubbs and his publisher were imprisoned by order of the Queen, and both condemned to have their right hands cut off. Crowds gathered in the market place at Westminster to see this done, and the people murmured against the Queen.

This grieved Elizabeth; but she had, in a moment of passion, sent for the Duke, and she dared not risk offending the French by allowing their royal family to be insulted while the Duke was actually her guest.

Philip Sidney—who was handsome, gifted and charming as well as being Robert's nephew—was one of the Queen's favourite younger men. He now wrote to her in a manner which was more insulting to the French Prince than even Stubbs had been.

"How the hearts of your people will be galled," he wrote, "if not aliened when they see you take as husband a Frenchman and a papist, in whom the very common people know this: he is the son of that Jezebel of our age, and his brother made oblation of his own sister's marriage, the easier to massacre our brethren in religion . . ."

Philip Sidney was banished from the Court.

There were storms in the Parliament. Some of her ministers were quite blunt, saying she was old enough to be the Duke's mother. Others, more politic, implied the same thing in a more courteous way: They did not wish to see the Queen risk her life by attempting to bear children.

And Elizabeth, when she was not flirting with Monsieur, or raging against Robert—or fretting for him—was thinking of what was happening in the Netherlands, and how Philip of Spain was gaining domination over the poor suffering people of that land; and she wondered what would happen when he had completely subdued them.

Then, all the world thought, and Elizabeth must think it too, his attention would turn to England, for was not his dream to abolish Protestantism throughout the world, and was not England a refuge for the Huguenots of France and the Netherlands?

Elizabeth could tremble when she thought of that day. The great dread of her life was war; and even now that dread seeped through her miseries caused by Robert's defection, and curbed her gaiety in the French Prince's wooing.

While her statesmen wondered how a woman of her age and genius could act with such girlish folly, simpering, giggling, urging her wooer on to what—in the eyes of Englishmen—seemed the most foppish folly, she was flattering him as he was flattering her. Not only did she lead him to believe that he was a very fascinating man, but she let him know that she considered he was born to command an army; and since it was the destiny of France to go to war with Spain, and she was sure there was a kingdom to be won in the Netherlands by a man of courage, spirit and genius, such as Monsieur undoubtedly possessed, she wondered why he did not seek his fortune in Flanders.

His brother, a young man, was on the throne of France; it was a sad thing, she knew from experience, to be near the throne and have serious doubts of ever reaching it. There were always plots and counter-plots;

it was a wise thing to make a kingdom for oneself; and if one were a man, brave as a lion, a military genius—as she was convinced her little Frog was—he should first win his kingdom, and then come for his bride.

She knew the man with whom she was dealing. He had need to assert himself. As little Hercule, the youngest of his family, he had suffered much humiliation. To be small and ugly and to have been marred by the pox was bad enough, but to be called Hercule into the bargain had been an intolerable insult which Fate had given him. Mercifully his name had been changed to Francois, but no one could change his face. His mother disliked him because he was his brother's enemy, and he believed that she had tried to poison him. He needed to show the world what a great man he was, and he was determined that all should see him as Queen Elizabeth had. He would go to the Netherlands and fight the Spaniards.

The Queen, he believed, was so much in love with him that she would help him to finance his expedition.

So the Queen sat smiling, and her ministers marvelled that the seemingly foolish woman was sending Anjou away in the utmost amity to fight England's war in the Netherlands. Should the money be granted? Indeed it should! This was a master-stroke of policy.

The Queen was so pleased with her plan—and glad in truth to say goodbye to her little Frog who was beginning to tire her—that she smiled on all the world.

He must have an escort to take him across the sea, she declared.

"Master Leicester has been idle too long. I will put him in command of my dear Frog's escort and make some use of the man."

This was a sign to all that once more she had forgiven Robert.

X

She took him back, but whenever she saw him with Lettice she was jealous and alert.

She was angry because the marriage seemed to be successful. Robert had ceased to look at other women. Was it his age? wondered the Queen. Or had that she-wolf some magic power? She was sure the wolf was capable of anything. Wolves were treacherous animals.

A son was born to them—another Robert Dudley—and Elizabeth did not know whether she was pleased or angry. He had once said that she should perpetuate *her* beauty. She thought: He has perpetuated his, mayhap, and I am glad of that, though I would the boy were not that woman's son.

Lettice already had one son, and the Queen could not help being attracted by him in spite of his mother, for young Robert Devereux, Earl of Essex, was the handsomest young man she had seen since the days when his stepfather had enchanted her.

Often she would look sadly at her Robert and think: We are getting old now—too old for jealousy, too old for enmity. She would compare him with the young man who had ridden to her at Hatfield on a white horse, to tell her she was Queen. Poor Robert, he had put on much weight; his face was over-red from too much good living; that sensuality which had been virility in youth became grossness in old age.

And she herself? She was a goddess; she would not be frightened by the encroaching years. All about her were men—men of Robert's age and others of young Essex's age—to tell her she was a goddess who—without Cornelius Lanoy's elixir—had found eternal youth.

Anjou had failed in the Netherlands, but William the Silent was waging furious war there for his people's freedom. All eyes in England were on the Netherlands; the outcome of that war for freedom was of the utmost importance.

And the eyes of the Spaniards were on England. What sort of a woman is this? was being asked in Spanish Councils. What sort of a country does she rule? It is only part of an island, yet she acts as though she rules the world. Her seamen are arrogant pirates. They are diverting treasure from Spanish coffers. They are bold and adventurous; they have no respect for His Most Catholic Majesty. They insult the Holy Inquisition itself.

There were names which were spoken of with horror and dread in Spanish ships and Spanish territories: Drake, Hawkins . . . the fearless ones. How could men be so fearless as these were? How could they always win? It was because they were in the pay of the Devil. They were not men; they were sorcerers.

Clearly these men and their arrogant Queen would have to be taught a lesson. Francis Drake came sailing home from Chili and Peru with all the treasure plundered from Spanish towns in the new world, and from Spanish galleons. He had rounded the Cape, and by so doing, the world. And what did the Queen do when this pirate arrived home? Did she hang him as he deserved? Did she treat him as a thief, a robber and a murderer of His Most Catholic Majesty's subjects?

No! He was a handsome man, and she liked him for that among other things. She liked his Devon burr and she liked his flashing eyes. He was a man after her own heart, for, in his country way, he could pay a gallant compliment.

The Queen told him that the Spaniards went in fear of him. They called him a bold and wicked man.

"Are you such a man, sir?" she asked. "I believe you may be, and I must perforce cut off your head with a golden sword."

She thereupon called for a sword, and bade him kneel that she might with all speed perform the task which would put an end to plain Francis Drake.

She laid the sword on his shoulders and she said: "Arise, Sir Francis."

He rose, bowed low and kissed her hand, and said that he would sail the world twenty times and bring back twenty times as much treasure for one smile from Her Majesty's lips.

There came a tragic year for Robert. His son—in whom he had taken great pride—died suddenly. They buried him in Beauchamp Chapel at Warwick. "Robert Dudley, aged 4 years, the noble Impe," were the words inscribed on his tomb.

Robert was distraught and the Queen forgot her jealousy and did her best to comfort him.

Kneeling at her feet he said: "It is a retribution. I went against Your Majesty's wishes in my marriage. This is God's justice."

"Nay," she said gently, "it is not so. The innocent should not suffer. Robert, we are too old and too sad to do aught but comfort each other."

She made him sit at her feet, and while she caressed his hair she dreamed that it was black and luxuriant as it had once been.

Robert tried to forget his loss by taking under his charge that other Robert, his son by Douglass. He railed against a fate which took his legitimate son and left the other—though he loved both boys and wished to keep them.

He was frequently ill. He had lived too well, and now that he had turned into his fifties he must pay the penalty.

He could not talk of his ailments to the Queen; she hated talk of illness.

More troubles came.

That year, Robert Parsons, a Jesuit, published a book in Antwerp. He was a Catholic, and Leicester was now known throughout the world as England's Protestant Leader. This book, which was printed on green paper, was referred to as Father Parsons' Green Overcoat. It was a scurrilous life-study of the Earl of Leicester; and as the Queen had played a large part in that story, she did not escape scandalous references.

Here was an account of the lust between the Queen and her favourite with no details spared. The numbers of children they were reputed to have produced were mentioned. Robert was credited, not only with the murder of Amy Robsart, but of Douglass's husband

and the husband of his present wife, Essex. Every mysterious death which had occurred—and some natural ones—were laid at the door of the Earl of Leicester and his professional poisoners.

The book was brought into England and secretly distributed. Copies were passed from hand to hand. The affairs of Leicester were discussed afresh in every tavern. He was the world's worst villain. He had contaminated the Queen with his own evil. He was the son of the devil.

Elizabeth raged and stormed and threatened terrible punishment on anyone found with a copy of this foul book, which she swore to be utterly false.

Philip Sidney, indignant on behalf of the uncle whom he loved as a father, wrote an answer to the base knave who had dared circulate such lies against a great nobleman of England.

He declared that although through his father he belonged to a noble family, his greatest honour was to know himself a Dudley.

But no matter what was written and what was said, the memory of Amy Robsart was as fresh now as it had been nearly twenty years before. And those who understood such matters knew that this was more than an attack on Leicester and the Queen. It was a preliminary skirmish in the Catholic-Protestant war.

In that year William of Orange met his violent death. The Protector of his country, the leader, who had inspired his countrymen to fight against the Spanish tyranny, was gone.

The Netherlanders were turning desperate eyes towards England, and Elizabeth was uneasy. War, which she longed to avoid, was being thrust on her. She wanted to hold back, to cling to the prosperity she was building up through peace in her land. But there was no shutting her eyes to the position now. Most of the wool markets in the Netherlands had fallen completely under the Spanish yoke, and the prosperity which had come to England through the wool trade was declining. New markets must be found; but would the English be allowed to find them? Philip had his eyes on England, and he was a fanatic with a mission. In his harbours he was building up the greatest fleet of ships the world had ever known—the Invincible Armada, he called it; and its purpose, all knew, was to sail to the shores of that land whose Queen and whose seamen had so long defied his might.

Elizabeth called her ministers to her. They were in favour of intervention in the Netherlands. They did not feel as she did. They were *men* who hoped to win power and glory through war. She was only a woman, longing to keep her great family of people secure, herself possessing that understanding which told her that even wars which were won brought less gain than continued peace would have brought, without waste of men and gold.

But she could no longer hold back, and the Netherlands were asking that one to whom they could look as a leader be sent to them, one whom they could follow as they had followed their own William of Orange. This was the man who had put himself at the head of the Protestant Party and was, as the world knew, so beloved of the Queen that she would never set him at the head of an enterprise to which she would not give her wholehearted support.

The Netherlands were crying out for Leicester.
And so she gave her consent that he should go.

As she bade him a fond farewell, she thought how handsome he was, how full of enthusiasm and ambition. He appeared to be almost a young man again.

He did not suffer at the parting as she did. He was going in search of honour and that military glory which had always appealed to him.

She must stay behind, following his exploits through despatches and letters, rejoicing in one fact only: if he were separated from her, he was also separated from his wife.

Robert rode in state through the clean little towns to the sound of rapturous applause. It was as though a lifelong ambition was at last realized. For so many years he had longed to be a King; and these people cheered him, knelt before him, as though he were more than a King—their saviour.

It was shortly after his arrival at the Hague that the greatest honour of his life was paid to him.

It was New Year's morning, and he was dressing in his chamber when a delegation arrived to see him. Without waiting to finish his dressing he went to the antechamber. There the leader of the delegation knelt and told him that Dutchmen, looking upon him as their leader, wished to offer him all those titles which had belonged to the Prince of Orange. He should be Governor, ruler, Stadholder.

Robert was overwhelmed with delight. He had longed all his life for something like this: his own kingdom to rule, a kingdom he owed, not to the good graces of the Queen, but to his own statesmanship and popularity.

This was the great testing time of Robert's life; and how was he to know that, when honours came easily, the hands did not grow strong enough to hold them, that it was by hard work and achievement only that such strength came? He had been carried up to greatness in a litter prepared for him by a doting woman; when he reached the top the air was too rarified for him without his litter to support him; and these Hollanders were asking him to stand on his own feet. Philip of Spain was close; the Duke of Parma was waiting; and in England there was the Queen, who must give her consent to his acceptance of such honours.

He hesitated. He wanted to accept, to take his laurels. He longed to ride through the streets and receive the people's homage. Dare he do so, and later persuade the Queen to support him? It was an irritating shock to realize that he could not maintain his position without that support.

He hesitated and succumbed to temptation.

He was the Governor of the Netherlands now. He was to be Stadholder, and the people called him Excellency.

The news came to England.

Lettice, seeing herself as the Queen of the Netherlands, decided to join her husband in his new kingdom.

Great preparations were made. Lettice would travel in state to the Hague, with all the trappings of a Queen.

Elizabeth, furious because he had dared accept his new position without even consulting her, was writing angry letters to him. He should at once renounce what he had dared to take up.

"How contemptuously we conceive ourselves to have been used by you, you shall by this bearer understand. We could not have imagined had we not seen it come to pass, that a man raised up by ourself, and extraordinarily favoured by us above any other subject in the land, would have so contemptuously broken our commandment . . ."

While she was writing, Kat came to tell her of the preparations Lettice was making to join her husband.

Elizabeth laid down her pen.

"She may prepare all she will," she sneered. "She shall never go."

"She plans to go in the state of a Queen, surpassing even Your Majesty's state."

Elizabeth's eyes blazed. "Let the she-wolf make her plans. She shall ere long wish she had not joined herself to a man whom I shall bring so low as I shall this one. This is the end of the kindness I have shown my lord of Leicester. That man, I promise you, shall wish he had never been born. As for that harlot, that she-wolf, we shall soon see her deserting him. He will see who his friends are. Does he think she has been faithful to him while he has been away?"

"I know, Your Majesty, there are rumours of that most handsome Christopher Blount."

"Years younger than she is!" snapped the Queen. "A friend of her son's. There is pleasant news for my lord! But I shall make him smart more than she ever can!"

She picked up her pen and wrote, commanding him

to lay aside his new-found honours. He would make an open and public resignation in the very place where he had accepted absolute government without his Queen's consent. He would show himself to his new "people" as a man of no account, a man unable to make a decision without the consent of his mistress—and most firmly she withheld that consent.

"Fail you not," she ended, "as you will answer the contrary at your uttermost peril."

Then she laid aside her pen and let her anger blaze, while she thought with furious resentment of the wicked woman who had dared betray him with a younger man.

Robert, in desperation, sent home two men to plead his cause with the Queen. The matter was too far gone for open withdrawal he pointed out. If she repudiated him, the people of the Netherlands would lose heart; and she must think what that would mean to England. He was contrite; he had offended her and he would rather have died than have done that. But for the good of England, she must give him time to slip out gracefully from his terrible blunder; she must see that public repudiation would be playing into the hands of Philip of Spain.

Her ministers agreed with that view. Robert had to be allowed to disentangle himself with as much tact as possible.

She was now in turn outraged mistress and apprehensive Queen. Worried by the state of affairs in the Netherlands, fervently she wished that England had not become so involved. She accused Robert of squandering England's money. To that accusation he made a magnificent gesture by selling his own lands and giving up a great part of his fortune to the campaign in the Netherlands.

But he was not suited to his task. He had been too long favoured, and had never learned to win success through tedious application. His experience of war was limited. He could sense approaching that military disaster, which lack of the Queen's support must mean.

His greatest source of consolation was his nephew, Philip Sidney, who was there with him.

He dearly loved Philip and trusted him completely. Philip had urged him not to send for Lettice, and Philip was proved right; for Robert, knowing Elizabeth, realized that the real cause of her anger was the fact that Lettice had arrogantly prepared to join him with the state of a Queen.

Philip had sent one of his players, who had accompanied them to Holland, with urgent messages to Walsingham—Philip's father-in-law—asking him to use all his influence to prevent Lettice making the journey.

Unfortunately the player had been a head-in-the-clouds fellow—a young man named Will, an actor from Stratford-on-Avon—and, said Philip, recalling the way in which this actor had performed his mission, it would have been a better thing if he had stayed in Stratford; for he had delivered the letters to Lettice herself instead of to Walsingham, and thereby much trouble had been caused which might have been avoided.

Robert was beginning to hate the Netherlands; he was longing for nothing so much as to return home. He wished he had never thought of leaving England and had not been tempted lightly to take that which had been offered.

His melancholy turned to bitter grief when, after the battle of Zutphen, in which he himself fought valiantly, the dead were brought in and he found among them the body of his nephew.

He listened to the accounts of how nobly Philip Sidney had died. This gallant young man had given part of his armour to another man, although he knew himself to be in need of it. When Philip had been fainting from wounds a cup of water had been put to his lips by one of his men; but Philip, seeing a soldier close by groaning in agony, had sent his man over to the sufferer that the water might be given to one who was in greater need of it than he himself. Robert was proud of his nephew, but he felt that he would have given everything that was left to him if he might have brought him back to life.

So Robert lived through his gloomiest hour. He felt in that moment that death would have been preferable to the plight in which he found himself.

When Robert was suffering in the Netherlands, news of the Babington Conspiracy swept through England. Babington, a young man fascinated by the charm of the Queen of Scots when he had been a page in her household, had been persuaded by a group of men to communicate with the Queen with a view to effecting the assassination of Elizabeth and the setting of Mary upon the throne.

Mary had lost none of her impetuosity during the years and, to her, plotting was an exciting pastime.

The conspirators had forgotten what elaborate spy-

Walsingham.

Walsingham understood what was happening in the early stages of the plot, for a priest, Gilbert Gifford, having been sent to England secretly to work against Protestantism with the help of the great Catholic families, was captured. Walsingham promised to spare his life if he would become his spy.

This the priest agreed to do and, when Mary was removed from Tutbury to Chartley, Gifford arranged with the brewer who supplied the Chartley beer to convey letters to and from Mary. These were wrapped in water-proof cases and put through the bung-hole of the kegs—letters going to Mary in full kegs; hers coming out in empty ones. Gifford took these letters and, before passing them on to those for whom they were intended, handed them to Walsingham, who, putting them into the hands of an expert decoder, learned their contents and was able to follow every twist and turn of the plot.

It was arranged that six men should assassinate Elizabeth. One of the six was to be Babington. If the deed were successfully carried out, these men believed that it would be a simple matter to set Mary on the throne.

Walsingham, as one of the leaders of the Protestant Party, had always deplored the fact that Mary had been allowed to live; and as soon as Mary's letter to the conspirators—in which she gave her full support to the assassination of Elizabeth—was in his hands, he lost no time in arresting the men and laying the whole plot before the Queen and her Council.

All England rejoiced as soon as the news was made

known. Bonfires were lighted; in the country there was dancing on the village greens; in the towns there was singing in the streets. The beloved Queen had narrowly escaped, and at last the Jezebel of Scotland was shown to her most merciful Majesty for what she was. There were services in the churches and on street corners.

Elizabeth noted these expressions of love and loyalty with deep gratification; but she knew that the people were demanding the death of Mary.

Seven of the conspirators whose names had appeared in the letters were placed on hurdles and dragged through the City from Tower Hill to St. Giles' Fields. Anthony Babington was one of the seven. After these seven had been hanged, they were cut down alive and disembowelled while still living. Such cruelties had been frequently witnessed during the reign of the great Henry; they were rarer in these days.

The agonized screams of tortured men were heard beyond St. Giles Fields, and many thought, as they listened, of the wicked woman whom they held responsible for the terrible suffering of these men whose crime was that they had attempted to serve her.

The next day seven more men were condemned to die in the same terrible manner; but Elizabeth, who knew the mood of the people, and who knew too that they expected clemency from her, commanded that the men should not be cut down until they were dead. The mutilations of their bodies should be performed after death.

There remained Mary; and Elizabeth knew that she must die, Queen though she was.

She was taken from Chartley to Fotheringay and there tried before the commissioners of peers, privy councillors and judges; and in spite of her protestations of innocence, her repeated cries that Walsingham had forged the letters which he had laid before the Queen and her ministers, she was found guilty of plotting against Elizabeth and condemned to die.

Elizabeth was even now reluctant to sign the death warrant. That Queens were above the judgement of ordinary men was a maxim she wished to preserve; but great pressure was brought upon her. The situation vis-a-vis Spain was recalled to her mind, and eventually she was prevailed upon to sign the warrant. But she did not despatch it; and as Walsingham was at that time indisposed, the responsibility for sending the warrant to Fotheringay fell upon a secretary, William Davison.

One February morning, Mary, dressed in black velvet, her crucifix in her hand, went to the hall of the castle of Fotheringay where the block and the executioner were awaiting her. Calmly she bade farewell to her servants.

"Weep not," she told them, "for thou hast cause rather to joy than to mourn, for now thou shalt see Mary Stuart's troubles receive their long-expected end."

The whole Catholic world was talking of the wicked Walsingham's forgeries, of the evil act of the Jezebel of England whose hands were red with the blood of her enemies.

Walsingham and Burghley would snap their fingers at their enemies. Not so the Queen. The threat of war was moving nearer; in the Spanish harbours work was going on apace in the building of that Armada which was to conquer the world; and its first victim was to be Elizabeth's England.

The Queen sought to placate her enemies. Her great desire was to hold off the evil day. Time was her ally—now as ever.

She chose William Davison as her scapegoat. She declared she had never meant the warrant to be sent to Fotheringay. She mourned her sister of Scotland. She had never wished for Mary's death.

She had Davison sent to the Tower. He was to pay a fine which would impoverish him. But she told him before he went that she would continue to pay his salary while he was a prisoner and, as he fell on his knees before her, she let one of her long slender hands pat his shoulder.

The Queen's reassuring touch told Davison that he was merely the scapegoat she was offering to Spain; and she herself hated Spain as fiercely as any in her realm.

As it turned out, Davison continued to receive his salary, for the Queen kept her word; and when he was shortly afterwards released, she did not forget to reward him.

So Mary Stuart died; but the Spanish menace grew and Elizabeth knew that the whole of England was threatened.

When Robert returned from the Netherlands he was greeted rapturously by the Queen. It was a year since she had seen him, and she felt a great and tender pity touch her as she looked into his face.

How he had suffered! His dignity was lost, and the great position for which he had longed was taken from him. She had heard that he was ill in the Netherlands and needed his English doctors. She had at once had them sent to him, for when she heard of his illness all her rancour had disappeared. Lettice was blatantly unfaithful with that young and handsome Christopher Blount. So how could Elizabeth scold him at such a time? How could she do anything but take him under her wing? He had lost dear Philip Sidney, that handsome and most clever young man. Life had suddenly turned cruel to Robert; and seeing this, the Queen knew the height, depth and breadth of her love which had flickered and flamed for nearly forty years and which, she knew, nothing could ever entirely extinguish.

Now she would keep him by her side. She would make up to him for the loss of his beloved nephew, for the loss of his honour, and for the unfaithfulness of his wife. Dear Robert, once the conquering hero, was now the conquered.

Elizabeth had believed that it would be impossible for her to love a man who was no longer handsome, who was no longer the most perfect, the most virtuous; nevertheless she found that she could not cease to love Robert.

The whole country was in a state of tension.

All along the south coast the watchers were alert for the first sight of a sail. The bonfires were ready. In Plymouth Sir Francis Drake was impatient to get at the enemy. Lord Howard of Effingham was begging the Queen for more supplies. The ships, even in the little harbours, were being hastily made ready all through the nights by the light of flares and cressets. The coastal fortifications were being strengthened at fever-heat; and off the Devon coast Ark and Achates, Revenge and Rainbow, Elizabeth Bonaventure and Elizabeth Jonas with their fellow escorts were waiting.

Burghley and Walsingham were frantically counting the cost of the preparations, demanding of one another whence the money was coming to pay for this and that. The Queen, who was always reluctant to spend money, was refusing permission to victual the ships, refusing the money to pay her seamen.

Elizabeth knew that she now faced the greatest peril of her reign, of her life; if her gallant sailors failed to beat off the invader, England would suffer worse than death. Elizabeth loved her country with a great maternal love, with a passion she had never given to any person. Her one idea had been to bring it through peace to prosperity; and this she had done; and this she would have continued to do had that tyrant of the Escorial allowed men and women to follow the religion of their choice. Let him have his priests and his Holy Inquisition—that unholy band of torturers—let him burn his own subjects at the stake; let him torture them on the *chevalet*; let him tear their limbs with red hot pincers in the name of the Holy Catholic Church; Elizabeth cared not that this should be. If they chose to follow such a Faith and such a King, let them.

But it was not as easy as that. They were sailing now steadily towards her shores—Andalucian, Biscayan, San Felipe, San Juan and many others; they brought the Spanish dons, the Spanish grandees, the Spanish soldiers and sailors; but they brought more than these: they brought their priests, their inquisitors; they

406

brought the instruments of torture from their dark chambers of pain. They hoped to bring, not only conquest, but the Inquisition.

She had been afraid, but she would overcome that fear. How could she lose? How could England be beaten? It was impossible. She had her men—her beloved men—who in the service of the goddess, the perfect woman, the Queen, the mistress, the mother, could never fail.

There was Lord Howard of Effingham, that fine sailor; there was the incomparable Drake; there was Frobisher, Hawkins; and there were all her dear friends: her Spirit, her Moor, her old Mutton and Bellwether—all those whom she loved; and above all there was Robert.

She had shown her confidence in him, and the return of all her love in this great emergency. He was forgiven the terrible calamity in the Netherlands for which she knew she must accept part of the blame; for if Lettice had not thought of joining him as his Queen, would Elizabeth have felt so insistent on robbing him of his new office, of destroying Flemish trust in England?

She had appointed Robert Lieutenant and General of her Armies and Companies. That would show everyone what she thought of him. That would make it clear that in adversity they stood together, as they had stood when Amy Robsart had died and he had been accused of her murder.

She trusted him; he was her beloved; he was again her Eyes; he was the only man she would have married if she had decided to take a husband.

Robert had divided his forces into two armies—one of which he had stationed at St. James's, the other at

Tilbury. They would be ready, those soldiers of his, to defend their country if the dons dared to land. But Howard and Drake and their men were determined they should never land. Would English seamen give the victory to English soldiers? Never! England owed her prosperity to her seamen—so said Drake—and he was bent on capturing the credit for himself.

Elizabeth wished to be with her armies at such a time—and was not Robert at the head of those armies? She sent a despatch to him, telling him of her determination to see and talk with her soldiers.

His answer came back.

"Your person," he wrote, "is the most sacred and dainty thing that we have in the world to care for, and a man must tremble when he thinks of it . . ."

He would have preferred her, he said, to have stayed in the safest place in England.

"Yet I will not that in some sort so princely and so rare a magnanimity should not appear to your people and the world as it is . . ."

She read the letter through many times; she kept it with her; she kissed it often, as she used to kiss his letters in the early days.

When she reached Tilbury, gay with flags, Robert met the barge to the sound of thundering cannon, and rode with her in a coach decorated with diamonds, emeralds and rubies.

She was truly noble as she went among her soldiers. This she knew to be the greatest moment of her country's history; therefore it was Elizabeth's greatest moment. Her fear had left her; she no longer believed in the possibility of defeat. The odds might seem against the English. The Spaniards had the ships; they had the ammunition; but they had not Elizabeth; they had not Drake; they had not—and this was their greatest lack—the calm knowledge that they could not fail.

There at Tilbury she mounted a great horse and, holding a truncheon in her hand, she sat more like a soldier than a woman; and thus she addressed them:

"My loving people, we have been persuaded by some that are careful of our safety to take heed how we commit ourself to armed multitudes for fear of treachery. But I assure you, I do not desire to live to distrust my faithful and my loving people. Let tyrants fear. I have always so behaved myself that, under God, I have placed my chiefest strength and safeguard in the loyal hearts and goodwill of my subjects; and therefore I am come amongst you, as you see, at this time, not for my recreation and disport, but being resolved, in the midst of the heat and battle, to live or die amongst you all, to lay down for my God, and for my kingdom, and for my people, my honour and my blood, even in the dust. I know I have the body of a weak and feeble woman, but I have the heart and stomach of a king, and a king of England too, and think foul scorn that Parma or Spain, or any prince of Europe, should dare to invade the borders of my realm; to which, rather than any dishonour shall grow by me, I myself will take up arms, I myself will be your general, judge, and rewarder of every one of your virtues in the field. I know, already for your forwardness, you have deserved rewards and crowns; and we do assure you, in the word of a prince, they shall be duly paid you."

This speech of the Queen's put courage into the hearts of all those who heard it. She was invincible, as she had always known she would be, for, foolish though she might be, vain, coquettish, ill-tempered, selfish—when the occasion arose, she had the gift of greatness.

And the Armada sailed into the English Channel.

It was Spain's tragedy that, with the finest ships in the world, with the best ammunition and equipment, she was doomed to failure. Her commander had no wish for the task which he had implored the King to give to another. His seamen were afraid of El Draque, the Dragon, that Englishman whom they believed to be no ordinary man, but one possessed of superhuman power, and destined to destroy them. They had seen him in action, and no ordinary man was ever so fearless as El Draque. He had sailed calmly into Cadiz Harbour and burned and pillaged the ships which lay at anchor there; he had delicately referred to this operation as "Singeing the Beard of the King of Spain." He had sailed the high seas, and he had come back with Spanish treasure rich enough to fortify his country against Spain. The Devil was at work here, and Spaniards feared the Devil.

It was England's glory that, with her little ships, ill-equipped, her sailors short of food, with sickness aboard and a tragic lack of shot and powder, she was invincible. She believed in victory. She had not the hope that she would win; she had the knowledge that she could not fail.

The fight was not of long duration.

The Spaniards were outclassed in courage and the genius of seamanship which the world had already seen displayed by Drake.

The battle raged. The fire-ships were sent among the Spaniards who were beaten before a storm arose to make their disaster complete.

England was saved. The might of Spain was broken.

The Inquisition would never come to the Queen's England.

It was the greatest hour of a proud reign.

The Queen of half an island had set herself against the mightiest monarch in the world; and a small, courageous nation had beaten and broken the power of mighty Spain.

All through the towns and villages there was rejoicing such as had never before been known. The church bells rang out. With the appearance of the first stars the bonfires were lighted. Revelry was heard throughout the land.

Robert wrote to the Queen that he longed to be with her, but the fever which had troubled him so often had returned and he was going to Kenilworth, and thence to Leamington to take the baths, that he might not present himself until he felt well enough to enjoy that which gave him more delight than anything in the world—the company of his beloved and gracious mistress.

In the course of his journey he paused at a mansion in Rycott, and there he wrote to her again.

"I most humbly beseech Your Majesty to pardon an old servant who is so bold as to write and ask how my gracious lady doth. The chiefest thing in the world I do pray for is for her to have good health and a long life. I hope to find a perfect cure at the bath and with the continuance of my wonted prayer for Your Majesty's

411

most happy preservation, I humbly kiss your foot."

She read this through several times and tenderly put it into the box where she kept his letters.

Then she went forth to the rejoicing.

It was September, less than a month after she had talked to her soldiers at Tilbury, when Kat brought the news to her.

Kat came and knelt before her and, lifting her face to that of her mistress, could find no words. Elizabeth looked into this dear friend's face and, seeing the tears flow slowly down her cheeks, she herself was afraid to speak.

She feared this news. She wanted to run from it; but she was calm as she would always be in the important moments of her life, whatever sorrow they might bring her.

"What is it, sweet Kat? Do not be afraid."

Still Kat could not speak.

"Mayhap I know," said Elizabeth. "He looked so sick when I last saw him."

"It was at Cornbury near Oxford, Your Majesty. It was the continual fever. It returned more violently and . . . he did not rise from his bed."

The Queen did not speak. She sat very still. She was thinking: So he died near Oxford—near Cumnor Place. It is twenty-eight years since they found her at the foot of the stairs. Oh, Robert, Robert . . . never to see your face again! But we have been so near, so close in all things. Dearest Eyes, why have I lost you? How can I be aught but blind to the joy in life without you?

"Dearest . . ." said Kat; and she threw her arms

about the Queen and sobbed wildly.

Elizabeth was quiet while the tears flowed down her cheeks. Suddenly she spoke: "In the streets they are still shouting Victory, Kat. I have a warm place in their hearts. They love me—their Queen—as they never loved King or Queen before me. Once I thought that was my dearest wish . . . so to be loved. Kat, by my own people. Our country is safe from danger; and I, who should be the happiest woman in the world, am the most wretched."

"Dearest, do not speak," implored Kat. "It hurts you so, sweetest Majesty."

"I will speak," she said. "I will speak through my tears and my torment. I loved him. I always loved him; and I shall love him till I die. Philip has lost his Armada, but mayhap he is not less happy this night than I. For I have lost Robert, sweet Robin, my love, my Eyes."

Now she began to give way to her grief, and her sobs were so violent that they frightened Kat, who threw her arms about the Queen once more and comforted her.

"Dearest, remember your life lies before you. You are a Queen, my darling. My dearest, there is much left for you. You are no ordinary woman to cry for a lost lover. You are a Queen—and Queen of England."

Then Elizabeth looked at Kat and, laying her hands gently on her shoulders, kissed her. "You are right, Kat. You are right, dear friend. I am the Queen."

Then she went to the box wherein she kept his letters. She took out the one she had received but a few days before, and calmly she wrote upon it: "His last letter."

She kissed it vehemently and put it quickly into the box. She turned, and she was smiling with apparent serenity.

Robert had gone, and he had taken much of the joy from her life, but when she faced Kat she was no longer the woman who had lost the only man she had loved; she was the triumphant Queen of victorious England.

MORE HISTORICAL NOVELS
FROM BERKLEY

(Please turn page)